The Men
and
the Girls

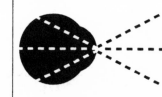

This Large Print Book carries the
Seal of Approval of N.A.V.H.

The Men
and
the Girls

Joanna Trollope

G.K. Hall & Co.
Thorndike, Maine

Published in 1994 by arrangement with Random House, Inc.

G.K. Hall Large Print Core Collection.

The text of this Large Print edition is unabridged.
Other aspects of this book may vary from the original edition.

Set in 16 pt. News Plantin by Penny L. Picard.

Printed in the United States on acid-free, high opacity paper. ∞

Library of Congress Cataloging in Publication Data

Trollope, Joanna.
    The men and the girls / Joanna Trollope.
        p.   cm.
    ISBN 0-8161-5919-X (alk. paper : lg. print)
    1. Man-Woman relationships — England — Fiction.
2. Conflict of generations — England — Fiction. 3. Large
type books.
I. Title.
[PR6070.R57M46   1994]
823'.914—dc20   93-40242

---

*For
Andrew*

Chapter One

Because he wasn't wearing his spectacles, he didn't see her pedalling painfully along the gutter beside him in the dark and the rain, and in consequence, he knocked her gently off her bicycle. He stopped the car at once, dead, and the rush-hour queue in Beaumont Street leant angrily on its collective horn, and blasted him.

He sprang out of the car, and hurried round the bonnet.

'I'm so sorry,' James said, stooping over her. 'I'm so desperately sorry.' Lit by his headlamps, she glared up at him from the wet pavement. He saw, with a shock of tenderness, that she was a true Oxford spinster, one of that dwindling band of elderly, dignified, clever women living out frugal lives in small flats and rooms sustained by thinking. He seized the handlebars of her bicycle, to free her, and, in so doing, emptied out the contents of her wicker bicycle basket.

'Oh God,' he said in despair. He attempted to pick the objects up; a plastic carrier bag of books, a bicycle lock and chain, a tin of cat food.

'Should you be driving?' she said furiously, struggling to her feet. She peered at him in the rain, through Schubert spectacles. Her glance

7

travelled to his grey hair. 'Are you safe to drive?'

Holding her bicycle awkwardly with one hand, he grasped her arm with the other.

'Are you hurt? Have I hurt you?'

'Only my feelings,' she said with emphasis.

'I forgot my glasses —'

'I'm not interested!' she cried, her voice sharp with shock. 'Why should I care?'

'Come home with me,' James pleaded. 'I live two minutes away. We'll put your bike in the boot. I can give you some brandy.'

'No,' she said. 'No. I have an appointment.'

'Let me drive you to it.'

'It's here. It's in Beaumont Street. I have an appointment with the doctor —'

'Then let me take you in and explain.'

She said something incoherent, scrabbling in her pocket. 'My handkerchief —'

'Take mine. Out of my breast pocket. I'd give it to you, only my hands are full.'

She shook her head. He began, with infinite tenderness, to guide her and her bicycle along the pavement.

A man wound down his car window and yelled, 'You just leaving that bloody thing there?' jabbing his thumb angrily at James's car.

'Yes,' James called.

'Oh dear,' the woman said suddenly. 'Oh dear, oh dear. I do so detest upsets, disagreeableness —'

'Me too. Even more if I've caused them.' He remembered he had left his spectacles in the lavatory at home, on the pile of old copies of *Private*

Eye. He could hardly confess this.

'It's here,' she said, pausing at a doorway, and pressing a plastic bell.

'Will you tell me your name? And where you live? May I come and see you, to apologise, to see if you are all right?'

She hesitated. Fright had made her cross and then tremulous. 'My name is Bachelor. Beatrice Bachelor.' She paused and then added, 'I live in Cardigan Street.'

James said, 'I live close to you, so close —'

The door opened. A receptionist in a jersey so vibrantly patterned it quite overshadowed her face said, 'Oh Miss Bachelor, what a night, whatever have you done to yourself?'

'It was my fault,' James said. 'I knocked her over.' He looked down at Miss Bachelor in the light. She had mud on her cheek and her headscarf had fallen back exposing thin grey hair that was escaping from its knot. 'My name,' said James, feeling the need to confess it as a pointless act of contrition, 'is James Mallow.'

'Yes,' said the receptionist taking Miss Bachelor firmly by the arm. 'Yes, I expect it is.' Then she shut the door on him.

When James got home, the house was still dark, except for Uncle Leonard's window on the first floor, which glowed redly. When Leonard Mallow had come to live with them five years before, Kate had asked him what colour curtains he would like and he had said at once, 'Oh red, dear. Really red. As red as you can get them.' He was a man of decided tastes. He loved cricket and the works of John Buchan and anchovy paste and Mrs Cheng, the small, impassive Chinese woman who helped Kate with the cleaning; he hated progress and materialism and girls with short hair. He had been a schoolmaster for almost fifty years of his long bachelor life and said, with the utmost benevolence, that he was sick of boys.

James let himself in. The hall was dark, but there was a line of light under the kitchen door and the thump of rock music. Uncle Leonard hallooed from upstairs. 'That you?'

'It's me. It's James.'

'Sodding awful night —'

'Telling me. I'll be up in a sec.'

'No hurry,' Leonard shouted amiably. 'Take your time. Never any hurry.'

James opened the door on the left and switched on the light. His study — his study now for over a quarter of a century — sprang to familiar and beloved life; the wide sash windows at either end, the green carpet, the lamps and cluttered little tables, the scuffed leather armchairs, the desk (his father's mahogany desk, brought from South Africa), and the books, the shelves and shelves and shelves of books, floor to ceiling, running unbroken down the two long walls of the room except for a space above his desk where a painting hung, a painting which Kate loved, of a sleek Mogul prince in a flowered coat and silver shoes. James went from one window to the other, pulling curtains. Mrs Cheng had hoovered the carpet today, and the grass-green pile lay in stripes, like a lawn. The room smelled as he liked it to, of leather and paper and polish. He looked at the leather chairs, and wished that Miss Bachelor was in one of them, warming her spinstery limbs at his gas fire, cradling a cup of tea or a glass of brandy in her not quite steady hands. He felt miserable with remorse. If he was going to knock someone over, why couldn't it have been a robust, resilient person who sprang up from the pavement and yelled healthy abuse at him? Why did it have to be a Miss Beatrice Bachelor in woolly gloves with legs like brittle sticks? He sighed. He wished Kate was at home; he needed her warmth and understanding.

Slowly, he went out of his study and climbed the stairs to the landing, switching lights on as he went. The door to Leonard's room was ajar, a sign that he was available for company. When he wished to sleep, or do the crossword, or perform the long, complex ritual of dressing or undressing, he closed the door firmly and shouted 'Go away!' if it was knocked upon.

'Ah,' he said, as James came in. He sat in his usual chair, an upright armchair of singular charmlessness, with wooden arms and a deep seat which looked as if it hid a po. 'Ah. You look all in.'

'I've just knocked someone over,' James said. 'Very slowly. I didn't hurt her but I frightened her. I feel awful.'

11

'Whisky,' Leonard said, flapping a long hand at a cluster of bottles on his chest of drawers. 'Help yourself.'

'I left her at a surgery,' James said, picking up Leonard's toothglass and inspecting it for signs of toothpaste before pouring whisky into it. 'I'll go and see her tomorrow. She lives near St Barnabas.'

'No, no,' Leonard said, flapping again. 'Soak my gnashers in that one. Perfectly good glass by the bottles.'

'Sorry.'

'Left your specs behind. Saw them in the lav.'

'That's why I knocked her over. That and the dark and rain.'

'Only sixty. Aren't you?'

'Sixty-one.'

'No call for things to drop off at sixty-one. Eyes should still work at sixty-one.'

'I'm not falling apart,' James said, settling himself in Leonard's other chair, a creaking basketwork bucket, with a lumpy cushion covered in cretonne. 'I'm as absent-minded as I ever was, that's all. I mean, I am permanently deep in thoughts unconnected with driving the car or mowing the lawn. It drives Kate mad. She says why can't I apply my intelligence as much to loading the washing machine as to writing and teaching.'

'Why can't you?'

'I suppose I'm not as interested.'

Leonard slapped the folded newspaper on his knee.

'Liked your piece today. Don't agree, of course. Can't stand subsidies. No wonder the theatre's gone all namby-pamby.'

'I wasn't entirely pro-subsidy in that piece. I said there should be a balance —'

'Best thing I ever saw,' Leonard said suddenly, 'was *Journey's End*. Wonderful stuff. Guts. That's what it had. Guts.'

'Where's Kate?'

'No idea. Here one minute, gone the next. Wham, bang, slam the door. You know.'

James regarded his uncle levelly. In all Leonard's life, nobody had ever been kinder to him than Kate. It was Kate's idea that they should take him in when it became plain that years of institutional living had rendered him totally unable to cope on his own. But Leonard, although he was keenly aware of what he owed Kate, and although he had come to love her, could not forgive her for two faults. One was her class. He knew he couldn't voice his opinion, and he knew he was unfashionable to hold it, but James had been born a gentleman, in Leonard's view, and Kate's father was a college groundsman; her mother was an emigrant Irishwoman from County Cork. These facts stuck in Leonard's mind like stones in sand, these facts — and, of course, that other one, which was more of a boulder than a stone.

'Leonard —' James said warningly. He finished his whisky. 'I'd better go down and see Joss.'

'We've done her homework,' Leonard said, picking up the paper to show James that he wanted him to go anyway. 'Polished that off in no time.'

'Is that a good idea? How does it help her in class, if you zip through her prep and create such a false impression of her capabilities?'

Leonard adored doing Joss's homework. He put his face into the newspaper. 'Mind your own business.'

James went out on to the landing. Kate had repainted it last winter, a pale, soft corn colour. She had painted it with her usual energy, and James had gone round after her, removing the splashes of yellow paint from the white woodwork, and tidying up the edges round light switches. She didn't mind, she never took things like that personally, she just laughed. The landing was one of the few things she had changed since she came; for the most part, she seemed either too absorbed by the business of living to fuss about décor, or too delicate in feeling to impose her taste on James's house.

It was his house. He had bought it nearly thirty years before, long before the carelessly built Victorian area of Oxford, called Jericho, had risen from a near slum to gentility. It was a low, double-fronted red house with a Gothic doorway and wide sash windows edged in blue-and-yellow brick. Above the door it said firmly in black, 'Richmond Villa'. It had perhaps been built for one of the master printers at the great university press in Walton Street, and James loved it. He loved, too, Kate's tact about it.

He went downstairs. The thump of music from

behind the closed kitchen door had given way to a sad, plaintive wail in a nasal voice, like a voice heard over a high wall in a North African souk. James paused. He put his hand on the doorknob. Behind the door, no doubt messily eating corn-flakes, on which she seemed to exist, he would find Joss, his stepdaughter. Except that she was not truly his stepdaughter since her mother, throughout the eight years they had lived with James in Richmond Villa, had staunchly refused to marry him.

Joss had a small white face and a horrible haircut. Her hair was the same reddish colour as Kate's, and she had had it cut brutally short, to appease the prevailing fashion in her class. Secretly, her haircut appalled her, so she defended it with hysteria. On her bedroom wall, she had stuck posters of girl rock stars with hair like convicts, but under her bed she kept a box of cuttings from magazines, photographs of fashion models with curtains of luxuriant hair, swinging and shining. Those girls wore beautiful shoes. Joss wore heavy black boots with thick soles and eyelets rimmed in brass.

'Uncle Leonard says he's done all your prep.'

Joss yawned. 'He can do it. I can't. So.'

James did not feel equal to a battle.

'Where's Mum?'

'I dunno. The home, I suppose.'

The home was a refuge for battered women, set up by a friend of Kate's, near St Margaret's Church. Kate helped there, on a voluntary basis, looking after the children and listening, endlessly listening. It was where she had found Mrs Cheng, looking like a little pansy with her yellow face blurred by purple bruises. She had given Mrs Cheng a part-time job at Richmond Villa, and had then found her a room in a hostel and a second job, cleaning a dentist's surgery in Beaumont Street. Mrs Cheng's gratitude manifested itself in tireless zeal for Kate, a zeal that took the form of trying to subdue the mountains of muddle that grew up round Kate wherever she alighted. Joss had been to Mrs Cheng's room in the hostel. She said it was very bare and smelled funny.

'What she'd really like,' Uncle Leonard said, 'is to live here, in the cupboard under the stairs, and cook fish heads in a bucket.'

'I'll start supper,' James said now, moving towards the fridge.

'Good,' said Joss. James was a better cook than Kate. His food stayed separate, in its own colours and textures. Kate's always tended to look and feel the same, so that the taste was a surprise; not always, either, a very nice surprise.

'I bought a hat,' Joss said suddenly. She had not meant to admit this, and blushed at her mistake. Her buying of hats from the second-hand shops in Walton and Little Clarendon Streets was a solemn passion which she tried to keep as secret as her photographs of hair and shoes.

'Did you?'

'Yeah.'

'What sort of hat? Can I see it?'

Furious with herself, Joss kicked a carrier bag towards James. It was an old supermarket bag, worn and crumpled. James picked it up and took out a little black velvet hat, like a Highlander's bonnet, with a coarse black veil pinned to it with two diamanté bows.

'It's lovely. Really glamorous.'

'I hate it. I wish I hadn't gone and bought it.'

James knew better than to call her bluff and say take it back then.

'I wish women still wore hats like that. So sexy.'

'Yuk,' said Joss.

James put the hat back in its bag. He opened the fridge — far too small, as it had been for eight years — and squatted in front of it.

'What about a giant stir-fry of everything I can see in here?'

Joss drew the hat bag towards her, with infinite stealth.

'I'm not hungry.'

'I am. Uncle Leonard always is. Mum's bound to be.'

'I'm going to take this hat back. It's gross.'

James stood up and began to unload things out of the fridge on to the table.

'Why don't you give it to Mum for her birthday?'

'What birthday?'

'Her birthday in two weeks. Her thirty-sixth birthday.'

'You said that hat was sexy —'

'It is.'

'I can't give a sexy hat to *Mum!*'

They stared at each other. Joss pictured Kate in the hat and James looking at her in it, and felt sick. James pictured the same thing and felt stirred. He was the first to turn away. 'Suit yourself,' he said, picking up a punnet of tired mushrooms.

The front door opened, letting a wild draught shoot in under the closed kitchen one, and then slammed.

'Ah,' James said with satisfaction. Joss stuffed the hat bag hurriedly into the black sack she used to lug her school books about in.

Kate opened the kitchen door and blew in, glistening with rain. She had put nothing on her head, and her wiry red hair held the drops like a maze of twigs.

'Disgusting,' Kate said, and dropped her bag on the floor, and a carrier of groceries, which sagged sideways and spilled tangerines and a huge tawny Spanish onion.

James went over to kiss her.

'Careful. I'll drench you. I'm wet through to my knickers. Hello, Jossie.'

'Have a bath. I'm about to cook supper. Have a bath while I do it.'

'Where've you been?'

'At the home. Where d'you think? Usual post-Christmas flood of the poor things. They all say they dread Christmas more than any other day of the year.'

James began to extract Kate from her mackintosh.

'You're quite right, you're soaked through. Joss, go and run Mum a bath, would you? And say supper in half an hour, to Uncle Leonard?'

Joss got up. 'Can I go skiing? Can I go with the school?'

Kate glanced at her. 'No,' she said, 'I haven't the money.' She gave James a quelling look to fore-stall his offering. 'You know I haven't. But I'm sorry. I'm sorry I haven't.'

'Yeah,' Joss said. She'd held out little hope in the first place, and, although she'd promised herself she would make a scene, she hadn't the heart for it when it came to it. She went out of the kitchen, leaving the door open, knowing that James would have to close it after her.

'I'm so glad you're back,' James said.

Kate squatted on the floor by her bags, a supple little figure in black dungarees. 'Me too. It was so sad today. I suppose it's as much the gloom of early January as anything, but somehow the home didn't feel like a refuge today, more like some sort of bleak waiting room, all form-filling and queues. And everyone was smoking. I'm ashamed when I feel ratty, but sometimes I do, really ratty.' She put the last rolling tangerines back in the carrier and stood up.

'Talking of shame,' James said, returning to his mushrooms, 'I'm full of it. D'you know what I did?'

'Tell me,' Kate said.

'I forgot my specs when I went out to fax my piece through to the paper. And I knocked a

19

woman over in Beaumont Street, not badly, not hard, but I knocked her off her bicycle.' Kate was listening, still, attentive. James warmed to her unspoken sympathy. 'The worst of it was that she was so vulnerable, one of those frail old academics with a bun. There was cat food in her bike basket. She was going to the doctor's, luckily, so I escorted her there, and of course I'll go and see her tomorrow, but in the meantime, I feel rather haunted, and so sorry.' He stopped, and waited for Kate to reassure him, even to come over and put her arms round him, and lay her damp cheek against his chest and tell him that it could have happened to anybody, particularly on a night like this. But she didn't. She said nothing and she didn't move. He looked across at her, surprised. She was regarding him with a look that was wholly unfamiliar, a cold, almost contemptuous look.

He opened his mouth to speak, but before he could utter, Kate said, in a voice that matched her expression, 'You stupid old man.' Then there was another silence, in which they regarded each other with horror.

Kate lay in her bath with her eyes closed. She had asked Joss to stay and talk to her, but Joss had said she'd got stuff to do, and clumped away to her bedroom. Kate couldn't blame her. Joss might only be fourteen, but she was no fool and could easily tell the difference between being asked to stay for a genuine conversation, and being asked to stay to prevent Kate's being left with

20

her own thoughts. 'Sorry,' she'd said, 'got stuff to do.' Her voice was faintly cockney, Kate's was faintly Oxfordshire, James's was, well, different; Kate's mother said James had an Oxford accent. James! Why had she said that to him? She hadn't meant to, she hadn't even realised she was going to. Stupid was all right, so was man, but old — Kate drew up her knees in the bath in agony. He'd looked stricken, as if she'd slapped him. She'd never slapped him, she'd hardly ever raised her voice to him; he wasn't that kind of man, nor she that kind of woman. Yet now she had called him a stupid old man, she realised with a shock that she meant it. It *was* the behaviour of a stupid, myopic, absent-minded old man to drive about in the dark and the rain without glasses and knock people off bicycles. Oh God, thought Kate, suddenly afraid of where her mind was going, what am I doing?

She never thought about his age when she met him. If anything, the twenty-five years between them had been something of a turn-on, and the whole affair had been so natural and so marvellous, she had never asked herself what she was doing. They had met in a pub off Holywell Street. James had been there with his lifelong friend Hugh Hunter, and Kate had been with a boyfriend, not Joss's father who had vanished back to Canada the minute he heard she was pregnant, but another boyfriend, with whom Kate was getting bored. Hugh Hunter had spilled a little beer on Kate's shoulder as he tried to push through the crowd, and James had been the only one with a handkerchief. He looked wonderful to Kate, big and relaxed in a polo-necked jersey under an old tweed jacket. She looked up into his face quite openly and thought of the Duke of Wellington; perhaps it was his nose. He said, mopping her shoulder, 'My name's James Mallow.'

'My mother comes from Mallow,' Kate had said. 'Mallow in County Cork. In summer, her parents took her and her sisters to paddle in the Glashaboy River.'

James took her telephone number. Next day, he rang and asked her out to see a film with him. Then he asked her to come and have Sunday lunch with him at Richmond Villa. He wouldn't let her help, but sat her at the kitchen table with a glass of wine, while he chopped and sliced. She sat there and watched his hands and forearms as he chopped, his shirt-sleeves rolled up to his elbows, until she couldn't watch any more, being so giddy with the longing to be in bed with him that she could hardly sit upright on her chair. After lunch, James did take her to bed, and it was extraordinary. It was, Kate told herself, like those sex scenes in novels that you scoff at for never happening in life. But this one did. That spring Sunday afternoon when Kate was twenty-eight and James was fifty-three (and Joss was six) the sex was sensational.

When at last it was over, James took Kate down to his study, and showed it to her. She was amazed at how clean everything was; not at the cleanliness itself, but because everything that was so clean was also so old. In Kate's childhood, apart from a few family treasures of her mother's, only new things had ever been clean. Old things were, by definition, worn, grubby, stained, decrepit. Here everything was the reverse. Old things wore a glow of health. Kate sat in James's spinning desk chair and looked up at the painting of the smooth, plump, pale-brown prince, with pearls looped in his turban and around his neck, and his hand resting upon a sword slung from a silken sash.

Two weeks later, she had moved in. She couldn't now remember if James had precisely asked her, but she was so consumed with longing to live with him, she'd have hardly noticed if he had asked or not. James painted a little bedroom for Joss, who had never slept on her own before and who wouldn't have the light turned off at night for two years. When he was working, writing articles at his desk, or tutoring pupils in his study, Kate crept about the house with excited reverence. Nothing must be changed, she must respect what James wanted. Even later, when she realised that he had grown to love her, and that she could be quite bold with him, she still had no desire to alter things. The villa was James. Kate, as James was quickly grateful to realise, did not judge; Kate had a huge capacity to accept.

She accepted the habits of a man accustomed for twenty years to living on his own; she accepted his desire for order, even if she could not match it in her own behaviour; she accepted the need, for James's sake, for Joss to lead a more disciplined life; she accepted Uncle Leonard; she accepted too, without asking him, that James would give her, in return, all the freedom she needed to do the things she wanted to do. One of those things was to stay single.

'I'm dead scared of being pitied,' Kate said. 'And I'm even deader scared of being a burden.'

'But you wouldn't be. I want to marry you because I love you and I want you to be mine. I want you to be a burden, if you put it that way. I want to be responsible for you.'

'Today, perhaps. Even tomorrow. But not for ever. I couldn't take the responsibility for disappointing you.'

'But you wouldn't. I know you. You're what I want.'

'All the same. No.'

'Your reasons are so flimsy.'

'Not to me. Clear as crystal and solid as rock to me.'

And so it went on, wrangle after wrangle. Gradually, he ceased to fear that if she wasn't married to him she would leave him. When she began on her voluntary work, with problem families, with young drug addicts camping out at Horsley, with battered women, she said it was the least she could do. 'I'm so lucky, I stink.' Three days a week she worked for a friend in a little pasta restaurant, waitressing, washing up, doing the books. It kept her and Joss in clothes and extras; she would have liked it to have kept them in food and household expenses too, but when she said this to James, he was absolutely adamant.

'No. I'm not even going to discuss it. You can call me antediluvian if you like but I want to support you both. If there ever comes a time when I can't, I'll tell you, but until then, shut up and eat up.'

Kate sat up in the bath and seized the soap. She began to wash vigorously, almost punishingly, as if she were scrubbing away something much more than tiredness and a day's wear on her skin. When she had finished, she let the bath water out and turned the shower on, to cold, and rinsed herself all over, for longer than was anything but purely unpleasant. Then she towelled herself dry, pulled on jeans, a huge old jersey of James's, and a pair of thick white seamen's socks, and padded downstairs.

James had laid the table, and put candles on it. He had also piled the tangerines in a green glass bowl, cleared the day's detritus off most of the surfaces and opened a bottle of wine. The air smelled deliciously of supper and Radio Three was kindly playing some Vivaldi. James turned it off when Kate came in, and looked at her.

Kate bit her lip. 'I'm so sorry. I don't know why I said it. I never meant to.'

He made a little gesture. 'Forget it. It doesn't matter. I expect it's true, anyway.'

They waited, to see if anything either of them had said would make things feel better. It didn't. The telephone rang. Out of habit, because James hated the telephone, Kate went to answer it. 'Hello,' she said. 'Oh hi. It's you. I know. Awful. I got wet through. Hang on, I'll get him for you.'

She held the telephone out to James as if it were a peace offering.

'It's Hugh,' she said.

Chapter Two

Hugh Hunter sat on a rush-seated bar stool in his perfect country kitchen, and talked into the telephone. The kitchen had been made perfect by Julia, who had an unerring eye for not over-doing things. It was a long, low room with white walls and a cork floor and just the right kind of wooden furniture and jars and racks of practical kitchen things. There were terracotta pitchers and cracked blue-and-white plates and old copper pans, but not too many and not obviously displayed. All guests to Church Cottage seeped gradually into the kitchen because the atmosphere was so alluring, and sat by the Aga in Windsor armchairs on patchwork cushions to watch Julia stirring a sauce or giving the twins their tea. Hugh had an office to telephone from, at the back of the cottage, and another telephone, comfortably beside an armchair in the sitting-room, but mostly, and particularly if the call was conversational, he found himself in the kitchen, on a bar stool, with his elbow and wineglass and ashtray on the waxed elm dresser beside him.

'I've rung to grizzle,' Hugh said to his oldest friend, James Mallow.

'It'll have to be a short grizzle then. We're about to eat.'

'Julia's left me boeuf Bourguignonne and gone off to record something. I should never have egged her on to try her hand at interviewing.'

'Rubbish,' James said, 'you're sick with pride.'

'True.'

'And quite right too.'

'Yup,' Hugh said. He was proud. In one way or another he had been proud of Julia all along. When she had produced boy twins for him, he had thought he would expire with pride.

'Look,' James said. 'You eat your boeuf Bourguignonne and read something improving, and I'll see you on Saturday, in the King's Head.'

'Condescending prat,' said Hugh, and put the receiver down. He thought a bit. James had sounded unrelaxed. Probably it was Joss, who was enough, if she tried, to unrelax the most lowly-strung of households. Why were most teenagers such helpless posers? Would the twins be? Would those dear little fair boys with their earnest four-year-old faces turn into stereotypes of elaborately anarchic adolescence? How sad, if so, how sad and how deeply, profoundly, boring.

Hugh opened the bottom door of the Aga. His casserole sat there in an olive-green glazed pot from Provence. He took it out carefully and put it on the rush mat Julia had left on the table, beside the place she had laid for him. 'Salad in fridge,' her note said. 'Then cheese. Could you bear to finish the Brie first?' That was typical of

Julia, firm but very polite and charming. They had been married for seven years and, during those seven years, Hugh had frequently been out in the evening without Julia, or in London for the night. Tonight, however, was the first night of their marriage, with the exception of the odd occasion when Julia went to see her parents, when the goose's accepted sauce applied to the gander.

Hugh turned on the radio. Vivaldi. He didn't feel like Vivaldi, he felt like something harsher, Walton or Britten, perhaps. Church Cottage had an elaborate music system, piped throughout the ground floor, but Hugh did not, somehow, feel like going to the trouble of finding the right disc, and feeding it into the player. 'It'll take two minutes,' he told himself. 'I know,' he said back. 'I know, I know, but I don't want to do it.'

He found his salad in the fridge, little curly fronds of dark and pale leaves sprinkled with walnuts. There was a brown baguette loaf too, and unsalted butter in a white rectangular china box with a cow reposing peacefully on the lid. He arranged his supper around the laid place at the table. It looked faultless; it smelled glorious. For some reason, Hugh wanted to pick up the butter dish lid by the china cow, and flick ash inside. He poured more wine into his glass — a thick, lovely glass which they had bought together in Venice — and splashed some on to the smooth blond surface of the table. He let the red pool lie there for a while, and then he drew in it with his finger and made it into a red snake. He thought of Joss Bain again. He was behaving like Joss. Joss made him think of James. He sat down on a patchwork cushioned chair, and began to spoon casserole on to his plate, and wished that James was there, eating with him, telling him not to smoke, looking at him with exasperation and affection.

They had met at Cambridge. They had been tutorial partners, both reading history. James had been born in South Africa, in Grahamstown, in the Eastern Cape, where his father, arriving there from England in the mid-twenties, was a schoolmaster. The family had returned to England just before the Second World War, and James's father had survived almost the whole war, only to die of a virulent dysentery in Italy, in a prisoner of war camp. His younger, physically frail brother, Leonard, had come to the family's rescue, helping with James's school fees and introducing his sister-in-law to the bursar at the public school where he taught himself, whom she subsequently married. James was brought up to believe that there was no career in life to be considered but schoolmastering.

Hugh was brought up very differently. His father, an asthmatic, throve commercially during the War — black market dealings, Hugh always suspected — and died in 1948, the year Hugh went up to Cambridge, leaving just enough money to pay his debts, and to pay off, in the shape of a passage to Australia and a small capital sum, a hitherto unsuspected mistress and eight-year-old

child. Hugh's mother, a brassy woman of unquestionable courage, sold the family house, gave
half the proceeds to Hugh, and took his sister to
live in a flat in her home town of Huddersfield.
A dressmaker by training, she set up a tiny business, which grew to be a bigger business and then
to be a significant shop. When she died, she left
most of her money to her daughter, who had inherited her father's asthma and was too frail to
do more than part-time work, and two hundred
thousand pounds to Hugh. With it, he and Julia
had bought and entirely renovated Church Cottage.

At Cambridge, James was as haunted by not
wanting to be a schoolmaster as Hugh was fired
by longing to be an actor. He was a member of
the dramatic company and after his degree (a
third) he joined a touring company, as a student
ASM for twenty-five shillings a week, which rose
after six months to the basic Equity wage of six
pounds and ten shillings. His mother disapproved
violently; in her view, the theatre was full of nancy
boys and show-offs. In all his three years in rep,
she never came to see a performance, and when
his delicate, breathless sister came, she had to pretend she had gone somewhere else. 'It wouldn't
be worth the row,' she'd say in her soft Yorkshire
voice, holding out a food parcel to Hugh. 'She
can keep a row going two weeks or more. I'm
not stopping coming, but I'm not confessing
either.' When independent television was born, in
the fifties, and Hugh got his first contract with

one of the major companies, his mother said without enthusiasm that that was more like it. She'd wanted him to be a lawyer, after Cambridge, she'd wanted him to better himself.

Hugh Hunter and television adored one another and he was made front man for one of the first national news and views programmes. He was known as Double H, by his colleagues and by the public; in due course, his programme was successfully rechristened *Double H Time* and won awards. He had a flat near the studios, an MG and a series of lovely sixties girlfriends with enormous painted eyes, and sometimes, at a weekend, he would put the current girl into the MG and drive her down to the old Oxfordshire rectory on the Windrush River, where James lived, with his wife.

His wife was much older than James. She was also quite wealthy. She had bought the house on the Windrush, and she paid most of its expenses, so that James was quite free to please himself as to what he did. He tried several things, opening a bookshop, writing a thriller, beekeeping to a commercial standard, but they did not satisfy him. He recognised that his dependence upon his wife probably accounted for his dissatisfaction, but he never blamed her for it. He was deeply fond of her; she had been a parent at the school where his stepfather was bursar and she had, in the truest sense, rescued him from Mallow expectations and tyrannies. They lived in great harmony in their riverside house, only disagreeing over one thing, which was Hugh Hunter. In the end, to keep the peace, Hugh stopped coming down to Oxfordshire, and James met him in London. When James's wife died, of a brain tumour, when James was thirty-two, Hugh was the first person to come to comfort him.

James's wife left him enough money to buy a modest house — the rest went to her children — and a letter in which she said she was afraid her wealth had done him no service, and that she wished him a fulfilled life from now on, and a very happy second marriage. On Hugh's free days from the studios, he and James prowled Oxford for houses, since James said he'd moulder if he lived in the country any longer. It took them four months to find Richmond Villa. 'It's a night-mare,' Hugh said. 'You can't live in a horror like that.' But James loved it at first sight.

The house had brought him luck. He found, to his chagrin, that he liked teaching, and got himself a job at one of the city's many tutorial colleges. He also found, that, even if he couldn't write fiction, he could write. He wrote some ex-perimental social and political pieces for national journals and newspapers and had them accepted. He altered Richmond Villa a little to make it more comfortable; he rather vaguely made a garden, he made friends. He developed, in a peaceable, ran-dom manner, a way of living which gave him, he came to realise, the first real freedom he had ever known. This freedom became very precious to him and so, although he embarked on a series of romantic and sexual adventures (he did not seem able to combine the two in any one woman), he felt no desire whatsoever to share Richmond Villa with anyone. Hugh scoffed at him; he said he was turning into an old armchair of a bachelor, that he had soup stains on his mind as well as on his tie. James, looking at Hugh's sun-lamped tan and ever younger girlfriends, said equably that, whatever he was, it was better than being a fossilised middle-aged trendy.

They took to meeting every week. In the early seventies — Hugh's heyday — *Double H Time* went out on most independent channels early on Thursday evenings, giving Hugh a weekend of Fridays and Saturdays. He invariably saw James each Saturday, driving down to Oxford because he said it took James a week to drive anywhere. Sometimes he went to Richmond Villa, but mostly, out of respect for their early days together at Cambridge, they went to the pub. Afterwards, James would walk Hugh around Jericho, or along the Oxford Canal, revelling in Hugh's horror that anyone could actually choose to live among low bleak brick streets within earshot of the railway line. James said, 'I love hearing the trains.'

Hugh was honest with James. He never tried to pretend, with James, as he did with everyone else, that he had known Richard Dimbleby — with whom he had in truth once had lunch in a party of ten — very well. He did not try, either, to hide his anxiety when *Double H Time* was switched to Mondays, then cut from forty-five minutes to thirty, then dropped altogether. After the age of forty, he grew palpably afraid of getting old, and would turn to James for reassurance. He always looked younger than James, younger and fitter and better cared for, but his growing anxieties made him tense in public, inclined to overact. He began to talk of London-based television as played out, of the provincial companies as the places to look to, for a future. James understood him very well.

It was a terrible shock to Hugh when James met Kate. He was unable to appreciate either her, or her beneficial effect on James, because his own sense of loss and betrayal obscured his vision. He stayed away from Oxford, and endured several alarming months in London, alarming because he was perfectly certain that both his professional and his personal life had ended in a yawning black hole. Then the telephone rang. It was an offer, the offer of presenting a similar kind of programme to *Double H Time* on Midland Television, whose chairman, Maurice Hirshfeld, had been a friend and colleague in those first happy independent television days in the late fifties and early sixties. 'We've come a long way,' Maurice said. 'We started in a converted cinema. Remember?' Hugh was offered a two-year renewable contract.

His production assistant on the new programme, *The Midlands Matter*, was a girl called Julia Ferguson. She was quite unlike the girls Hugh had used to tear down the motorway with, a cool, collected girl with smooth hair drawn back, and huge pale spectacles. She wore suits, and very little jewellery; she could speak French and Spanish and she read Latin American novels; she turned Hugh hot and cold by alternately seeming oblivious of him, and seriously asking for his advice and acting upon it. Within a year, they were married without having once properly discussed the discrepancy in their ages; Hugh because he was afraid to, Julia because she didn't need to.

Hugh's mother died two months after the wedding, of which she disapproved. She said Julia was a cold fish. With her legacy, they set about finding a house half-way between the Midland Studios and Oxford, because Julia intended that there should be children who would need educating in Oxford. They found Church Cottage standing in its acre of orchard and garden, a sixties conversion of a seventeenth-century cottage in which some dated echoes remained, the odd wall of hessian wallpaper, or a stray abandoned curtain after a design by William Morris.

Julia was orderly, a planner. The house was reorganised to eighties standards with a careful nod to its seventeenth-century origins, in two years. Once that was done, Julia stopped swallowing the pill and became pregnant. Two days after Hugh's fifty-seventh birthday, Edward and George were born in the John Radcliffe Hospital and two days after that, Hugh's contract was once again renewed. On his first programme after the twins' arrival, Hugh made an impromptu, emotional and very successful speech to the viewers about each of us having, once in our lives, an unexpected *annus mirabilis,* and the true, and dare he say it, almost religious thankfulness this inspired. He got sackfuls of letters after it, and the management of Midland Television, which had been sharply divided as to the wisdom of renewing his contract, relaxed a little.

James wrote to Hugh when the twins were born, and the friendship fell back into its old ways with relief. Kate and Julia, it was assumed, would get on. Each was, for different reasons, slightly disconcerted by the other, but it was not in Kate's nature to dislike. In any case, there were the twins. Fair, square and cheerful, the twins had, without the least effort, collected a fan club which even included Joss Bain.

'Are you jealous?' James had asked Kate, anxious for her. 'Are you jealous of Julia?'

'I'm not jealous of her for having babies,' Kate said. 'But I'm jealous of her for having the twins. You'd have to be made of stone not to be.'

As far as the twins were concerned, Hugh was made of putty, or butter. Julia was the one who administered discipline, vitamin supplements and early reading practice; Hugh administered play and adoration. If he was worried, or irritable or in need of distraction, he would either go and find the twins, or think about them. His office at the Studios was full of photographs of them; the whole staff sent them birthday cards and at Christmas they came to the first half-hour of the Studios' party and were handed about like puppies.

37

They were tremendously good-natured about this, as they were about everything, as long as they remained in sight of one another. Sometimes, simply thinking about them when he was in one room at Church Cottage, and they were only in another, could cause Hugh to want to weep.

They were, of course, Hugh's solution to the present evening. A glimpse of them under their blue-and-white striped duvets, turned towards one another across the space between their beds, would soothe and mollify him. At the thought, Hugh repented of his sulks. He put his plates and cutlery docilely into the dishwasher, replaced the butter in the fridge, ran hot soapy water into the Provençal pot, wiped away the dried trail of the red-wine snake and shut his cigarettes firmly into a drawer which he would not open again, he said sternly, until an emergency. Then he lowered the lights — all the lights at Church Cottage were harnessed to dimmer switches — and went upstairs. He would, he decided, wash his hands and brush his teeth before he went to look at his sons.

His sons. They lay as he had pictured them, George's cheek on a knitted pig, Edward's deep in his pillow. Julia disapproved of pillows, but Hugh had fought for them, on the grounds of psychological comfort.

'They don't need that. They aren't like single people. They're twins.'

'Even so,' Hugh said, 'they're still individuals, they need their own territory, and personal comforts, whatever they are, are part of that territory.'

He stooped over them. They were still young enough to smell of babyhood, rather than of the rankness of boy. Julia kept them perfectly, clean and trimmed in bright, soft clothes. They always looked brand-new from their gleaming fair heads to their polished leather boots; Julia would not allow them trainers, but bought French boots for them in scarlet and navy-blue.

'Oh twins,' Hugh breathed, gazing down on them.

George stirred. His eyes opened. He looked at his father. 'No pig,' said George and flung the knitted pig to the floor. He was asleep again immediately, shutting Hugh out. From downstairs — Julia always unplugged the upstairs one in the evening — the telephone rang.

Hugh went down without enthusiasm. 'Over fifty,' he often said to Julia, 'you learn to dread the brute.' He didn't go into the kitchen but into the sitting-room, the calm and elegant sitting-room, floored in pale sisal matting and hung with kelims.

'Yes?' Hugh said. 'Hugh Hunter.'

'Hugh. It's Maurice.'

Hugh felt in his trouser pocket for his cigarettes. They were in the kitchen drawer.

'Sorry to ring you so late, I wanted to tell you personally —'

'What?'

'The good news,' Maurice Hirshfeld said loudly. 'The *good* news.'

Hugh swallowed. He tried not to think about

39

his cigarettes. 'Which is?'

'We've got him. He's agreed. He signed to-night.'

Hugh sat down in the cream calico armchair beside the telephone.

'Kevin McKinley.'

'Yes. It's wonderful. As I've said to you often, having a man like Kevin as our Managing Director can only raise our image.'

Hugh said, 'He's made one series, *one* series, Maurice, that's been a huge success, that's all —'

'He's the right age, he's got the right contacts, he's worked in America —'

'And I expect he sees Midland as a stepping stone to the BBC, to being Director General. What sort of a deal has he got?'

Maurice said, 'You only get monkeys if you pay peanuts.'

Hugh said nothing.

Maurice went on. 'We'll all benefit, Hugh. We've got the franchise renewed, and now we've got Kevin.'

Hugh took a huge breath and closed his eyes. His long acquaintanceship with Maurice was his strongest card at Midland Television and Maurice would — he hardly dared think about it — be retiring in two years, two years before Hugh, had he been an accountant or a solicitor, would have been retiring too. He must, for his own sake, betray nothing.

'Jolly good,' Hugh said, filled with fear. 'So pleased. Great news.'

'Knew you'd be pleased. That's why I wanted to tell you myself.'

Lies, lies, the whole conversation lies.

'He wants to meet all the key people next week. Can you make Tuesday?'

'Of course —'

'Excellent,' Maurice said. The relief that the call was almost over lent warmth to his voice. 'See you Tuesday. Have a good weekend.' He suddenly remembered. 'Boys well?'

'Blooming.'

'Good. Well done. Jolly good.'

Hugh put the telephone down and went into the kitchen. He opened the drawer and found his cigarettes, and then he retrieved his glass from the dishwasher and filled it again. He sat down with both, on the bar stool. He could picture it all, Kevin McKinley naming his own salary, huge holidays, a chauffeur-driven car, Kevin McKinley saying, 'And you'll pay my full pension.' The Kevin McKinleys of this world, Hugh thought, were not disposed to look kindly upon presenters of over sixty, even presenters who looked well under sixty (and unconsciously took two or three years off their ages when asked to state it) and whom the public liked. 'They do like me,' Hugh said, staring down into his wineglass. 'They do. They write and tell me so.'

Car tyres crunched softly over the gravel outside the window. Julia. Hugh was not sure he was ready to face Julia, he felt — he felt — what did he feel? Distressed, that's what he felt, unhappy

41

and afraid and shaken. He didn't like Julia to see him like that, even though inevitably, in seven years, she sometimes had. With a life as precarious as his, how could it be otherwise? It couldn't, but that didn't stop him disliking it. He sat on his bar stool and ground out his cigarette and waited for her quick light step from the garage.

'Oh Hugh,' said Julia coming in, bright-eyed. 'How forlorn you look.'

He held his arms out to her. 'No good at evenings on my own —'

She clicked her tongue but she allowed him to hold her for a moment. He said, 'Did it go well?'

She nodded. 'I went out with a fire engine. It was fascinating.' She turned her head away and said modestly, 'They said I was fine.'

'You mean they said you were bloody marvellous.'

She removed herself from his embrace. 'I'll have to get contact lenses. I can't go on wearing these goggles.'

'I love your goggles.'

'You're not a television camera. How are the boys?'

'Dead to the world.'

She took the kettle over to the sink to fill it. 'Was supper all right?'

'Delicious.'

He watched her. She hadn't taken off her narrow, dark-blue overcoat and her pale hair — the twins' hair — hung down the back of it, its edge cut as levelly as a curtain's.

'It was such a revolting night. I had to stand under an umbrella and I'm sure my nose was red. They've decided to call the series *Night Life*. Next week, it's a travelling soup kitchen in Oxford.'

'Better tell Kate. Derelicts are her speciality, she'd know where to find them.'

'I think,' Julia said quietly, plugging in the kettle, 'I'd rather find my own. Tea?'

'No thanks.'

She looked at him.

'What's the matter?'

'Maurice rang,' Hugh said.

Julia took off her coat and folded it over the back of one of the wooden armchairs. She wore a polo-necked jersey and a short skirt and her admirable legs were clad in narrow suede boots. She came over to Hugh and put her arms round him.

'Oh Hugh. It's Kevin McKinley, isn't it?'

'Not really.'

Julia said nothing. After a while, Hugh said against her shoulder, 'My contract's up for renewal again in the summer.'

'I know.'

'Kettle's boiling —'

'It'll switch itself off.'

'Maurice is a good friend,' Hugh said, a little heavily.

'He's as weak as water,' Julia said. 'Only serving time now until retirement.'

'Still Chairman, sweetie —'

Julia let go of Hugh, and went over to the kettle. She unhooked, as she passed it, a blue-and-white mug from the dresser and dropped into it a sachet of camomile tea.

'Maurice won't let me down,' Hugh said.

Julia poured boiling water into her mug.

'Know something?' Hugh said. He had straightened on his bar stool and now took a confident swallow of wine.

'Tell me,' Julia said, her mind winding itself lovingly about the memory of her evening, about the director's praise . . .

'The Kevin McKinleys of this world,' Hugh said, looking straight at Julia with that directness of gaze so effective on camera, 'come, and go. Mostly go, having no bottom. But you can be sure of one thing, absolutely sure. And that is that the tide in the affairs of television is swinging back my way.'

Long after Hugh had fallen asleep, Julia was still wakeful. When she heard the long case-clock in the hall strike two, she realised that it was a serious wakefulness, and slid quietly out of bed and went down to the kitchen.

The kitchen was warm, even at two in the morning, because of the Aga, the dark-blue Aga which Julia had chosen with such grave care. Hugh had teased her about it; Hugh was one of the few people in her life who had ever teased her, and she had stopped feeling shy about it, had grown even to like it. 'Miss Immaculate Conception,' he called her. 'Miss Perfect Understatement. Miss Shiny Shoes.' He could still, with light-hearted physical suggestiveness, make her blush.

She had blushed that evening, out of pure pleasure.

'Great,' the director had said to her, when they had finished. 'I've hardly a complaint. What it is to work with someone who uses their intelligence.' Later still he said, 'You'll be going places, Julia.'

'No,' she said. 'No, this is just an experiment. I'm really a mother of two.'

They had both laughed. He'd said, 'You mean mothers aren't people?' and then he said, 'See you next week. I'll look forward to it.'

Julia sat down in one of the Windsor armchairs and put her slippered feet against one of the Aga's heavy hot doors. She had not, she reflected, been quite truthful when she told the director that she was experimenting. She was not, by nature, an experimenter. It had become perfectly plain to her, since the twins were born, that Hugh's career was going to run out of fuel quite soon, and glide gently to a halt. This was going to be a fearful blow to him, and Julia, while bracing herself for it, was not quite sure how best she could help him bear it. In her eyes, his fading glamour as a television face had had nothing to do with falling in love with him; she'd done that because he wasn't in the least afraid of her, and he made her laugh. He was more musical than she was, more broadly educated, inevitably more experienced. He also had, in all kinds of directions, truly catholic tastes. Once, when they had known each other only a week or so, she had asked him what kind of music he liked best and he had said at once, quite seriously, 'Mozart for the morning and Tina Turner for the afternoons.'

'What do you see in him?' Julia's mother had demanded. She had wanted Julia to marry a country landowner and have Labradors.

'He delights me,' Julia said.

I wouldn't mind if he didn't work at all, Julia told herself now, moving her feet to a cooler door, I'd only mind for him. But we've got to live, and we've got to live properly, I'm not going backwards. We've all got to be clothed and fed and the twins have got to be educated. It's as simple as that. Hugh's got no pension and no capital outside this house. It's up to me.

Her thoughts, which could never help themselves, began to form into a plan. If the *Night Life* series was generally considered a success, and led to something else, preferably under contract, then she would look about for a responsible girl who could drive, to look after the twins . . .

The kitchen door opened. Hugh said, 'Can't stand not sleeping.'

Julia put a hand out to him.

'What are you up to,' Hugh said, 'sitting down here looking all of fourteen? What are you plotting?'

'I'm not plotting —'

'No?'

'I'm planning.'

'Yes,' Hugh said, his voice dropping. 'Yes. I was afraid of that.'

Chapter Three

'My lotus flower,' Uncle Leonard said to Mrs Cheng. 'My little yellow peril, where the bloody hell have you put my slippers?'

'Under bed,' said Mrs Cheng. 'Alway' under bed.'

'And how,' said Leonard, leaning on his stick and snorting at her down his nose, 'how am I, with a gammy hip and a ticker on the blink, supposed to get them? Grovel about on the floor to find the sodding things?'

Mrs Cheng went on dusting, flick, flick, like a mechanical doll.

'Alway' do.'

'Never do. Shall I spend the day in my bleeding socks?'

'S'pose so.'

Leonard was very happy. He adored the days Mrs Cheng came, and heaven knows, this week needed a little light relief.

'There's been an atmosphere here,' he said confidingly. 'An atmosphere like nuclear fall-out. James knocked some old bat off her bike and pow — mushroom cloud.'

'Not interested,' said Mrs Cheng. She began to move all the pill bottles off the glass shelf above Leonard's basin.

'Mind you,' Leonard said, poking about under his bed and fishing out his slippers with the hooked end of his stick, 'it was a pretty damned stupid thing to do, driving without specs.'

Mrs Cheng ran water into the basin and began to polish the taps.

'He's gone to see her again today, the old bat. Kate doesn't like that. Now, why doesn't she? Loves the halt and the lame but doesn't like James trotting round to see a harmless old bat. What's the reason?'

'None of your business,' Mrs Cheng said. 'Want coffee?'

'Yes, but not yours. Never yet met a Chink who could make coffee. Do you realise what filthy coffee you make?'

Mrs Cheng put the pill bottles back.

'Good 'nough for you.'

'Love a woman with spirit,' Leonard said. 'Love a bit of fight. Kate's got spirit. D'you think she thinks James and Old Bat Bachelor have too much in common as to age? Hah!'

'You older than either,' Mrs Cheng said. 'You more trouble than all put together.'

Leonard looked pleased. 'You bet I am. Where's my coffee? It's ten past eleven. What does Kate pay you for, you useless peasant?'

Mrs Cheng picked up her dusters and cloths and began to wind the flex round the Hoover handle.

'I paid double,' she said, 'to put up with *you.*'

49

Miss Bachelor kept the very dull biscuits she offered James with his coffee in an octagonal tin patterned with vaguely oriental herons and peonies. It was a very battered tin, as battered as everything else in Miss Bachelor's crammed, first-floor bed-sitting-room, except for her precious radio, which was brand-new, and on which she could, to her delight, get the BBC World Service during her long, sleepless nights.

Her room was not only crammed, but cheerless. She had no more idea of how to make it charming than she had of how to dress, and she calmly knew it. 'As you observe,' she said to James, 'I seem to have no practical visual sense. The rapture I feel in seeing beautiful things is something I am quite unable to translate into my life.' Her furniture was either late-Victorian, heavy and overbearing, or what James's mother would have called boarding-house, gimcrack and slightly fancy, overlaid with a varnish like thin gravy. Her bed had a counterpane of tired maroon candlewick, and her unwelcoming chairs were covered in terrible blankets of sewn-together crochet squares, in the screaming colours associated with acrylic paint. The carpet was muddy, the sad curtains unlined; only the walls relieved the ugliness, being covered with postcards and larger reproductions of all the Italian works of art Miss Bachelor so loved — paintings by Bellini and Giorgione, statues by Michelangelo, bas reliefs by Ghiberti and della Robbia.

Miss Bachelor's sister-in-law owned the house in Cardigan Street, and allowed her the room. She had opened the door to James three times by now. She was a depressed, grim woman, a widow, who lived only for her hypochondria. She resented Beatrice's cleverness just as she had resented her husband's, and for Beatrice to have a personable male caller bringing sherry and a pot of hyacinth bulbs just coming into flower was a fine cause for fresh resentment.

'Mrs Bachelor,' said James heartily to her on the third visit. 'How exceptionally well you're looking.'

'You will have annoyed her exceedingly,' Beatrice said.

'Will she take it out on you?'

'She will try. She will hide my butter or shut my cat out, but I have developed a mantle of imperviousness to defend myself. It irritates her beyond all telling.'

Beatrice had several dark bruises on her legs, visible through her unlovely stockings. James had vowed he would keep coming until those bruises had vanished. After the first few minutes of the first visit, Beatrice had said she didn't want the accident referred to again.

'It involved us both in a loss of dignity, and we shall only suffer it anew if we remind ourselves of it.'

She was tremendously pleased with the hyacinths, and shy about the sherry. 'There was a period in my life,' she said unexpectedly, 'when

51

I drank a great deal of it, a very great deal. It coincided with a time of going to Greece alone, and of having adventures. The memory of that time is rather — stimulating. But it disconcerts me too.'

James leaned forward. 'What adventures?'

Beatrice looked away.

'Lorry drivers?' said James.

Beatrice said nothing.

'Oh Miss Bachelor,' James said. 'I begin to feel so glad I knocked you over.'

She was, he discovered, sharp as well as brave and unconventional. She had taught classics at an Oxford girls' school, but had had to retire early to look after her old parents who both took an interminable and fretful time to die. 'I loved them,' she said serenely to James, 'but I didn't like them in the least.' They had left a tiny estate, just enough for Beatrice's brother and his wife to buy the little Jericho house, and give Beatrice a room in it. 'My brother was hopelessly impractical, an antiquarian and, I must confess, a very weak character. My sister-in-law kept him by working as a secretary in a solicitor's office, and I contributed out of my pension which, I have to admit, is very nearly invisible to the naked eye.'

'Not enough to go to Greece any more?'

'Greece,' said Beatrice, 'never cost me very much. Not, that is, in money.'

James longed to share this with Kate. 'Do you think she had a series of rough-trade romps? Do you think they paid for her? Took her all over the Peloponnese in the cabs of their trucks, and fed her ouzo and olives and made love to her under taverna tables?' But Kate wouldn't respond. She looked mulish and cold. She said she thought James was making a fool of himself and of Miss Bachelor, and then she said she didn't want to hear any more about it.

'Jealous,' Uncle Leonard said.

'Jealous? Of Beatrice Bachelor? Don't be daft.'

'I'm not daft. I'm a wiser old bugger than I'm given credit for.'

'You're certainly an old stirrer.'

Leonard put down the paper and looked at him.

'You're an odd cove, James.'

Was he odd? Was it odd to feel curiously at peace in this ugly room, with its little banners of beauty and civilisation pinned to the walls, in the company of Beatrice Bachelor? Was it any odder than spending time in the places Kate chose to frequent, the places inhabited by all those poor wretches whom modern society had made so hopelessly dependent? And if he was odd — or she was — why wouldn't she talk about it?

'I live with a woman twenty-five years younger than I am,' he told Beatrice. 'She has a fourteen-year-old daughter. And we also have my eighty-five-year-old uncle.'

'A rich household.'

'Yes. Yes, I suppose it is. When you live something, it doesn't of course feel rich, it merely feels commonplace.'

'You must learn to value dullness,' Miss Bachelor said. 'And you must send me that fourteen year old. I like girls. I particularly, having been one myself like difficult girls. Fourteen year olds, if they're worth their future salt, are always difficult.'

'I won't go,' Joss said.
'Of course you don't have to,' Kate said. She felt tired and irritable. She had spent the day helping in the restaurant kitchen, because the chef was off sick, and she had chopped up a mountain of chillies without rubber gloves, and her fingers and cuticles blazed and throbbed.
'I hate old women. What's the point, anyway?'
'I said, you don't have to go.'
But Joss wanted to. 'What's he on about? Why does he want to make me?'
I'm lonely, Joss thought. She turned the little silver stud she had just had inserted in the side of her nose. Uncle Leonard had said, 'Good God. Looks like a bloody great boil,' sending Joss flying to the bathroom mirror. 'It looks great!' she'd shouted. She spun it carefully now, defiant and uncertain.
'I'm not going. I'm not. He can go if he wants to, but I'm not.'
I wish, Kate thought, holding her burning hands under the kitchen tap, I wish he didn't want to. I wish he wasn't so fascinated. It makes him seem so peculiar, somehow, a bit dotty, *old* dotty. I know I'd go mad if he fancied anyone young, but

somehow this mental fancying of someone old has got me too, it really has, and I shouldn't feel it, I shouldn't.

'I'm not —' Joss began again.

Kate spun round, Kate who never shouted, and shouted, 'Oh for God's sake, Joss, go away!'

Joss stared. Then she swore. Kate turned back to the sink, trembling. The kitchen door banged behind Joss, and her aggressive boots went up the stairs with challenging thuds.

I'm tired, Kate thought. It's January and I'm tired. I don't suppose I'm worth much more than four pounds an hour but, at the end of a day like this, I can't help feeling that there must be easier ways to earn twenty-five pounds. In between chopping chillies, she had helped in the restaurant, waiting on the three back tables which the regular girl, Susie, disliked because no one could see her, away from the front window, and she lived in hope of being seen, and, as a consequence of being seen, of being rescued from being a waitress and taken away to be a princess instead. Nobody interesting had come to Kate's tables that lunchtime, only a dull pair of tidy women, and a man on his own with a book, and three whispering students, but two couples had come to the front tables who had, in their various ways, upset Kate even more than the savage chillies. That poor man, Kate thought now, taking her dripping hands away from the stream of water to see if they still hurt, that poor young man. And then Julia.

The young man had come in first, a postgraduate, perhaps, not young enough to be an under-graduate, with a dramatic girl in bold earrings and thigh boots. She was laughing as they came in and Kate thought how lovely, what a relief on a glum day like this to see people so happy that they're laughing. But she wasn't laughing with him, she was laughing at him, and soon, even while they wound up forkfuls of tagliatelle alla Carbonara, they were quarrelling. It seemed that the girl not only liked quarrelling, but she liked doing it in a public place where other people, even the lone man with a book, could look up and see her flinging her hands out, tossing her hair. The young man had not been much more controlled. Kate had heard him say, 'Not here. You mustn't say these things here.' Finally the girl had leapt up and thrown herself out into the street, and the man had said no thank you, he didn't want any coffee, and had paid the bill and followed her.

Five minutes later, while Susie was downstairs in the kitchen and Kate was pouring out coffee for the two tidy women, he came back in. Kate thought he had forgotten something. He came up to her, by the espresso machine, and she looked at him enquiringly. He said, 'I've just come back to say sorry.'

'What?'

'We were very anti-social.' He turned to the restaurant. 'I'm so sorry, everyone. It was extremely rude.'

They gazed at him.

'It's nice of you to come back,' Kate said.

'I feel badly, I feel —' he stopped. He had a narrow face and thick dark hair and his eyes were, Kate thought, so sad. He said, 'I'll go now. I just wanted to say that I'm sorry if we — if we spoiled anyone's lunch. That's all.' He backed away. Kate smiled at him. He smiled too and his smile illuminated his face and made it puckish, delightful. He gave a little nod to Kate and opened the door to go out just as two other people pushed at it to come in. They were a man in a black leather jacket, and Julia.

Julia came straight up to Kate. She was smiling. She said, 'I brought Rob here deliberately. He said he was Italy-sick, so I said I knew where to go.'

'Good,' Kate said faintly. Julia wore grey flannel trousers and a tweed jacket and a cream jersey and pearl earrings. Kate thought of the sauce stains down her apron and her red unhappy hands.

Julia said, 'Rob is my director.' Rob smiled at Kate. He had a friendly, crumpled face and tinted spectacles.

'Of course,' Kate said. 'Where would you like to sit?'

'Not next to the lavatory door,' Rob said.

'Here then,' Kate said, leading the way. 'Here. Susie will look after you.'

'Not you?' Julia said. Her face was open.

'I'm supposed to be skivvying in the kitchen. I shall offend the hierarchy otherwise —'

Julia smiled again. 'What do you recommend?'

'The gnocchi,' Kate said, 'made an hour ago.'

'How's Joss?'

'Dear, but horrible. I expect the twins are just dear.'

'Yes,' Julia said. 'Yes, they are,' and then Kate had felt she should melt away, so she had melted, to watch Julia and Rob intermittently and covertly while they ate and talked, with utter absorption, and Rob made copious notes in a reporter's notebook.

When they left, Julia had kissed Kate and said give her love to James and Kate had been left standing oddly on edge. Why, she asked herself stacking plates in the dishwasher, why, when it all too evidently wasn't a remotely romantic occasion? Why should it affect her that Julia should have lunch with a television director in this patently above-board and businesslike way, any more than that James had found an innocent human curiosity that amused him for the moment? He might be getting older, Julia might be setting out on a career, but so what? Kate had always known James would get older, and that getting older would probably change him a little, just as getting middle aged would doubtless change her. She had always felt affectionately about this, knowing that the essence of James would never change, and believing that the periphery didn't matter. As for Julia, Kate and James had often talked about her, and her very real competence, and how heaven-sent it was that someone like Hugh, with career prospects dependent on age, should have someone like Julia to take over quietly when he was forced to stop. Now, faced with Julia appearing to be embarking on doing exactly that, and James behaving with all the imagination and warmth of heart that she had always so loved in him, why wasn't she rejoicing? *Why?* She always rejoiced at other people's achievements, she always had, she relied upon being able to do so. But stacking plates in the restaurant's basement scullery that afternoon, and standing at the sink at Richmond Villa now, she felt cold with resentment. She also felt scared by her feelings.

She dried her hands and inspected them. 'Little hands,' James always said, folding the pair of them up in one of his. They looked wretched. She thought she would go upstairs and find the cream that the doctor had prescribed for Leonard the winter he had had bronchitis, to prevent his getting bedsores. Kate had nursed him then, at least, as much as he'd allowed her to.

'I've got my dignity still, though I mayn't have hair or teeth. When I look at myself in the bath I think: Leonard, old boy, you need ironing. And I'd rather only I saw that.'

Kate went out of the kitchen and along the hall. James's study door was shut, and from behind it came the steady reluctant drone of a pupil reading an essay, a gloomy, stooped boy, trying to retake his A-level English examination, to whom James, being James, was very encouraging. Kate went up the stairs slowly and tiredly. The split in the carpet on the seventh step was widening, exposing old-fashioned, matted brown underfelt. The usual music was hammering away behind Joss's door and the radio news quacking behind Uncle Leonard's. Kate knocked.

'Wait.'

Kate waited. There was shuffling and grunting and the radio was turned off.

'Come!' Leonard shouted.

'Look,' Kate said, holding out her hands.

Leonard peered. 'You need my bum stuff. What've you been doing?'

'Chopping chillies.'

Leonard began to rummage in a drawer. 'You'd earn more money on the streets.'

'I know.'

'James back?'

'Yes.'

'Know where he's been?'

'Yes,' Kate said steadily.

Leonard found a huge white plastic pot with 'Oily Cream B.P.' stamped on the side, and held it out to Kate. 'Why d'you reckon he goes?'

'She interests him and he feels guilty.'

'Why don't you like that?'

Kate looked at him. 'I don't know.'

'But you don't.'

'I'm tired,' Kate said. 'It's January.' She unscrewed the lid of the pot and took out a dollop of cream on her finger. 'I'd forgotten what slimy stuff this is.'

'Kate,' Leonard said. He watched her sliding her hands round and over one another in the slippery thickness of the cream. 'Kate. If you'd only bloody marry him, you'd have the authority to object.'

Julia was home ten minutes before she had promised to be. Thursdays were Hugh's empty days, and he had agreed, without particular grace, to look after the twins while Julia had lunch with Rob Shiner. Julia had thought of asking Hugh to come too, for his sake, and then had decided against it, for her own, and for the sake of their future. She had left a shepherd's pie in the bottom oven, vegetables ready prepared in saucepans, and a tub of Greek yoghurt in the fridge which her note said the boys could have for pudding with a teaspoonful of clear honey. Hugh told them they didn't have to have honey. They always had honey, so at first they didn't know what else to suggest until Hugh said what about jam, which they were seldom allowed. Then the possibilities of this game dawned on them and they thought of marmalade and peanut butter and then (much funnier) bubble bath or mud and then (so funny that George fell off his chair and lay shaking on the floor) poo. After that, they became extremely wild and silly and rushed round the kitchen like express trains shouting lavatory words, and Edward put a cushion on his head in order to be the bees knees of a joke and it fell off into the puddle of yoghurt he hadn't eaten. That sobered them all up, because the sticky cushion made them think of Mummy. Sticky cushions and Mummy didn't somehow go to-gether.

'I'll wash it,' Hugh said.

The twins dragged up chairs to the sink to help him and squirted washing-up liquid all over the cushion in looping yellow squiggles and the cushion went from being a light, soft, coloured, dry, comfortable thing to being a sad, dark, heavy wet lump. They squeezed it and shook it, and laid it on the hot lid of the Aga, where it flopped like an omelette.

'It'll be fine,' Hugh said. 'When it's dry, it'll be just like before.'

The twins weren't sure about this. When Hugh took them into their little playroom — bright and clean with a big cork pinboard, and a huge low table for playing trains and painting on — for an after-lunch story, they became babyish and jostled all over him and put their thumbs in. They didn't really listen to their story, a particularly soppy tale they had insistently chosen about a bad puppy and a good kitten, being far more intent on their wriggling battle to occupy the prime place on Hugh's lap. After the bad puppy had chewed a little girl's new bedroom slipper, Hugh gave up and said they were going out for a walk. They immediately shouted 'Yeah, yeah, yeah' and began to stand on their heads. For a fraction of a second, even Hugh had to remind himself that he loved them.

The walk was not a success. George had a sock that wouldn't stay up in his gumboot and Edward said his ears hurt in the wind but he wouldn't wear his hat. It was a sullen, raw day, with the flat Oxfordshire fields in a mid-winter sulk. By the river they met a disagreeable swan and an ordinary duck or two, but the landscape was otherwise devoid of interest and life. Hugh plodded on for a dutiful mile while the twins skirmished round him tripping him up, or trailed in the rear, grizzling about their socks and their ears, and these were, he told himself, his good, cheerful, biddable twins who were universally agreed to be the least trouble it was possible to be if you were four, and a boy, and multiplied by two.

When they got home, the twins clamoured for television, which they were allowed to watch on selected days only. Hugh felt rebelliously that he didn't care if it was a selected day or not. He turned it on — the boys were forbidden to touch anything electrical — and a purple gorilla lunged out of the screen and brandished a panga at them, shouting 'Kill, kill, kill!' Sighing with rapture, the twins subsided in a heap together on the carpet and put their thumbs in. They looked as Hugh imagined he used to look long ago, when he smoked dope, serene and inwardly concentrated.

He went out to the kitchen. After the post-lunch rampage, the chairs had been left all anyhow, like abandoned dancing partners, and half the crockery they had used was still on the table among the spills and smears. On the Aga, the cushion had baked into a thin dry biscuit. Hugh picked it up and shook it, and the feathers inside rustled like cornflakes and fell into a little heap at one end, leaving him holding an almost empty bag. He tried to pump it full of air, and then arranged it artfully back in its Windsor chair and casually threw a folded newspaper across it.

He began to clear the table. Everything seemed coated with stick, even the rush mats. He aimed washing-up liquid at the table, to unsticky it, but it was the concentrated kind, and the surface of the table vanished under a dense blanket of unconquerable foam. Hugh rinsed and rinsed and rinsed. The foam dissolved into clouds of bubbles which were lighter but thicker, and began to blow about the room and make him sneeze. He scraped them off the table surface with a fish slice, and then dried it vigorously with several clean, ironed tea towels, and stood back to admire the effect. The surface of the table, usually as pale and gleaming as the twins' and Julia's hair, looked dull, smeared and unhealthy.

'Bloody, fucking hell,' Hugh said.

He lit a cigarette and began to slam things into the dishwasher. He broke the handle off a mug. From next door in the sitting-room, the roars of the gorilla were mounting and it suddenly struck Hugh, for no reason, that, in the three and a half hours since Julia had been away, the telephone had been completely silent. It seemed the last straw. He dreaded it when it rang, but he was desolated when it didn't. Prompted by nothing

64

more than impulse, Hugh pulled the bar stool up to the dresser, settled himself there with his ashtray, and dialled James's number.

'Richmon' Villa,' said Mrs Cheng.

'Is Mr Mallow there, please?'

'James out,' Mrs Cheng said.

'And Miss Bain?'

'Kate workin'.'

'When will Mr Mallow be back?'

'Don' know,' said Mrs Cheng. 'Never say. You want to leave message?'

'No,' said Hugh. 'No. I don't want to leave a message. I want to *talk* to someone.'

Then Julia came home. She brought an apple tart from the French baker in St Giles. She said, 'Oh Hugh, have they been awful?' and he said with miserable thankfulness that he thought it was his fault, he'd egged them on. He managed to ask if her lunch had been a success. It had.

'We planned the next three programmes. It's so amazing, the way that talking to someone who's brimming with ideas makes you have ideas too. I remember thinking that when I met you, I remember thinking that it was all right to think things that weren't conventional.'

'And now you're used to me.'

'Of course I am, in a sense, because you aren't a stranger any more. What happened to this cushion?'

'It was the victim of a game. Don't be cross with them.'

Julia looked from the cushion to him. 'I'm

65

seldom cross with them. I explain things. Has any-one rung?'

'Not a soul.'

Julia put the cushion down. She went over to Hugh and put her hands on his shoulders. Her eyes, behind her huge spectacles, were huge too, and serious.

'Darling Hugh, I know this is hard for you, I know it's hard to change. But we've got to live, haven't we? We've got to live and educate the boys and have the nice things we're used to and the holidays and so on. I suppose it was inevitable that our roles would change a little, over time, that we would have to adapt, that the emphasis would shift. I can cope. I don't mind shouldering more. I don't feel any differently about you if I shoulder more. But I don't think I can shoulder your resentment as well.'

'I'm not resentful. I'm simply in mild despair.'

'But why? You've had a wonderful career, you've been a household name, you've still got a very good job, why do you feel in despair?'

Hugh took her hands from his shoulders and held them a little and then dropped them. 'Be-cause, my darling child, I am simply not effective any more. And when we cease to be effective, then it is that the iron enters into our souls.'

While Julia was bathing the twins, and washing their hair which she always did on Thursdays, she remembered she had not told Hugh about seeing Kate. Kate, Julia thought, had not looked very well, she'd looked pinched and tired, though her manner had been as sweet as ever. Privately, Julia thought working in Pasta Please was a tiny bit affected, though she genuinely admired Kate's voluntary work. Well, she would tell Hugh about Kate at supper, and then she would have a serious, constructive talk with him about things he could do in life which would restore to him this sense of being effective that he said was so vital.

After supper at Richmond Villa, Kate's friend Helen rang. Helen ran the home for battered wives. She spoke for a long time, explaining how the money-raising side was claiming more and more of her time and attention, and that she really did need someone prepared to help much more with the administration, though of course she couldn't pay such a person more than pocket money, so it would have to be a person well circumstanced enough to feel they really owed it to society to do something difficult for nothing. Then she paused and waited for Kate to volunteer. Kate, winding her legs round the legs of the kitchen chair she was perched on, and feeling a rat, didn't volunteer. Helen then admired Kate. She said she had such understanding and compassion and humour and that her days at Mansfield House (named after Katherine Mansfield whom Helen particularly respected) were days everyone there looked forward to. Then she stopped again, and waited.

'I'm sorry,' Kate said. She tried to say something

else, she tried to say that she would love to help, and, even more, to mean that she would love to, as she would have done, she told herself only recently, but nothing came.

'I've rung you,' Helen said, not troubling to hide the reproach in her voice, 'because I thought I could rely on you to see how I'm situated and to want to help.'

'I do want to, but I can't.'

'Why? What's happened?'

'There are,' Kate said carefully, 'a lot of changes here.'

'Don't tell me. Don't tell me James is throwing you out —'

'No. No. Nothing like that.'

'Then —'

'Helen, if I could explain myself properly, I would. I'll go on helping on my usual days, but I can't do more. I'm sorry, but I can't.'

'I see,' said Helen, who didn't, and put the telephone down.

Kate drew her knees up so that her feet were on the seat of her chair, and wrapped her arms round her shins. I'm changing, she said to herself, I'm changing. How could I say no to Helen when I know what she does, how hard she works? How could I? But I did, and I don't want to ring her and take it all back, either. What's happening? I feel I'm losing all the things in myself that I value, that I'm hardening, that I'm trapped. Is it because I live with someone a bit inflexible, someone a bit old? I'm mad. Sixty-one isn't old.

68

Sixty-one's nothing. It's very wrong of me to think of James as old. And it's very wrong of me not to want to help Helen. Help, Kate thought, pushing her knees into her eye sockets, help. Where is all the loving going?

The door opened. James put his head round it.

'Kate. Are you all right?'

She raised her head. She looked at him. She managed a smile.

'I've just been very unhelpful to Helen, on the phone.'

'Good,' James said, who thought Helen was bossy.

'No,' Kate said, shaking her head. 'No. Not good at all.'

Chapter Four

The Penniman Agency in London occupied two small but graceful rooms in Bedford Square. Vivienne Penniman, who had been a Rank starlet in the days when Hugh Hunter was first entering television, had set up the agency with all the shrewd realism of an actress whose career manifestly had a certain lifespan, and no afterlife. The purpose of the agency was to organise money-making public appearances for celebrities, in order that they might be able to put something by for the bleaker days ahead when the public, reminded of them by a chance remark, would say, 'He's never still alive! Heavens, I thought he'd copped it years ago, you never see him now, do you?'

Actors and actresses, television personalities, footballers and lesser tennis players came to Vivienne Penniman to be offered things to open or promote, supermarkets, garages, sports complexes, leisure centres. Depending upon the position their star currently occupied in the popular firmament, she could offer them either a four- or more often a three-figure sum for an appearance of not more than two hours, minus her ten per cent. Some of her clients were realistic and cheerful about this, enjoyed joshing around with the public, and had no illusions about the ephemeral nature of their best success. Others were resigned, but professional, and regarded the whole business as a necessary evil, with whining about it being out of court. Yet others felt diminished and resentful, unable to pass up several hundred pounds an appearance, and equally unable to reconcile themselves to how it was earned. Being of this latter group, Hugh Hunter had so far resisted joining Vivienne Penniman's agency.

But Julia had talked to him. She had been very sweet, not in the least patronising, only sympathetic and firm. Hugh had been surprised at how firm she was. She had said look, there's this problem and here are some of the ways I think we could help solve it. If you have better ideas, fine; if you don't, perhaps you would look at mine. Julia had reminded Hugh about Vivienne Penniman.

Hugh reminisced about Vivienne for a bit. 'She was fearfully pretty. I remember her coming in to the studio with a whole lot of other Rank girls, and it was like having a bunch of flowers sitting there. They were asked to predict their futures, and told that we'd look at them again in ten years, and see where they'd got to. It was terribly funny, not just because they were so innocent and hopeful, but because of the cameras. We only had one set in the studio then, of course, and we had to use them for everything. They'd been taken out on the Solent the day before, filming ocean races, and every time the turret turned you could hear a layer of sea salt crackling.'

Julia was not deflected. 'Hugh,' she said, in the kind, steady, adult voice she used when the twins were on the verge of doing something awful.

'I know,' he said. 'I'll go. Don't bully me.'

'I'm not. I'm simply trying to focus you.'

'And you're right. I know you're right. But it is terribly, painfully, difficult to go against one's instincts.'

'I do understand.'

Hugh filled his wineglass again and took a gulp. 'Please don't,' he said. 'Please don't be so sweet and understanding and reasonable. Please, my darling Julia, don't be so fucking perfect,' and then he had taken himself and his glass out to his little chill study at the back of the cottage, and hunted about among the files of thirty-five years for Vivienne Penniman's telephone number.

'Hugh,' Vivienne said. She was standing up behind her desk, her hands held out to him in a clash of bracelets. The girl like a flower had matured into a formidable magnificence of bosom, and strong, shapely legs and richly tinted hair. She wore black, and too many pearls for the morning. 'My dear Hugh. After all these years.'

She leaned across the desk and gave him a kiss whose powerful fragrance took him abruptly back to all those dear departed theatrical dressing-rooms of the fifties. 'And what a success you've been.'

'Past tense significant.'

'I don't allow that kind of talk in here. I wouldn't

have agreed even to see you if you weren't still going strong. Mind you, you should have come years ago. I could spank agents, really I could. A business like mine is no skin off their noses, but they won't urge their people my way when it's to their best advantage to do so. I like to get someone when they're rising, bully them into investing what they earn with me and then, when they're fading, hey presto, there's a nest-egg.'

'I'm a late starter,' Hugh said.

Vivienne looked at him as if she were appraising a prize pig. 'You certainly are. But there's mileage in you yet. Certainly mileage in the Midlands.'

'Garages in Bicester, businessmen's hotels in Birmingham —'

'Exactly so,' Vivienne said crisply. She pressed a buzzer on her desk. 'I'll give you our details, and we'll look and see what we've got that might do for you.'

A girl came in, a lively girl, all hair and exuberance, and put down some papers in a plastic folder on Vivienne's desk. Hugh looked at her. She gave him a wide, remote smile. He looked at the plastic folder. Vivienne had spun her chair away from him towards a computer screen behind her.

'See you,' the girl said, and went out.

Vivienne tapped and pattered on the computer keys. Hugh watched her. The telephone rang and was intercepted in the other room.

'What luck,' Vivienne said, without turning. 'What luck. There's a delicious new golf course, sponsored by Japanese car people, just outside Wolverhampton. It's the real thing, thirty-six holes and all the trimmings. They've got a golfing star to open it, and they want a well-known telly face to be his sidekick, ask him things.' She swung back. 'You can do it with your eyes shut. They'll pay all your expenses, and three hundred pounds.' She looked at him. Her expression changed. 'Smile, please, Hugh,' she said.

Joss knew it had to be Miss Bachelor. She had that old-fashioned posh sort of voice, and she was wearing a dire coat, and she was asking Mr Patel in the grocer's for Nice biscuits. Joss didn't think that was how you pronounced them, she'd always thought they were called that because they weren't nice at all, but boring.

'And oxtail soup, if you please,' Miss Bachelor said to Mr Patel. 'Just one tin, and some brown boot polish and a pint of milk.'

Mr Patel was very polite to Miss Bachelor. Other customers, trained by supermarkets, collected their groceries in a wire basket, but Miss Bachelor didn't seem to have cottoned on to such independence, and Mr Patel humoured her. Mr Patel was a second-generation Christian, his father having been converted, in Rawalpindi, before the Second World War, by a missionary who had looked very much like Miss Bachelor, and whose photograph was glued into the Patel family album. It would have distressed Mr Patel very much to know that Miss Bachelor was an atheist.

'Is that everything now?' said Mr Patel, putting a carton of milk on the counter. He was keeping an eye on Joss, juggling her chewing-gum packet in her hand. She was just the age, in Mr Patel's experience, for the least scruple about shop-lifting.

'A quarter of humbugs,' Miss Bachelor said. 'And a tin of Mousemix.'

'Meowmix,' said Mr Patel gently.

Joss snorted. Miss Bachelor turned round. She looked at Joss for some time, then she said, 'I wonder if you are Josephine?'

Joss froze. Nobody ever, ever, called her by her real name, her gross, obscene, shameful name. 'It's Joss,' she growled.

'As we have never been introduced,' Miss Bachelor said, 'I am hardly in a position to use your nickname, am I?'

Joss didn't know what to do. She looked at the floor and wished she had enough hair to hang over her face in a protective curtain.

'Put that gum with my groceries,' Miss Bachelor said. 'I will pay for it. I dislike it personally, but clearly chewing it is preferable to smoking.'

'I don't want you to pay for it,' Joss said.

'But I do, because I want you to carry my shopping for me.'

Mr Patel thought it was just as well there was no one else needing serving. Joss took a step forward and dropped her gum packet on the counter. She looked stunned.

'Now,' said Miss Bachelor, pulling out of her pocket a purse whose size and air of pathos would

75

have distressed James very much, 'the grand total, if you please.'

Mr Patel put the groceries into a carrier bag left over from Christmas, bearing a picture of two smudged children building a snowman. He handed it to Joss. Miss Bachelor counted out her money with infinite slowness and care and laid it on the counter.

'Two more pence, please,' said Mr Patel patiently.

Outside in the street, Joss was seized with the violent apprehension that she might be seen accompanying Miss Bachelor. Few of her schoolfriends lived in Jericho and, in any case, darkness had fallen at teatime, but Joss thought she would keep her head down, all the same. Awkwardly, with her one free hand, she wound her black muffler high around her cheeks and ears.

'I'm truly pleased to meet you,' Miss Bachelor said. 'I asked your stepfather to send you to see me.'

'He isn't my stepfather.'

'Then how would you describe him?'

Joss couldn't think.

'Would you prefer it if I were to call him your mother's lover, which is what, I suppose, he literally is?'

Joss certainly wouldn't. She gave a little involuntary gasp. She said, in a slightly strangled voice, 'He's called James —'

'I didn't think you would come, of course,' Miss Bachelor said. 'I thought you would be determined not to. I am, after all, so very unfashionable. But I thought we would somehow meet, even if I didn't think it would be so soon.'

'What for?'

'Explain yourself.'

'Why d'we have to meet?'

'We don't have to. But I thought we might like it if we did. I knew I should like it and I imagined you could put up with it. I have a cat, and even if you don't like me you will like my cat.'

They turned the corner into Cardigan Street. A sharp wind met them and Miss Bachelor stooped into it. 'I detest the winter.'

'Yeah,' Joss said. She planned to dump the carrier bag, say hi to this cat, and run. Miss Bachelor said, 'I will turn on my gas fire, and we will make toast.'

'I got homework,' Joss said.

'You will do it better after toast,' Miss Bachelor said. 'And another time, we might do it together.'

'I don't need that,' Joss said rudely. 'I've got Uncle Leonard for that.'

Miss Bachelor stopped in front of a narrow door, and fumbled inside her coat for a key on a string round her neck.

'I shall keep you fifteen minutes, Josephine, and then you may go, and if you dislike it that much you need never come again.'

Joss was late for supper. She was not only late, she had clean forgotten it was going to be something of a celebration, because it was Kate's

77

birthday. It was only when she burst into the kitchen and saw the three of them sitting there, with candles and a bottle of wine, that she remembered. They all looked up when she came in.

'Where've you been?' James said.

'Doesn't matter,' said Kate quickly.

'Where've you been?' Uncle Leonard demanded as if James hadn't uttered.

'Miss Bachelor's,' Joss said. She drooped. 'I forgot.'

She had forgotten, completely. She had spent the first ten minutes of her allotted fifteen minutes looking steadily and pointedly at Miss Bachelor's clock, and then she hadn't remembered to look at it again until Miss Bachelor had remarked that it was half-past seven.

Kate pulled out the chair beside her. 'Come and sit down. James has done a chicken, roasted a chicken.'

There was a lump in Joss's throat. She said, 'I'm not hungry.' She wasn't, she was full of toast, packed with it, slice after slice toasted on an old-fashioned fork, like a devil's fork, in front of Miss Bachelor's gas fire. Miss Bachelor let her spread the butter straight from the packet.

Kate said in a slightly tight voice, 'Did you have a nice time?'

Joss nodded. It was weird, but she'd liked it, she'd liked it from the moment Miss Bachelor had said, 'We have something in common, you and I. We are both regrettable to look at, but you are going to improve. Indeed, you are going, in the end, to be lovely, and believe me,' Miss Bachelor said, waving her hand at her postcards and pictures, 'I am a judge of loveliness.' Joss had knelt on her bed and looked at the Marys pinned above it, Mary after Mary in blue robes, and golden robes and rose-coloured robes, each one holding her Jesus. Joss didn't like some of the Jesuses. She thought Jesuses ought to look like George and Edward Hunter, with soft round baby faces and fair hair, and some of these Jesuses looked middle aged, heavy and knowing. But the Marys were beautiful. Joss supposed Miss Bachelor was churchy; old women like her were always churchy.

'I am an atheist,' Miss Bachelor said to Joss, 'but I am thankful to the Christian religion for the inspiration it proved to be to the masters of the Italian Renaissance.'

'What's an atheist?'

'Look it up,' Miss Bachelor said, pointing to a dictionary in her shelves. Joss did, with difficulty, not being adept with dictionaries, and then she was amazed.

'You don't believe in God!'

'In any god. Once I was that most Victorian of creatures, an agnostic, but then I came to believe in a certain spirituality, just not in a god.'

'I'd be scared not to,' Joss said.

'That,' said Miss Bachelor, 'is superstition.'

They had an argument then. Joss had liked it, because it never seemed to get personal, even though she couldn't seem to see anything except

79

from her own point of view.

'Stop saying "I" all the time,' Miss Bachelor said.

'I can't —'

'Yes, you can. You can with practice. You must learn to stretch the muscles of your mind.'

Joss grew excited. 'Dim,' she was used to Uncle Leonard shouting. 'Clod-hopping dim. *Stupid child.*' She knew he didn't mean it, that from Uncle Leonard insults were endearments, but all the same, whizzing across her maths homework with exasperated ease and speed, he made her feel dim.

'I'm thick,' Joss said to Miss Bachelor.

'Arrant nonsense,' Miss Bachelor said back. 'Piffle. All your brain lacks is exercise.'

'What did you talk about?' James said now, putting a plate of chicken in front of her. There were peas on it too, and roast potatoes, and little rolls of bacon and a splodge of bread sauce. Joss's eyes bulged.

'God,' said Joss.

'What?'

'I can't eat this —'

She looked up at Kate. Kate was looking desolate. Joss said, 'Oh my God, your present —' and shot from the room.

'Don't be cross with her,' James said to Kate.

'I want a looksee at Old Bat Bachelor too, you know,' Uncle Leonard said to James.

'I'm not cross,' Kate said in a quiet despair to her plate.

Joss returned with an old crumpled supermarket bag. She thrust it at Kate. 'Sorry it's not wrapped up, sorry it's late, sorry it isn't new, sorry —'

Kate drew out the black hat with its veil and glittering diamanté bows. 'Oh!'

'Isn't it delicious?' James said. He picked up his wineglass. 'Put it on.'

'No,' Kate said. 'No.' Her face was working. She held the hat away from her. 'Thank you,' she said to Joss.

'You don't like it —'

'I do, I do —'

'You don't!' Joss shouted. She tried to snatch the hat. Uncle Leonard shot out a bony hand and gripped her arm. 'Behave yourself.'

'She hates it —'

'I don't,' Kate said. Her voice was almost a whisper. 'Oh Jossie, I don't, it's lovely, it's a lovely present.'

'Then put it on,' James said. He glanced at Joss, green-white and still imprisoned by Uncle Leonard. Poor Joss . . .

'I can't,' Kate said. She lowered her head and laid the hat carefully on Joss's empty chair beside her. Then she got up and walked slowly out of the room, closing the door behind her.

Leonard dropped Joss's arm. 'Of all the —'

'Shut up,' James said. He went round to Joss. They never touched, it was part of their unspoken mutual code of conduct not to touch, but now he longed to put his arms round her. 'It's not you,' James said to Joss, 'and it's not the hat. It might be me, and it might be something quite other, but it's definitely not your fault.'

'You said to give it her,' Joss cried defiantly.

'I know.'

'And now look —'

'Go after her,' James said, 'go on. She'll be feeling awful. She'll want to talk to you.'

'I don't want —'

'Joss,' James said.

She looked up at him with her father's eyes in her mother's face, under her mother's hair.

'Go on,' James said gently.

She turned away, sighing like a tornado, and slumped out of the room. The door crashed behind her.

Uncle Leonard held out his wineglass. 'Good riddance,' he said, 'to the whole boiling of them.'

'I didn't go because I wanted to,' Joss said to Kate, 'she asked me. She asked me to carry her shopping, in front of Mr Patel, so I had to.'

'Of course,' Kate said. She sat on the edge of her bed, her and James's bed, and screwed a tissue up into a scruffy little ball. 'It was kind, to go.'

Joss stood on the old Afghan rug in front of Kate, and jabbed at a hole in it with her boot toe. 'The hat was only a joke —'

'It's lovely. I said so. I love it.'

'It's awful. I'll take it back.'

'Please not,' Kate said. She wanted Joss to come a little nearer, so that she could hold her, in this cold bedroom, in her misery. 'I'm behaving so badly,' she said. 'I don't know what's the matter. Miss Bachelor —'

'She's OK,' Joss said, in the encouraging, re-assuring voice she sometimes used with the twins.

'Why does James want to go?'

'I dunno.'

'What's it like? What's her room like?'

'Dreary,' Joss said. 'Old-looking. Everything's old.'

Old, Kate thought. She shivered. She held her arms out to Joss. 'Give us a hug.'

Joss came and stood stiffly against her.

'I wish I was fourteen again,' Kate said into Joss's shoulder, 'like you.'

Joss said nothing. She only ever thought about age in tiny amounts, like whether a boy you fancied was three months younger or older than you were. Kate was thirty-six now, but that didn't mean anything, it was just the sort of age mums were.

'We must go down,' Kate said. 'James bought me a cake. I'll — I'll put my hat on, for the cake.'

'Jesus,' Joss said, pulling away. 'Jesus, don't do that!'

Kate stood up. She pushed her hair away from her face, and her bangles, the Indian bangles made of shell inlaid in brass that Joss had given her for Christmas, clacked together.

'I do like that hat, Joss. I do. I just couldn't bear it when I took it out and I saw James —'

She stopped. 'Come on. Come downstairs with me and help me eat my cake.'

Later, while they were washing up, the telephone rang. As usual, Kate went to answer it.

'It's Hugh,' she said, holding the receiver out to James. 'He sounds pissed.'

'I am pissed,' Hugh said to James, 'pissed and pissed off.'

James manoeuvred a chair towards the telephone with his foot and sat down.

'What now?'

'Want to hear about my new career?'

James closed his eyes. He held the receiver a little way from his ear and Hugh's voice came clearly out of it.

'I'm going to open garages, James, garages and bowling alleys and lavatories for the disabled. I'm going to be Hugh Hunter, the megastar of the minimarket, I'm going to pull them in in their tens, I shall make hundreds. Oh James —' Hugh's voice cracked. 'Oh James, what's it all been bloody *for*?'

James opened his eyes and looked at Kate. She finished drying a handful of forks and put them down on the table with a soft clatter. She didn't look back.

'Where are you?' James said. 'At home?'

'No. No, I couldn't stand it, I wasn't fit company for anyone. I'm in the boozer, our local.'

'Stay there,' James said. 'I'll come.'

'You're a friend —'

'But you are *not* to get sentimental.'

'Promise.'

'Twenty minutes. I'll be twenty minutes. Don't drink any more.'

He put the telephone back and stood up. 'I'm so terribly sorry,' he said to Kate, 'and on your birthday.' He paused. On Kate's birthday, and his birthday, as well as on numerous other particular days and days of no consequence at all, they made love. If he drove over to Hugh, he would not now be back again until after midnight, and Kate would be asleep, or at least, sleepy, too sleepy for sex. He said, 'I'm painfully conscious this has been a thoroughly wrong-footed birthday from start to finish. I'd hoped I could at least get one thing right, later on, but Hugh —'

'Doesn't matter,' Kate said, interrupting.

'Give me a kiss. Give me a kiss before I go.'

She came around the table and kissed him quickly, impersonally.

'You're cross.'

'No.'

'What is the matter, then? Shall I ring Hugh back and tell him to pull himself together and I'll see him some other time?'

'No.'

'Kate —'

'I don't like birthdays,' Kate said. 'I don't like milestones. You go to Hugh. Poor Hugh.' She gave James a shaky smile. 'Drive carefully.'

He said, 'Katie, I wish you'd talk to me.'

She turned away and unhooked the car keys from

their home on a high cupboard knob. 'I expect I'll be asleep when you come home.'

'Will you? Couldn't we —'

'I'll be asleep,' Kate said quickly. 'I'm pretty tired. I've got the restaurant tomorrow. Thank you for my dinner, my birthday dinner.'

When James had gone out to the street to find the car, Kate climbed the stairs with a heavy heart. Leonard's door was half open, and Kate could see Joss, sitting on the floor on the red rug Mrs Cheng had found for Leonard at a jumble sale. Joss was wearing the frayed tweed coat she used as a dressing-gown.

'Ask her round,' Leonard was saying. 'Ask her to see me. I'll give her atheism.'

'She's a good arguer,' Joss said.

'So'm I,' said Leonard.

'She doesn't lose her temper —'

'Nor do I.'

'Yes, you do. You get baity all the time. And you say "I" all the time too.'

'Cheeky baggage —'

'You should learn to stretch the muscles of your mind,' Joss said.

'Hah!' Leonard cried. 'Caught you out. You never thought a thing like that. Too sodding stupid. You're just parroting Old Bat Bachelor.'

'Don't call her that —'

'Oh,' said Leonard suggestively, maddeningly, joined the James camp, have we?'

Kate crept past to her own room. She turned the handle softly and opened the door on to a chill wall of cold air. She put the light on, and closed the door behind her, and leaned against it. She looked at the bed, the bed which she and James had shared, for sex and for sleeping, since before she was thirty. Now she was thirty-six. In four years, she would be forty; and James would be sixty-five. She looked at the bed with apprehension. It's all my fault, Kate thought, all this not understanding each other, this coldness, this atmosphere. It's something that's happened to me, that's the matter with me, and I'm making everyone miserable. How dare I? I haven't got real troubles, not troubles like Hugh, poor Hugh with no future.

She crossed the room slowly, and looked at herself in the mirror that hung above the chest of drawers where James kept his clothes. She had to stand on tiptoe, because James, being so much taller than she, had hung the mirror at his eye-level. She didn't like the look of herself. Her hair looked dry and her face looked pinched and the dark-lashed eyes she had inherited from her mother looked like black beads. I'm going to hurt something soon, Kate thought. I'm going to damage something because something in me has got broken, and until it's mended I'm a liability to everyone else and I mustn't be that, nobody should ever inflict their brokenness on other people, on the innocent.

She went over to the windows to pull the curtains across. The street was empty, blue-black with pools of ugly orange light from the street lamps.

In the house opposite, the white man and the black woman who lived on the first floor and who never drew their curtains, were sitting either side of a table, among papers and files. The woman had plaited her hair with little coloured beads and they shone in the light over her head. Kate was filled with envy of her, working away across the street so peaceably, with her exotic beaded hair and her absorbed companion. She drew the curtains across abruptly, to shut the scene out, and hung there, gripping the edges, her forehead against her fists.

'The only thing,' Kate whispered to herself, 'the only thing that I can do now is simply to go away.'

She let go of the curtain and slid down to the floor. So what, really so what? She'd always known she'd have to, in the end.

Chapter Five

Beatrice Bachelor sat on a blue velvet sofa in the Randolph Hotel. She didn't think she had been inside the hotel in twenty years, despite living ten minutes' walk from it, and so she had, in its honour, put on new stockings and her Cairngorm brooch.

James Mallow had asked her to have tea there, to meet a friend of his who needed, James said, to have his sense of proportion restored to him. Beatrice, whose social horizons had widened dizzyingly in the month since James had knocked her over, had found herself agreeing to tea in the Randolph Hotel.

'You're an old fool,' her sister-in-law said sourly. She stood in the kitchen doorway and watched Beatrice tie her everyday Paisley headscarf over her grey knot of hair. 'You're being made a monkey of.'

Beatrice said nothing. She looked at herself in the hall mirror without affection, and hummed a little tune, 'O Lord and Father of mankind'. How irritating hymns were, burrowing about persistently in one's subconscious when one didn't subscribe to a word of them.

'I shall be home by six,' Beatrice said. 'Cat is

in my room. Please don't let him out.' Cat was not, in fact, in her room, but safely in the airing cupboard, on the clean towels, and Beatrice knew it. 'Goodbye, dear Grace,' said Beatrice annoyingly to her sister-in-law.

She did not, to her surprise, feel a fool at all, sitting in the Randolph Hotel. She felt perfectly ordinary, and rather pleased. Tea was a meal she liked in any case, and always had. If you ate enough tea, you didn't need to trouble with further sustenance that day, which allowed for a wonderfully long, uninterrupted evening. These had never alarmed Beatrice, accustomed as she was to associating evening with books and music and solitude. It was, however, delightful to think of eating a hotel tea in company. When James came in, he stooped over Beatrice and kissed her cheek. He had never done such a thing before, and, for a few seconds afterwards, she was disconcerted, and stumbled over her greeting of James's friend, a glamorous man, a healthy-looking, rather brightly coloured man, in smart clothes.

'You must have a forgiving nature,' Hugh said to Beatrice, 'to allow this idiot anywhere near you, after he knocked you flying.'

'Only flat,' said Beatrice, recovering herself, 'not flying.'

Hugh smiled his wonderful smile at her. 'I want a real tea, don't you? The works. Proper tea.'

Beatrice gave him a clear look to indicate she declined to be either humoured or patronised. 'Naturally,' she said.

'So dull,' James said, picking up a menu. 'It's a standard set thing, selection of this, selection of that. I'm going to find a waitress to say that we'll do the selecting, thank you. What sort of sandwiches?'

'Cucumber,' said Beatrice.

'Egg and cress,' said Hugh, still playing his role, 'and a cream horn. Or an éclair.' He sat down in an armchair.

'Be firm with him,' James said to Beatrice, and left them together, taking half of Hugh's audience away with him.

'I feel,' said Beatrice, 'that I am meeting James's friends in the wrong order. I think I should have met Miss Bain before I met you.'

'Haven't you?'

'No.'

'Kate's wonderful,' Hugh said exaggeratedly. 'Kindest heart in Christendom.'

'I hope her heart is not exploited.'

'Why should you say that?'

'Because in my experience,' said Beatrice, 'people assume that a kind heart in someone else is a bottomless well into which it is their right, almost their duty, to dip. My mother, when she was dying, once said to me, "How fortunate it is, Beatrice, that you have an opportunity to exercise your cherishing gifts." I went down to the kitchen after that, and simply shook with rage.'

Hugh forgot his wonderful smile, and leaned forward. 'You were nursing her?'

'And my father. They took seven years, between

them, to die. It was quite unnecessary.'

'Unnecessary?'

'They were both afflicted with cancer. Their lives dwindled to mere existences, but they resisted me, all the same. They preferred pain and humiliation and loss of all bodily and mental appetites to the obvious solution.'

James came back to hear Hugh say, 'What obvious solution?'

Beatrice glanced at James. Then she said calmly to Hugh, 'To euthanasia. I believe in euthanasia. I helped my brother to die.'

'God Almighty,' Hugh said, and fell back in his armchair.

James sat down silently, and stared at Beatrice.

'I joined the Voluntary Euthanasia Society in 1937,' Beatrice said, 'when I was twenty. I was taken to an asylum in Esher by a university friend whose brother was confined there, and the spectacle of those wretched inmates caused me unutterable anguish. I was an agnostic then, so of course I did not recognise human spirituality, but now that I do, I am even more convinced of the wrong done to damaged humanity in prolonging a life that has neither autonomy nor any capacity for the pleasures.'

A small Malaysian waitress appeared with a laden tray and began to unload cups and plates.

'If you would put the teapot here,' Beatrice said, 'I shall pour out.'

The men said nothing. The waitress put down cucumber sandwiches and egg and cress sandwiches and a plate of biscuits. 'Sorry,' she said to Beatrice, 'no éclair. No cream cakes.' She smiled. Half her teeth were gold.

'It's of no consequence, thank you,' Beatrice said. She began to pour the tea. The waitress moved away and Beatrice said, 'I appear to have disconcerted you.'

'Of course you have,' James said. 'I'm reeling.'

'You helped?' Hugh said with difficulty. 'You helped your brother to die?'

'Milk? Sugar? Indeed I did. At his request and with the help of a most excellent doctor. My brother had cancer too. His experience of chemotherapy left him unwilling to endure it again for what could only be another few years of diminished life. He died in his sleep, without pain. I cannot imagine how we have plunged into these deep waters.' She picked up the egg and cress sandwiches and offered them to Hugh. 'I think you should eat one of these, and I also think we should change the subject.'

'On two conditions,' Hugh said, seeming to pull himself together. He took a sandwich.

'Oh?'

'That we can return to it one day. And that you will consider, even for a moment, talking about it, on television.'

'Hugh!' James said, outraged.

'Why not?' Hugh said to Beatrice.

She looked at him. She thought of her brother's face that last evening, the calm on it, the relief. He had held her hand. 'Thank heavens it's nearly over,' he'd said. 'Don't ever tell Grace, don't ever tell her, or you will suffer, and no one who has acted as you have done, with such courage and understanding, deserves to suffer.'

'Why not indeed,' Beatrice said. 'After all, it is a very private matter, but it is not a secret. And there is a world of difference between the two.' She helped herself to a sandwich and inspected it. 'How excellent. They have cut off the crusts.'

For some reason, Pasta Please was full, all day. Customers had begun to come in as early as midday, and there were still people spooning sugar crystals out of the bottom of their espresso cups at four o'clock. Susie the waitress went home early, complaining of agonising period pains.

'Her stomach cramps,' the owner of the restaurant said to Kate. 'Happen quite regularly in the first week of every month when a certain software salesman is in town. I'd sack her, except she's quite good at her job the rest of the time, and, to be quite honest, my heart fails me at the prospect of looking for someone to replace her.'

'You wouldn't have to look far,' Kate said.

The restaurant owner, who was called Christine, and who had met Kate during a series of sessions at the Marston Ferry swimming pool, stopped writing out a bill. 'What do you mean?'

'Me,' said Kate. 'I need a full-time job.'

'Wait,' Christine said. She put the folded bill on a saucer and weighted it, as was the restaurant's custom, with two Italian almond biscuits done up in screws of tissue paper. Then she went across to the last of the customers and put the saucer on their table. 'I do hope,' Kate heard her say, 'that you enjoyed your meal.'

Yes, they said, polite and obedient, they had. Lovely ravioli, one of them added. Christine said it was all fresh, you see. She unhooked their coats from the bentwood hat stand by the door and helped them into them, then she opened the door to let them out. When they had gone, she closed the door, and bolted it, and turned the 'Open' sign back to front. Then she came back to Kate.

'What's happened?' she said.

Kate began piling plates to take down to the kitchen.

'Stop that,' Christine said. 'Stop fiddling about and tell me.'

'I've got to leave James,' Kate said. 'I'm doing no good staying. I'm going to hurt him soon, and I couldn't bear to do that. I've got to be on my own, I've got to live on my own. To sort myself out.'

'Oh Kate,' Christine said, with a degree of exasperation. She too was a single parent, and she too lived with what she firmly described as a partner. She had met James. She liked him. He looked a loyal type, and, after her own experiences, Christine set great store by loyalty.

'I'm not being neurotic,' Kate said. 'This isn't self-indulgence. It would only be self-indulgence if I stayed.'

'You haven't lived on your own for years.'

'I'd have Joss. I wouldn't be quite on my own.'

'Is this temporary?'

'I don't know. I just know I don't have a choice.'

'But if I'm going to offer you Susie's job I have to know it isn't temporary. I can't create all the upheaval just to have you turn round and say you don't need the job after all, you've sorted it out with James. I'm not saying I wouldn't like to employ you, because I would, you're much better than Susie in every way, but I'd have to have a commitment, Kate, I'd have to.'

Kate said, 'I'd be happy to give you one.'

'A year,' Christine said. 'At least until next Christmas.'

Kate swallowed. It shouldn't be this easy, getting a job, it ought to be part of the punishment that getting a job should be difficult, miserable. 'Thank you.'

'It's long hours, Kate.'

'I know.'

'And no software salesmen.'

Kate shook her head, trying to smile.

'Where will you live?'

'I haven't sorted that out yet.'

'You won't get even a room under forty pounds a week, you know. And that'll be a student sort of room. Dead grotty.' Christine thought of Richmond Villa, which she had visited several times. 'You must be mad.'

'Probably,' Kate said, 'but insanity's preferable

96

to guilt, any day.'

'Why on earth do you feel guilty?'

'Because I've changed. I've changed, for some reason, into someone I don't like at all, and while I'm like this I'm upsetting everyone.'

'Too young for *the* change, I suppose.'

'Yes,' Kate said, 'I can't blame it on anyone but myself.'

'What about Joss?'

Kate thought. 'Poor Jossie. She's used to me, and she's nearly as impossible as I am herself. James will be thankful to see us go.' She picked up the plates and moved towards the basement stairs.

'Don't you be so sure,' Christine said. She followed Kate down to the kitchen, where the chef was changing his blue-and-white-checked working trousers for jeans. 'Sleep on it, Kate, sleep on it. We'll talk about it on Friday.'

'She's coming out with me, Friday,' the chef said. 'Aren't you, Katie? Going for something young and virile.'

'That rules you out then, Benjie.'

'You should see me,' the chef said, 'when I gets going. I really gets going, Fridays.' He zipped up his jeans and reached for his leather jacket. 'Bloody women. It's you what drives me into the arms of other blokes, you know. It's you bloody women.' He stopped to give Kate a garlic-breathed kiss. 'Ta-ra.' The basement door slammed behind him.

An hour later, Kate followed him up the steps

to the street. She and Christine had cleared up and laid the tables for the evening almost in silence, only speaking briefly about Christine's son, Justin, who might be good enough to get into the junior team to fence for Oxfordshire. When Kate finally took off her apron and put on her jacket, Christine said, 'Now you think seriously and we'll talk again on Friday,' and Kate said, 'You're a real friend.' Christine had smiled and said, 'The sisterhood,' and they'd laughed. Then Kate climbed up the basement steps to the street, and sniffed the February dusk, and felt a sudden small lightness of heart, as if a burden was slipping from her.

'Excuse me,' someone said.

Kate turned. It was a male someone.

'I didn't mean to frighten you, but I've been waiting. For you, I mean. I couldn't get the hang of the days you worked here, so I've done a lot of loitering about, and it was always that other girl, the blonde —'

'Susie,' Kate said. The street light, and the light above the restaurant's fascia board, revealed the young man who had come in with the sneering, flamboyant girl. He was wearing the same loose, dark coat, with the collar turned up.

'Oh. Susie.'

'Can I help you?' Kate said. 'Did you leave something?'

'Oh no. No. It was just that you were so kind —'

'I don't think I was,' Kate said firmly. 'I don't

think I said anything. I was too surprised to say anything.'

'You *looked* kind. It meant a lot. I was feeling pretty awful, as you can probably imagine.'

'Well, I'm glad,' Kate said. She took her gloves out of her jacket pocket and began to pull them on.

'It wasn't just that you were kind,' the man said. 'It was more than that. I really liked the look of you. I do, I really do.'

Kate took a step away. 'I've got to get home.'

'Please,' he said, putting a hand out. 'Don't be alarmed. I'm not a nutter, I'm just not doing this very well because I've never done it before. My name is Mark. Mark Hathaway. I'm head of the English department at a private tutorial college. Perfectly on the line, you see.'

'Well,' Kate said, laughing, 'how do you do, Mark Hathaway.'

'And you?'

'Kate.'

'Kate what?'

'Kate Bain,' Kate said.

'May I walk you home, Kate Bain?'

Kate hesitated. Now that the evenings weren't pitch-black by four-thirty, Leonard didn't draw his curtains so early, but sat at his window, like an elderly heron, watching the street for incident.

'I don't think so.'

'Are you married?'

'No.'

99

'Then what is the harm in my escorting you home?'

'This is all happening in the half-dark,' Kate said. 'It feels peculiar.'

'I think it feels exciting.'

She took a step away. 'I'm going,' Kate said. 'Thank you for your offer, but I'm going now. Alone.'

He followed her. 'Please may I see you in daylight? Will you have lunch with me?'

'No,' Kate said without conviction.

'Coffee, then. Meet me for coffee. Please.'

'I don't think so —'

'Look,' he said, and he took her arm. 'Please just look. I'm a straight bloke who happens to be charmed by your appearance and your manner. Meet me for coffee, just once, and if it isn't a success I will never trouble you again, cross my heart and hope to die.'

Kate removed her arm. 'All right,' she said. Just one cup of coffee.'

'Thursday?'

'Yes.'

'I'll meet you at the entrance to the Golden Cross. Eleven-fifteen.'

'Why aren't you teaching?'

'I am. But I'm not at eleven-fifteen on Thursday.' He stepped back and the light from a nearby street lamp fell on his rumpled dark head. 'Goodbye, Kate Bain, Miss. Till Thursday.'

When she reached Richmond Villa, having

paused to buy chops for supper and collect James's only suit from the cleaners (who would collect his suit in future? He would, of course. Oh God. Don't think about it), Leonard was waiting. James had been in, and gone out again, with Hugh, for a drink, and Leonard was bursting with news.

'Give you three guesses —'

'What about?' Kate said. She looked round the kitchen. Mrs Cheng had left it as she usually did, with the floor and taps and surfaces gleaming, and all the room's intractable muddle of living piled in a reproachful heap on the table.

'Mindless yellow peasant,' Leonard said, poking the pile. A small avalanche of opened letters slid to the floor.

'Don't call her that. Not even as a joke.'

'She doesn't mind. Adores me. Hide like a rhino. Guess what.'

Kate began to transfer little heaps of the muddle back on to the dresser and worktops, where it usually lived.

'Can't possibly guess.'

Leonard craned forward on his stick. He'd had a lovely day, first three hours of Mrs Cheng, now a really first-rate morsel of gossip.

'Old Bat Bachelor believes in euthanasia!'

Kate had paused to read part of a letter from Joss's school, saying that they were trying to arrange a student exchange with a high school in Kiev, and could they please have parental co-operation over this.

'Euthanasia?'

'Euthanasia, my dear, half-educated dimwit, is the term commonly applied to the direct painless killing of the incurably ill or insane.'

Kate looked up. 'I know.'

'James and Hugh took old Beatrice out to tea. Randolph, no less. I said to James, "What did you talk about?" and he said, "Euthanasia. She believes in euthanasia." '

'So what,' Kate said rigidly.

'So nothing. Just thought you'd like to know.'

'Why should I want to know?'

'Just thought you'd like to keep tabs on James.'

'Stop it,' Kate said furiously. 'Stop it. I never have and I never will. What James does is no concern of mine.'

Leonard hesitated. He had gone too far. He craned towards Kate.

'Marry him,' Leonard pleaded. 'It's what he wants. It's what you want. Do it. Marry him.'

Kate turned away. 'I can't,' she said.

'Why? Why the devil not?'

'I can't explain. You'd never understand.'

Leonard let his breath out in a windy sigh. Then he limped to the door. 'In that case,' he said, as he creaked out, 'you ought to leave. It's the only decent thing you can do.'

Late that night, sitting in the bath while James brushed his teeth at the basin, Kate said, 'I gather you had tea at the Randolph.'

James spat and stooped for a mouthful of water from the cold tap.

'I took Hugh to meet Beatrice. It was meant to be a distraction and actually it was rather successful. He's dreading his golf course.'

Kate began to wash one foot with exaggerated thoroughness.

'Leonard said you talked about euthanasia.'

James peered at his teeth in the mirror above the basin.

'These may all be my own, but they don't half look like it. Do I look sixty-one or a hundred and sixty-one?'

'So you won't tell me about Miss Bachelor,' Kate said, starting on the other foot.

James turned to look at her.

'What would you like to know?'

Kate glared. 'Nothing.'

'My darling Katie,' James said, 'I'll tell you anything you want to know. You know that.'

'I wouldn't have known about this tea party, except for Leonard —'

'I didn't tell you because you've made it abundantly plain you don't want me to. There is nothing in the least furtive about my friendship with Beatrice, except your attitude to it. Yes, we had tea. Yes, we talked about euthanasia, and Hugh is now all fired up about a telly programme.' He came to kneel by the bath. He put out a hand and touched Kate's breast. She flinched.

'Katie.'

She shook her head.

'Why not?'

She turned her head away.

'Oh Katie,' James said sadly, getting up. 'How I wish you'd at least talk to me.'

Kate bowed her head. 'I would if I could.'

'You don't laugh. I haven't heard you laugh for weeks.'

'No,' Kate said. She clenched her hands round the sponge until her knuckles gleamed white. 'No. I've forgotten how.'

The Rapswell Golf and Country Club sent a car for Hugh, a Mercedes with a polite driver who asked diffidently for Hugh's autograph, for his daughter. Hugh had had a discussion with Julia, and then several more with himself, about what he should wear, and ended up in a blazer that he said made him look like a game show host.

'Too many buttons. All I need is a toupee and a redhead in a backless dress.'

'You look great,' Julia said seriously.

'Where are your golf bats?' George asked.

'I'm going to talk about golf, not play it.'

'Don't you be so sure, Mr Hunter,' the driver said later. 'They'll have you up to all sorts of stunts. They're a very lively crowd up at Rapswell.'

Hugh made faces of mock panic. 'I couldn't hit a golf ball. I couldn't hit a beach ball at two paces.'

They drove peacefully through the north Cotswolds. Hugh, who had chosen to sit beside the driver in an effort to appear approachable

('Good old pro,' he told himself), began to feel happier as the miles rolled by, less resentful and more as if he were approaching a performance. His feelings had also, without question, taken an upward turn after the extraordinary tea party in the Randolph Hotel, and he had spent much of the night after it planning a memo on a projected programme for a mate of his whom he could trust to be executive producer. He had no intention of telling Kevin McKinley, not, at least, until the programme was about to go out, and it was too late to halt it, to fuss about consulting the ITC, and risk having it stopped. He'd also thought a good deal about Miss Bachelor. He saw, now, why James had made a friend of her. You could say typical spinster of Beatrice, you could say she was dried-up, dusty, bookish, sexless, but for all that she had a powerful appeal, the appeal of someone with intellectual poise and the zest added by originality and by wit. 'Why not indeed,' she'd said to Hugh about his proposal that she should appear on television. No fluster, no old-ladyish demurring and terror of being conspicuous. 'Why not indeed,' she'd said. Bravo, Hugh thought, bravo, Miss Bachelor.

'Nearly there, sir,' the driver said.

Hugh looked out of his window at the landscape which had abruptly turned from being a nondescript succession of fields and bungalows to being a manicured series of small green hills and curved yellow sandpits.

'Cost millions,' the driver said proudly. 'Best

course in the Midlands. All-weather greens, club house with jacuzzi and gym, you name it. Those bunkers are filled with sand brought in from Saudi Arabia.'

'Is Saudi sand better than our sand?'

The driver looked shocked. ' 'Course, sir. They had to fly it in. It wasn't just dug up at Bournemouth.'

The car turned in between curved walls ending in huge stone gateposts crowned with lions holding shields. Chiselled stone tablets pronounced, 'Rapswell Golf and Country Club. Members Only'.

'There's a waiting list of hundreds,' the driver said. 'Half Birmingham wants to get in.'

The smooth drive was edged with smoother verges, the latter protected by a spiked chain looped between short, varnished posts.

'It looks very tidy,' Hugh said.

The driver said reverently, 'I tell you, Mr Hunter, it's the last word.'

Outside the club house, a vast verandahed structure which would have looked perfectly at home in Texas, the club chairman and committee waited in violent agitation. The scheduled golfing star had been stricken by a gastric virus and had cried off only an hour before. They were in despair. They had telephoned every substitute they could think of but no one was available at such short notice, no one, that is, of any distinction. They clustered round Hugh, almost pawing him in their anxiety and disappointment.

'Well,' Hugh said. 'You will simply have to make do with me.'

'Mr Hunter,' the Chairman began. 'Forgive me but —'

'Why not?' said Hugh, smiling at him. 'Why not? I'm game for anything. I've never played golf in my life, but I've been performing for over thirty years.' He waved to the television cameras waiting at the edge of the group. 'Morning, lads!'

One of the cameramen, who knew him, waved back. The committee looked at one another.

'You haven't a choice, really,' Hugh said. 'You've half an hour to kick-off. I'll carry it, I promise you, I'll open this club like no club has ever been opened before. Which of you is going to give me a golf lesson, on camera, that is? Then we'll do a tour of the facilities. I'll have a wallow in the jacuzzi if you like. Anything.' He leaned forward and patted the Chairman's arm. 'Come on,' he said, 'trust me.'

George and Edward Hunter, wearing identical dark-blue dressing gowns piped in scarlet, shared a bean bag in front of the television. They were not usually allowed television as late as this, but tonight was an exception because Hugh was appearing on *Midland Miscellany*, the daily round-up of news items from around the region. Behind George and Edward, Hugh and Julia sat on a cream-coloured sofa. Hugh had a tumbler of whisky in his hand; Julia, a glass of white wine diluted with soda water.

The screen filled with some stone writing. Julia read it out. It said, 'Rapswell Golf and Country Club. Members Only'. Then a voice said that the television personality, Hugh Hunter, had opened the club earlier in the day and there had been a crowd of over eight hundred people. There were pictures of a huge, house-like thing, and then some of a room full of sofas and a lot of men standing about holding glasses, and a girl with a lot of teeth wearing a bathing suit under a towelling dressing gown, and then there was Hugh.

'You took your jacket off!' Edward said reprovingly.

'I had to,' Hugh said, 'watch.'

They watched. They saw Hugh being taught how to hold a golf club by a man with a grey moustache. They saw Hugh swing the club at a ball and miss and go spinning about, clowning, apparently out of control, and then fall over. They saw him pick himself up and do it again and land up in the arms of a lady in a red suit who was laughing so much she could hardly stand up herself. Then they saw him flailing away at another golf ball in a sandpit and then trying to kick it nearer the little hole in the middle of the green, and being told off by the man with the moustache, except the man with the moustache was laughing all the time and didn't sound very cross. Then they saw Hugh running into the huge building chased by a crowd of people, and jumping into a sort of enormous bath, and then the camera got faster and faster and Hugh went scampering in and out of rooms, pursued by all these people, and there was very loud, very fast music and suddenly there was a great banging chord in the music and the camera stopped dead on Hugh, flopped out in an armchair, with his eyes crossed. The twins cheered and squealed and fell off the bean bag.

'I have to tell you,' Hugh said to Julia, 'I was an absolute wow.'

'I can see —'

'They want me to go back and host the Christmas dance.'

'Will you?'

'They doubled my fee, you know. I could bear the Christmas dance for another double fee.'

'Oh Hugh,' said Julia, taking his hand and smiling at him.

'Long ago, before you were born, I did that kind of thing in a pantomime at Kidderminster. I'd forgotten I could.' He leaned forward towards the rolling, giggling twins. He felt tremendously happy. 'Well, then. Was I funny?'

'Yes!' shouted Edward. He scrambled to his feet and began to tear round the room. 'This is you, this is you, this is you!'

George joined him. A lamp, its flex caught by their flying passage, tottered on its table.

'Stop it!' Julia said, but she was smiling.

'Here's you!' George yelled, leaping into an armchair and scattering cushions. 'Here's you in that bath!' He collapsed on his back and kicked his legs about.

'Amazing,' Hugh said, watching him, holding Julia's hand, 'amazing, isn't it, to be paid six hundred pounds and a case of champagne for doing exactly that?'

'But they loved you, you can see that, they loved you.'

He looked away for a minute and then took a gulp of his whisky.

'Yes,' he said. He sounded pleased and confident. 'Yes, they bloody well did.'

Chapter Six

Mark Hathaway bought Kate a *cappuccino* with grated chocolate scattered on the foam. He wore blue jeans and a black jersey of indefinable elegance and he looked, to Kate, like a French film star. He also looked young. His age worried Kate; he might turn out to be younger than she.

He said, sitting down opposite her, 'You look terrific.'

'Could we,' Kate said, 'start with a more ordinary conversation?'

'Like what?'

'Like details about ourselves.'

'Specification?'

'If you like.'

'Right,' he said, grinning. 'Five foot-ten inches, eleven stone, and thirty-two. Born in Hereford, chorister at the Cathedral, minor public school, Oxford, teacher training college, more Oxford, single. Father dead, mother still living, one brother married with two children. Salary adequate, prospects ditto. Restless. Your turn.'

Kate swallowed. 'Thirty-six, single, daughter of fourteen, born in Oxford, educated at a comprehensive in Oxford, no further education, no professional qualifications. Both parents living, but hardly see them because my mother is a Catholic, and disapproves of the fact that I've lived with someone for eight years and haven't married them. Two older brothers, one in London, one in the North. Five foot-three and seven and three-quarter stone. Restless.'

'Wow,' Mark said. He looked at her. She drank a mouthful of her coffee and looked back.

'Of course you know the bit I'm most interested in,' Mark said.

'My living with James,' Kate said, without co-quetry.

'Yes. Eight years. It's like a marriage.'

'I know.'

'Why haven't you married him?'

'I never thought it would be right.'

'Right? What kind of right? Morally right? Emotionally right? Appropriate?'

'All that,' Kate said. 'Everything.'

'And you still don't?'

'More than ever, just now.'

'Thank God for that.'

'He's much older than me. Twenty-five years older than me.'

'Lord. Like a father. Don't you —' He paused, then he said, 'Don't you miss being with someone young, someone your own age?'

'I don't know,' Kate said. 'I haven't been, not for eight years. I've just been with James.'

'Am I allowed to ask if you're in love with him?'

'I was.'

'And now?'

'You can't ask any more,' Kate said, 'I don't know you.'

'Then I'll tell you about me, shall I, to help things, to help you to know me?'

She looked at him. He was smiling but his eyes looked anxious, almost pleading.

'All right.'

'I didn't really want to teach,' Mark said, 'but I couldn't bear to be away from Oxford either, and you know what Oxford is, what a bullying kind of place, and stuffed with education. I've got a little house at Osney and I let a couple of rooms in it, and I have this nice enough job. The girl you saw me with was an affair of the loins rather than the heart — I've hardly ever been in love, only once, perhaps, several years ago. I like jazz and the cinema and cooking and now I like red-headed women.'

Kate smiled at him. 'I can't reciprocate. I haven't got a neat little catalogue like that.'

'I don't want you to. I'd rather find out. In time.' He glanced at his watch. 'Which I've now run out of.' He looked at her. 'I have a half-day on Monday. Can I see you on Monday? Did I pass the coffee test?'

She hesitated. He stood up and pulled on his coat, and then bent over her for a moment.

'Come on,' Mark said, 'come on, Kate. Take your fingers out of your ears and hear the call of the wild.'

Kate caught a bus out to North Oxford. She

hadn't been to Mansfield House for over a week and her conscience was heavy with the knowledge of her neglect. In addition to that, she felt that Mansfield House would set her in order, put her the right way up again, by reminding her of familiar patterns and priorities. She could also talk to Helen.

That Helen was wonderful went without saying. Strong-minded, tireless, colourful, she aroused admiration in those who wanted to help her and terror in those who didn't. She had never had children, and her marriage had foundered under the demands of the causes she espoused, leaving her believing that men, on the whole, simply weren't up to relationships that required them to fulfil a fair half of a bargain. Being sexually energetic, however, a series of lovers passed through her hands, mostly much younger lovers who were apt to wear expressions of stunned acquiescence during their spells of being in favour, but none of them lasted long. After their dismissal, they would hang about Mansfield House for a while, hoping for a glimpse of Helen, or they would waylay Kate or any available inmate, to ask, uh, if, uh, she could help a bit with what went wrong. Kate had learned that, harsh though it was, the kindest thing in the long-run was to tell the truth.

'Sorry, Matt. She got tired of you.'
'*Tired* of me?'
'Yes.'
'But she doesn't get bloody tired!'

'Not of Mansfield House, not of her work.'

'Just me —'

'Yes, Matt, just you.'

'What if I got a job?'

'It wouldn't make any difference. When she's tired of someone, that's it.'

'Tired of blokes, that is. She doesn't get tired of *women* —'

'No.'

'So she's a bleeding dyke.'

'No.'

'I give up.'

'Yes. That's what you've got to do. Give up and go away.'

Kate had grown fond of Helen. She was the kind of woman who can only lead, who is poor at follow-through. Kate didn't mind following through, didn't mind taking orders, being second in command. At least, for five years she hadn't minded that. There was, after all, the luxury in waltzing into Mansfield House knowing that at the end of the day she could waltz out again; indeed, that very knowledge had driven Kate to feel that she must come as often as she could. It was also, without question, something she was good at; she was calm, unbossy, patient in persuading the women to run the refuge for themselves in order to give them the independence to learn to run their own lives again.

'You don't know what it's like,' the women said, often and often. 'You don't know how it feels to have such a low opinion of yourself that you never look higher in life for anyone than another woman-beater.'

She didn't know, of course. How could anyone living with courteous, warm-hearted James, know, with the thumping blood of experienced recognition, what it felt like to live with such self-disgust, with such nauseating apprehension?

'It was always a relief when he hit me,' someone once said to her, 'because at least then the waiting to be hit was over. The waiting was always the worst.'

Nobody had ever hit Kate. Nobody had ever hit Helen either. 'That's why,' Helen said to Kate, 'it behoves us to help.' Kate had always agreed, had done more than agree, had felt powerfully that she was thankful to have a chance to help. But now . . . Now, sitting on the bus as it toiled its way up the Woodstock Road, she felt reluctant, not eager. It wasn't that she wasn't sorry for battered women any more, any less that she couldn't see what was excellent in James any more, it was just that she couldn't really feel either. 'I can get my mind round it,' she said to herself, 'I just can't get my feelings round it too. I'm not afraid, am I? I'm not afraid of helping Helen? I don't think so. But I am afraid of age, suddenly, I'm terrified of it. I don't know why. All I know is that it makes me draw back from James.'

The bus stopped close to the end of St Margaret's Road. Kate got off and stood for a moment on the bleak, late-morning pavement. She was filled with an irrational envy of the rest of the people

on the bus, sailing cosily on northwards to cov-
etable humdrum lives that weren't racked with
confusions and anxieties. There was a sharp wind,
and it blew little eddies of grit and litter about
Kate's ankles. She thought of Mark. Mark was
thirty-two. Four years ago she had been thirty-
two, and when she was thirty-two she had been
happy. Oh, she thought crossly, you whingeing
cow, you spoilt, whingeing cow. She swung her
bag on to her shoulder, and set off towards
Mansfield House.

Mansfield House was in uproar. A husband, a
small, pale husband whom a casual observer
would not have thought physically capable of
even swatting a fly, had taken advantage of the
front door being left open by mistake, and had
come to claim his wife. He had found her in the
bedroom she shared with her children and another family, and she had been alone, with only
a toddling child, making the beds. First he had
pleaded, and then he had shouted, and, although
she could resist his pleading, she crumbled at the
shouting and had been finally rescued as she was
towed sobbing downstairs. It had taken three
women to get him off her and out of the door,
and all the children in the house had seeped out
of other rooms to watch this spectacle that was
so familiar and so terrible to them, and one of
the husband's small sons, in an agony of confusion,
had attempted to go with his father, and the row
had redoubled.

When Kate reached Mansfield House, the

husband was sitting outside, on the pavement, shouting for his son. 'Come to Daddy, Paul, come to Daddy. Daddy'll look after you, Paul. Daddy loves you, Paul.' Kate stepped over him.

'Bitch,' the man said.

Inside, the staircase was swarming. Everybody was agitated; nobody could find Helen.

'Kate!' someone shouted. They turned to her. She looked up. She stood in the hall, just inside the front door, and looked up at the mass of faces, the mass of crying, distracted faces. The din rose and rose.

'Kate!' they cried. The mass seemed to surge forward, as if it would pour down the staircase and engulf her in all its despair and greedy dependency, all its noise and helpless brokenness. She stepped back.

'Kate! Oh, thank God you've come. Oh Kate —'

She put a hand out to feel for the doorknob behind her, turned it and, twisting round, pulled the door open and fled down the steps to the pavement, almost stumbling over the man, still waiting there. Then she ran.

The man looked after her. 'Bitch!' he shouted.

Beatrice Bachelor sat in the basket chair in Leonard's room. Joss had brought her. Joss had arrived at the house in Cardigan Street and explained that Leonard wanted her to bring Beatrice to see him.

'What is your uncle like?' Beatrice had said.

'He's not my uncle.'

'What, then,' said Beatrice, turning the tables on Joss's literalness, 'is your mother's lover's uncle like?'

'Thin,' Joss said. 'Old.'

'And as to personality?'

'I don't know,' Joss said. 'Old. A bit weird.'

'How banal you are. How dull your conversation is. How limited.'

Joss watched Beatrice tying on her headscarf. She didn't mind somehow, when Beatrice was sharp with her, though she couldn't think why. She nursed Cat, who clung to the slope of her knees with claws like scimitars.

'Ow,' said Joss.

'It's your idleness of mind I can't be doing with,' Beatrice said. 'The way you just let your brain loll around with its tongue hanging out.'

Joss grinned. 'It gets you worked up, though.'

'If you wish for such a cheap goal, you have reached it, of course —'

'Don't be cross,' Joss said. She laid her cheek on Cat's broad-striped head. 'You can be cross with Uncle Leonard. He loves arguing.'

Leonard did not intend arguing with Beatrice. He wanted to inspect her. He couldn't imagine what kind of person she could be to have caused such waves of unease at Richmond Villa. He sent James out to buy a fruit cake and he tried to make Joss make sandwiches.

'Make them yourself.'

'Idle hussy. What else are women for?'

He limped down to the kitchen and made a crumby, buttery mess and got jam on his cardigan. His pile of sandwiches looked like a tent that had collapsed with a whole lot of people inside. There was jam on the underside of the plate.

'Sodding cooking,' Leonard said, carrying his efforts upstairs.

'Did you slice or spread first?' said Beatrice Bachelor, looking at her rhomboid sandwich.

'Sometimes one, sometimes the other,' Leonard said. He grinned at her. She was no looker, that was for sure, and never had been. Like taking a bag of golf clubs to bed, he shouldn't wonder. Leonard's experience of sex had been very limited, but as he grew older he believed more and more that what he wished had happened actually had, with those deep-bosomed, shapely legged women he had always fancied, slightly brassy women with ginny voices who knew what was what. The last time he'd been on a train, he'd sat opposite one, plumply stuffed into an elaborate blue suit with gold buttons. Throughout the journey, she'd read a copy of the *Reader's Digest*, and steadily eaten milk chocolate buttons out of a shiny plastic envelope, while Leonard devoured her with his eyes and imagined her in her corset thing, a corset thing with suspenders. Beatrice would never wear a corset.

'I rather hoped to meet Miss Bain,' Beatrice said.

'Gone to her refuge. Won't be back till suppertime.'

'Refuge?'

'Battered women. Goes to listen. And take the children to the lavatory.'

'How very good of her.'

Leonard took a bite out of a sandwich and the jam oozed out at the sides and fell in small dark blobs on his trousers.

'You know she won't marry James.'

'Should she?'

Leonard scowled. ' 'Course.'

'Because it's tidier?'

'No,' said Leonard, scrubbing at his trousers with a disgusting handkerchief, 'no. Because they won't relax until they do.'

'Ah,' said Beatrice. She leaned back and looked at Leonard. To her eye, he resembled a drawing by Ronald Searle. 'I have never been married. Have you?'

'Never!'

'Then perhaps neither of us knows very much about it.'

Leonard looked faintly sneering. 'What do you know about, then?'

'Old age,' said Beatrice.

He stared at her. Then he leaned forward. 'What d'you think of it?'

Beatrice took a sip of tea. 'I think old age is treacherous.'

'Nothing to be said for it?'

'Very little.'

Leonard drooped. 'I know,' he said. 'Detestable. Terrifies me sometimes.' He eyed her. 'That's why I wanted you to come.'

Beatrice waited. She watched his mouth working loosely for a while and then it was no surprise to her at all when he said, 'I want to talk about euthanasia.'

Later, Leonard waylaid Kate in the kitchen. Kate had been walking, endlessly walking, all across Port Meadow in its gloomy, late-winter drabness, and had come home tired and on edge. Leonard said, 'Guess who I had to tea.'

'The Queen,' Kate said, wondering if half a pound of minced beef could be made into a) enough for four and b) something that might fool everyone it wasn't just mince again.

'Nope.'

'The Pope,' Kate said. 'Marilyn Monroe.'

'Close,' Leonard said, 'very close. Beatrice Bachelor, actually.'

Kate said wearily, 'You don't give up, do you, you never give up —'

'Thing is,' Leonard said, craning towards her, 'she's nothing to be alarmed by. Nothing. Old stick of a thing. Old schoolmarm.'

'I know.'

'She's got courage, I'll grant you. And spirit. Cracked a joke or two. But she's just a funny old woman, Kate, that's all.'

'I know.'

'Then what in the devil's name is there to get worked up about in James being kind to a funny old woman?'

Kate looked at him.

'Exactly that,' she said.

James was not, by nature, confiding. He was perfectly open, but not inclined to offer private information. In his relationship with Hugh, he had invariably been the listener, except on the very rare occasions, such as the death of his wife, when he found he needed to say a great deal, and a great deal of the same things at that, over and over. Now, perplexed and unhappy about Kate, he found he didn't much want to talk to anyone, not even to Hugh. What was there to say, after all, except that he was perplexed and unhappy, and that he believed Kate to be so too? The only person he wanted to talk to was Kate herself and she either wouldn't or couldn't. James missed her. He lay in bed beside her and sat across tables from her and missed her.

'I love you,' he had said to her, trying to catch her in a doorway. 'I love you. Isn't that any comfort? Isn't that enough?'

Sadness lay on James like a cold cloak. Sometimes he thought it was worse than sadness; it was grief. He imagined, writing his articles, teaching his pupils, going about the usual daily round of domestic chores, of talking to Leonard, of trying to talk to Joss, that his cloak was only visible to himself. It was therefore a great surprise to him to have Hugh come to Richmond Villa. He took him into his study.

Hugh looked buoyant. He walked up and down James's green carpet and told him about Rapswell,

123

and what a success it had been. He'd got a supermarket to open next, and then a health club, it was actually all rather a doddle.

'Now,' Hugh said, swinging round to face James.

'What?'

'You.'

James waited.

'I want you to help me, James. I want your help on this euthanasia project. My producer likes it. Likes it a lot. Beatrice has agreed to talk, once we've got the lawyers cleared. And guess who else. Guess who rang me yesterday.'

'Tell me.'

'Leonard.'

'*Leonard?*'

Hugh smiled. 'Says he's been converted.'

'He's just longing to be on telly.'

'Does it matter? Will you help? Will you persuade Beatrice to go further, find other people, best of all, a doctor?'

'Why are you asking me?' James said. 'You never have before. Why now?'

Hugh regarded him. He put his hands in his pockets. 'Because there's no remedy for sorrow like work.'

'I'm not sorrowful,' James said.

'No?'

'I'm fine.'

'So you're not interested —'

'Of course I'm interested, it's a — a fascinating subject —'

124

'Friendship's a two-way thing, James. You have to take as well as give, and vice versa. I'd be the better for having you. And you'd be the better for working with me and so might — Kate.'

'Kate.'

There was a silence. Then Hugh said, 'Come on, dear fellow. Come on. What've you got to lose?'

Mark Hathaway's house at Osney seemed to Kate full of charm, a light-hearted charm, a kind of gaiety. It was in West Street, facing a narrow canal, and across the canal was a triangle of grass, between the water and St Frideswide's Church. The scale was tiny, like a play place. Mark had made himself a flat out of the first floor, and the two ground-floor rooms were let out to an Indian postgraduate from Edinburgh, and a girl who worked for a firm of Oxford architects.

Mark had made one room out of the two principal bedrooms. When Kate walked in, there seemed to be light bouncing in from all directions, and falling on the clean, new modern furniture, and the bright rugs, and the bronze bust of someone who was wearing an American baseball cap.

'Robespierre,' Mark said. 'I bought him in the market for a tenner.'

There were posters by David Hockney on the walls, and sophisticated, moody black-and-white photographs of street landscapes, and other landscapes of human limbs, and all the books lived in bookcases which looked like cages of scarlet-painted steel.

'D'you like it?' Mark said.

'Oh yes.' She turned slowly, taking in the brilliant Latin American embroideries, the shining wood floor, the air of economy. 'Oh yes. It's lovely. You can breathe.'

It was like being on a balcony, Kate thought, or a ship. She walked about, touching chairbacks and cushions, marvelling.

'It's all so light.'

'That's being up a floor.'

'I've never done up a house,' Kate said, suddenly realising that it was true. 'Not like this, I mean, not from scratch. I've just taken on other people's things. It never seemed to matter —' She stopped. She picked up an Indian candlestick of twisted brass. 'It must be wonderful, getting somewhere of your own to look as you want it to, to be yours.'

'It is,' he said, watching her.

Kate put the candlestick down. 'Trouble is, I'm too chaotic. I make a frightful mess. James —' She hesitated a moment and then went on. 'James gave me a plate with "Only dull women are tidy" painted on it. Perhaps if I'd ever made something of my own, I'd be tidier, I'd want to be.'

'Where did you live before James?'

'In a flat. I shared it. There were five of us. We never changed anything.'

'Why not?'

'I didn't mind,' Kate said, 'not then. It didn't

seem important. What was important was Joss —'

'Joss?'

'My daughter. I had a Canadian boyfriend. He buggered off when I told him I was pregnant.'

Mark said, 'There are stages in our lives when different things seem important. Don't you think?'

She looked at him. 'I was twenty-two when I had Joss.'

'So I'm younger than you, but I've already had ten years more freedom.'

'I wouldn't be without Joss —'

'That's not what I'm saying. I'm just saying you might be due your freedom later than sooner.'

'Due,' Kate said. 'Freedom.' She picked up a pink-and-scarlet cushion embroidered with rough wool birds and hugged it. 'This room feels free.'

'It is.'

'Sometimes,' Kate said, 'sometimes, you can get so covered with people, you can't breathe. I've always thought that listening to people, helping them, is the very least you can do, the very least, if you're OK yourself. But at the moment —' Her voice trailed away. She laid her cheek on the cushion in her arms.

'As I said,' Mark said, watching her, 'there are different stages. You don't stay the same for ever. You're organic after all.' He came across to where she was standing. 'You don't have to lie down and just take things, you know, you don't simply have to accept. You can turn protagonist, you have the right to decide your own life. Thirty-six isn't very old. It certainly isn't too late to start.'

Kate sighed. She released the cushion and laid it back with its fellows on the low sofa.

'I want to take you to bed,' Mark said.

'Now?'

'Preferably.'

She gazed at him. He was charmed by her lack of flirtatiousness.

'I won't claim you,' he said. 'I won't just add to your pile of people.' He waved his arm at the room. 'Here's proof: my life, my separate identity.' He held his hands out to her and he was laughing.

'Come on,' he said to Kate, 'come on. We'd have a lot of fun.'

She shook her head.

'No.'

'Don't you fancy me?'

She hesitated. She certainly felt a longing but she was aware it wasn't lust.

'You're really attractive,' Kate said. 'Really. But —'

'Not yet?'

'Maybe.'

He turned away, clenching his fists. 'What a disappointment.'

'Is that why you asked me here?'

'Partly,' he said, his back still towards her, 'and I wanted you to see where I live.'

'I love it. I think you're — lucky.'

He gave himself a little shake, and turned round again.

'What do you want to do, then?'

'I'd like to look at the rest of Osney.'

'It'll take you ten minutes.'

'Fine,' Kate said. She felt uneasy, anxious to be gone.

'Tell you what,' Mark said, 'you go out for a quarter of an hour and I'll make some tea. I'll have tea ready when you come back.'

'Lovely,' Kate said, 'great. Thank you.'

She went down the stairs. In the hall, the Indian postgraduate was talking on the communal telephone in his strong Scottish accent. Kate slid past him and went out into the street, the street whose further side was in part so charmingly provided by water. There was a moorhen on the water, and a coot, and, on the grassy triangle on the far side, a patch of snowdrops. There were also trees.

Kate walked Osney's live little streets with mounting delight and incredulity. How, she asked herself, could she have lived in Oxford all her life and never known that just beyond the station lay this little water-girt place, these cottage streets of brick and painted stucco with their oddly, unmistakably foreign air, an island of distinct character protected from the surrounding schools and factories and newspaper offices by the quiet, olive-green barriers of river and canal? There were several pubs, a closed bric-à-brac shop, a little supermarket, a milkman humming past in his float, and, in those front windows right on the narrow pavements, were spider plants and giant shells and families of brass and china animals. In South Street a child waved to her from an upstairs window; in East Street she met a man carrying a bird cage and a loaf of bread; and in Swan Street, a tiny cul-de-sac ending in a white bridge over the water, she met an exotic woman in a brocade hat leading a vast and fluffy white chow on a strip of purple leather. Kate returned to West Street glowing.

'It's so lovely! I never knew it was so lovely!'

Mark had made China tea in a pot with a bamboo handle.

'After Jericho, it's like another world,' Kate said. 'The water, the light, the atmosphere! You can't breathe in Jericho —'

Mark said, 'I owe you an apology.' He held out a thin black mug of tea to her.

'Forget it.'

'No,' he said. 'I shouldn't have asked you to sleep with me. Not yet. And I shouldn't have reacted how I did when you refused.'

'It's all right,' Kate said. Her eyes strayed to the western window, to the water and the white-faced coot idling about on it.

'Thing is,' Mark's voice deepened, 'I'm so scared of being rejected. I rush in and then I can't stand it when I don't succeed.'

'I didn't reject you,' Kate said, 'I just postponed you.'

'I know, I know. I'm not blaming you, I'm blaming myself.'

Kate sipped her tea.

'Let it go,' she said. She felt happier than she had felt in weeks. 'Lovely tea.'

'Will you come again?'

'Of course.'

She walked to the eastern window. Across two tiny gardens were the backs of the Bridge Street houses, and at a first-floor window directly opposite a young woman was hanging curtains.

'Look,' Kate said. 'Mark. Come and look.'

He came to stand beside her. Kate pointed across to the woman.

'I wish,' Kate said suddenly, 'I wish that was me.'

Chapter Seven

Helen had always declined to have an office at Mansfield House. It was one of her abiding principles that the refuge was both the home and the democratic responsibility of the inmates, and therefore there should be no particular room where problems might be brought. 'It stops people dealing with their own,' she said, 'and makes them prone to the seduction of buck passing.' When she was at Mansfield House, she was usually in the kitchen where she could guarantee that nobody could corner her alone.

It was a big kitchen in the back wing of the house that stuck out into the neglected garden. A series of assorted cookers stood against one wall, there was a vast table in the centre, and double glass doors, smeary with fingerprints for the lower four feet, opened out on to a rough rectangle of paving stones on which a sad, black barbecue stood, awash with winter rain. The room was never empty; it filled the function, in every sense, of a common room.

When Mrs Cheng had fled to Mansfield House, the kitchen had much shocked her. The almost tribal sharing of everything from instant coffee to children, the noise, the cluttered table and full ashtrays and unswept corners filled her with dismay and confusion. Living, as she always had, in a tightly — and in her case, brutally — controlled family environment above a takeaway shop down the Iffley Road, she was initially quite at sea in this humming and free-form community. Cleaning up the kitchen became an anchor for her, a spar to which she clung in those first few weeks when she wondered if she had only escaped one hell for another, albeit of a different kind.

'Leave it,' the other women would say, as she vigorously washed away at the floor around their feet. 'Don't keep on. Let it go. We don't care.'

It was Kate who understood what the kitchen represented to Mrs Cheng, who saw that for her the cultural strangeness of her new life held alarms almost as great as the systematic violence of her old one. She had fled from the takeaway shop (pretending to be going next door to the newsagent, to buy a racing paper for her husband, his sole reading matter) because she had believed that soon she would quite simply be killed. She had gone to Mansfield House because, only a month before, she had stood at a city centre bus stop where a torn, hand-printed poster about the refuge had been crudely pasted across the glassed-in timetable. The two decisions had quite drained her and had robbed her of all sense of identity. Keeping the refuge kitchen as orderly and clean as she had once kept both the takeaway shop and the rooms above it was a desperate attempt to remember, by repeating a familiar function, who she was.

Before her scrubbing and polishing drove the rest of the Mansfield House insane, Kate took Mrs Cheng away to expand her energies on Richmond Villa. It was soon after Leonard's arrival, and the house had not yet assimilated itself to his presence, nor to his depressing underclothes appearing in the laundry, his faddishness about food, his lingering, peppery, elderly smell.

'I need you,' Kate said to Mrs Cheng, 'I need your help. Everybody in this house requires different things and I can't manage alone.'

Mrs Cheng had certainly been needed before, as slave labour, but she had never been needed in a human way. Being childless — one of the many reasons her husband gave for beating her — her instincts for nurturing lay dormant. Leonard seized at once upon them, greedily, like a cantankerous baby, but it was Kate who really needed them, Kate who, Mrs Cheng came to see, to her astonishment, required support.

Kate also paid her. Mrs Cheng had never been paid a penny for anything, in all her forty odd years. She carried her first wages from Kate around with her for a week, incredulous, joyous, and terrified they would be taken from her. In time, James gently managed to teach her the ways of a savings account, but only because he presented it to her as a way of keeping her squirrel's hoard safe; the handing of her first notes across the building society counter was terrible to her. What guarantee was there she would ever see them again?

'You ask,' the girl said, smiling.

Mrs Cheng held out her hand. 'Give,' she said.

The girl passed the notes back to Mrs Cheng. Mrs Cheng held them in her hand for a long time, staring down at them, and wrestling with herself. Then she slid them under the glass screen again.

'You keep,' she said to the girl, 'you keep safe.'

Five years on, Mrs Cheng would hardly have recognised her earlier self. She had her own room, solid savings (these had now become a passion) and a talent for dealing with Leonard. She walked rather than scuttled, had put on a little weight, and belonged to a Chinese women's group which met regularly on Wednesdays and Saturdays. All that had not changed was the fervour of her feelings for Kate.

Kate's present state of mind weighed upon Mrs Cheng like a stone. Given the circumstances of Kate's life, her misery was incomprehensible to Mrs Cheng, but that in no way invalidated it for her. At the beginning of the change in Kate, Mrs Cheng had attempted to help by ever more thorough cleaning of Richmond Villa, moving heavy pieces of furniture to dust behind them, polishing unlooked-out-of windows, dousing lavatories with so much bleach that the house smelled like a public swimming bath. Not only did these exertions seem to go unnoticed — except by Joss and Leonard who complained bitterly at the dustless order of their rooms — but Kate looked and seemed no better. After a while, Mrs Cheng resolved that something more must be done, another approach tried altogether. Accordingly, she went up to Mansfield House to find Helen, and to convey to her, as best she could, that Kate wasn't — wasn't *well*.

Helen was sitting at the kitchen table with a child on her knee. The child was laboriously drawing on an old newspaper with a felt-tipped pen. He breathed heavily as he drew, and his fingers were blotched with blue and green.

'Talk private,' Mrs Cheng said to Helen.

'Come on,' Helen said, 'you know the rules.' She patted the stool next to her. 'Sit down and tell me.'

Mrs Cheng admired Helen, but had never warmed to her. Helen was too big, too bright to look at in her dramatic peasant clothes and clashing peasant jewellery, too expansive in gesture and manner.

'No,' Mrs Cheng said, 'Kate.'

'Kate?'

Mrs Cheng nodded. Helen looked up at her. The refuge had been much thrown by Kate's bolting away a few days previously. 'She looked panicked,' someone had said, 'as if she couldn't cope, couldn't stand it.' Helen rose to her feet, exuding a cloud of jasmine oil. She set the child down where she had been sitting.

'OK,' she said to Mrs Cheng, 'OK. We'll go and sit in my car.'

'I've got some things to say to you,' Helen said. She was treating Kate to a bowl of French onion soup in a bistro above the covered market. Kate did not seem to be eating her soup, but was simply pushing the croûtons in it round and round like a child playing with ducks in the bath.

'I want you,' Helen said, 'to stop feeling so racked with guilt.'

Kate found an onion ring and looped it over her spoon.

'And I want you to eat that soup.'

Kate ate the onion ring.

'Listen,' Helen said. She arranged her elbows on the table and brought her hands together in a rattle of bracelets. 'We are in a transitional stage in the relationship between men and women. There's a long way to go yet, and it's when things are in transition that people get scared and lose heart. Opinion gets polarised. People retreat back into the status quo because, even if that's not what they like, it's what they know.'

Kate waited. Long practice in listening to Helen had taught her that, if you didn't interrupt, Helen reached her goal sooner. Kate ate another onion ring and a tiny piece of croûton.

'I think,' Helen said, 'that your relationship with James has simply come to its natural end. James doesn't want to face that, so he is pretending that you are having a little funny phase, and everything will be just the same as before, when you come out of it. You don't want to face it either, so you are taking refuge in guilt. He hasn't thumped you or raped you or persecuted you mentally, so you are falling back into the old stereotyped thinking of being afraid that you have no good reason for leaving, therefore you are the guilty party.'

Kate picked up her mineral water and took a slow mouthful.

'It's more often the case than not,' Helen went on, 'that women put far more into relationships than men. Men find marriage much easier than women do, for exactly that reason, and your and James's relationship is a marriage, after all, in all but name. The thing is, Kate, you have just given too much of yourself away. You are psychologically worn out. If you stay, you'll be worse than worn out, you'll be damaged.'

She paused. She began to eat her own soup rapidly and Kate realised that it was now her turn to say something.

'I like looking after people,' she said lamely. 'At least, I did.'

'Of course. That's exactly what I'm getting at. You have given too much and now you're paying the price.'

'But James doesn't ask for anything. And he looks after me.'

'Dear me,' Helen said, spreading a piece of French bread lavishly with butter, 'your thinking *is* confused.'

'No, it isn't. It's sad, but it isn't confused.'

'So what are you going to do?'

Kate hesitated. Helen leaned back and surveyed her.

'Well?'

'I've found a couple of rooms in Osney.'

Helen said nothing. She pushed up the sleeves of her wildly exuberant Peruvian jersey, and then she took the leopardskin-patterned plastic combs out of her abundant dark hair, and put them back in again, at a different angle.

'Kate. Is there another man?'

Kate pushed her soup away. 'There's a man I know, but I'm not in love with him. I'm just a little in love with how he lives, where he lives.'

'I suppose Osney's a safe choice —'

'Don't sneer,' Kate said, suddenly cross.

'You could always live at Mansfield House —'

'No. Thank you, but no. I'm going to work full-time for Christine and I'm going to live in Swan Street.'

'With Joss?'

'Of course with Joss!'

Helen regarded her. 'So we won't be seeing much of you at Mansfield?'

'Not for a little bit, not until I feel less —' she stopped. She did not want to tell Helen about the change that had come over her feelings for James, her shrinking from him.

Helen waited. Kate said nothing more. After a while, Helen gathered up her huge embroidered sack bag from the floor, and patted Kate's hand.

'You are doing exactly the right thing. One has to call a halt to bullying and tyranny oneself, because nobody is going to do it for you.'

Kate looked at her levelly.

'Exactly,' she said.

Back at Mansfield House, there was a stranger in the kitchen, a fair, tidy stranger in spectacles who said her name was Julia Hunter.

'I'm a friend of Kate Bain's,' she said.

'Is that why you're here?' Helen said. Julia looked to her deeply, dangerously conventional, the kind of together woman who would urge Kate to marry James rather than leave him.

'No,' Julia said, smiling, 'I just knew where to come because of Kate. I work for Midland Television, actually.' She paused for a second and then said with a shade of self-conscious pride, 'We're making a series called *Night Life* and I'm interviewing for it.'

All the women in the kitchen had stopped stirring things and hissing at their children. Everyone was looking at Julia and Helen.

'Television,' someone said. All the eyes that had been examining her clothes were now fixed on her face, and her smile hid a lurch of inward panic — and pity — at the contrast between the children in the kitchen and George and Edward, safely and cosily at their irreproachable nursery school's Easter party.

'The aim of the programme,' Julia said as gently as she could, 'is to look at all sorts of lives that go on when more conventional lives have gone home from work and consider everything finished until the morning.'

There was some laughter at this.

'Never bloody stops here.'

'You want to come and film bathtime?'

'It's when the telephone begins, after six —'

'Would you pay us?' Helen said, regarding Julia. 'We have no income here. We can't afford to do anything for free, even though we'd like the publicity.'

Julia opened her mouth to say that such a decision was the producer's, and said, 'Of course,' instead.

'OK,' Helen said. She gestured at the women standing round them. 'Let's talk. Let's discuss it.'

Much later, Helen walked Julia out to her car. Her opinion had shifted a little while listening to Julia, away from feeling that Julia was a kind of undercover policewoman, and towards an appreciation of Julia's usefulness to the refuge.

'You said you know Kate,' Helen said now.

'Yes,' Julia said, 'our husbands are lifelong friends.'

Helen eyed her. If anything, she looked even younger than Kate, though this could be accounted for by her childlike colouring.

'Another one —'

'Sorry?'

'Another child bride.'

Julia took her car keys out of her bag. To her mind, Hugh bore no resemblance to James and their mutual age was merely coincidental. James after all, hadn't taken any care of himself for years, and it showed.

'What an impertinent and uncalled-for remark.'

'Is it?' Helen said, unperturbed.

Julia put the car key into the driver's door, and turned it. This Helen person, so big and bohemian and sure of herself, was just the kind of woman Kate wouldn't mind, might even like. Julia swallowed. Perhaps you couldn't do a splendid thing like run Mansfield House if you weren't pushy and three-cornered. She gave Helen the best smile she could manage.

'I'll be in touch to firm up dates,' she said, across the roof of the car.

'And the money,' Helen said.

She watched Julia drive away. Interesting. What was it that made some women choose men old enough to be their fathers? Was it, Helen wondered, climbing the steps back to Mansfield House front door, could it be that women like Kate, like this Julia Hunter, hoped that by so doing they could always think of themselves as girls?

Julia collected the twins from their party. They were scarlet with over-excitement, their shirts had come untucked in an unaesthetic frilly manner and they were clutching party bags adorned with Easter rabbits with daffodil-yellow fur and sticking-out teeth.

'Pow!' George yelled at the sight of Julia.

'I do hope they've been good,' she said anxiously to Frederica MacBride, who ran the nursery school. 'Perfectly,' said Frederica, who said that to all the mothers in order to emphasise that no child ever misbehaved with *her*. Julia knelt to tuck in Edward's shirt while he jiggled up and down and biffed her lightly on the head with his party bag.

'Enough,' Julia said quietly, looking at him.

He gave a loud sigh, and let his party bag fall to his side.

'Pow!' shouted George again, rushing up. Julia looked at him too, and so did Edward. 'Pow,' said George in a smaller voice, and then, in a whisper, 'Pow.'

On the way home, Julia asked them what they had done at the party and what they had eaten. They said they'd had sausages and cake and played musical cushions and had an Easter egg hunt. She asked them if they'd had a nice time and they said yes. Then she asked them a whole lot of other things and they said yes, yes, yes to her, because they were really preoccupied with taking off their trousers and their pants, impeded both by their child-safety belts, and by keeping their four round blue eyes fixed on the driving mirror in order to meet Julia's if she glanced at them. When they arrived at Church Cottage, they were haphazardly dressed again, and strangely serene. Julia unbuckled them from their seat belts and they stampeded into the house, to find Hugh in the kitchen, roaming about at the end of the telephone cable, and laughing and talking into the receiver. He was wearing jeans, and a pink shirt with the sleeves rolled up, and he was smoking and his hair was ruffled, and Julia coming in and seeing him so confident and happy felt a rush of love for him and, in addition, that pleasurable internal sinking that heralded a hope he would think of making love to her.

Hugh fielded the twins inadequately with one hand. 'Must fly, the team's home. Sure, sure. Wonderful. Ready to roll, then? Good to hear you. Ciao.' He put the telephone down and scooped up the boys.

'Don't burn me!' Edward shouted, squirming theatrically away from Hugh's cigarette.

'I will if I like,' Hugh said, kissing him. 'I'll do anything I like. I'm the father.'

He glanced at Julia. Her shy, excited expression was unmistakable. He came across the kitchen to her, still holding the twins, and bent forward to kiss her.

'Anything I like?'

She coloured and laughed.

'Oh Hugh —'

'Had a good day?' he said, his face still close.

'Oh yes. Kate's refuge has agreed to be filmed. It's run by a terrifying woman, one of those bossy independent women who think men are pathetic, but it'll make wonderful television.'

'Did you talk to her about Kate?'

'Down,' Edward said firmly. He slithered out of Hugh's grasp to the floor.

'Me too,' George said, following.

'No, I didn't. Should I have?'

'James is very worried. Kate seems miserable. She's withdrawn.'

144

'Oh dear,' Julia said, but she wasn't thinking about Kate. 'Was — was that a good call?'

'It was. It was the final budget assessment for the programme. Well within limits.'

'Oh good —'

Hugh leaned across to the table and stubbed out his cigarette in an ashtray painted with a blue cockerel, that they had bought on holiday in Portugal. Then he took off Julia's glasses and put his arms round her.

'Am I right,' he said into her hair, 'in thinking that you aren't listening to a word I'm saying?'

She gave a tiny giggle.

'Because you are, aren't you, simply calculating how long it will take you to get the twins to bed, so that —' His hands moved down her back to her bottom.

'Stop it,' she said happily, wriggling.

He pushed his fingers between her legs. 'So that I can get you to bed and fuck the hell out of you?'

'What?' said George.

'Fuck the hell out of Mummy,' Hugh said, more conversationally.

'*Hugh!*' Julia said, enchanted and scandalised.

'I can see Mummy's pants,' George said.

'Can you?' said Edward, hurrying over.

They looked.

'Black ones,' Edward said to George.

Julia wrenched herself free and tugged her skirt down. She was flushed and laughing.

Hugh looked down at himself. He grinned. He

looked back at Julia.

'Come on,' he said, 'these boys are going to have the century's fastest bathtime. At least bathing children is something I can do perfectly well bent double.'

Joss lay on her bed in the early spring dusk. She thought that, for the very first time in her life, she might very nearly be the least little bit happy. As this was not a sensation she was either used to, or had trained herself to admire (it being much more cool to be depressed), she was not quite sure what to do with it, so she was lying on her bed in the dim room, without music, for once, just doing a little savouring.

The weird thing, the really bizarre, weird thing, was that the beginning, the first cause of this wonderful feeling, lay with Miss Bachelor. If it hadn't been for Miss Bachelor, Garth would never have noticed Joss and Joss would not now be lying on her bed vowing not to bite her nails again and conjuring up his face in the dusky air. There she'd been, taking Miss Bachelor and her usual awful shopping home, when what she'd always dreaded had happened, and someone from school had suddenly appeared, out of the delicatessen in Albert Street, and what's more, it was that new American boy from the first-year sixth, that really cool boy who looked like Tom Cruise. Joss had wanted to die. She'd wanted to murder Miss Bachelor and then just die, shrivel up and simply disappear down one of the drain grids in the gutter.

Garth had bought a French loaf from the deli. He'd got it propped against one shoulder, like a rifle. For a second, Joss thought he wouldn't see them and, if he did, he'd never recognise her because she was just one of the fourth year and looked gross anyway, she knew it, just gross. But he'd stopped in front of them, and smiled his beautiful, wide, white American smile and said, 'Hi, there.'

Joss had gone purple. She could think of nothing except that she was holding this bloody basket with the lavatory paper and the biscuits and the tins of soup and that Miss Bachelor was wearing her belted brown overcoat which made Joss die of shame just to walk beside.

'How do you do?' Miss Bachelor said.

Garth's smile was still there. 'I'm just fine,' he said. 'Can I help carry that basket?'

He gave 'basket' a short 'a'. Joss was ready to faint. He said, to Miss Bachelor, 'We're at school together. My name is Garth Acheson.'

Miss Bachelor looked at Joss.

'Josephine?'

Joss whispered, 'I c'n manage —'

'You sure?' Garth said.

'It's most kind of you,' Miss Bachelor said, looking penetratingly at Joss, 'but I think Joss can totter as far as my front door. She has, after all, often done it.'

Garth held out his hand. 'Pleased to meet you, then, ma'am.' He bent a little towards Joss. 'See you tomorrow, Joss.'

Her name! He'd said her name!'

'You have the manners of an alley cat,' Miss Bachelor said, when he'd gone. 'And a very gauche alley cat at that.'

Joss didn't care. She went home that night in a daze, a daze which turned to a waking dream the next day when Garth approached her coming out of the dining-hall and said he thought she was great to help that old lady.

'I liked that,' he said, 'I really liked that.'

She ventured the smallest glance up at him. He blazed above her like a god.

'I like your stud,' he said, 'I really go for it. When you see a girl with a nose stud, you know you've got a really funky babe on your hands.'

Joss said, 'They hate it at home.'

'Of course they do,' he said. He paused. He gave her a long look. Then, 'You're cute,' he said, and asked her to go to the movies with him.

'OK,' she said, in a voice tight with joy.

Now, lying on her bed, the prospect of the cinema hung before her like the gates to paradise. He was sixteen. Sixteen! He'd been at the school since September and he hadn't asked anyone out, except Sue Fingall, and everyone asked Sue Fingall out as a matter of course, she was so stunning, so it hardly counted. Now he had asked her, Joss Bain, and, if she hadn't been so entirely convinced of her physical repulsiveness, she would have been able to be sure she was happy. As it was, she had just this evening to look forward to, this one evening before he discovered how boring she was, as well as repulsive, and inevitably decided not to have anything more to do with her. Joss turned on her side and felt under the bed for her cuttings box. She dragged it out on to the rug, and pulled out the photographs that lay on top, two of them, cut from magazines printed on laminated paper. She looked at the girls in the photographs. They had long, shining hair and firm flexible bodies in tiny, clinging clothes. Joss sighed. Her own body was only to be borne if shrouded in layers of ragged black, shirts and T-shirts piled on in gloomy, holey layers until, as Uncle Leonard said, she resembled a bag lady. Panic gripped her. She dropped the photographs. The one and only evening of her entire life was twenty-four hours away, and what was she going to *wear?*

Next door, Leonard sat and wondered at her silence. She had come in to see him, after school, and they had quarrelled mildly over the last chocolate biscuit in his tin — 'You ought to give it to me because I'm your guest.' 'You aren't a guest, you're an infestation' — and he thought she had looked very, very slightly pretty. Nobody, of course, could look even half-way pretty with hair like a nailbrush, and a scowl and navvy's boots, but none the less Joss had looked a little better than usual to Leonard. He'd even said so, and she had raised to him a glance of unquestionable happiness, a dreamy glance, full of light.

Was she smoking something? He shouldn't wonder. Kate was so absent-minded these days, Joss might as well not have a mother, for all the use Kate was. Leonard fretted about it, just as he fretted about running out of denture powder with no one in the house to send out for more, or about the time, soon coming, he feared, when his gaunt old arms simply would not pull the rest of his gaunt old self out of the bath any longer. The only thing at the moment that diverted him from fretting was the television programme. It was fascinating, he hadn't been as interested in anything for years; he couldn't remember, either, when anyone had been as interested in him, in what he thought, in what he had to say.

That Hunter chap, friend of James, had been here for hours already, with a camera and all the paraphernalia and a crew (that's where all the chocolate biscuits had gone), and before that, there'd been all the discussions with Beatrice and with James, and a few lovely rows about God, whom Beatrice had no time for but who Leonard suspected was probably lurking about somewhere, built into the fabric of things, like cricket and the rule of law, a sort of institution. They'd had one quarrel on camera. Beatrice had wanted it cut afterwards, but Hugh had talked her round.

'You're naturals,' he kept saying to them, 'absolute naturals.'

Hugh was talking to a doctor, too, and several people Beatrice had put him on to. They'd had surprisingly little trouble getting people to agree, not even the old people's homes where they were going to do the opening shots, all those poor old vegetables just sitting there, smelling of pee and staring at the telly with their mouths open and no teeth in. Leonard shuddered.

'I'll take the poisoned umbrella any time,' he'd told the camera. 'Stuff the medics. Whose sodding life is it anyway?'

'Have you ever been close to death?' Hugh asked him. 'Have you ever been in an accident? Or the War?'

Leonard bared his teeth at him. 'The closest I've ever been to death is now. And I'll tell you something. I don't mind the look of it as long as I'm allowed to pull my own plug.'

'Do you really mean that?' Hugh said, off camera.

Leonard looked away. He had fallen in love with his screen personality. 'Mean what I say,' he mumbled.

Then there had been the lawyers. Beatrice had been amazing, no other word for it, quoted Section 2 of the 1961 Suicide Act at them and said that, even if she was now prosecuted, the most she'd get was a suspended sentence because she'd helped her brother at his own request.

'I'm not encouraging anyone to commit suicide,' she'd said, 'I'm simply putting the case for euthanasia.'

Once, she told Leonard privately, the Voluntary Euthanasia Society ran a helpline for would-be suicides. They sent a man round with a plastic bag and a box of pills. Leonard's eyes had bulged. Hugh didn't want that put in the programme.

'We can be as controversial as we like, but we mustn't commit an offence. Any mention of methods might be an offence.'

Leonard got up from his chair and crept to the wall that divided his room from Joss's. He pressed his ear to it. No sound.

'What the hell are you doing?' James said from the doorway.

Leonard jumped.

'Why are you spying on Joss?'

'She's so bloody quiet. Can't hear that infernal music.'

'You ought to be thankful.'

Leonard straightened up. He looked at James. 'Where's Kate?'

'Why,' said James tiredly, 'why do you always ask that?'

'Where is she?'

'I don't know.'

'Whisky?' Leonard said.

'I'm drinking too much —'

Leonard limped over to his clutch of bottles. 'Medicinal.'

'Temporarily, I suppose.'

'What've you come up for?'

'I don't really know,' James said. 'It just felt rather empty downstairs. That's all.'

Leonard handed James a tumbler.

'Bloody madhouse,' he said. 'Kate never in, Joss

gone dead quiet, you like a wet week. What's the matter?'

'With me?'

'No.'

'Who, then —'

Leonard sat down in his comfortless chair and looked at James fixedly.

'I see,' James said. 'You mean, what's the matter with Kate.'

Leonard waited. James swirled his whisky round and round its glass for a little, and then he said carefully, 'The matter with Kate, Leonard, is that I have suddenly become too old for her, and she doesn't know how to tell me.'

Chapter Eight

The two rooms Kate had found in Swan Street were strictly speaking a room and a half. They looked north, along the gardens by the canal, and the smaller one, the cupboard-sized one that Kate had set aside, in her mind, for Joss, had only a slice of window, cut off by a partition wall. Because there was only space enough in this second room for a bed and a chair, Mr Winthrop downstairs, who owned the house, said he would only charge Kate forty-five pounds a week, exclusive of services, for both.

Mr Winthrop had been a dealer in antique maps and prints. He dealt a little still, but mostly now he mended old clocks in a tiny creaking conservatory at the back of the house. He played big band music while he worked, the saxophones mingling with the hoarse blast of an electric fan heater which he kept going from dawn to dusk, except in summer. He showed Kate an alcove on the landing where a little old electric cooker stood for her use, with a cracked sink beside it. Then he showed her the bathroom she and Joss would have to share with him. Kate had not entered such a bathroom for a decade.

'Who cleans this?' she said to Mr Winthrop.

'You do,' he said, 'if you care.'

Her rooms, on the other hand, were quite cheerful. The light was cold, but there was plenty of it, and a previous tenant had almost covered a plainly violent wallpaper with cream emulsion. The furniture, though neglected, was Victorian and solid, and there were two comfortable chairs. Kate sat in one and tried to picture Joss in the other, with the electric fire burning cosily and a jug of flowers on the table. Telling Joss was one of the two major hurdles ahead. The other one was telling James.

Mr Winthrop said he didn't mind if she painted the rooms and changed the curtains. Kate made plans and wrote a list. She thought she and Joss might go shopping together for paint and curtain material, and she would borrow Christine's sewing machine. Joss could paint her cupboard room any colour she liked, and cover it with her posters and photographs, and she could have an armful of Indian cushions on her bed to make it, by day, into a sofa. Perhaps Kate might afford a rug for her, too, and a brass lamp. Perhaps, on the other hand, the lamp would have to wait. Kate went out to the supermarket in Bridge Street and bought cleaning things, and a bucket, and a packet of blue-and-white disposable cloths. A sense of a new beginning filled her with elation.

'I feel,' she said to Mark Hathaway, half embarrassed at herself, 'that I'm starting to tell the truth.'

He offered to help her paint, in the evenings. 'When I've told Joss.'

'Joss,' he said. He was very uncertain about Joss. What greater obstacle to a budding relationship could there possibly be than a girl of fourteen, a girl too old to send to bed and too young to send out into Oxford? 'I hope she'll like me,' he said, meaning the opposite.

'Of course she will,' Kate said. She looked at Mark. His appearance was everything Joss would admire; so was his taste, his modern, fresh, fashionable taste.

'It's wonderful you're coming,' Mark said, 'it's just wonderful. You look different already, so much happier.'

'I am,' Kate said. She felt it. She couldn't believe how happy it made her, in a simple, carefree way, to clean the windows and polish the furniture in Swan Street. Mark bought her a poster, a reproduction of a watercolour of a cane chair on a bare floor by french windows opening on to a southern landscape, hazy-blue and gold. Kate was enchanted with it; it seemed a symbol, a symbol of her feeling that she was stepping out of some kind of restriction into an environment that wasn't just free, but natural to her as well, natural to her age and personality. Only when she thought honestly about James, about how his life would be without her, did her spirits sink. She was going to hurt him, but not as much, she told herself firmly, brushing at the Swan Street carpet, as she would if she were going to stay.

Walking back to Jericho one day, from one of these furtive visits to Swan Street, a car stopped beside Kate and the passenger door opened.

'Kate!' Julia said, leaning across from the driving seat. She was smiling, and wore a pair of dark glasses pushed up on her head in place of a hair-band. Kate stopped to peer in.

'You look quite different —'

'Contact lenses,' Julia said, laughing. 'The new me.'

'Hello,' the twins shouted from the back seat. 'Hello, Kate, hello, hello, Kate, hello —'

She beamed at them. They wore yellow jerseys. 'You look like ducklings.'

'Get in,' Julia said, 'get in and I'll drive you home.'

'It's fine, really, I'm only ten minutes —'

'Come on. I haven't seen you in ages, so much to tell you.' She patted the passenger seat. 'Why are you walking by Hythebridge Street any-way?'

'Just a variation,' Kate said, buckling her seat belt, her head bent.

Julia put the car into gear and moved it into the traffic. 'We were at the station. Weren't we, boys? What were we doing at the station?'

'The girl went on the train,' George said, 'that blue girl. You know.'

Julia glanced at Kate. 'I've succumbed to help at last. I think I've found the perfect person. She was nice, wasn't she, boys?'

'She was a bit fat,' Edward said doubtfully.

'But it's rather cosy to be fat, isn't it —'

'And she had funny hair.'

'Not *very* funny —'

'It was fat hair.'

'She had a blue jersey,' George told Kate.

'And fat hair.'

'She was a dear,' Julia said to Kate, 'a farmer's daughter from East Anglia. So capable, drives and everything. She was sweet to the boys. Wasn't she, boys? She'll be a life-saver, quite honestly, with me getting busier all the time and things picking up so quickly for Hugh. I mean, suppose the twins were ill?'

Kate turned round to look at them. They grinned at her. 'I never saw two chaps look less ill in my life.'

'No, but suppose they were. There's been a bout of chicken pox at their nursery school, Frederica's been quite frantic, and they could be incubating it right now.'

'All spotty,' George said, opening his eyes wide.

'Sam is spotty, isn't he?'

'Up his nose, he's spotty —'

'And,' Edward said reverently, 'inside his *bottom.*'

'Lord,' said Kate. She winked at them. They began to giggle.

'I advertised for help,' Julia said, 'then I interviewed the best-sounding four, and this one was perfect. She's called Sandy.'

George said scornfully, 'Sandy is a silly name.'

'No, it isn't. It's a pretty name. It's short for Alexandra. Now, Kate, tell me what's up with you?'

They were only a minute from Richmond Villa.

'Nothing to compare with contact lenses and nannies —'

Julia laughed. 'Isn't it absurd? Twenty-five years in specs and now I've got these, I think I must have been mad to have endured glasses all this time, but Hugh says he misses them —' She sounded suddenly coy.

The car slowed. 'Come in,' Kate said, turning to the twins again, 'come in and see Joss.'

'Joss!' they clamoured at once, straining at their seat belts. 'Joss! Joss!'

'We really ought to get back,' Julia said, 'I'm expecting several calls —'

'Just a quick cup of tea?'

'Joss! Joss!'

'All right,' Julia said, relenting, switching off the engine. 'Ten minutes. When Sandy comes, of course, I won't know myself, all that lovely freedom.' She smiled at Kate. She was quite extraordinarily pretty without her glasses. 'Isn't it exciting when life does this, just takes a lovely new turn when you're least expecting it?'

There was no Joss at Richmond Villa. The kitchen was empty, so was James's study, and there was no point even looking in the neglected sitting-room because no one was ever in there, except at Christmas. 'My front room,' James called it. The table in the kitchen was dotted with notes, weighted down by marmalade jars and cotton reels.

'Darling,' James's note said, 'am out with Hugh, seeing the lawyers. Back sixish. Hope refuge not too depressing.'

'But you weren't at the refuge, were you?' Julia said, reading the note over her shoulder. 'Wrong direction —'

'Gone to the cinema,' Joss's note said, 'back late.'

'I forgot,' Kate said. She turned to the twins. 'I'm so sorry, twins. I forgot that Joss was going out to see a film with her new boyfriend.'

'Wow,' Julia said, 'boyfriend!'

'He's an American. Lovely manners. Her — her first date, I suppose.'

'Can you believe it! Little Joss.' Julia looked at the twins. 'Ten years and it'll be you and girls, I suppose.'

'Joss coming soon?' George said hopefully.

'Oh darling, I'm so sorry, but not for a long time. I quite forgot. I'll find you a biscuit.'

'Look,' Julia said, 'there's another note.' She pushed a scrap of paper at Kate. It said:

Out to tea
With old BB
What a spree
For ancient me.
P.S. Gone in a taxi.

160

'That's Leonard,' Kate said shortly.

'Who's BB?'

Kate found a tin in a cupboard and bent down with it in front of the twins so that they could choose a biscuit.

'You know,' she said, 'the heroine of Hugh's programme.'

'Oh,' Julia said with emphasis, 'her. The famous Miss Bachelor. I'm dying to meet her. What's she like?'

'I don't know.'

'Haven't you met her?'

'No.'

'Why not?'

'It hasn't arisen,' Kate said, straightening.

'Pink,' Edward said in satisfaction, peering at the filling in his biscuit.

'Sorry,' Kate said, 'not very health foody —'

'Once in a while doesn't matter,' Julia said kindly. 'Does it?' She looked round the kitchen. Quite apart from the clutter, it had a forlorn look, as if no one was paying it much attention. 'Really Kate, isn't it lucky that you have all your interests, with the household so preoccupied with its own concerns? To tell you the truth, I always thought I was perfectly happy being a mum at home, but, now these chances have come up, I really am appreciating being able to stretch my wings a bit. I feel terribly sorry for women who just can't be themselves at all, don't you? I mean, what would you do, Kate, if you really felt you were trapped?'

At supper, James made a private resolution that he would tackle Kate later and confront her with her own fears. He decided this quite suddenly because she looked so haunted when she handed him a plate of one of her curious curries.

'How nice,' he said, to encourage her.

Uncle Leonard scowled at his helping. He was in an exhibitionist humour, having been out of the house for the first time in over a year and having managed to upset Beatrice Bachelor's sister-in-law by telling her she looked in the pink of health. He shook hot chilli sauce all over his curry and said he expected Joss was, at this moment, being raped in a multistorey car-park.

Kate and James ignored him.

'She looked really nice when she went out,' James said. 'I saw her.'

'What was she wearing?'

James thought. 'Jeans, I think. And something white? The whole effect was much less lugubrious than usual.'

'He seems nice,' Kate said, thinking that she should have been at home herself to admire Joss in her jeans and something white.

'He called me sir,' James said. 'Amazing. He looked clean enough to eat off.'

'That's being American.'

'Not eating this,' Leonard said, pushing his plate away.

James looked at it. 'You've drowned it in fire-lighting fluid, that's why.'

'Cake. Full of cake. Battenburg.' He pushed his chair back. 'Not really hungry.'

'Leave it, then,' Kate said, bending her head. She was seized with a sudden, violent longing to be in Swan Street, away from this charade of meaningless talk and ritual. She pictured the table by the window, and the view down the gardens fading in the fading light, and craved it. She jabbed her fork against a pile of rice on her plate and then dropped it. 'It isn't up to much, I'm afraid.'

James handed Leonard his stick.

'You're a rude and ungrateful old sod.'

'That's me,' Leonard said, unrepentantly, heaving himself to his feet. 'Old Beattie says I'm the original curmudgeon.'

'There's no call to sound so pleased about it.'

'Hah!' Leonard said. He limped to the door. Then he turned back for a moment. 'Sorry,' he said to Kate and crept out.

'I'm so sorry,' James said, too. 'I really am. He's intolerable.'

Kate shook her head. She was terribly afraid she was going to cry. She attempted to pick up her fork, but missed it, and it clattered off her plate on to the table. James stooped over her and put his arms round her shoulders.

'Julia came,' Kate said, seizing an excuse. 'She came with the twins. She's got contact lenses and they're hiring a nanny —'

'Come with me,' James said. 'Come into the study, and tell me all about it.'

'You want to leave me,' he said. 'Don't you?'

Kate sat in the swivel chair by his desk, and looked up at the plump young prince. 'Yes,' she said.

James was sitting behind her in his usual chair, the chair he sat in to read the paper and to teach and, sometimes, to sleep in after lunch. He said, 'Could you explain why?'

His voice sounded careful, as if he were controlling himself. Kate heard him get up, and then she heard the hiss of gas as he turned on the fire, and then the soft plopping ripple of it igniting. 'Tell me, Kate,' James said. 'Turn round and tell me.'

She swung the chair. He was standing by the fire, slightly stooping, waiting for her.

'I've changed,' Kate said.

'I wonder,' he said. He crossed the hearthrug back to his chair and sat down in it, so that his profile was presented to her. 'I wonder if it's you, or me. I rather thought I had become too old for you. I mean,' he said, looking up at her, 'it's not very jolly for you here, with me over sixty and Leonard so difficult. I've been thinking perhaps that it's no longer any place for you. Or Joss.'

Kate swallowed. It was going to be impossible to explain if James was going to be so nice. She said, almost without meaning to, 'I've got so tired of helping people.'

'I know.'

'Do you?' said Kate, suddenly irritated. 'Do you? It seems to me that clever people like you always make the mistake of thinking that stupid people like me are much more stupid than we are.'

He said with some energy, 'I'm not so patronising.'

Kate didn't speak. She pulled her feet up on to the seat of the chair and wrapped her arms around her knees.

'Is it the order we all impose on you?' James asked. 'Is it the demands? Is it —' He stopped for a moment, and then he said, 'Are you in love with someone else?'

'No,' Kate said.

'Sure?'

'Only a room. I'm in love with a room. I want to live in it, away from here.'

'I see,' James said. He leaned forward. 'Could we talk about age?'

Kate said, 'I don't want to be hurtful, I don't want to damage anything. That's why I must go away.'

'Are you afraid you'll have to look after me?'

She dropped her eyes.

'Do you love me?' James said. 'Do you love me still, at all?'

She looked up. 'I don't know. I'm afraid of you.'

'You're afraid of yourself,' he said. 'You see in me what you will become and you're afraid of that.'

She cried, 'But that doesn't make it any less

real for me! You can't just talk away a feeling!'

He put his hands briefly over his face. 'Oh Katie,' he said.

She released her knees and gripped the arms of the chair. 'I know I seem mad to you, and cruel, and selfish. But you know, don't you, what it is to feel that you have to do something just — just to save yourself? Even if it hurts someone else?' He stared at her. She went on, almost crying. 'I'm so bad at explaining, I can't find the words, but I feel if I can't go and live my own life I won't have any meaning, that I'll just break up, literally, into little bits and pieces —'

'A younger life,' James said.

She took a long breath; then she nodded. She said, her voice faltering because the words she was about to say did not seem at all adequate for expressing what she felt, 'James, I'm trying — I'm trying to do what's *right.*'

He said gently, 'I suppose I was always expecting this, with part of my brain.' He glanced up at her. 'I'm sure you've thought of Leonard and me going on here, without you. But have you thought of you, without me?'

She gave a little gasp. A fleeting dread seized her, but a second later it was swallowed up in the larger, now familiar dread of having to stay at Richmond Villa.

'Nothing will be easy —'

'Oh,' he said, 'nothing ever is, in the end, nothing worth having, that is. What will you do for money?'

'I'm going to work full-time for Christine.'

'You'll get exhausted —'

'No.'

'Let me give you a cheque —'

'No.'

'Please, Katie, let me help you, let me —'

'No!' she screamed, putting her hands over her ears. 'No! I've got to be free!'

He stood up. 'Of course,' he said.

She said, 'You'll have Mrs Cheng to look after you, and Joss'll come in to see you. We aren't going far.'

'Joss!'

'Yes, of course. Joss will come with me —'

His face twisted briefly. He put a hand out and lightly touched Kate's shoulder.

'Of course,' he said, 'of course Joss will go with you.'

'I won't,' Joss said.

She was so angry with Kate she could hardly speak. She stood in front of her, in the kitchen, the light of her evening out quite extinguished from her eyes, and glared.

'Jossie —'

'I don't want to,' Joss said. 'Right? You can do whatever bloody stupid thing you want, but you're not making me do it too. I'm not coming.'

'You have to,' Kate said gently. 'You're under sixteen and you're my daughter, and you have to come and live with me.'

'Look,' Joss said. Her mind, for the last six

hours so full of delight, felt fragmented and scattered, as if it wouldn't work properly. She made a huge effort to make her position plain. 'You may have gone off your head, but you can't make me come. You can't. I don't know what you're saying but I do know that I'm not coming. I'm staying here with James.' She stopped. Garth had said James was neat. His tone of voice suggested that it was an excellent thing to be neat, and besides, neat or not, Joss's bedroom was in James's house and she knew her bedroom, like she knew James, and Uncle Leonard. 'You're mad,' she said to her mother.

Kate tried to take no notice. 'It wouldn't be the same here for you, without me. Households without mothers, without women, just aren't. You can't imagine how it would be, of course, but I can promise you that you wouldn't like the feeling here if I wasn't here.'

Joss was triumphant. 'Anything'd be better than the feeling round here recently with you being such a pain —'

'Don't speak to me like that —'

'Same to you!' Joss shouted. 'Same to you! Don't speak to me like that! Don't tell me I've got to do some shitty stupid thing just because it's what you want!'

Kate gripped the edge of the kitchen table. She couldn't look at Joss. She said, 'James couldn't cope with you, Jossie. He couldn't manage, really he couldn't.'

'I'll go and ask him!'

'All right,' Kate said tiredly, 'you ask him, and you'll find he'll say just what I've just said. It's no good screaming at me, you just have to accept. That's all. Just accept.'

James heard the kitchen door crash deafeningly shut, and then came the subdued clatter of all the pictures hanging in the hall reacting to the slam. This was followed by a brief silence. He sat in his chair in his study, and watched the closed door to the hall. After twenty seconds or so, the handle of the door turned, and the door opened six inches, and then stopped.

'Joss,' James said.

Nothing happened.

'Come in,' he said.

Very slowly, she sidled in. She looked awful; she looked, indeed, very much as he felt.

'Come and sit down.'

She hovered far away from him, just inside the door, behind a chair.

'Mum isn't mad,' James said, 'nor wicked. She's a young woman, and it's perfectly natural.'

Joss whispered something.

'What?'

She looked up at him for the first time, her face sick-white. 'I want to stay —'

'Jossie,' he said gently, 'you can't do that. You have to live with your mother. I'm not even your stepfather, legally. It would be, I think, wrong if you stayed. Do you see?'

'No,' Joss said.

James leaned forward. 'You'd miss Kate, I promise you. You're angry with her tonight, but when your anger's died down you'll find that you'd be really unhappy without her.'

Joss cried suddenly, 'Don't make me, don't make me —'

James looked away. Why did Joss, so thorny and unapproachable and frequently purely disagreeable, have to be so touching?

'Joss, I don't know if I could handle you.'

'I'll be good,' she said idiotically, beginning to cry, 'I'll be good, honest —'

James stood up. He came over to Joss and waited beside her awkwardly, wishing it was easy and natural to put his arms round her.

'It isn't my job to bring you up, Jossie. We may have lived together a long time, but I've never had a child of my own. Kate's always had responsibility for you, you see.'

Joss muttered something. He stooped.

'What?'

'I like you,' Joss said.

He said, as kindly as he could, 'You mustn't blackmail me.'

'Please,' Joss mumbled. She raised her head and looked at him with wet eyes in dark blotches of smudged mascara. 'Please, please, please, please —'

Much later, Joss lay in bed under her duvet, with the light on. The house was very quiet. Kate was in her and James's bed, and James had gone to sleep in the spare bedroom. Uncle Leonard had been listening to the radio, but now he had switched it off, and had finished gurgling away at his wash basin, and was quiet too. Joss thought she would probably never be able to sleep again, she felt so wide awake. She'd made, in the end, a bargain with James. She could stay, on trial, for three months. She had tried for six, but he had said no, and from the way he said no she could tell that he might go back on the whole deal if she pushed him. Kate had looked ghastly when they told her, and furious with James, and then they'd gone off into the study and Joss had heard Kate crying and crying and James talking and talking. They went on for so long that Joss grew restless and lonely and went up to see Uncle Leonard, who wasn't his usual self, all horrible and funny, but pathetic, sad and shaky with runny eyes.

'I'm to blame,' he said to Joss. His voice croaked. 'It's my fault. I said to her, "Marry him or get out." So she's going. It's all my fault.'

Joss poured him some whisky. She half-filled a tumbler and didn't put any water in and he choked and spluttered. 'Sorry,' Joss said. She was trembling and the smell of the whisky made her feel sick.

'She doesn't want to get married,' Joss said. 'She just wants to live in this room.'

'What room?'

'A room in Osney. I'm supposed to go too, but I'm not going. James says I can stay.'

Leonard stiffened. 'You can't stay. A young girl and two old men? You can't stay.'

Joss's voice shook. 'I've got to. I want to.' She looked up at Leonard from where she knelt on the hearthrug. 'It's where I *live*.'

He stared at her for a long time. His face wobbled. Then he said slowly, 'Yes. Yes, I suppose it is.'

This is where I live, Joss said again to herself now, looking up at the ceiling where all the cracks ran about. This is where Garth came to collect me this evening. I didn't want him to, I didn't want him to see, but he just came and he said it was great. He said James was neat. Mum wasn't here. Joss caught her breath. Mum — wouldn't be here, either, in the future. James had said, 'You can go and see her every day. You can stay the night when you want to. It's only a walk away.' Joss suddenly felt very shy of James, he seemed different to her, not so familiar. She yawned. She wondered if Uncle Leonard was still awake, lying quite straight in his bed, as he did, in those weird pyjamas that he buttoned right up to his chin. She leaned across to their common wall and tapped it. Silence. She knocked again. Silence. Pity. She would have liked, she discovered, to tell Uncle Leonard that Garth had put his arm round her in the cinema and said, 'You know something, Joss? You know what? You're a real lulu.' She wanted to laugh out loud thinking of it. A lulu! Well, one thing was certain and that was that she bloody well wasn't going to tell Kate.

Beatrice Bachelor was also awake. She was not in her bed — it was Cat who was comfortably in her bed — but in a chair by the fire. She had never been much good at sleeping, but, at the moment, with so much to think about, sleep was more elusive than ever. It didn't trouble her. She had, after all, she told herself, the kind of rational personality that wasn't prey to 3 A.M. bogeys and glooms.

All the same, she was anxious. She wasn't in the least anxious about the television programme, being perfectly certain both about her views and her legal position, but she had grown anxious about James's household. None of them had openly confessed to dismay or unhappiness, but an open confession was hardly necessary. It was quite plain that things were simply falling apart, and in a way that Beatrice's logical and decided mind did not care to dwell on, any more than it cared to dwell on the precise nature of her feelings for James. Uncharted waters, those, uncharted and dangerous waters where the map of reason that Beatrice swore by wasn't much use.

It all hinged, it seemed, on this person Beatrice hadn't met, this young woman, Kate Bain. James had shown her a photograph and Beatrice had seen a small, supple woman with a sharp, appealing face and slightly slanting eyes and a wild mop of hair. James said her hair was red, pale-red. 'Carrots,' Beatrice had said to herself. It had become very apparent that Kate was avoiding her, somehow, and Beatrice, although intellectually so confident, did not feel socially confident enough to force a meeting on anyone so patently reluctant. Yet she knew she ought to because she also knew, with that intuition which she so despised as being unworthy of an academic mind, what was the matter with Kate. Kate felt as Beatrice herself had felt, though for different reasons, when she was nursing her parents. Kate plainly felt herself to be a victim, and, when you feel that, Beatrice thought, you believe that you have lost power over your own life and that is the very worst thing you can possibly feel, and is one of the reasons why I believe so strongly in euthanasia because you must, you *must*, have that power to the end.

She looked across at her bed. Cat had burrowed under the quilt, leaving only the end of his fat striped tail showing. The quilt heaved gently with his satisfied slumbering.

'Can't stand cats,' old Leonard had said that afternoon, and then, twenty minutes later, wistfully, 'Wish I had a cat.'

Wishing! What did she wish! Beatrice got up and looked at herself in the unhelpful little mirror behind the door. The trouble about the dreadful frailty of being human was that one went on, stupidly, wishing.

'Grace is right,' Beatrice told her grey-pig-tailed reflection. 'Quite right. You're a foolish old woman.'

Then she switched off the light, turned out the fire, and padded across the worn carpet to join Cat under the covers.

Chapter Nine

Sandy the nanny arrived in the Easter holidays, and was given a pretty room at Church Cottage with its own wash basin and a view over the garden and the sheep-filled fields beyond. She brought very little luggage — her wardrobe seemed to consist solely of jeans and sweatshirts — and was downstairs within ten minutes of having been shown upstairs, calmly unloading the dishwasher. The twins, eating their tea at the kitchen table, solemnly watched her large denim bottom bent over the dishwasher, and mutually, instinctively, resolved to withhold a large measure of their co-operation.

Julia was anxious that Sandy shouldn't know she had never employed anyone domestically before, except for Mrs Phelps, who came two mornings a week from the village to help clean the house. Julia and Mrs Phelps saw eye to eye in the matter of tidiness and gleaming surfaces, and Mrs Phelps was also a fan of Hugh's, and had gained great stature at the village Wednesday Club meetings by working for a television personality. Mrs Phelps was not talkative, and prided herself on never sitting down, so she had been, in terms of efficiency, a most trouble-free employee. Watching Sandy stack clean plates in the cupboard as instructed, Julia hoped and prayed that she would turn out to be as effortless as Mrs Phelps.

Julia explained to Sandy about the twins' diet. She then explained about the washing machine and the necessity of handwashing all woollens in liquid soap and about the days the milkman and travelling fishmonger called. Sandy listened with every appearance of good humour and then she said to the twins, 'Come on, then, lads. Time for the telly.'

The twins caught their breaths.

'Only on Mondays and Thursdays,' Julia said.

Sandy gazed at her. 'What do they do on the other days?'

'They draw and paint and play with their toys, and in summer they play in the garden.'

'And what do I do?'

'You,' said Julia crisply, 'play with them.'

Sandy scratched her head. Then she grinned. 'OK,' she said, 'I'll give it a whirl.'

The twins got off their stools and looked at her. She looked back at them. 'Right,' she said, her comfortable Suffolk voice overlaid with the merest hint of mocking gentility, 'let's go and play, then, shall we?'

'She's wonderful,' Julia said to Hugh.

'No beauty —'

'What does that matter? The boys think she's heaven. You should have heard them in the bath.'

He smiled at her. They were having such a happy time together just now, so optimistic and confident. He leaned sideways on the sofa and bit her ear lightly.

'Ouch.'

'Nonsense.'

'Isn't it amazing,' Julia said, 'you and me down here having drinks in this civilised way, with Sandy doing all the chores. She offered to get supper, even. She says her mother's the star cook for their local WI and she's taught Sandy.'

'Hurray,' Hugh said. He looked admiringly at Julia. For the first few weeks of her new contact lenses he had missed her spectacles — or at least, he had missed taking them off before he kissed her — but now he loved her new, free face. She looked pretty enough at the moment to verge on the beautiful. He said, 'I'm a lucky dog.'

She blushed. She looked down into her champagne glass. They were drinking champagne to celebrate Sandy's arrival, and the conclusion of the highly successful editing of the euthanasia programme — 'It is, quite frankly, a corker,' Hugh said. It was to be transmitted at the end of April, and at the beginning of May Hugh's contract was due for renewal; it would now, of course, go through on the nod. In addition, the preview of the first series of *Night Life* had pleased so many people that Rob Shiner, Julia's producer, was planning a second. There were, indeed, myriad reasons for drinking champagne. They had offered some, of course, to Sandy but she said no thanks, she only drank lager. At bathtime, Edward had cried because he didn't want to sit on her knee

and become physically involved with her rolls of
stomach and bosom, but Sandy said nothing of
that to Julia. 'You'll get used to it,' she told Edward. 'I've had to, and you will.'

'Poor James,' Hugh said suddenly.

'I know.'

'Seems wrong, somehow, toasting ourselves in
fizz while James is left coping with all that.'

'I gather Joss begged to stay. I suppose you
can't blame her for wanting to cling to what she
knows. She's only fourteen, after all.'

Hugh frowned at his glass. 'You know James.
Won't let on, won't say his household is a living
hell, but what else can it be? Have you seen Kate?'

'No,' Julia said carefully. 'I know she's stopped
going to Mansfield House because when I went
there no one had heard a word from her for three
weeks.' She stopped. She didn't want to say that
Kate was irresponsible and selfish, because Hugh
was always so defensive about James and anything
pertaining to James, and it was, amazingly, plain
that James had not himself said one derogatory
word about Kate.

Hugh grinned at her. 'Penny for your thoughts.'

'Stop it —'

'Irresponsible is one thought, isn't it? Selfish
another.' He adopted a teasing, mocking voice,
imitating an outraged suburban housewife. 'How
she could leave a kiddy, I don't know, and with
no call to go either. It's that women's lib, that's
what it is. Me, I've always been proud to keep
a lovely home.'

179

'Shut up,' Julia said, but she was laughing.

Hugh put his glass down, and swung himself sideways to lie down on the sofa with his head on Julia's lap. 'Let's have a party.'

'A party!'

'Yes. You know. You cram a whole lot of people and bottles into a room and let them out again after midnight.'

'We haven't had a party for ages —'

'We haven't been this successful and happy and perfectly wonderful for ages, either.'

Julia smiled down at him. 'OK, then.'

'Can we have balloons?'

'No. Nor party poppers either.'

'Darling. Why are we so silly? Could it be because we're happy?'

Julia stooped so that she could kiss him and her hair fell silkily over his face. He put his tongue in her mouth.

'You're awful —'

'I know. You love it. Let's ask James.'

Julia sat up. 'James!'

'Yes. Why not? Do him good, poor fellow, to forget his troubles and come to a party.'

Every day seemed to James like an endurance test that had to be painfully completed before he was allowed the brief oblivion of a night's sleep. It wasn't simply the pain of Kate's absence, but also the additional administrative burden her departure had laid upon him. He had grown used to her domestic sustaining, however haphazard, of Richmond Villa, and was appalled to discover how much there was to do. A greedy demanding procession of meals and laundry and shopping bore down on him in the day, and haunted his sleeping-pill-induced dreams at night.

He had not spoken to Kate for almost a month. He had seen her once, by chance, as he was driving up the High Street, and she was coming out of the covered market. She had looked young and carefree, wearing a cream jacket he didn't recognise, and black trousers and a lot of silver jewellery, and her palpable air of happiness struck at his heart's core. Joss had been to see her once, but would say nothing about it, except that she didn't like the room and she didn't like Osney. She declined to add that she had met Mark Hathaway, and that she didn't like him either, on principle. If it hadn't been for the benevolent influence of Garth Acheson's continuing, if inexplicable, interest in Joss, James thought he might have strangled her.

She was, as James came to suppose she always had been, just an inert lump in the household, a creator of mess and washing, a consumer of food at all times but mealtimes. Infatuation with Garth caused her to monopolise the bathroom, locking herself in for hours to perform such rites as dying her hair purple which she did very badly, managing, in the process, to spatter the towels, the curtains and James's toothbrush with random splashes. As Garth understandably objected to the purple, she repeated the process with henna and left the bathroom looking as if it had been rinsed in tea. James lost his temper and shouted, so Joss sulked and stayed out, as was strictly forbidden, until eleven. Only two months to go, James told himself, hauling a spaghettilike tangle of socks and tights out of the washing machine. Only eight weeks, and then I'm shot of her.

Leonard, on the other hand, he couldn't be shot of. Kate's absence was making Leonard querulous. He fussed and made objections, and poked suspiciously at his food.

'What's this, then?'

'Chicken.'

'Could have fooled me.'

'It's the kind of chicken I've been cooking for you about forty per cent of the time you've lived here.'

'Doesn't look the same.'

'Smells funny,' Joss said.

James shouted, 'Go to hell, the pair of you!'

They stared at him.

'C'n I have ketchup?' Joss said.

James sighed. 'I don't care. Have what you want.'

'Wicked,' Joss said, squirting ketchup.

Leonard watched her. 'I'll have some of that.'

James went into the study and sat in his chair with his eyes closed. Kate, he cried to himself, oh Kate, oh Kate. He opened his eyes and looked at the swivel chair by his desk, the chair she had sat in the first day she had come to Richmond Villa, and again the day she had agreed with him,

182

yes, she did want to leave. He couldn't blame her, but oh how could she have left him to this terrible, pointless, miserable wasteland of time and life? I've got to go on, James told himself, but by God, I don't want to. How could anyone want to, with the great sustaining love of their lives having removed itself elsewhere? Perhaps it's a punishment for not having valued her enough, not having loved her enough, or told her I loved her enough. But I did, I do. I yearn for you, James told the absent Kate, I yearn for you to be here in my arms and content to be there, as you used to be. He turned his head sideways and his glance fell on a book Miss Bachelor had lent him, a translation of the odes of Pindar. Perhaps Beatrice was right in her beliefs; she certainly seemed so at the moment. At the moment, James thought, at this very moment, all I want to do is to die.

Kate's guilt — 'your ball and chain', Mark Hathaway called it — had gone through a metamorphosis. Instead of feeling guilty about making other people's lives, and particularly James's, unhappy, she now felt guilty at being so happy by herself. It was like putting down a great burden, or feeling a chronic headache lift and the subsequent sensation came very close to joy. Kate felt as if she had come in a huge weary circle through life, back to her true self, to the person who could decide for herself, plan for herself, make things happen in a way that was both right and comfortable. Even Joss's absence didn't trouble her, because it was obvious that, at the end of the trial period at Richmond Villa, Joss and James would say goodbye to one another with nothing but relief. The only thing that troubled her was the knowledge, brought by Mrs Cheng, that she had left behind her a misery as profound as her own new delight.

'He too old for this,' Mrs Cheng said of James. 'He tired right out.'

'It'll be better when Joss comes here —'

'There's still the old devil,' Mrs Cheng said.

Kate looked round her room. 'I can't go back.'

Mrs Cheng said nothing; her loyalty was badly shaken. Who, in their right mind, would forsake the solid comfort and security of Richmond Villa for a room in a poky house which resounded all day to Glen Miller or The Four Freshmen? Yet, perplexingly, Kate looked better, younger, happier. Her eyes shone. Her room, as Mrs Cheng's appraising eye fell upon it, wasn't tidy, certainly, but it looked the room of someone who was pleased to be in it.

'I love it here,' Kate said.

It was true. From the moment she opened her eyes in the little segment that would shortly belong to Joss to the moment she closed them again to the sounds of faint late traffic in the Botley Road, she loved it. She loved walking to work, she loved working, she loved the feeling that what she earned was hers to administer so that she seemed to inhabit and to rule a little kingdom of her own. Every week, she sent James a cheque for Joss.

He never acknowledged it, and she suspected he didn't spend it on Joss, but saved it for her.

Twice a week, by arrangement, she rang Joss from a call box, and once a week they met for lunchtime sandwiches or a teatime doughnut. Joss looked strange to Kate, half surly, half elated. Kate was in a hurry for the last two trial months to be up, so that she could begin to share her new independence with Joss, and to teach her the value of staying free, and in control. Mark had typed out a quotation for Kate, from an American professor of addiction: 'The lack of a fully realised perception of personal power and meaning is destructive to anyone.'

Kate loved that, too. She had tucked it into the corner of the mirror in her room, the mirror that reflected a face she was startled and enchanted to be pleased to see. Mark had said he was falling in love with her. Was she, he asked, falling back?

'Give me time,' she'd said, 'give me time, just to be me.'

In the end, Hugh and Julia decided on a Sunday lunch party.

'More gravitas,' Hugh said.

He intended to ask everyone of significance in his life, all his past real cronies from television, as well as those upon whom his future depended. He would include Maurice Hirshfeld and his exhausted long-term wife (but not his current short-term boyfriend), Vivienne Penniman, and even Kevin McKinley, who was married to a formidable-sounding girl, the editor of a magazine for working women. Julia suggested her own producer, Rob Shiner, and Helen, and Frederica, who ran the twins' nursery school and regularly bought the magazine edited by Fanny McKinley. There would be twenty of them in all, which Julia reckoned she could accommodate in two halves, ten in the kitchen and ten in the dining-room.

'Oh, and James.'

'Gosh, nearly forgot. Of course. Poor James.'

Sandy could indeed cook. Julia took a vicarious pride in this, and consciously allowed Sandy to help her decide on the food. Sandy said she made a very nice chicken dish with orange and tarragon, and that nobody ever refused her chocolate roulade. Because of this, Julia decided to overlook the fact that she had shrunk Edward's Fair Isle jersey and bought the twins packets of brilliantly coloured chewy sweets at the village shop. Sandy made a trial roulade and Julia told herself that anyone who could cook like that was perfectly entitled to shrink the odd jersey.

In the week before the lunch party, Julia made lists. She made a wine list for Hugh, a shopping list for herself, and a cooking list for Sandy. She worked for Midland Television three days and two evenings and was astonished to discover that she was relieved and pleased to come home and find that the twins were in bed and that something had been done towards supper. True, the kitchen didn't always look as immaculate as she liked it to, and Sandy had an irritating preference for using the tumble dryer rather than the line in the orchard, as well as a stubbornness about ironing underclothes and not eating chocolate in front of the boys, but really, you couldn't have everything, could you? There had to be give and take, after all, just as there had to be a willingness to learn. Julia had learned something recently, from Hugh. Hugh had said that life was unendurable if you didn't feel yourself to be effective, and although Julia had dismissed this at the time, she now knew, being so very effective herself, how very true it was.

James was late for the lunch party. He had forgotten that, if he were out himself, Leonard and Joss still needed to be fed, and there had been a last-minute panic, with Leonard saying 'Don't mind *me*' with heavy sarcasm and Joss saying she was going out anyway. Then there were cuff buttons missing from his favourite blue shirt — who cared? — and a telephone call to discuss a newspaper piece on a possible Lost Eden philosophy behind the Green movement — who cared about that, either, at this precise moment? — and a hunt for the car keys. In the end, hurtling out of the house leaving Leonard muttering resentfully over a saucepan of baked beans, 'How the hell do I know when they're ready, sodding things?' James felt that the last thing he needed was any form of social life, and if it hadn't been Hugh's party, he would have cried off.

He drove too fast. It was a pretty, late-April day, and once outside the city the hedges were fuzzy with new green. These were difficult to appreciate properly since James had dropped his spectacles on the kitchen floor two nights ago, and cracked a lens, so that any view resembled the jagged medley at the bottom of a kaleidoscope. He took his glasses off as he approached Church Cottage, anxious to look neither neglected nor half-witted. Getting out of the car, which he decided to leave in the lane, he observed ahead of him a sleek couple in their late-thirties or early-forties, and hastily tucked into his jacket sleeve (should he have worn his suit?) the flapping untethered cuff of his shirt.

Church Cottage looked ravishing. The daffodils in the garden were almost over, but a huge old prunus tree, with its greenish and oriental bark, was extending a vast umbrella of pale blossom among new red leaves. The gravel path was raked, the lichen on the stone urns of dwarf tulips was artistically dappled, and smoke rose hospitably from the brick chimneys set so charmingly in the thatched roof. James surveyed it all in dismay, and wanted to go home.

He tried very hard to dawdle so as not to arrive at the front door at the same time as the sleek couple, but they suddenly took it into their heads to wait for him, and the woman, ferociously urban and elegant in a suede tunic over a brief skirt, turned and held her hand out to him with a wide smile and said that she was Fanny McKinley. She then indicated the saturnine man with her and said that he, of course, was Kevin.

'Of course,' James murmured. He took her slim, cool hand. He was clearly expected to react, but there was nothing he could think of to say except, 'Lovely day,' lamely. His clothes felt as if he had not only slept in them, but had had several nightmares in them too.

The front door opened, and there was Hugh, blithe in a gingham shirt.

'Kevin. Terrific to see you. And the delectable Fanny. Am I allowed a kiss? And James. You've met, I see. Come in, come in. Seize a glass and fight your way into the mêlée.' He took two glasses of champagne from a tray on a small table in the hall and handed them to the McKinleys. 'To me, men! In we go!'

James helped himself to a glass and followed them. The sitting-room seemed very full, not only of people, but of the steady braying sound of a party working itself up from cold to a cruising speed. Julia, completely pretty in a soft, pale jersey and trousers, came quickly over to him and kissed him with tender solicitude, as if he had fallen over and hurt his knee. She smelt of lily of the valley.

'Come and meet Frederica.'

Frederica was dark and highly coloured, in a brilliant fuchsia sweater.

'Oh,' she said to James, turning bright eyes on him. 'James Mallow! I love your pieces. I agree with every word you say.'

'What a pity,' James said. 'Now we can't argue.'

189

'I wish you'd write more about education. I'm terrifically committed to education, you see.'

'I'm afraid I know nothing about it.'

Frederica's voice softened. 'Don't you have children?'

A sudden, absolutely unbidden homesickness for Joss thickened James's throat. 'Not a child.'

Frederica was very startled. 'But,' she said, trying to retrieve the situation, 'you look like a father.' She turned to the man standing on her other side. 'Doesn't he?'

The man was about James's age, thin and yellow-toothed in a pink shirt under a fancy tweed jacket. He winked at James and put a hand out. 'Terence Gray. Old chum of Hugh's.'

'Me too,' James said.

'Surely not television?'

'No. Nothing to do with television.'

Terence Gray clasped his hands round the bowl of his champagne glass and rolled his eyes heavenwards. '*Sensible* man. It always was a madhouse and now it's a purgatory.'

'It's been enormously influential in education,' Frederica said.

Terence eyed her. 'Has it, sweetie?' he said languidly. 'Like our friend here, I know nothing about it. Do you think I look like a father? Too amusing.'

'I think you look like an actor,' James said.

'Do I? Bull's-eye, actually. Actor turned freelance director. In my next life, I shall come back as a highly paid employee with a chauffeur-driven

190

car and a pension plan.' He dropped his voice and indicated Kevin McKinley's sharply clad back three feet away. 'Like him.'

'Who's he?'

'My dear,' said Terence Gray, leaning forward and showing his yellow teeth, 'he's the reason for this party. He's the new man at Midland Telly. Hugh's whole future hangs on Mr McK.'

At lunch, James found himself in the kitchen at a table beautifully laid in white and pale yellow with posies of narcissi down the middle, between Frederica and a worn-out looking woman who said she was Zoë Hirshfeld. James thought Frederica neither attractive nor interesting, so he decided to leave her to another of Hugh's cronies on her far side, a vastly overweight man with dark hair almost to his shoulders who had gained a national reputation for his producing of comedy series. Across the table, just too far away to speak to, sat Kate's friend, Helen. She looked at James as if he were both despicable and pitiable and James resolved to avoid her. He looked down at his plate. On it lay a little golden pouch of pastry filled with something white and speckled.

'Goat's cheese,' said his neighbour.

He turned to her. She was probably about his age too, and had the dry, faded air of an exhausted moth. Her face and hair and clothes were all palish and fawnish, and her eyes had no life in them at all.

'How elegant.'

'This house is,' Zoë Hirshfeld said. 'Isn't it?'

'If a cottage can be elegant —'

'Julia's elegant.'

'Oh yes.'

She poked at her pastry with a fork. 'And young,' she added.

'Is elegance a matter of age?'

'*Everything's* a matter of age. And sex.' She put a fragment of cheese into her mouth and stared at him. 'I mean, are you happy?'

'No.'

'There you are, then. I bet you were happy when you were Julia's age.'

'Yes, I think I was.'

'I was,' Zoë Hirshfeld said. 'I'd only been married a couple of years and I thought television was wonderful. I can't bear experience, I can't bear what you have to learn, and age brings experience whether you like it or not. This needs black pepper.'

James looked down at his plate. It was empty.

'I don't seem to have noticed —'

'Which is your wife?'

'I haven't got one.'

'I should have known,' Zoë said. 'I shouldn't even have asked. You'd think I'd have learned, wouldn't you, after all these years mixing with telly people —'

The fog cleared. 'I'm not gay,' James said.

Zoë looked at him again. 'Well, why haven't you got a wife?'

James couldn't bring himself to mention Kate.

He said, 'I had one. She died.'

After a long time, Zoë took her eyes away from his face. 'I'm looking forward to widowhood,' she said.

'You won't like it.'

'You're quite wrong there,' she said. Her voice dropped. 'It's all I'm hanging on for, it'll be my revenge.'

James drove home in the lowest spirits. Full of irreproachable food, and generous drink, he felt nothing but downcast by his first foray into social life on his own without Kate. His table at lunch had gradually been taken over by Hugh's cronies who had begun, during pudding, on an interminable sequence of anecdotes of the old days, when television had been the preserve of the autonomous amateur. They bellowed with laughter and lit cigarettes and blew smoke all over their neighbours and went into a schoolboy teasing routine with Hugh when he came in with a bottle of brandy and a fistful of glasses. Frederica had made many brave attempts to lure James into the irresistible topic of primary education, and Zoë had pushed her food around her plate and told him that the only thing worth living for was finally getting even with someone who'd ruined your life, until James could bear no more and had escaped, with his coffee, into the dining-room. There he had been captured by Fanny McKinley. She talked at him for a long time about the aspirational markets for modern magazines, and he sat and looked at her and thought how perfect she was, like something carved and polished, and also how her eyes lacked all vulnerability, all humanity, and that this made her, in the end, repulsive.

'Had a good time?' Hugh said, as James was leaving.

'Lovely,' James said.

Hugh looked unnatural, shining with an exaggerated bonhomie. 'You OK?'

'Yes,' James said.

'I'll be in touch,' Hugh said, and slapped him on the shoulder.

It was a relief to be back in the car, in his ruined glasses, and to be leaving the Hunters' cosmetic corner of the countryside for beloved, ugly Jericho. For a brief moment, he thought of turning the car south, to skirt the city towards Osney, and then he thought that this would be the emotional equivalent of prodding an aching tooth, and continued homewards. When he got home, he told himself, he would go out into the garden for an hour and maybe prune something. It was Kate who had done the pruning in the past; Kate, who liked the garden.

Leonard had left his beans saucepan congealed and unwashed up on the draining board. He had left his dirty plate on the table too, and a scatter of Sunday newspapers, and he had helped himself to a glass of red wine, leaving the cork out of the bottle. It was difficult to decide whether he or Joss was the more chronically adolescent.

How, James wondered, running water into the saucepan and jabbing at the clinging mess in it with a wooden spoon, did women stand families? No wonder housewives sometimes clamoured for payment; who could think of a sum adequate to recompense for the steady attrition of the nerves consequent upon living with two people like Joss and Leonard?

He went up to Leonard's room. Leonard was doing the crossword with exaggerated concentration.

'Couldn't you even have cleared up?'

Leonard took no notice. He began to hum, just faintly.

'Where's Joss?'

Leonard scented a welcome deflection from his own guilt. 'Still out.'

'When did she say she'd be back?'

'Didn't.'

'Any more of this,' James said, 'and she's going to Osney, and you're going into a home.'

Leonard drooped. The hand holding the newspaper shook.

'I mean it.'

Leonard squinted at him. 'You wouldn't have the heart —'

'If you had any consideration whatsoever for my heart,' James said, 'you'd be doing something, just some tiny thing, that showed even an atom of consideration. You can get your own tea.'

He marched out and slammed the door.

'Going to anyway,' Leonard muttered to the crossword.

Joss was not back by eight, her Sunday-night deadline. She was not back by nine, either, nor by ten. Leonard was sulking, and would not share first James's concern, and then his anger.

'Should I ring the police?'

'Not your child —'

'No, but a child in my care.'

'Ring Kate.'

'Kate!'

'Her child, after all. Her wretched child.'

Shaking with weariness, anxiety and emotion, James dialled Mr Winthrop's number in Osney.

'Yes?' said Mr Winthrop, shouting above the strains of the US Navy Band of Sam Donahue.

'I wonder if I could speak to Kate Bain?'

'She's out,' yelled Mr Winthrop. 'Gone to a party.'

'Do you know when she'll be back?'

'Couldn't say, couldn't possibly say!'

James put the telephone down. Then he put his head down on the telephone. He stayed like that for some moments, eyes closed, fists clenched. Then he raised his head and crossed his study to his desk and found a piece of scrap paper and wrote on it, blackly.

'Door locked. Don't ring the bell. Go to Osney.'

He carried the paper and a drawing pin outside and pinned the note in the centre of the front door where it was plainly visible. Then he went inside, shot both bolts and fastened across the door the heavy, old-fashioned security chain that he had hardly used in thirty years.

Joss stood unsteadily on the pavement. It was one-thirty, and she had definitely had too much rum and Coca-Cola as well as a drag on some joint someone had passed her. She felt sick and tired and very much in need of the consolation of her own bedroom.

The note was so black-and-white that it was perfectly easy to read by the light of the street lamp without even going up the steps. It frightened Joss a little; James hadn't even signed it. She began to whimper, rubbing her party-impregnated sleeve across her eyes. There was no light in Uncle Leonard's window and there was something sufficiently uncompromising in the tone of the note to deter even Joss from chucking up a stone against the glass to wake him.

She subsided, snuffling, on the pavement and leant against the street lamp. She could go back to the squat, where the party had been held, which was inhabited by a shifting population of drop-outs from Oxford's private schools — drop-outs elaborately defying their middle-class upbringings — but she was, without Garth, a little apprehensive of doing that, and Garth had gone home to his liberal, academic parents in Observatory Street. She might go there, except that she'd never met his parents, and parents could be funny about being woken at two in the morn-

197

ing. Joss felt uncertain of her social adequacy in braving Observatory Street.

'Go to Osney,' the note said. She certainly wasn't going to do that. She'd rather climb the fence at the side of the house, and break into the decrepit shed where the lawn mower and the deck-chairs lived and spend the night there than go to Osney. She didn't mind seeing Kate on neutral ground, but she jolly well wasn't going to have anything to do with Kate's so-called new life. She'd been once, because they'd gone on at her so, but she wasn't going again.

She stood up. She felt awful. Garth had been a bit, well, he'd tried something at the party, he'd tried to — Joss had known he would, sooner or later, and had thought she'd like it when he began, but she hadn't, and at the same time had been too scared to tell him to stop. He hadn't got very far, because someone had interrupted them, and then he'd been too stoned to start again. Joss thought of her pillow and her duvet locked inside the house and slow tears of self-pity rolled down her face and dripped on to her jacket.

She stumbled over to the fence and looked for hand- and footholds. It was made of overlapping upright panels, and it was absolutely smooth, there wasn't a cranny or a crevice. Joss leant against it, and thought: I'll just stay here, I'll just stay here until the morning, I don't care, I don't care about anything, when another thought struck her. She straightened up, and considered it for a moment. Why not? Why not give it a try? Pulling

198

her jacket round her, Joss moved away from the fence, and set off at a steady trot for Cardigan Street, and Miss Bachelor.

Chapter Ten

'I don't eat porridge,' Joss said.

'This morning,' said Miss Bachelor, 'you do.'

Joss sighed. She was, she knew perfectly well, in no moral position to object to anything of any kind, nor had she the energy, even over porridge. It lay in her cereal bowl in a grey-fawn pool; her punishment.

She had spent the night on the sofa in Miss Bachelor's sister-in-law's sitting-room, under Cat and a mound of crocheted blankets. Miss Bachelor had seemed unsurprised to see her, and remarkably equable about being disturbed at almost two in the morning. She had made Joss a mug of disgusting cocoa, full of powdery lumps.

'I am distinctly short of maternal instincts,' she had said to Joss, 'but if you wanted those, you should have gone to Osney.'

Joss had slept heavily and woken to a hammering headache. Now there was this porridge. What she craved was glasses and glasses of cold blue water and a very dark place to drink them in. She jabbed at her porridge and made lakes and bays for the milk to run into.

'When you have eaten that,' said Miss Bachelor, spreading jelly marmalade on a triangle of toast, 'we are going round to Richmond Villa together.'

'Can't,' Joss muttered. She inserted a tiny spoonful of porridge into her reluctant mouth and held it there, in disgust.

'Do you wish to continue living there?'

Joss swallowed. Tears surged into her eyes. From upstairs came the sound of ferocious plumbing, as Grace Bachelor performed her lengthy morning ablutions. 'I do live there.'

'Not necessarily,' Miss Bachelor said.

Joss dug again at her porridge. 'I do. James said I could.'

'Only temporarily. If you misbehave and are selfish and troublesome, he will turn you out.'

'He won't.'

'He will. You are being elaborately childish.'

Joss felt childish. She gulped another spoonful of porridge and seized her cup of tea to wash it down.

'If you do not behave with more co-operation and generosity, you will be turned out, and quite right too. He has no obligation towards you. You are not his child nor even, as you insist upon telling me, his stepchild. He is not responsible for you.'

Joss raised her head and looked at Miss Bachelor.

'If you want to stay in Richmond Villa,' Beatrice said, 'you will have to earn your right to stay. There is no relationship on this earth worth having that does not have, in some way, to be earned.' She stood up. 'I am going to telephone James and tell him that you are safe, and that I am escorting you home. And when I return, you will have eaten your porridge. If I find the porridge in the waste bin, I shall order you a taxi for Osney.'

Joss gazed at her. On her white exhausted face there was an unmistakable mixture of resentment and relief.

'Thank God,' James said.

'I am sure you were worried.'

'I didn't sleep at all. How dare she? How dare she make me lose a night's sleep? Is she at all sorry?'

'I believe so. She does, of course, lack any grace of expression, but I sense fear and a mild repentance.'

'I'm not sure,' James said, changing the telephone receiver to the other ear, 'I'm not sure I can go on coping with her. Not her and Leonard.'

'Then you must give her up.'

'Beatrice, it isn't so easy, I feel responsible, I feel I've been involved in making this insecurity for her —'

'Nonsense,' said Miss Bachelor. 'She is her own person, she is not simply a victim.'

'But she's so young. I feel I ought —'

'Stop it,' said Miss Bachelor, interrupting. 'Just stop it. Clear your mind of conscience. Why is it up to you to put this right?'

'Because I suppose I think every child has a right to a proper family life. And I feel guilty.'

'Guilty?' shouted Beatrice.

James held the telephone receiver away from his ear.

'Nonsense!' shouted Beatrice. 'Don't behave as if you were the first! Agamemnon had a terrible family life, remember! It isn't original sin!'

She banged the telephone down.

'Who was that?' Leonard called.

'Beatrice. She's got Joss —'

'Damn,' Leonard said, dizzy with relief.

'She says my troubles aren't a patch on Agamemnon's —'

'Hah!' Leonard said. He began to laugh, his wheezing, creaking laugh. James leaned against the kitchen wall beside the telephone and closed his eyes. He would have given, at that moment, anything to feel frankly, luxuriously, furious with Kate.

Kate was humming as she laid tables in Pasta Please. Downstairs, in the basement kitchen, Benjie was cursing steadily into a new batch of pizzaiola sauce, working off simultaneously a weekend hangover and a reluctance for Mondays. They had the restaurant to themselves as Christine had gone to watch her son in some county fencing trials. She had telephoned in her instructions, which Kate had taken down with precision. Now, laying the tables and putting a new spray carnation in a glass tube on each one, Kate was pretending that the restaurant was hers.

She had been, the night before, to a wonderful party. She had been to wonderful parties very occasionally, long, long ago, but not for ages, ten years or more. She had forgotten how a party could make you feel, how elated and free and happy, and full of air after all that dancing. After the party, she and Mark had walked home through quiet Sunday midnight Oxford, singing the words of the songs they had been dancing to. Oxford seemed magical then, full of sleeping life that would burst out in the morning and spread energy along all the streets, like sunlight. She had held Mark's hand, and made him run with her down Queen Street, past the foolish posturings of the mannequins in shop windows. The most modish of them had no heads, only polished wooden knobs, like tailors' dummies, and for some reason this had seemed terribly funny.

'Look at me,' Mark had said beseechingly to one of them through the plate glass. 'Just one look from those bewitching eyes —'

Of course, he had come home with Kate, taking off his shoes and matching his tread to hers up the stairs.

'Does old Winthrop care? Why should he care? You pay the rent, you do what you like —'

'I want there to be no bother about having Joss here, no chance of bother.'

'Oh,' Mark had said. 'Joss.' He kept hoping that the Joss question would simply resolve itself by dissolving. He had thought Joss, in their one brief encounter, most objectionable, and, at the same time, disconcerting. He did not like thinking of Kate as a mother; he wanted to think of her as an independent spirit, a caged bird that he had set free. Free, that is, for himself.

She was not, however, proving entirely tractable about becoming his. She was delightful with him, carefree, light-hearted, but he had got to the stage of wanting her to express more commitment. This she seemed disinclined to do, either verbally or in bed. She was acquiescent in bed, but Mark wanted more than that, much more, even a little violence, which to himself he called abandonment. 'Trust me,' he said to Kate, urging her further, 'trust me.' But she didn't seem to. Once he had yelled, 'Are you thinking of bloody James?' and she had looked amazed and said, 'Of course not,' but he wasn't sure. Last night he had made a huge effort to be slow and gentle, but, as usual, he couldn't control or pace himself. 'Ow,' Kate said at one point, and then a bit later, 'Not so fast, not so fast.'

Thinking about it now, laying the tables, Kate resolved to give herself a week without sex with Mark. It wasn't that she didn't find Mark attractive, nor that she didn't like sex with him (or did she really?) but simply that she didn't want sex with anyone just now, she wanted to live peacefully, with herself, alone. She was working four evenings this week anyway, and was going to the cinema with Helen on another (this was a daunting prospect because of her desertion of Mansfield House, but it had to be gone through, otherwise there'd be an irretrievably bad feeling between them), so there wasn't time to see Mark, since two evenings out of seven to oneself were perfectly reasonable in anyone's book. And on the eighth evening, she'd arranged to see Hugh's euthanasia programme with Mark anyway, in his flat. Until then, Kate told herself, her life would be hers, and it was this thought that made her hum.

Benjie's head appeared up the spiral stairway from the basement.

'Guess what, Katie?'

Kate knew Benjie. Without turning round from the table where she was spiralling napkins into wineglasses, she said, 'You've had a sex change.'

'No such luck. Try again.'

'Princess Di's just rung —'

'Give over,' Benjie said, 'I've run out of bloody oregano. *Oregano*. I ask you.'

'So?'

'So I haven't time to go and get any more, Katie darling, precious, sweetheart, love, sexpot.'

'I see.'

'Four ounces minimum. Freeze-dried.'

'You're useless.'

'Not at some things,' Benjie said inevitably. 'You ask the lads.'

He disappeared downwards. Kate raided the petty cash box for change and went out into the street, still humming. It was a charming day, pale, clean blue sky and cotton wool clouds, an optimistic day. Turning down the side street in which Pasta Please stood, Kate made for Cornmarket Street at a run.

She dashed across it, and through the arcades of the Clarendon Centre into Queen Street, pausing on the pavement there to wait for a gap in the traffic. Then she saw them. They were standing on the opposite pavement also waiting to cross, James and Joss, laden with supermarket food bags. Elation died out of Kate in an instant. James and Joss stood there together, opposite her and not seeing her, not looking particularly happy or at all pleased to be together, but looking — and this tore at her heart — just bored and deeply ordinary and natural, like, oh God, thought Kate, like any old fed-up father and daughter sent out to do the shopping together. They began to cross the street and James put out an instinctive, burdened, protective arm in Joss's direction. Kate turned on her heel and fled.

The Hunter twins were in Julia's wardrobe. They had climbed in, in order to hide from Sandy, but the doors were heavier than they had supposed and had swung shut behind them. Being imprisoned didn't trouble them at all, since they were together in the warm, Mummy-smelling darkness, and the wardrobe was in Julia and Hugh's bedroom, so release was ultimately certain. Also, at the moment, they were beautifully occupied by listening to Sandy blundering about yelling for them, and by putting their heads up Julia's skirts and trouser legs and feeling rude and mischievous.

'Poo, poo, poo,' said George, muffled in black chiffon.

Edward fell out of a tweed jacket, giggling helplessly.

'Fatty Sandy, fatty Sandy, fattypoo Sandy,' said

George, much encouraged.

Edward stiffened. 'Shh —'

Heavy footsteps came along the landing and paused. Even Sandy, with her cosy smiling insolence, was reluctant to enter Julia's bedroom. The door opened very slowly. The twins held their breaths, and Edward, lying on the wardrobe floor, watched, through a crack under the door, Sandy's clumsy, trainer-clad feet treading uncertainly over the polished boards and the white Greek rugs. They paused by the bed, and by Julia's dressing-table. The twins could hear things being picked up and put down, pots and bottles, click-click on the glass surface under which Julia kept pictures of them, taken from the time they were just little shrimps in a doll's bath, to now. Sandy seemed to be taking a long time, a terribly long time, and a mutual longing to laugh and to pee began to cramp their muscles. Then Sandy said, 'Bloody kids,' and went out.

George slid out of Julia's evening dress and lay beside Edward. They clutched each other and shook and then the giggles came over them in a vast, irresistible wave and swept aside all control of their bladders. They peed and laughed until they were empty of everything and the pee ran out of the wardrobe and lay on the clean, shining floor outside, in little pools.

Sandy was not at all afraid of Julia. 'I went to the toilet. That's all. That's all I did. Three minutes.'

'Have you looked everywhere? Absolutely everywhere?'

' 'Course I have.'

'Even in my bedroom?'

'I wouldn't go in there,' Sandy said, much shocked.

Julia took a deep breath. She was determined that Sandy shouldn't see how terrified she had become, especially as Sandy had said calmly, 'It's only a lark. They'll come out when they're hungry enough.'

Nothing like this had ever happened to Julia. She had never been lost herself, or lost anyone significant. Her own fright frightened her, made worse by the fact that she had had such a wonderful day, that everything was going so well. Fanny McKinley had telephoned to say she wanted to do an interview with Julia for her magazine, and Hugh had heard that his progamme (now titled *Is the Choice Yours?*) was being syndicated across the independent channels simultaneously, and that the press were beginning to sniff enticingly around, and now . . .

'Shall I put the kettle on?' Sandy said. 'I'll fry some bacon. They'll smell that.'

'No,' said Julia, but by mistake she screamed it.

Sandy stared at her.

'I'm going upstairs,' Julia said. 'I'm going to search upstairs. They'll — they'll come out for me.'

'OK,' Sandy said.

Julia went out, trying to believe that Sandy's

indifference was calm.

'Boys?' she called, running up the stairs. 'Boys? Twins?'

She hurried along the landing, opening doors and calling, coming at last to her own door.

'George! Edward! Darlings, where are you?'

She went in. The room was quiet, so quiet the silence sounded positive. I want Hugh, Julia thought, I can't manage this, I need Hugh. She threw her jacket on the bed, and ran round it for the telephone. She stepped in something; she looked down. She had trodden in a puddle of something on the floor below the wardrobe, a puddle of — She put her finger down, gingerly, into the puddle, and from inside the wardrobe, tired out and sodden-trousered, the twins began to cry.

Hugh thought it was funny. He held Julia, and laughed and laughed into her hair, and then he went upstairs into the twins' bedroom, to tick them off, and went on laughing up there.

'Sandy was quite right,' he said, unwisely in front of Sandy.

'I feel such a fool —' Julia said when they were alone.

'Don't, darling one, darling maternal thing.'

'I screamed at Sandy.'

'She's like an ox. Screams bounce off her like pebbles. I should scream some more, if I were you. Did they pee in your shoes?'

'Only one.'

'Oh Lord,' Hugh said, collapsing into laughter again. 'Oh Lord. It's just perfect. What a give-away —'

'I was really frightened. I was just going to telephone you.'

He looked at her. 'Were you?'

'Yes.'

'How dear and dependent. I like that.'

Julia said, 'I didn't like the way Sandy didn't seem sorry, either. It scared me.'

'But I thought you said Sandy was wonderful —'

Julia hesitated. She had, she did think Sandy reliable and competent, she did. She just hadn't liked Sandy's expression in the kitchen. She put her chin up. 'I expect she was as scared as me and it made her surly, because she felt responsible.'

'Darling,' Hugh said, putting an arm round her and his face close to hers. 'Darling. It wasn't a big deal, was it? Come on now. They weren't even lost.'

Julia turned huge eyes on him and then bent her head to rest on his shoulder. 'No. No, of course.'

'We're on a winning streak,' Hugh said firmly. He took Julia's hand and led her downstairs to the kitchen. The table had been laid for the two of them, and a note from Sandy lay beside the pepper mill which read, 'Stuffed pancakes in bottom oven. Gone out to play darts.' On a pad of newspaper on the Aga, like a peace offering, lay

Julia's shoe, the shoe the twins had peed in, washed and drying.

'There,' Hugh said in triumph, indicating it. 'There you are! What more could you ask for than that?'

Leonard began to wash up. It was plain, on Joss's return, that things in Richmond Villa had to change a little, and washing up, he decided, would be his contribution, being both a public activity and one that offered plenty of scope for pantomime. Several times a day, he dragged a three-legged stool up to the sink to sit on, and made a tremendous mess and performance with water and soapsuds, drying everything afterwards with the same tea towel, day after day.

'There are plenty of clean ones —'

'Wicked waste. What's the matter with this one? I only dry clean things, and any germs are our germs. If you can't take your own sodding germs by now, you're a poor fish.'

He liked best to wash up in the afternoons, listening to radio drama. He shouted at the characters in plays and sometimes threw his sodden tea towel at the radio in rage. Mrs Cheng, who saw no point in his washing up since he was so incompetent that most of it had to be done again, regarded the radio as an ally since it deflected so much of Leonard's abuse from her. She moved swiftly about the house with her cloths and brushes, listening to the roars and crashes from the kitchen with the detachment she felt about everything except Kate. After her early visit, she could not bear to go back to Osney again. It had terrified her to see Kate so happy in a situation which only seemed to her mad and wrong. All she felt she could do about it was to look after Richmond Villa with redoubled zeal, and particularly Joss's bedroom. It was noticeable, even to Mrs Cheng, that in the last week Joss had been much less ungrateful about her straightened bedroom, much less inclined to plunge into the mild order Mrs Cheng imposed and recreate chaos.

'Don't touch her room,' James said to Mrs Cheng. 'Leave it. It's an expression of anarchy and the only thing to do is to ignore it.'

But Mrs Cheng couldn't do that. The thought of what lay behind Joss's bedroom door goaded and drove her until she had confronted it and attacked it with her desire for cleanliness and regularity. In the school holidays, this was made even more difficult by Joss's intermittent presence, and, when the first day of term came, and Joss's consequent absence, Mrs Cheng opened the bedroom door with the exalted, pent-up zeal of the true reformer. There was a hump in the bed.

Mrs Cheng went over to the bed and peered. Joss's eyes were tightly closed. Mrs Cheng prodded her.

'Why you not at school?'

'I had a headache,' Joss whispered. 'They said I could go home. Miss Gale sent me.'

'Why you have headache? You have period?'

213

'No,' Joss said, 'just headache.' She turned her face into the pillow.

Mrs Cheng went out and downstairs to the kitchen. Uncle Leonard was drying forks and shouting, 'Don't give in, you fool, don't give in!' at a dramatisation of *The Forsyte Saga* on Radio Four. Mrs Cheng hurried across the kitchen and turned it off.

'What d'you do that for?'

'You hear Joss come in?'

'No. Joss is at school. Turn that back on. Never heard anyone so bloody wet as Michael Mont —'

'She upstairs. With headache.'

'Joss?' Leonard dumped his handful of forks down. 'Latest wheeze, I suppose. Blasted child. Playing truant.'

'Look pale,' Mrs Cheng said.

Leonard reached for his stick. 'She'll look paler when I've finished with her.'

Mrs Cheng watched. Leonard limped out of the kitchen and she heard him go slowly and painfully up the stairs. After a while, she heard a bit of shouting, and then his stick and his shuffle went along the landing to the bathroom and back again. Then, very slowly, he came downstairs and back to the kitchen.

'Given her an aspirin.'

'Call doctor?'

'Certainly not. Doctors are for the dying, not for adolescent malingerers.'

'Where James?'

'Gone to the library. He'll be back at six. I,'

said Leonard drawing himself up and looking down at Mrs Cheng with an air of superiority, 'I am going out at six. To watch myself on the television screen, with Miss Beatrice Bachelor, on her sister-in-law's television. I am taking a bottle of sherry. Tonight, my lychee-faced bamboo shoot, my little oriental half-wit, tonight is my big night.'

Mrs Cheng took no notice. 'Won't leave Joss alone in Villa?'

'Certainly not,' Leonard said. 'I know my responsibilities.'

Mrs Cheng put away her cloths and hung the broom behind the cellar door. Then she buttoned and buckled herself into the shocking-pink mackintosh she had bought after much agonising between it and one in lime-green, and let herself out of the front door. When she had gone, Leonard picked up the kitchen telephone and asked the nearest taxi service to collect him at a quarter to six and take him to Cardigan Street.

The house was quite silent when James let himself in, a little after six. He stood in the hall and listened for the familiar sounds of Leonard's radio, and Joss's rock music. There were neither. He went down the hall to the kitchen where the results of Leonard's washing up lay strewn about the table in what was rapidly becoming a familiar medley of inconsequence; teacups sitting in pudding bowls instead of in each other, big plates balancing on little saucers, spoons lurking in the teapot. He put his briefcase down on a countertop, and opened the cupboard where the drink lived. There was an inch of whisky, two cans of beer and half a bottle of a red wine from Turkey which was all Mr Patel seemed to offer.

'Another customer says it is very muscular,' said Mr Patel, who didn't drink alcohol despite his Christianity.

James poured the whisky into a glass and sloshed water in after it, from the tap. Then he carried it into his study. Leonard had plainly, in his excitement over *Is the Choice Yours?*, gone out early, and Joss, equally plainly, in defiance of the tiny concessions to more civilised behaviour James believed she had made in the last week, was out also, and not doing her homework. He drank a gulp of whisky. It was difficult to decide if he was depressed anew by Joss, or simply resigned to her, beyond caring, counting the days until she could go to Osney and that would be that. The trouble is, James thought, staring down into his glass, that part of me, which I do not understand at all, doesn't want that to be that.

He put the whisky glass down on the pile of books by his armchair, and lit the gas fire. Then he went upstairs to change his jacket for a jersey, and, as he reached the landing, he became aware that a cat had got in somewhere and was shut in, and was crying. He stopped, turning his head, and realised that the cat was in fact a person, and the person was behind Joss's bedroom door. He leaped forward, flinging the door open, and the noise of

216

the crying rose to a great wail of misery.

'Joss!'

She reared up at him, swaddled in her duvet, her face distorted with weeping.

'Oh Joss,' said James, much shocked. He sat on the edge of her bed, and seized her wadded body, pulling it on to his knee. 'Oh Joss, what is it, what is it?'

She clung to him. Her arms, emerging skinny and naked from a grey T-shirt, crept out of her duvet and fastened themselves round him. Then she turned her hot, slippery face towards him, and clamped it into his neck.

'Is it Kate, is it Mum, do you want to see Mum?'

'No!' Joss shouted, choking, rubbing her face violently against him. 'No!'

James took one hand away from holding her, and prised her face from him so that he could look at her. 'Joss,' he said gently, 'is it Garth?'

She gave him a look of utter desolation, and tears began to pour down her cheeks again in a stream. James laid her face back against him and began to rock her, back and forth, back and forth, like a baby with wind.

'Oh Joss, I'm so sorry, I'm so sorry.'

'Immature,' Joss said incoherently, her voice muffled, 'he said I was. Just a kid, a little kid. He said I was boring.'

James went on rocking. He found he had a lump in his own throat. He said unsteadily, 'People often call other people rude things when it's what they

217

are themselves, you know.'

'I — I *liked* him!' Joss cried in a strangled scream.

'Of course you did. I know. But there'll be others.'

'Never,' Joss said.

'Jossie! What nonsense. Come on, now. Nose-blow time.'

She sat up a little straighter, and smeared her face with the back of her hand.

'Don't be so disgusting. Here. Have my handkerchief.'

The telephone began to ring. Joss stiffened slightly.

'Telephone —'

'Leave it,' James said. 'If it's important they'll ring back. It can't be as important as this, whatever it is. Come on, now, tell me what happened.'

'He said it after lunch,' Joss said, sounding a bit stronger. 'In front of everyone. They all heard. Everyone heard.'

'What a coward.'

Joss shook her head. 'I knew it wouldn't last.'

'Another one will.'

'Never!'

'Rubbish.' He put out a hand and ruffled her short, damp hair. 'Well, old thing. We're in the same sort of boat, aren't we?'

She made no move to get off his knee, but sat there swaddled, sniffling, and regarding him. Then she leaned forward and bumped a clumsy kiss on his chin. He swallowed.

'You know what we've got to do?'

'What —'

'We've got to go down and watch Uncle Leonard and Miss Bachelor talking about death, that's what.' He touched Joss's cheek. 'I feel about ready for a good laugh like that, don't you?'

Joss leaned forward and laid her cheek on his chest again, and began, very weakly, to giggle.

'Great stuff,' Mark Hathaway said, pressing the 'Off' button of the television remote-control panel. 'Amazing. Amazing old woman.'

Kate said nothing. She was trying to adjust herself to having, as it were, met Miss Bachelor for the first time on television. Miss Bachelor had been most impressive: clear, calm, and even, at times humorous. 'Not at all,' she had said crisply to Hugh, the unseen interviewer, several times, and once, briskly, 'Absolute nonsense.'

'What did you think, Katie?'

'I feel a bit stunned —'

Mark got up from the sofa. He said sharply, 'You were stunned when you came in.'

It was true, she had been. She had tried to ring Richmond Villa, to speak to Joss, and the telephone had just rung and rung, not even Leonard had answered it. For some reason she had no logical explanation for, Kate felt that they had all been in the house, and had heard the telephone and, suspecting it was her, had conspired not to answer it. Such behaviour went against everything she knew of all three of them, but the feeling

219

persisted in her like nausea. She had told Mark this, and he had looked withdrawn and unhelpful, as he had looked when she told him about seeing James and Joss in Queen Street. He was angry with her, she supposed, for refusing to sleep with him for a week. She looked at his marvellous, elegant jawline as he moved about making coffee, and couldn't help but observe that it was set and taut. Damn and blast, Kate thought, more soothing ahead, more explaining and reassuring.

'I imagine,' Mark said, holding out a coffee mug to her, 'that your cordon sanitaire is still in operation.'

'If we can't even be very civil to one another out of bed, why should we be any better in it?'

He looked down at her, still sitting on the sofa, with contempt. 'Sex is a prime form of communication, in case you hadn't realised.'

Kate stared down into her coffee mug. He had made, as he always made, beautiful coffee in a cafetière, and the aroma rose richly upwards and seemed to mock her, as Mark's room suddenly did, for being unable to be a true child of her times.

'It doesn't matter,' Mark said, turning away, 'I couldn't make love to a woman who can't think about anything but her damn kid. A kid she abandoned in the first place —'

Kate shut her eyes. In her ears rang Hugh's familiar tones from the television programme, and Beatrice Bachelor's decided ones, particularly when, at one moment, she had rebuked Hugh for suggesting an element of self-dramatisation among the supporters of euthanasia.

'I will quote Doctor Johnson,' Miss Bachelor had said with some severity. 'He said that those who do not feel pain seldom think that it is felt.'

Kate looked up at Mark again. He had turned back and was staring at her, challenging her to react to him. The trouble about pain, she thought suddenly, was not so much the insensitivity of the pain-free, as the wild variations among the sufferers. She tried a small smile, and held her hand out. 'Sorry,' Kate said.

'I congratulate you,' Kevin McKinley said. His desk was strewn with newspaper cuttings. 'TV Death Show' said one of the headlines Hugh could read upside down. 'TV Programme Defends Our Ultimate Choice', 'Nationwide Protest at Death Plug'.

Kevin McKinley smiled. He had kept Hugh waiting for nearly twenty minutes — 'I'm in no hurry to see the old fart,' he'd said to his secretary — and was not intending to offer him a drink or even a cup of coffee. *Is the Choice Yours?* had earned viewing figures of eleven million, and headlines in every single newspaper. If Miss Bachelor and Leonard Mallow had not, on advice, remained anonymous, they would have been, by now, under siege from the press in Jericho.

'Great old lady,' Kevin said.

Hugh nodded. He was bursting with pride and relief, and was holding himself in with every nerve

221

and muscle in order to suggest that pulling off a success like this was something he was extremely accustomed to.

'I don't think we'll have any trouble from the ITC. They can always say they were never told about it, which of course is no less than the truth. I didn't tell them on purpose.'

'Quite.'

Hugh's eyes fell on the cuttings again. He couldn't see the one that he very much wished brought to Kevin McKinley's notice. It was a comment piece, from a well-known journalist who specialised in the media, admiring not only the programme but Hugh's presentation of it, and interview technique. 'If Midland have any sense,' the journalist had written, 'they will capitalise on the unexpected depths revealed in a hitherto light-weight presenter.' Hugh wondered how he might discover if Kevin had seen the feature.

'Have you seen all the press?'

'The main stuff —'

'There's an excellent piece in the *Telegraph*.'

Kevin gave a little bark of laughter. 'If I ever read the *Telegraph*, I'll be in a bath chair.' He stood up. Hugh had had his five minutes. 'Mustn't keep you, Hugh.'

Hugh hesitated. Was there going to be no further word, no mention of a follow-up programme, no — even — general jolly remark like, Keep it up? Apparently not. Hugh squared his shoulders and smiled broadly.

'Nice to keep the opposition hopping, anyway.'

'Oh yes,' said Kevin.

The door opened.

'I've got Los Angeles on the line for you,' Kevin's secretary said.

' 'Course —' Hugh said.

'Bye, then —'

'Bye,' Hugh said, still smiling. 'Bye.'

Then he went out into the corridor and Kevin McKinley's office door was shut behind him so quickly that it almost caught his heel.

Chapter Eleven

Kate had asked Joss to meet her after school in the covered market. She had chosen the market because it was only two minutes from the restaurant and because it was busy. After her last telephone call to Joss, some instinct had told her that to meet in a busy place would be better for both of them. Also, Kate had something she wished to say to Joss. She intended to suggest that Joss come to Osney at once, that they abandon the farce of Kate and Joss living apart, now that Joss had made her statement of independence, and had had it honoured for two months.

She had said she would meet Joss by the hot little shop that baked huge American cookies on the spot, which you could carry away, warm and scented, in an excitingly unEnglish kind of paper bag. Joss was late. Kate put her hands in her trouser pockets, and leaned against a blind wall of the cookie shop, and watched the people throng past, the local people buying cabbages and pounds of sausages, and the tourists, drifting in the mildly, aimlessly inquisitive way peculiar to all tourists. Everybody was carrying something, bags and cameras and plastic carriers and folded mackintoshes and babies and books and newspapers and paper cones of flowers and . . .

'Hi,' said Joss. She too was burdened. Over her shoulder was slung her black school sack, and in one hand she held a plastic bag out of which protruded the bright leaves of a head of celery, and the end of a cucumber. Joss was wearing a pink sweatshirt which startled Kate as much as if Joss had been naked. She let Kate kiss her.

'What's all that?' Kate said, indicating the vegetables.

'Celery,' Joss said, 'a cucumber.'

Kate gave her a broad, deliberate smile. 'I can see that. I mean, why are you carrying it?'

'Why not?' Joss said. 'James can't do all the shopping and Uncle Leonard's so rude to Mr Patel we can't let him go in there.'

Kate remembered Mr Patel's perfect courtesy with a sudden pang.

'Tea?' she said to Joss.

'OK,' Joss said, 'but I can't be long.'

'Nor can I —'

Joss looked at her. 'Well, that's all right then.'

Across the tiny, plastic-topped table in the café, Kate said, 'You look different.'

'No, I don't —'

'Yes, you do. Brighter, somehow.'

'Thanks a million!'

'It's nice to see you in pink.'

Joss plucked at her sweatshirt with scorn. 'It's Angie's. We did a swap.'

'Angie? I don't know Angie —'

Joss took a messy bite of bun and said through

225

the crumbs and sugar, 'She's at school.'

'New?'

'Nope.'

Kate leaned forward. 'What's she like?'

'She's OK.'

'Joss.'

'I told you,' Joss said, sucking her fingers, 'she's at school, she's OK, she swapped this sweatshirt.' She paused, then she added, 'She's coming to supper. She's a veggie.'

'She's coming to supper! At Richmond Villa!'

Joss stared. 'Why not?'

'You never brought anyone home —'

'Well, Angie's coming.'

Kate said bravely, 'What on earth will Uncle Leonard say to a vegetarian?'

'Oh,' Joss said dismissively, 'you don't want to take any notice of him.'

'Joss,' Kate said. 'Joss, I want to ask you something, suggest something.'

Joss looked wary.

'It's about you and me.'

Joss ducked her head. 'Don't get heavy —'

'It's not heavy, but it's serious.'

'That's heavy,' Joss said, pushing back her metal chair.

'Please —'

'Leave it, Mum,' Joss said, 'just leave it.' She stood up and began to gather up her burdens.

'Joss, you must listen to me.'

'No, I mustn't. I got to go. Honest.'

'Don't you miss me?'

Joss looked appalled. 'I said, don't get heavy —'

'I don't know what's going on any more,' Kate cried. 'I don't know what you're doing, who you're seeing! What about Garth?'

'Garth?' Joss said, almost sneering.

'Yes, yes, are you still seeing Garth?'

'Not him,' Joss said, 'I wouldn't see *him.*' She shouldered her sack.

'What happened?'

'Can't remember,' Joss said. She stopped to brush her face against Kate's in the echo of a kiss, and her bag crashed against the table.

'Careful —'

'See you, Mum,' Joss said. 'Take care.' Then she was gone.

'He wants to see you,' the secretary said.

'Are you sure? Are you sure it isn't my husband he wants, my husband Hugh?'

'No,' the secretary said. Her eyes ran over Julia's clothes as if she were labelling and pricing every garment. 'He said he'd be grateful if you'd spare him ten minutes before lunch. Twelve-thirty, he said.'

'Of course.'

There was a little pause. The secretary, who had come down to Julia's office rather than telephone on the off-chance of seeing Rob Shiner, on whom she had her eye, waited to be thanked. All Julia did was smile. Snotty cow, thought the secretary, and went out. Rob Shiner's office door stood open, but he was not inside. Who cares,

227

the secretary said to herself, who bloody cares? Not me. She walked slowly back to the lift. Julia dialled Hugh at home.

'He's sent for me!'

'Kevin?'

'Yes. At lunchtime! He actually sent his secretary down to ask me to go up and see him before lunch!'

Hugh blew kisses down the telephone. 'Hold on to your hat, my darling!'

Kevin McKinley's office had been redecorated, under Fanny's eye, to suggest being both in power and in touch. It contained sleekly sculpted plywood furniture, magnificent black-and-gold curtains printed with a neo-classical design, and banks of telephones and computer screens. The only pictures were Francis Bacon prints. By the window, an immense weeping fig in a terracotta urn cast dappled shadows on the carpet.

'Good to see you, Julia,' Kevin said. He stood up behind his modern maplewood desk, and held his hand out to her. He was smiling. 'I wanted to see you personally.'

She inclined her head. The room made her feel elated and apprehensive all at once. She took his hand, and then the chair he indicated.

'I've been talking to Rob Shiner. I hear good things.'

Julia waited. She suddenly remembered sitting in her headmistress's study at school when she had thought she was going to be made head girl and she hadn't been, only deputy head. It had been a salutary lesson, and one that she had taken to heart. Kevin McKinley was going to say that he was pleased with the *Night Life* series, but that he didn't want to over-egg the cake and therefore there wouldn't . . .

'I want to offer you a contract, Julia. Two years.'

She gazed at him.

'You don't look very thrilled.'

'Oh, I am, I am —'

'I want more documentary stuff, you see, and from a nineties angle, a softer, more serious approach. You fit the bill.'

'I'm delighted, absolutely delighted —'

He gave her part of a smile. 'So glad.' There was a little pause, and then he said, 'We can't renew Hugh's contract, you see. On account of his age. But at least this way, it keeps it in the family. Don't you think?'

Hugh was very quiet but Julia didn't think he was asleep. As for herself, she felt sleep was for ever out of the question. There simply couldn't, ever, have been a more terrible evening for any couple anywhere, not because of quarrelling, but because of agony. It was an agony that had begun in Kevin McKinley's office and had grown as Julia drove home and then had grown and grown still further all evening until it had landed them in bed, silent, separate, and wretched.

'Shall I refuse it?' Julia had said. 'Shall I turn it down?'

Hugh shook his head. 'What good would that

229

do? He'd never hand it to me instead. It's you or nothing. You go for it, sweetheart,' he'd said, not looking at her. 'You go for it.'

Once, Julia had believed that she would be able to go for it, when she had to, and that she would firmly, kindly, make it plain to Hugh that he had to accept it. She remembered sitting by the Aga, and planning the future calmly and sensibly to herself. She couldn't do that now, not because she had lost her sensibleness, but because she hadn't taken into account how she would feel to see Hugh crushed. She felt so badly, so keenly, about it that she wasn't sure she could bear it, but the one person she wanted to turn to in her pain — Hugh — was the one person she couldn't turn to. He hadn't shouted or sworn or cried or hit the bottle. He had even tried to eat his supper, and he had certainly tried to be generous.

'I am proud of you.'

'Don't —'

'Julia, I am. This is great news.'

'Please —'

'Every dog has his day.'

In her turn, she had been as understanding as she knew how, as gentle and sympathetic as possible. It was no effort, because she felt it; she wanted to hold him and soothe him and admire him. But he hadn't seemed to want that. He hadn't touched her or let her touch him. He lit cigarette after cigarette and sat staring across the room. Julia had tried to analyse Kevin McKinley's reasons for giving her the contract, to reassure Hugh that he was the victim of cockeyed malevolence and not a failure, but Hugh wouldn't let her.

'I mean, it's mad, you got eleven million people watching and they haven't even shown *Night Life* yet!'

'Leave it, sweetie.'

'I'm sure you can argue. Why don't you ring Maurice, why don't you —'

'Julia,' said Hugh, looking at her, 'there is nothing to be done. This has been coming at me for years, and now it's arrived.'

'But you've still got your supermarkets. And that health club.'

His face twitched. Was he smiling? 'Yes. I've still got those.'

'I love you,' she said to him later, over and over. 'It doesn't matter what you do, I love you. And I need you. I can't manage without you. When I thought the twins were lost, my first instinct was to telephone you —'

'Shh,' Hugh said, not unkindly.

'Nothing need be different between us, nothing can touch that.'

He looked at her. His glance was quite affectionate but also a little appraising. She felt suddenly young, young and uncertain and a trifle silly. She put a hand out to him. 'Hugh?'

He took her hand and kissed it lightly. Then he gave it back to her and stood up. 'I'm going to look at the twins.'

'I'll come —'

'No. No, I'll go alone.'

He went upstairs and she sat and looked at the full ashtray by his chair, at the dented cushion that had held him. She felt so full of love and pain for him that she could scarcely endure it. She got up and went out into the hall and looked up at the pretty cottage staircase. The twins' door was open. She stood and waited for a long, long time and then Hugh came on to the landing and saw her, looking up.

He said, gently, 'Don't watch me.'

'But I'm worried —'

'Don't be. I'm fine.'

She started up the stairs. 'Of course you're not, how could you be, Hugh, oh please —'

He leaned down towards her. 'I'm going to have a bath. Alone. I just need to be alone.'

'Of course,' she said, thankful to be able to do something he wanted, even if it was to stay away from him.

He went into their bathroom and locked the door. Julia climbed the remaining half of the stairs and went into the twins' room. They lay as they always did, turned towards one another, and Edward had thrown off his duvet so that Julia could see he was wearing mismatched pyjama tops and bottoms. She found she didn't care; she couldn't help noticing, but she had no urge to go and find the missing co-ordinating half. She knelt on the floor between the beds.

'Poor Daddy,' she said in a whisper to the sleeping boys. 'Poor darling Daddy.'

Hugh was in the bathroom for almost half an

hour, and when he came out he went straight to bed. Julia followed him, to ask him if he would like some tea, or some whisky, but he smiled and shook his head, and slid down under the sheet, turning off his bedside lamp in a way that made it plain he still wanted to be alone. So she had locked up the house, leaving the back door unbolted for Sandy, and plumped cushions, and swept crumbs off surfaces, and switched off lights, and had then gone to have a bath herself.

She wondered if it would help to have a tremendous cry in the bath, to sob and wail in the steam and the privacy; but she found she couldn't cry, she couldn't even let go sufficiently for that. She washed conscientiously and cleaned her face and brushed her teeth and hair hoping for the small comfort of ritual, because it was quite beyond her previous experience to feel so desperate. She found a clean nightie and pulled it over her head, then she went through to their bedroom, and very quietly slipped into bed beside Hugh. She put a hand out to touch him, tentatively. He didn't move.

'Hugh,' Julia said, so softly it was hardly a whisper. Silence. She reached out to her bedside light and turned it off, and then she lay there, beside him, and felt his suffering and her own to be like two identical magnetic fields, repulsing one another.

They were often in the kitchen now, when Joss got back from school, and sometimes Miss Bachelor had made sandwiches, or brought some really dull biscuits, like petit beurre or Marie. It was, Joss thought, a bit like having grandparents waiting for you, except that average grandparents, from what she gathered, didn't grill you about the precise academic content of lessons or tell you that you were certifiably stupid. Joss didn't want tea — or rather she didn't want their kind of tea — but she discovered that she quite liked finding them there, messing about with cups and saucers and jars of horrible fish paste.

'You never used to come down,' Joss said to Leonard. He had made James buy him a yellow knitted waistcoat — 'For the sodding spring, you fool' — and had spilled soup down it the very first day, and, as nobody knew how to wash the soup off, they left it there.

'I never came down because there was never anybody bloody *in*.'

Miss Bachelor came most days. She had taken to cleaning the brass door-handles and to pruning and weeding the garden and to opening the door to James's pupils, who were terrified of her. While she was in the house, Leonard sat at the kitchen table, or, on fine days, on a kitchen chair just outside the back door, and argued with her. She tried to give him small tasks to do, but he was resistant to doing anything helpful unless it was on his own terms. He preferred to watch her weeding the narrow borders, kneeling on a folded towel to protect her knees, and shout insults at her. One day he went too far and said she had an arse like a camel, and she went home for three days. He missed her. He was so abusive about her that in the end Joss realised what was the matter and went round to Cardigan Street.

'Is she coming?' James asked when Joss got back.

'She said never again.'

'I see,' said James, 'so she'll be here tomorrow.'

Hugh had given them a video of *Is the Choice Yours?* and Leonard wanted to watch it, over and over. Beatrice refused.

'I know what I think, I know what I said and I have neither wish nor need to remind myself of either.'

Joss agreed with her. She thought the programme creepy, as well as boring. She'd watched it with James because he wanted to watch it and she had felt obliging — no, more than obliging really, almost affectionate, as if she wanted to sit next to him and be with him whatever he was watching. She found she agreed with a lot of what Beatrice said, even if she would never have dreamed of admitting it.

'Look at you,' Leonard said to her one day, 'just look at you. What a bloody mess. What a scruffy sight. 'Course, can't blame you, I suppose, poor sodding child. Broken home and all that. Nowhere to identify with.'

'Rubbish,' said Miss Bachelor, who was doing the newspaper crossword. Leonard could scarcely bear the fact that she did it so much faster than he did.

Joss, eating a bowl of chocolate-flavoured cereal

while propped against the fridge in her usual semi-slouch, waited for more. Leonard leaned towards Beatrice.

'Not rubbish. What'll she think of her mother when she grows up? Or her useless father? Or James? What notion of home life has she got? No wonder she's got no sense and no manners.'

Beatrice filled in seven-down. 'She has sense and she's learning manners. As for a home —' She raised her head and looked at Joss. 'Children make their own homes.'

Leonard snorted. Joss stopped chewing.

'She was at home in the womb, and she had to leave. I expect she was at home in her pram, and she had to leave that too. I imagine her home now is her room here, and her school, and as she gets older she will make homes all along the line. Society will be her home.'

Joss thought about this. Leonard said, 'Her home ought to be with her mother.'

'Ought?'

'It's only bloody natural —'

'What do you think?' Miss Bachelor said, turning to Joss.

Joss was embarrassed. 'I don't want to say —'

'Of course you don't. Why should you? One's sense of home is rightly private. I have no doubt your mother could tell you that.'

'My mother —'

'I am sorry,' Miss Bachelor said, 'that I haven't met your mother.'

'You haven't —'

'No. I have never met your mother.'

'She's a good woman,' Leonard said unexpectedly.

They both stared at him. He looked suddenly very sad. He caught them looking. Joss waited for him to shout at them, but he didn't, he just sat there, looking. Then Beatrice picked up the crossword again, and Joss went to the larder to find potatoes to scrub and bake for supper.

'Good evening, sir,' Garth Acheson said to James.

James had come out of Mr Patel's shop with a box of groceries. He gave Garth a nod. Garth was wearing an American baseball jacket and very clean jeans and an expression of imperfect confidence.

'May I help you with that?'

'No thank you,' James said. The sheer healthiness of Garth Acheson's face seemed to him a mark of insensitivity.

'Sir,' Garth said, 'may I come round and see Joss?'

'I shouldn't think so,' James said.

'You wouldn't wish it?'

'I think she wouldn't wish it.'

'I'm really sorry,' Garth said. His shoulders sagged a little. 'I never meant —'

'Don't bleat,' James said crossly, interrupting him. 'You can't inflict a hurt and then whine because the consequences are disagreeable.'

'She's a great kid.'

'I know. Now, if you would excuse me, I'm going home.'

He set off down Walton Street. Garth ran after him for a pace or two.

'Would you give her — would you tell her you've seen me?'

'I saw Garth,' James said to Joss while they unpacked the groceries.

Her head went up. 'What did he say?'

'He wants to come and see you.'

'Wow.'

'Do you want him to come?'

Joss stared down at the bag of carrots in her hand. 'No. But I don't mind him wanting to.'

James reached across the kitchen table and ruffled her hair. 'That's my girl.'

Joss tried to duck his hand. 'Geroff,' she said.

It was Sandy's day off. Julia sat on the playroom floor while the twins climbed over her aimlessly and whined. They had whined a good deal recently, and clung to her legs and done ludicrously babyish things like wanting a spoon to eat with, or failing to get to the lavatory in time, when they had been perfectly trained to forks and the lavatory for well over a year. Though as gleaming clean as usual, they didn't somehow look as robust as they used to and their clothes, in Sandy's care, had an air of being well-used, almost over-used, the fabrics faded and rubbed.

'Don't,' Julia said tiredly, as Edward's sandal buckle caught her leg. 'Please be careful.'

Edward dragged himself across her, and lay with his thumb in across her knees, pressing them painfully to the floor. George began to crawl up her shins and across Edward.

'Hurts,' Edward said, on a long, drawn-out grizzle.

'Doesn't,' George said at once.

'Does, does, hurts, Mummy, hurts, Mummy —'

'Shh,' Julia said. She pushed George away and lifted Edward off her legs and on to the floor. Then she scrambled up and sat on the sofa where, on happier days, she nestled with the twins for a story. They crawled inexorably after her, gurning.

'Stop it,' Julia said suddenly, furiously. 'Leave me alone. Just *stop* it.'

They halted, briefly. Then Edward began again, and Julia burst into tears.

'Don't!' George said in panic. He lunged at her, his own mouth trembling dangerously.

She gave herself a shake and sniffed loudly. 'Sorry, darlings, sorry —' They regarded her apprehensively. 'I'm a bit tired, Mummy's rather tired. That's all.' She blinked down at them and managed a hopeless smile.

'Not cry,' George said uncertainly.

'No, of course not. Silly Mummy.'

They looked relieved. 'Silly Mummy!'

Julia stood up. 'Let's go and find some tea, shall we? Shall we make toast?'

The telephone rang. Julia flew. It might be Hugh, it must be Hugh, having finished opening his supermarket, ringing to say it had been terrific and he was on his way home . . .

'Mrs Hunter?'

'Yes —'

'Julia, it's Vivienne Penniman here.'

'Oh,' Julia said, smiling into the receiver, 'how nice. How are you?'

'Well, thank you,' Vivienne said. 'I wonder if I could speak to Hugh?'

'I'm afraid he isn't back yet. He went to Coventry, to that —'

'I know,' Vivienne said. Her voice was not particularly friendly. 'The supermarket has just telephoned me. That's why I was ringing Hugh.'

'Is he all right?' Julia said in sudden panic.

There was a tiny pause, then, 'There's nothing to worry about, dear,' Vivienne said, much more cosily, 'just some little administrative hitch. Could you get him to call me, when he gets in?'

'Of course.'

She put the receiver down. The twins were dragging chairs across the kitchen towards the cupboards on which stood the bread bin, and the toaster.

'Don't touch the bread knife —'

The chairs collided and crashed and there was a shriek as George caught his fingers between them.

'Ow, ow, ow, ow —'

Edward tried to move the chairs apart and moved them the wrong way. George gave a piercing scream. Julia fled round the table, and, as she did so, heard through the wails the slow crunch of tyres on the gravel. Hugh was home, thank God, thank —

'Bleeding!' screamed George.

'No, it isn't, darling, it's just bruised, poor fingers, just bruised. We'll put them in hot water and it'll make it better —'

'Not me!' Edward wailed. 'It wasn't me!'

'I know it wasn't, darling, I know it was a mistake.'

The back door opened, slowly. They all turned in relief. Hugh stood there, supported as if he were an invalid, by the driver who had taken him to Coventry, and from their attitudes and expressions it was immediately plain that Hugh was not ill, but hopelessly drunk.

Chapter Twelve

'Shh,' said Benjie. He sat on a kitchen stool and held his head.

'What's the matter now?' Kate said. She had an exasperated affection for Benjie on account of a clumsy innocence that his wayward ways could never quite dispel, but his constant preoccupation with himself was very trying.

'Went out on the piss,' Benjie said.

'Oh, not again. Why are you so stupid?'

'It was me birthday. You never remember me birthday —'

'I didn't know it was your birthday. And why get drunk on your birthday?'

He looked offended. 'I always get drunk on me birthday.'

'More fool you.'

He gazed past her at the wide stainless-steel mouth of the pizza oven. 'Tequila slammers,' he said dreamily.

'What?'

'You put in the tequila and then you add the lemonade and then you slam it down on the bar and you have to drink it all quick before it fizzes right over. I had dozens. Dozens and dozens and dozens.' His eyes swung slowly away from the oven and took in Kate. 'You'd love a tequila slammer.'

'What does it taste like?'

'Dunno. Can't remember. Hey,' he said, his blurred gaze suddenly focusing, 'you don't look up to much.'

Kate was refilling the wooden pepper-grinders. Her hands didn't seem very steady and stray peppercorns kept bouncing off the sides of the mills and pattering down on to the counters and the floor. 'I'm OK. I just didn't sleep very well.'

'Trouble with lover boy?' Benjie said, for whom trouble always came in the form of booze or lover boys.

'No,' Kate said, though this was not strictly true. Mark was busy being offended at the moment, touchy and wounded, and Kate couldn't give him the attention he wanted because of her other, greater, preoccupation which was Joss.

'Money?'

'Not really,' Kate said. 'I mean, I can't not think about it, but it isn't keeping me awake.' She paused. There was no particular point in telling Benjie about Joss, since family life was as relevant to Benjie as life on Mars would have been; but there would be no harm either. And it would be nice to tell someone, someone who was not another woman with, invariably, strong female views. She had begun on the subject of Joss with Helen, at the cinema, and Helen had been emphatic. 'You must get legal help if you can't retrieve Joss any other way. Tomorrow. Start tomorrow. Honestly, Kate, what's the point of making a bid for freedom if you don't use that freedom and *act* independent?' Kate had attempted to explain that Joss's wishes had to be taken into account, and that she, Kate, had, somehow, got wholly out of touch with James, but that had only made Helen angry. What was worse was that Kate understood her anger. Of course she was being pathetic and feeble, or at least, of course that was how she seemed, but equally strongly, she felt that she couldn't, as Helen did, just march about all over other people's lives instructing them as to what they should do and think. Helen and Kate had parted that evening with a technical friendliness that had no heart to it.

'I asked my daughter to come and live with me,' Kate said now, 'and although she didn't say so in so many words, she turned me down.'

Benjie drew a long breath in through his teeth. He got up, his hangover apparently forgotten, and began his practised chef's ritual of assembling boards and pans and knives.

'She still with James, then?'

'Yes. I think —' Kate stopped and then said sadly, 'I think she likes it there now, I think —' She stopped again.

'How old is she?'

'Fourteen.'

'I expect,' Benjie said, reaching for his rope of garlic, 'she just wants to get up your nose. She says she likes it there just to aggravate you, give you a bit of grief.'

'James is kind, you know.'

'He's old, though, i'n't he?'

'No,' Kate said, without thinking. 'He isn't very old.'

'I seen him,' Benjie said, chopping rapidly and minutely. 'He's got grey hair.'

'Joss has known him since she was six.'

'Yeah. But she's known you since she was born. She's just trying to get at you. I did it all the time, get at me mum. Now she's gone, I wish I hadn't, but when she was here I never gave over tormenting her. You want to call Joss's bluff.' He turned round from his board and gave Kate a direct look. 'Don't you take it, Katie. You go round there and have it out with both of them, face to face. Everybody needs their mum, whatever they say.'

The May sunshine lay like a blessing on the garden of Church Cottage. In the borders, planted by Julia, were bright clumps of colour, cushions of polyanthus and pansy, ranks of tulips, spikes of rosemary. Julia had planted the garden very deliberately as a cottage garden, referring to countless books. 'Nothing too formal,' she had said. 'Nothing too sophisticated.' Hugh had agreed, without really listening. He was not, and never had been, a gardening man. 'Give me a nice terrace,' he'd said, to tease Julia, 'something you can dust rather than mow. Something with plenty of flat surfaces to park my drink on.'

He sat now in a sheltered corner, a straw hat tipped over his eyes, and looked at Julia's garden. It was exceedingly pretty, as she was pretty, and its very prettiness was, to his present state of mind, a reproach. It lay before him, charming and innocent, exactly as she presented herself to him just now, understanding and forgiving, innocent of his folly yet an automatic and helpless victim of it. She had uttered no word of censure, not a syllable of criticism over his behaviour at Coventry, and had staunchly taken his side in the face of Vivienne Penniman's furious condemnation. He had told her how they had reached Coventry early, and how he had told the driver he'd go to the Cathedral for an hour, but had not, and had gone to a pub instead, and drunk whisky steadily, and how the effect of the whisky hadn't really hit him until he was at the supermarket when he had felt the full force of it, and of his anger and unbearable disappointment with Midland Television. 'I did everything reprehensible,' he told Julia, 'except throw up. Everything.' She had sat and listened, her eyes full of pity. Vivienne said later on the telephone that she doubted she could get Hugh more work immediately, and Julia's eyes had filled with tears then, tears for Hugh. All that evening, all that night, and all the subsequent days and nights, she had been perfectly, utterly, sweet to him. Looking at her garden, sitting uselessly in his deck-chair, Hugh thought he couldn't stand any more of her sweetness, he simply could not take it.

It was, he knew, a reflection of his own sense of guilt and shame. The better she behaved, the worse he felt he was behaving by comparison. She had never been as spontaneously loving to him as she had been recently, and he couldn't lay his hand on his heart and say with any honesty that she was loving because he had become the shorn Samson. There was no triumph in her love, no sense of power or superiority; if anything, she seemed more dependent, more pliant, less sure of herself. In the face of this openly demonstrated love, this ideal, romantic-story love, it made him feel even more of a bastard to realise that he didn't want this kind of perfect emotion just now, this absolutely beautiful behaviour. It was more than that, too. He felt that the beauty of her behaviour did him, obscurely, an injury, and then he was consumed with guilt for the glaring injustice of this feeling.

'Mr Hunter!'

He raised the brim of his hat and turned his head. Sandy stood outside the open garden door, drying her hands on a tea towel and shouting. She always shouted, never came close enough to be able to say anything.

'Yes?'

'Telephone.'

He struggled up. Even the telephone seemed only a threat now, never a possible messenger of hope. He plodded tiredly into the sitting-room and picked up the receiver.

'Hugh Hunter.'

'Hugh, it's Maurice —'

'Maurice!'

'I meant to ring a week ago but we've been

so frightfully busy. I just wanted to congratulate Julia and say how sorry —'

'That's quite all right,' Hugh said interrupting.

'— absolutely not my wish, as you know, but of course I don't have the executive power I'd like —'

'I'm thrilled for Julia,' Hugh said. 'She deserves it. What does it matter which of us has it?'

'Splendid,' Maurice said, relieved. 'I knew you'd understand. I told Kevin —'

'He seemed to like *Is the Choice Yours* —'

'Oh yes, absolutely, loved it —'

'So I don't quite see —'

There was a small pause. '*Anno Domini*, Hugh. Simply that. Me next.' He gave a tiny laugh. 'I'll be joining the club in the autumn. What are your plans?'

'Plans?'

'Why don't you get away for a bit?' Maurice said. 'Take a break.'

'Julia's so busy —'

Maurice, who had not shared a holiday with Zoë, by mutual consent, for nineteen years, said, 'I didn't mean with Julia. She's too busy as you say, anyway. Why don't you go off by yourself?'

'I'm not very good company for myself just now,' Hugh said, suddenly tired of pretending he was all right. His voice shook a little. Maurice heard the tremble and prepared to end the call.

'Go and find a friend, then. That's what friends are for. Find a friend and go off and make hay, get a new perspective. Trouble with this television world of ours is that you get so close to it you can't see a damned thing. We'll meet when you're back, have a drink. Chin up, old boy. And my congratulations to your lovely wife.'

Hugh put down the receiver. He was shaking and felt cold and unsteady. The room was dim and cool, but through the windows he could see that bright and sunny garden, that heartless garden, heartless like all the world was, who didn't know what it was like to be turfed out at sixty-one with the door barred against you.

'Mr Hunter?'

He turned to the door. 'Yes?'

'I'm just off to collect the twins and then after lunch, Mrs Hunter said, would you mind them for a couple of hours while I go to Sainsbury's?'

Kate stood on the doorstep of Richmond Villa and rang the bell. James had tried to make her keep a key but she had refused, feeling it was not proper, as she was closing the Richmond Villa chapter of her life. When she had telephoned to say she would like to come and see him, James had sounded startled; startled, but pleased. 'Come on Tuesday,' he said. 'Come for a drink.' And then he had paused. 'Leonard will be out. He's taken to going out on Tuesdays, to play bridge, of all things. Beatrice takes him somewhere, in a taxi.'

On Tuesdays, Kate knew, Joss now stayed late at school for drama club, a development which had resulted from her friendship with Angie and someone called Emma who Kate hadn't met either. This was all quite convenient since, Kate had worked out, if she arrived at Richmond Villa at about five-thirty, she could have it out with James before Joss got home at six, when they could both talk to Joss. Kate did not dare hope that Joss would come home with her that night, but she had thought the hope several times before she had put it from her.

It was not easy, standing on the doorstep, in fact it was dreadfully difficult and Kate was stiff with apprehension. She had not seen James for almost three months, at least not to talk to, and so much had happened to her and to her feelings in those months that she felt he was now a stranger. When he opened the door to her, the shock was not of strangeness at all, but of familiarity. He put out a hand and took her arm and drew her in, smiling. 'Katie,' he said, and then he stooped to kiss her cheek. She turned her head away and his mouth caught only her hair.

'Oh dear,' James said.

She glanced up at him and said with bright friendliness, 'How are you?'

He gestured. 'As you see.' He looked exactly the same, neither fatter nor thinner, older nor younger. He wore a blue checked shirt she recognised (it had a mend in the elbow, she remembered) and the rust-coloured corduroy trousers she had given him two Christmasses before. Had he, she wondered, dressed deliberately?

He said, 'You look lovely.'

She turned her head aside. This was not what she had come for, not what she had bargained for; she had come to talk about Joss.

'When will Joss be back?'

'About six,' James said. He moved past her to open the study door for her as if she were a stranger. 'Come in.'

His study looked exactly the same too, and smelled the same. It was the smell that afflicted Kate with an unbidden nostalgia. She looked round quickly, to distract herself and stifle the nostalgia; the grass-green carpet, the plump prince, the battered chairs, the ragged piles of books and papers, all as they had been eleven weeks ago. The only thing that was unfamiliar was a bowl of peonies on the cluttered table by the window at the garden end. These had been given to Joss by Garth Acheson's mother, who rejoiced in the name of Bluey, and who had grown them in her garden in Observatory Street.

'Take these home to your mother,' Bluey had said. 'They've such a short life we all have to make the most of them.'

Joss had not troubled to say she hadn't got a mother at home to give them to. She had simply thanked Bluey, and given the peonies to James.

'I've never been given flowers in my life,' James said, very pleased.

'Haven't you?'

'No. I don't think men, on the whole, get given flowers. Not English men, anyway.'

'Well, I don't want them,' Joss said graciously,

'so you might as well.'

'Lovely flowers,' Kate said formally, like a guest.

'They came from the mother of a friend of Joss's.'

'Angie?'

'No, not Angie. Garth.'

'Garth! I thought Garth had thrown her over!'

'Garth,' said James with an in-the-know satisfaction that irritated Kate, 'is trying to throw himself back. She's handling him with wonderful cool.' He crossed the room to his desk, on which stood a small tray with a bottle of white wine and two glasses, all ready-prepared. 'Let me get you a drink.'

'Thank you,' Kate said. She sat down in one of the armchairs by the fire. She was beginning to feel better, stronger, more resolute. Something about James's manner, the assumptions he seemed to be making, was reminding her anew of why she had left.

'Do you know,' James said, handing her a glass of wine, 'do you know, I'm really beginning to appreciate Joss. I've always been fond of her, of course, but now I value her, I really do.'

Fury flared in Kate. How dare he? How dare he sound so — so proprietary? She took a swallow of wine and temper and said shortly, 'That's why I've come.'

He smiled. He seemed not to understand her. He stood looking down at her, holding his own wineglass. 'Sorry?'

She looked back at him. 'I've come to take Joss

home with me. This charade has gone on long enough. She's my child and we should be together. She's only trying to provoke me by staying here, and you shouldn't encourage her.' She stopped suddenly, conscious of an expression of utter dismay on James's face. He turned away from her and went to the window.

'Well?' Kate demanded.

He said nothing. She couldn't see his face now, but the set of his shoulders and back was eloquent of profound emotion. My God, Kate thought, My God, he thinks he's going to keep her, he thinks he's going to fight me for her! My daughter, *mine!* She said out loud, in a rush, 'I wouldn't stop you seeing her, James, she could come here as much as she wanted, but we can't go on like this any longer, it was stupid to set the three months, like being on trial at a new job. She's had her way, she's been treated like an adult so there's no loss of face. But she has to come and I rely on you' — dear heaven, thought Kate, I sound like Helen — 'I rely on you to make it easy for her, not to make her feel she's being treated like a child, or that she's got to divide her loyalty between us —'

'Shut up,' James said.

Kate sprang up from her chair. 'How *dare* you tell me to shut up! We are talking, James, about *my child* —'

He said, turning, 'I'm not arguing with you. I shall miss her like anything but of course she should live with you. I thought so at the beginning and I still think it.'

'Then —'

'Kate,' James said, looking at her with a face full of love, 'I hoped you wanted to come and see me for quite another reason.'

She was horrified. 'Oh no,' she said, stammering. 'How could you — no, I didn't, I don't — James, I can't —'

'No,' he said, 'I see you can't. I shouldn't have hoped and I'll try not to do it again, for my own sake as well as for yours.'

Kate subsided on to the arm of the nearest chair. 'I'd no idea, I feel awful, I'm so sorry —'

'Don't be sorry.'

'I don't want to hurt you. I never have, it's just that —'

'I know,' he said. 'You think you'd like it better if I didn't love and miss you. If it's any comfort to you, I think I'd like it better too. But don't worry. I've coped this far, and I'll cope further, just as you will with other things.' He put his wineglass down on the tray. 'Kate. I'm going out now. I'm going to leave you here to wait for Joss, and I won't be back until after seven. Say seven-thirty.' He paused. He was about to say, Tell Jossie to come any time, but he stopped himself, considering it unfair. Instead he came over to Kate and stooped and kissed her forehead. 'I'll take a key,' he said. 'Just slam the door when you both go.'

James walked. He thought, as he left Richmond

Villa, that he would go into one of the pubs, like the King's Arms, which could be relied upon to be rowdy with undergraduates, and drink there until seven-thirty, and then return home and drink there until there was no more drink or he passed out, whichever was the sooner. But the evening was lovely, with that late-spring light that is at once soft and clear, and in any case, James discovered that he just wanted to *be* drunk, that he didn't want to be bothered with the process of getting it. He thought of his usual, favourite walk, along the canal, but then he thought that the river would be better for his melancholy, the river that on a fine May evening would still have university rowing crews practising on it, shouted at by coaches pedalling along the towpath and bellowing through megaphones. The sight of hearty, unemotional activity, James decided, would be beneficial to one in such a state as he was.

It was a long walk. It took him through the heart of the city, and then through the quadrangles and cloisters of Christ Church out into the Meadows where the fading sunlight lay mellow on the grass and the wide paths. He walked slowly, impeded by his sadness, stopping every so often to look at a prospect or an angle or a pinnacle silhouetted against the sky. He felt he was seeing nothing, that he was removed from the throb and pulse of life because he was, quite simply, now bereft.

He had never, resolutely, thought of Joss as his. He knew he had no business to, and he knew now, too, what came of thinking that someone else was yours, as he had finally, fatally, come to believe Kate to be. But something had grown up recently between him and Joss, something that was not yet in any way intimate, but which was certainly there and which they both undoubtedly liked. She wasn't any more graceful to live with, or courteous, or charming, but she was aware of him now, and that awareness made her conscious of his rights in their joint existence, as well as her own. She had grown more confident with him, more confiding too, as if he were not to be automatically distrusted just because he was an adult. He thought her brave. She also, these days, constantly ticked off by him or by Leonard or by Beatrice, bore surprisingly little resentment. Indeed, if it had not nagged at him all the time that she should be living with her mother and not with him, James might have dared to say that she was happy.

He came to the towpath, and wandered along it past the modern college boathouses. Several had their doors still open, with people messing about slowly inside, or sitting in front of them on the concrete, idly chatting.

'I mean, I said look, I can't possibly read the whole of *The Faerie Queene* by Friday, and he said —'

'And I turned round and there was this weird girl —'

'There just isn't any point in writing an essay from such a positive angle —'

'Anybody want a jelly baby?'

'Look at that. Rolls of blubber. No wonder we can hardly heave the boat along with you on board —'

'God, you sound absolutely pre-Socratic —'

James dawdled past. They weren't very old, those lounging young, not more than five or six years older than Joss. When Joss was their age, he would be not far off seventy and Kate would be over forty and Leonard might well be dead. He paused at the last boathouse and sat down on the bank, with his feet on the gently heaving pontoon from which the boat crews embarked. The sky looked mild and soft, and from across the water came faint, echoing bursts of people's voices, people walking on the further towpath, people with ordinary evenings ahead of them filled with supper and the pub and the news on the television. Well, James thought, leaning his elbows on his knees and gazing past his rocking feet at the river, I just have to go on. No doubt something will happen, there will be changes and developments I haven't foreseen, but I mustn't plan on those, even hope for them. I'll see Joss and I'll always have had Kate, even if I can't have her now. Grief doesn't go away, I know that of old, but you get used to it, you learn how to live with it.

He stood up and balanced there for a moment on the movement of the water under the pontoon. Then he climbed on to the bank and set off northwards, back to Richmond Villa.

In the last hundred yards home, he had a wild

hope. He thought, with a sudden leap, that Joss would have refused to go with Kate, that there would have been another row and that he would find Joss in the kitchen, eating cereal and reading a rock music magazine, looking mulish and triumphant. But he knew, as soon as he turned the key, that the house was empty. He went into his study, and then the kitchen, and found that Kate had rinsed their wineglasses, and left them upside-down by the sink to drain, and put the rest of the bottle of wine in the fridge. The kitchen table was quite clear of everything except the huddle of marmalade and honey jars that now lived permanently in the middle. He went upstairs. Leonard wasn't back, wouldn't be back until at least nine, and his door was shut. Joss's was open. James went in. It looked as if she had packed in a tearing hurry, leaving drawers and cupboards open with garments trailing from them. James tried to visualise her as she had done it; had she been screaming at Kate, or excited, or simply resigned? He noticed she had taken her duvet, leaving her bed looking denuded and impersonal, and couldn't decide whether this was a bad sign that she had finally departed, or a good one that she had taken it to comfort her in strange surroundings.

He went round the room, looping T-shirts and jerseys back into drawers, and closing them, picking up socks and knickers and magazines from the floor, chucking screwed-up balls of chocolate-bar foil into the already stuffed wastepaper basket.

He started to strip the bed and abruptly couldn't bear it. It reminded him of the night Kate had actually gone, and he had climbed into their bed later and foolishly, helplessly, put his face into her pillow, still redolent of her. Mrs Cheng could deal with Joss's room. James dropped the armful of dirty laundry he held and went out of the room, and closed the door. Bloody Joss. Bloody Kate. They might at least have left him a note.

He went down to the kitchen and opened the cupboard where the drink lived. The Turkish wine still stood there, but it stood alone. Something about the Turkish wine made James think of bird-and-bottle parties of the sixties, and that thought was thuddingly depressing. He closed the cupboard. Instead of just drinking, he would eat. He would make himself something to eat, and drink the remaining white wine with it, and then Leonard would come home and he, at least, would be a diversion. James wondered how he would tell Leonard that Joss had gone.

He opened the fridge. There was a sad chicken carcass, a glum lettuce, and several dispirited odds and ends in bowls and dishes. There were also several idiotic yoghurts Joss had bought, in pots with little plastic feet. James shut the fridge. This was no evening for a martyred sandwich; he would go out and buy fish and chips and a bottle of stout. He went to the little wooden barrel on the counter where the change for housekeeping lived, and was picking it up when the doorbell rang.

259

Damn, James thought. He glanced at the clock. Seven forty-five. The witching hour for Mormons and Jehovah's Witnesses and other pests. He remembered Hugh opening the door to one once, and the missionary had said earnestly, 'Do you know God?' 'Intimately,' Hugh said. 'I am He,' and shut the door. James went down the hall, and opened the door with his, Not this evening or ever, ready on his lips, and it was Hugh, Hugh with a chic dark canvas bag in one hand and a bottle, wrapped in brown paper, in the other.

They sat there together in the failing light, in the two armchairs in James's study. The fish-and-chip wrapping, translucent with pools of grease, lay on the floor between them. The whisky bottle was half empty. In the spare bedroom upstairs, the companion front room to Leonard's, Hugh's canvas bag lay on the bed, where he had thrown it.

'You can't stay,' James had started by saying. 'You must go back. To Julia and those little boys. You can't run away simply because she is behaving like a dream.' But later he had gone combing his bookshelves in search of something, and had at last found it, a volume of Sylvia Townsend Warner's letters.

'Listen,' he said to Hugh, finding the page. 'Listen to this. Is this the trouble?' And then he read a passage. ' "I say it with my true heart," ' James read, ' "the worst injury one can do to the person who loves one is to cover oneself from head to

260

foot in a shining impenetrable condom of irreproachable behaviour." '

'Yes,' Hugh said, nodding, 'that's it. That's it exactly.'

'Thank God,' James said, 'thank God you came, even if it's only for a night. While I had Joss, I not only had her, I had Kate too, in a sense. I was pretty deep in self-pity when you came, and if there's any quality I detest, it's self-pity.'

They looked at each other for a long moment. A car drew up in the street outside.

'Leonard,' James said. 'Leonard and Beatrice. She brings him in, has a cup of tea and then I walk her home.'

Car doors slammed and voices came unevenly up the steps.

'What happened?' Leonard said. 'What happened to her?'

Beatrice's reply came clear and crisp. 'What do you think? Men invariably opt for convenience. He simply cast her aside, like a shilling glove.'

'He'll be in his study,' Leonard said, 'sozzling, no doubt.'

The door opened; James and Hugh looked up as the two old faces came round it in enquiry.

'What's going on?' Leonard said. 'What's he doing here?'

James stood up, and came towards them. 'I'm sorry to tell you that Joss has gone,' he said. 'But I'm glad to tell you that Hugh has come.'

Chapter Thirteen

Joss lay in the not-quite dark, clutching her duvet. It was reasonably quiet, but not as quiet as Richmond Villa, where her room was at the side, not the front as here, of the house. She didn't want to think about her room at Richmond Villa, but it lurked about in her mind and upset her because it made her feel babyish and inclined to tears. This room was weird. If she sat up on the left-hand side of her bed, she could pretty well touch the walls on both sides; and the window had been cut off by the partition wall and was much too high for its width. Through the partition wall, on the sofa in the bigger room, Kate was sleeping.

Kate. Joss felt in such a muddle about everything that she didn't know if Kate was Mum any more or just Kate, now. When she had found Kate, to her utter amazement, washing up glasses at the sink in Richmond Villa, Joss had felt a sudden surge of being Kate's child again; there Mum was, in context, familiar and expected, washing up at the sink where she had washed up since Joss was just a little kid. It had knocked Joss off balance to see Kate like that, and made her vulnerable and responsive, so that, when Kate said they were going back to Osney together, Joss had nodded and said OK, then, no fighting or screams. They had packed together, and Kate had telephoned for a taxi, and it was only when they were getting into the taxi that Joss remembered her duvet.

'But you don't need it, Jossie, I've got you a new one —'

'I do,' Joss said, suddenly desperate. 'I've got to have it, I've got to —'

She tore back into the house and up the stairs. Her room looked awful, as if it had been burgled, violated. Panic seized Joss. She couldn't go, she couldn't leave her room and — and James and Leonard, and then she didn't want the taxi to drive Kate away from her either. She stood gibbering faintly in the centre of her room, immobilised. From the street, the taxi blew its horn. Joss gasped. She took a deep breath and seized her duvet, and plunged her face into it. 'Help,' Joss said into its muffling folds. 'Help.' The taxi horn sounded again. Clasping her duvet like a treasured animal, Joss flew down the stairs and out of the door.

'You gave me a fright,' Kate said. 'I thought you'd changed your mind. I thought you weren't coming.'

In silent pain, Joss bowed her head and buried it in her bedclothes. She couldn't look at Kate; she couldn't look at anything until, what seemed like hours later, Kate said gently, 'We're here.'

Kate had put flowers everywhere, and there was a new, black-hooded sweatshirt for Joss in a carrier bag from her favourite shop. 'You can change it,' Kate said, 'if you want something else.' They had gone out, after they'd made up Joss's bed, for a pizza and Joss had had some wine and felt rather better, though it was an odd kind of better, giddy and a bit hysterical. They'd laughed a lot and Kate said, 'Oh, we're going to have such a good time!' and Joss began to think that perhaps they were. There were several people in the pizza restaurant who knew Kate and they came over to talk, and were introduced to Joss, and Joss felt excited and at the same time unhinged, because Kate hadn't known any of these people or talked like this, when she was just Mum, at Richmond Villa.

The whole evening was OK really, until Joss was alone in bed, alone with her duvet. Then she began to worry. How much longer was it going to take to get to school and which bus would it be? How would Angie be able to come here, and Emma, and what would happen all the nights Kate was working at Pasta Please and left Joss alone with gross old Mr Winthrop who reminded her of something that had got left in a damp corner and gone mouldy? And how would she fit in the rest of her stuff, and where could she be by herself and what did James and Leonard think when they came back and she wasn't there? Abruptly she remembered the yoghurts she had bought, in the little walking pots, the yoghurts in all the flavours James hated and she loved, like banana and chocolate and fudge. The thought of the yoghurts waiting for her in the fridge at Richmond Villa was too much for Joss. Very quietly, with clumps of duvet stuffed into her mouth to muffle the noise, Joss began to cry.

Kate could hear her. The sofa wasn't very comfortable, and was scarcely long enough even for Kate, and the various tensions of the evening hadn't been conducive to a quiet mind. It was odd, because Kate had got what she wanted, had achieved what she had set out to achieve, and with surprising ease at that, but the end result simply refused to feel natural. Here she was, lying in her dear room, through whose window she often saw the canal boats that never failed to thrill her, with Joss lying safely tucked up only feet away from her, just as she once used to be, before James, only this was better, and yet it didn't feel entirely right. I expect, Kate thought, turning once again in search of a sleep-inducing position, that we are too excited, and that we mustn't hurry getting used to each other again, after so long. But three months isn't very long, and we've seen each other every week . . . She strained her ears. Joss was still crying, but more quietly now. Kate slid off the sofa and tiptoed to the dividing door.

'Jossie?'

Silence.

'Jossie, don't worry. It'll be fine, you know, it's just that it's been a bit of a shock, something you weren't expecting. That's all. And don't worry about school. I've ordered you a taxi for tomorrow, until we've worked out the buses.' She paused. 'It's lovely for me to have you. To have you back.'

'Yeah,' Joss said faintly. She had stopped crying.

'Sleep well. Croissants for breakfast.'

Croissants, Joss thought. Why croissants? At Richmond Villa, they only ever had them as a treat, on birthdays, except of course for Uncle Leonard's birthday. He'd only ever tried one croissant. 'Stupid bloody thing,' he'd said, looking at the explosion of buttery flakes down his front. 'Trust the perishing French.' Joss set her jaw. She would not think about Uncle Leonard.

'Sleep well,' Kate said again, her voice very loving.

Joss took a breath. 'You too,' she said.

'I just wondered,' Bluey Acheson said, 'if you could use a few of these? They're Boston Bay cookies.'

With a wide smile, she held out a box. James had found her there, on the doorstep, when he went to answer the bell, thinking it might be the postman, with a parcel.

'I'm Garth's mother —'

'Ah!' James said, smiling back. 'The provider of the peonies.'

'That's me!'

James held the door a little wider. 'Do please come in.' She stepped past him, a neat figure in jeans and a scarlet cardigan. 'I'm afraid we're in awful disorder —'

'I'll confess,' Bluey Acheson said. She had shining brown straight hair tied back with a red-and-blue checked ribbon. 'Garth told me. He said

266

you'd all got in a bit of a pickle, so as Randy's away I thought I'd just come round —'

'Randy?'

'My husband,' said Bluey Acheson without enthusiasm. 'He's a physicist. That's why we're in Oxford. He's gone to lecture in The Hague or someplace.'

'Mrs Acheson —'

'Bluey, please.'

'Bluey, I'm afraid my uncle is still in his dressing gown.'

He was. He sat at the disordered remains of the breakfast table, and muttered at the crossword. Across the table Hugh, in a cashmere polo-necked jersey with the sleeves pushed up, was smoking and writing an illustrated letter to the twins with coloured felt-tipped pens he had found in Joss's room. The kitchen door to the garden was propped open to the temperate May sunshine, in which Miss Bachelor, firmly in her brown overcoat still, was pruning off the dead-flowered spikes of a forsythia.

'Attention please,' James said, 'I would like to introduce to you Mrs Bluey Acheson, Garth's mother, who has most kindly brought us some biscuits.'

Bluey beamed at them. Hugh leapt to his feet and held out his hand. 'You should never be in here, Mrs Bluey Acheson, you look far too hygienic.' He gestured to Leonard. 'Get up, you insanitary old heap.'

Leonard didn't move. He eyed Bluey. She smiled

at him. 'Have you brought Joss?' Leonard demanded.

Her face fell. 'Only cookies —'

'It's been ten days,' Leonard said accusingly, as if Joss's going to Osney was Bluey's fault.

Bluey sat down. Leonard was wearing a singularly repulsive old plaid dressing gown open over his pyjamas. He hadn't yet shaved. Bluey looked at him just as if he were shining with care and cleanliness.

'Garth's been to see Joss,' she said. 'He took her to the movies. I think she's doing fine.'

'No, she's not!' Leonard shouted. 'She's no business to!'

Bluey looked down. Garth had not in fact said Joss was doing just fine, he'd said she was homesick for Richmond Villa but that she felt she owed it to her mother to stay in Osney. 'I'll feel guilty wherever I am' she'd said to Garth, and then, though he had not told Bluey this, he had tried to take advantage of her temporary frailty by kissing her, and she'd socked him in the face with a fist uncomfortably armoured in new Indian rings. 'Don't you think she ought to be with her mother?' Bluey said now.

Leonard looked miserable and furious. He shook the paper at Bluey. 'What about me?'

James put a mug of coffee down in front of Bluey. 'You must make allowances for my uncle. He affects rudeness and temper to cover a heart of marshmallow.' Bluey smiled. She sipped her coffee and looked round the kitchen. It was sensationally untidy and looked, Bluey thought, just wonderful; human and imaginative. 'I love it in here,' she said.

Hugh goggled at her. 'You *couldn't*,' he said, remembering, though he had forbidden himself to, the ordered charm of the kitchen at Church Cottage.

'My kitchen's so dull, compared to this,' Bluey said. 'No books, no chairs, no —' she paused.

'Bottles?' James suggested.

She laughed. 'Only such *serious* bottles, you know! Olive oil and balsam vinegar and all the things *Gourmet Magazine* says I should have.'

James and Hugh pulled their chairs closer to her. She looked like a newly picked Alpine flower in the chaos around her.

'Her husband's called Randy,' James said to Hugh.

Hugh said to Bluey, 'You can't be serious.'

She nodded, delighted. 'It doesn't mean the same thing in the States.' She hid her face behind her coffee mug, giggling. 'My sister's called Pokey, and *that* doesn't mean the same thing either.'

James and Hugh watched her, smiling; she was charming, a pretty, sweet distraction blown in through the front door like a present. Leonard got up with difficulty, grunting and puffing like an old hippo. He found his stick and limped towards the garden door.

'And while Randy does physics, what do *you* do?' Hugh said.

Leonard made his way unevenly out into the

garden. Beatrice heard him coming and deliberately did not turn until he was almost wheezing in her ear.

'Why aren't you dressed?'

'It's sodding Saturday!' He thumped his stick down on the lawn. It needed mowing. 'They've got a woman in there.'

Beatrice turned round properly, a handful of whispering dead petals in her grasp. 'What *do* you mean?'

'Garth's mother. Looks like a doll. Made us some biscuits.'

'How very kind.'

'Kind!' said Leonard. 'Huh! News gets round that there's three men on their own at Richmond Villa and bingo, there's droves of bloody women. First you, now her.'

Beatrice flushed. 'How crudely you talk.' She turned back to the forsythia. It was ten-thirty and she had been slightly hoping that James might bring her a cup of coffee and pause to talk while she drank it, but she was not going to say so. Instead she said, 'Why don't you dress? You look inappropriate.'

He leered at her, from the side.

'Mustn't inflame Mrs Acheson with my *déshabillé?*'

Beatrice snorted. Chuckling, Leonard tottered back across the grass. Do believe,' he told himself, 'do believe the old boiler's jealous. Must be in love with me.' He lurched into the back door. Bluey was telling a story and James and Hugh were laughing at it. Nobody took any notice of Leonard. 'Bloody fools,' he said, quite loudly, and limped past them, to go upstairs and dress.

Kate paused at the top of the spiral stairs that led down to the kitchen of Pasta Please, to allow Christine to come up. Kate was carrying dirty plates; Christine was carrying two dishes of rigatoni in tomato sauce, sprinkled with parmesan and pine nuts.

'There's someone come in to see you,' Christine said disapprovingly. 'Please be quick. I told them you were working.'

'Who?' Kate said as they passed one another. 'A man or a woman?'

'A woman, of course,' Christine said crushingly, sweeping on.

It was Julia. She stood against a wall, where Christine had clearly driven her, so that she couldn't engage Benjie in distracting conversation at close quarters. She looked pale and thin, but her appearance was as clean and carefully thought out as usual, with her hair in a thick, perfect pigtail.

'Julia!' Kate said, putting plates down on the nearest surface and running over.

Julia put her arms out. They had scarcely even bumped cheekbones in token kisses before, but now Julia held Kate tightly, like a sister.

'Oh Kate. I'm so sorry to come here, but can I see you?'

'Of course —'

271

'When do you finish, when is lunch over?'

'I can get away about half-past three, I think. And Joss won't be home' — oh, the pride of being able to say that again — 'until about six.'

Christine's feet began to descend the spiral staircase. Julia's eyes swung in her direction, and then back to Kate.

'I'll come back for you about three-thirty, then. Can I?'

'Of course —'

Julia bent and kissed her cheek. 'Thank you. Oh thank you. I'll wait outside for you. On the pavement.'

When she was gone, Christine said, 'Don't I know her?'

'She's been in once or twice —'

'No, no. Not here. On the telly.'

'Yes,' Kate said, 'yes, you have. She presents *Night Life.*'

Christine had a headache, and a meeting with her accountant later that day. She scowled at Kate. 'What does she want with you, then?'

'I don't know what to do,' Julia said simply. 'I just do not know what to do next.'

She sat with Kate in the window of a big café in St Giles, and pressed a slice of lemon down to the bottom of her cup of tea.

'He says he is desperate without the twins and that he loves me, but he won't come home because my attitude is killing him.'

'What is your attitude?' Kate said. She felt fond

272

of Julia and sorry for her and, by comparison, for once strong and capable.

'I just want to help,' Julia said. 'I love him and I miss him and I just want to help him come to terms with this terrible unfairness. And —' she stopped.

Kate waited. She took a mouthful of warm, sharp tea and watched Julia. At last, as if after a little internal wrestle with herself, Julia said, 'You see, I can't cope without him. I thought I could but I can't. There isn't any point to anything without him. I need him. I've discovered that.'

'Have you told him so?'

'He won't let me,' Julia said sadly. She had telephoned constantly, for brief unsatisfactory conversations, and once she had gathered up all her courage, and gone round to Richmond Villa, which had seemed to be full of people and very lively, with an American woman in the kitchen showing Leonard how to make real hamburgers with a little plastic mould. Leonard had looked like a happy child in a sandpit. James had been sweet to Julia and Hugh had been kind, but politely kind, and she hadn't achieved anything.

'I begged him to come home,' Julia said now, remembering. 'I went round there and simply asked him outright. It was difficult to see him alone because there were so many people there, including an American woman I didn't know. I said please come home for the twins' sake even if you won't for mine. He said it was too soon. I tried to talk about the twins but he got terribly upset,

273

and I don't want to upset him.'

Kate, meaning to say something sympathetic, said instead, by mistake, 'What American woman?'

'The mother of a boyfriend of Joss's, I think. James said she was a woman designed to do charitable work and that they had become her charity. She didn't seem to mind when he said that. She laughed.'

Kate pulled herself together. 'And the twins? How are the twins?'

Julia swallowed. 'Terribly difficult. They keep asking when Daddy's coming home and every time the phone rings they rush at it shouting "Daddy, Daddy, Daddy". And they've started wetting their beds. I thought Sandy was wonderful —'

'Isn't she?'

'I think she's exploiting me, now Hugh's away.'

'Julia,' Kate said, leaning forward, 'can you work?'

'It's a relief,' Julia said solemnly. 'It's the only thing that's ordinary, that's all right.'

'So you're OK for money —'

'Oh yes,' Julia said, 'I'm earning more than Hugh did.' Her face twisted briefly. 'I'm so ashamed of myself. I used to think money mattered so much, that it was security, that our kind of life depended upon having enough of it. But now I've got enough of it, and I haven't got Hugh, I feel —' She stopped again.

'He'll come back, you know,' Kate said gently.

Julia gazed at her. 'But *will* he? You should see him and James together.'

Kate looked up. They stared at one another.

'Was there ever any, I mean, did they ever — ?'

'No,' Julia said, 'I don't think so. But the way they love each other is worse than sex, somehow, it's got more of a hold, they're such *friends*.' She spread her hands. Her big, beautiful old engagement ring from Hugh, a half-hoop of opals and tiny diamonds, glittered and gleamed. 'I feel shut out. Did you ever? Did you ever feel Hugh mattered to James more than you did?'

Kate thought. If she was scrupulously honest, it was only at the end that she had been irritated by James's affection for Hugh, and by then she had been ready to be irritated by anything. 'Not really.'

'I feel that at the moment I can't compete, that I've become smug and prissy and I haven't a sense of humour. Beside me, James is so warm and easy and human, and he doesn't make Hugh feel as if he'd let him down. I don't feel that Hugh's let me down either, but he feels he has and it's somehow my fault. It's like being in a maze,' Julia said, fishing out her lemon slice and dropping it in an ashtray. 'It's like going round and round the same paths in a maze, and never getting to the middle, and never getting out, either.'

'I think you just have to wait.'

'Do you? Do you honestly?'

'I did,' Kate said, 'I waited and waited for Joss, and then the time was suddenly right to act, and I acted. It was Benjie, the chef at work, actually, who suddenly spurred me to act. The same

275

will happen to you.'

'Will it?'

'Oh yes. Because, you see, Hugh will be missing you. He mightn't be able to feel it but he is. He's too wounded to feel anything just now, but he will in time.'

Julia put out a hand and took Kate's. 'You do comfort me. How can you be so sure?'

A shadow crossed Kate's face. She said, 'I'm not proud of this, but I know for certain that James is still missing me. Hugh will be just the same. And now I've got Joss —'

Julia smiled. 'It's so lovely, that you've got Joss back.'

'Yes,' Kate said. 'Yes. Lovely's the word.'

James asked Mrs Cheng to work extra hours at Richmond Villa; he said Mr Hunter would pay her. Mrs Cheng disapproved of Hugh. She liked Beatrice Bachelor, whose age, in any case, made her worthy of respect, and who treated her with courtesy and had asked her how to say several simple things in Cantonese; but Hugh was another matter. He made stupid jokes and he kept James up too late and there were too many empty whisky bottles. Mrs Cheng ironed his shirts — much better quality than James's — and cleaned his room and wiped over all his bottles and potions and lotions in the bathroom, but she did it purely and entirely for the money. She would do nothing extra for Hugh, and she wouldn't speak to him either.

'Bloody rude,' Uncle Leonard said.

'You fine one to talk.'

'What've you got against the poor sod, anyway?'

'Shouldn't *be* here.'

'Why not?'

'Not right,' Mrs Cheng said, brushing clots of fluff out from under Leonard's bed. 'Not right, all you men. Should be Kate back. Should be Joss.'

'We've got Bluey now,' Leonard said, to be annoying.

'Not same.'

'No,' said Leonard, thinking of Kate and Joss, 'not the same at all.'

Mrs Cheng had spring-cleaned Joss's room. She had washed the windows, and then the curtains, and prised all the chewing-gum off the carpet with a kitchen knife. She had made the bed up with everything but the duvet, and then covered it with a clean old double sheet, to be ready for Joss. When she couldn't bear Hugh, she went into Joss's room for a quiet moment. Although she had no concrete reason for suspecting it, she sometimes thought James did the same thing. James had only spoken of the matter to her once, and then in a roundabout sort of way, but all the same, Mrs Cheng knew what he meant.

'When things change,' he'd said, 'you simply have to learn to adapt to them, don't you? And I suppose, if you're lucky, you might learn to like the change, or at least get perfectly used to it.'

James, Mrs Cheng told herself, had a lot of

assets. Who would leave such a man? Kind man, she said to herself, steady man, and wise. Her father had been wise; he had told her not to marry Mr Cheng, but her mother had wanted it because of the takeaway shop. Her father had been wise, but weak. James Mallow, Mrs Cheng had come to believe, was wise and not weak at all.

'James grown up,' she said to Leonard. She swept a handful of dead flies into her dustpan. 'He not spoilt old baby like *you*.'

Mark Hathaway noticed that he was losing weight; not much, perhaps only a few pounds, but enough for his extremely expensive Italian jeans (he had been to London to buy them) not to sit on his waist and hips with quite such perfect snugness as they once had. He also thought his face looked thinner, but that suited his mood, to look mildly haggard and melancholy. What average man after all, would not look haggard and melancholy if messed about quite as appallingly as Kate was messing him?

The trouble was that he was in love with her, he was certain of it. He had never been so preoccupied with a woman; it amounted almost to an obsession. He couldn't satisfactorily analyse to himself precisely why she held so powerful an allure for him because, if he was ruthlessly candid, she was neither as intelligent nor as good-looking as almost every other girlfriend he had had. But she had a mixture of fragility and sturdy independence that was tremendously attractive, and she was gentle and seldom lost her temper, and she had a wonderful capacity for happy enjoyment of things and for making him enjoy those things too. He also felt, in a slightly strutting way, proud of having released her from the sterile habit of a worn-out relationship, and set her free. It frustrated him that she had never turned her extremely appealing slanting eyes on him and said thank you quite directly, for doing so.

But even that didn't frustrate him as much as Joss did. There he and Kate were, just getting through the first sticky patch inevitable in any relationship, and then along comes Joss, quite unannounced by Kate. Very, very occasionally on the nights Kate wasn't working, Joss would be out too, but usually Kate was with Joss on those nights because that was, she said, where she wanted to be. Of course, Mark could join them; he'd be more than welcome. She had to be joking. Joss and Mark made it perfectly plain to one another, without actually saying so, that there was to be nothing warmer between them than a truce.

There was nothing for it, Mark discovered to his dismay, but to wait for Kate outside Pasta Please, like some travesty of a stage door johnny, and walk her home. He started these walks by complaining to her of her neglect of him, but then she simply refused to speak to him at all, and his resentment at her preferring Joss was engulfed by a genuine fear of losing Kate altogether. He burrowed beneath all the feelings that seethed in the forefront of his mind for some genuine charm.

'OK,' he said to Kate, taking her hand, 'I accept that your being a mother must come first. But may I ask, in spirit of the sweetest reason, what comes next, for us?'

Kate was uncertain. She didn't want Joss to have the smallest excuse for thinking life in Osney was boring or that she was being ignored, yet she didn't, either, want to say goodbye to Mark Hathaway. She liked him and enjoyed being with him and he represented something very significant to her, a person to have a relationship with who did not simultaneously become dependent. 'I won't add to your pile of people,' he had said. But he had added to her experience; he'd given her modern novels, and music, and taken her to jazz clubs and Irish pubs and a tapas bar in Bristol. These things, and his friends, and his radical ideas and opinions, had made Kate feel that she had, in some way, been given back eight years of her youth. She wasn't at all ready to give up this source of mental stimulation and pleasure, and the growing self-esteem that went with it.

She said, 'Joss has only been with me two weeks. We're just getting somewhere, in fact, I think I owe quite a lot of the improvement in our relationship to you because I'm so much happier and she catches it. Can you be patient a bit longer? She'll be fifteen in a month and I expect she'll start staying with friends more soon —'

She had, in fact, asked if she could stay away already. She had asked if she could stay with Angie, and Kate had said of course, although she had been horrified to discover how much she didn't want to say it. Then Angie's mother had had to go into hospital suddenly, and the household was thrown into turmoil and Joss didn't go. She hadn't made a fuss about it either, to Kate's relief. In fact at the moment she was making almost no fuss about anything, and Kate almost dared to believe that she was happy.

'Look,' Mark said. He swung Kate's hand across him so that he could hold it in both of his. 'Look, I accept all that. Great. But I must point out that there is me, too. And us. So how does the timetable for the future look?'

'I don't know,' Kate said.

'One month? Two? My thirty-fifth birthday?'

'I can't tell. I wish I could, but I can't.'

'Do you *want* it to go on like this?'

'No,' Kate said candidly.

'Ah. Well, at least that's something.'

'But I do want to be with her and have a good relationship with her.'

'And — me?'

'And you.'

'So how are you going to resolve it?'

'Why do *I* have to?'

'Because it's your dilemma and you made it.'

Kate wrenched her hand free and marched ahead of him. He was seized, quite suddenly, with the urge to spring after her, and slap her. He rammed his hands into the tight hip-pockets of his jeans, and broke into a run until he had caught up with her.

'Kate. Sorry.'

'You said you wouldn't be possessive. You said you were an individual, that you were free —'

'I am. I'm not possessive.'

She stopped and swung round. The light from the street lamp turned her face pale-green and her hair bronze; she looked like a nymph or a dryad.

'Oh Kate,' Mark said in longing, 'have some pity.'

She watched him.

'I miss you,' Mark said. His voice cracked a little. Bother the charm, the manner, why shouldn't she see what she was doing to him? 'I love you, I'm mad about you. I know about Joss, but can't you, just occasionally, imagine what it's like for me, wanting you, thinking about you, planning things we can do together? I'm not asking for now, Kate. I'm only asking for soon. Surely you haven't the heart to refuse me that?'

She moved forward slightly. He took his hands out of his pockets and put his arms around her. Then he bent his head down and kissed her with no hurry whatsoever. Oh, Kate thought, sinking into the kiss, oh magic, and then, help, no, Joss is waiting . . . She pulled back abruptly.

'What now?'

She could have cried. 'Joss,' she said.

He stepped back. 'Of course,' he said politely, coldly, 'Joss.'

'I'll decide,' Kate said. She felt thoroughly shaken up. 'I promise I will. I won't keep you hanging about. I'll work something out soon. Honestly I will —'

'Good,' he said.

Joss saw them pause on the corner of Swan Street; then she let the curtain fall back in case they kissed each other good-night, which she certainly didn't want to see. She looked round the room, which she had tidied for Kate, and then made up her bed for her, on the sofa, as usual. Then she went to her own bed, and pulled from under the mattress a rectangle of cardboard cut from a cereal box. On the blank side, she had drawn a grid of little squares. Some were coloured in, about half. Joss coloured in one more. Fifteen nights now, fifteen nights in Swan Street.

Chapter Fourteen

Randolph Acheson came home from his lecture tour of Holland, and found that his wife Bluey had made a group of new friends. He was mildly surprised to find that they all seemed to be between twenty and forty years older than she was, but that was as far as his adverse reaction went. It was a relief, if the truth be known, that she had made friends because she was by nature gregarious but at the same time hadn't seemed able to get the hang of Oxford socially. Randolph was afraid it was because Bluey was a lapsed academic and all Oxford could see it. The budding marine biologist he had married seventeen years before had gradually exchanged her laboratory and scientific dissertations for recipe books and clothes catalogues. Although she had never confessed it openly, Randolph suspected now that Bluey had never, ever had a truly academic mind, and that she had only been to college because all the girls of her age and class in the affluent Chicago suburb where she grew up went to college. What Bluey really liked was baking, and people, and parties. As she got older, Randolph noticed, she was getting to have no shame at all, either, about acknowledging this.

Her new friends meant that she was out a good deal. This scarcely figured with Randolph since he was in the laboratory by eight-fifteen in the morning, and often — if he dined in the college to which he was attached — not home until ten-thirty. His clothes were still admirably laundered; the supply of fresh oranges in the icebox to be squeezed for his breakfast juice didn't run out; the little house they had rented collected neither dust nor faded flowers. The only difference was that Bluey didn't beg Randolph to take her to the movies or out to supper or to London. All in all, Randolph felt that for Bluey to have found her houseful of elderly English eccentrics was only a good thing.

'They're really neat people,' Garth said to his father. 'You'd really like them. They're like something out of a novel, something else.'

Bluey had started by thinking they were like something out of a novel herself, the sort of novel set in another, intriguing, age and society. Richmond Villa held her spellbound, with its muddled layers of living, its walls of books and curious pictures, its abundance of sagging comfort, its disregard of fashion. To find James and Leonard and Hugh in this house, and then Beatrice and Mrs Cheng, had seemed quite fitting to Bluey, as if she had stumbled upon a stereotype of a vanished kind of life, and had then discovered that it had breath in it, after all. But as she spent more time in Richmond Villa, she learned all their histories, and her heart went out to them all because she discovered that they had suffered variously in their lives with all the acuteness that she had suffered, in finding herself married to a man whom the passing years only seemed to make more impersonal, more remote, duller.

She had been deeply dismayed to observe Randy's shock as her interest in marine biology declined after Garth's birth, and she had turned, as a refuge, to domestic things, simple things, that seemed to represent a warm reality beside what now appeared to her the cold sterility of science. She knew perfectly well that Randy despised her for making patchwork cushions and reading cookery books, and she had told herself for several years that she didn't care about his opinion. But when she found that James and Hugh were not simply admiring of her skills, but even interested in them, she admitted to herself that she had been starved by Randy, that she had been dreadfully lonely. To spend an afternoon in the kitchen at Richmond Villa making blueberry muffins and sewing on myriad shirt buttons, while people spoke to her with gratitude and imagination, was like coming out into the sunlight after a long time in the cold and rain.

The sunlight was particularly warming if James was at Richmond Villa. James had not spoken to Bluey of Kate, but Hugh had. He had also spoken about Joss. Bluey had not initially thought Joss a very appropriate girlfriend for Garth, who was a handsome, well-set up, clean-cut boy and looked, to Bluey's proud eye, too good for a grumpy little scruff like Joss. But if James was devoted to Joss, and Hugh assured Bluey he was, then there must be more to her than met the eye, however maternally proud. Bluey would have liked to ask Hugh how devoted Hugh thought James remained to Kate, but delicacy forbade that. She had to comfort herself by reflecting that James looked, on the whole, well and happy, and not like a man who was pining. You couldn't say the same for Hugh. He was terribly attractive, Bluey thought, even if he was too charming to be trusted, but he looked, without doubt, as if he were pining. Bluey had seen his pretty, sad wife and James had told her about the adorable twins. It seemed inevitable that, given time, Hugh would, quite properly and naturally, go home to his wife and children and then James would be left alone in Richmond Villa with only Leonard for permanent company, and James might, in consequence, feel lonelier then, and gladder than ever of somebody to be sweet to him.

He often said she was sweet. 'You're a sweet thing,' he'd say, looking at the Waldorf salad she'd made for their supper, or a newly darned jersey of Leonard's or a posy of blue pansies on his desk. 'I feel rather awful, you doing all this for us.'

'But I like it.'

'I know. That's what's so sweet.'

'I haven't anything else to do. I don't have a job. Randy and Garth are out all day. Do I get in your way?'

'Not in the least. I simply feel that it isn't a very equal bargain, and my conscience troubles me about that.'

She gave him a clear glance. 'It's a fine bargain for me.'

'Thank you, then,' James said. He leaned forward and kissed her cheek. 'Truly, thank you.'

The only disconcerting element at Richmond Villa was Miss Bachelor. She wasn't there all the time, but when she was, Bluey felt a little afraid of her. She made Bluey feel rather as Randy made her feel, and there was something else besides. If Miss Bachelor hadn't been so old, Bluey would have said she had a soft spot for James, but Miss Bachelor was not only too old but too scholarly and rational to have anything so sentimental as a romantic weakness for anyone. Yet when Bluey looked at James, at his benevolent, human, experienced face, and his thick, never tidy hair, and his hands and the set of his shoulders and his air of being quite comfortable, thank you, with his own body, then she understood with an instinct that had nothing to do with reason that neither age nor cast of character had any effect whatsoever on a susceptibility to romantic weakness. This curious life, this strange foreign life in Oxford that had, until recently, seemed unassailable to Bluey, had suddenly become not only interesting, but explicable. I'm back in the human race, Bluey told herself, brushing her gleaming hair in front of her bedroom mirror, I'm plugged back into the system. I'm in love.

A week before her fifteenth birthday, Joss filled in the last empty square on her cardboard chart. Then she cut the chart up into a great many neat, small pieces, put them on to an old paint-tin lid she had found on the landing in a pile of Mr Winthrop's junk, and burned them. Then she did some desultory revision towards the coming school exams — no GCSE until next summer — and waited for Kate. Kate was not working that evening and had said she would be home about five. She said she would bring supper, which meant something from the restaurant. Joss liked pasta, but you could have too much pasta, like you could have too much of other things you put up with for someone else's sake. Joss had learned a great deal about that sort of endurance in the last month, and she had come to the conclusion that such sacrifice only had any point as long as you knew you were getting somewhere.

When Kate came in, soon after five, she flopped down in their most comfortable chair and kicked her shoes off and said it had been a nonstop day with the restaurant full of tourists, including what seemed like half a busload of Japanese who all ordered exactly the same thing which put Benjie in a temper. Joss made Kate some tea.

'Bless you,' Kate said gratefully, holding the mug and sipping, with her eyes closed. Joss watched her for a while. She'd had her hair cut a bit differently, a little shorter, and it suited her. Prior to the last month together, Joss had never looked at Kate dispassionately, as a person rather than just as a mother, but now she did, often, she couldn't help it even though she didn't like it much because it wasn't comfortable. Emma had told Joss she thought Kate looked quite trendy and Joss had been pleased and proud and disconcerted, all at once.

'Mum —'

Kate opened her eyes.

'Yes?'

'Mum,' Joss said, getting astride an upright chair and leaning on its back. 'Mum, I've got to go now.'

Kate said easily, 'I didn't know you were going out. Where are you going?'

'I'm not going out,' Joss said steadily. 'I mean, I've got to go home now. Back to Richmond Villa.'

Kate stared. She put her mug of tea down carefully on the floor beside her chair and leaned forward.

'Joss. This is home.'

Joss didn't flinch. 'For you,' she said, 'not me.'

They looked at each other.

'Haven't you been happy with me? I thought you were. You seemed to be.'

Joss said nothing.

Kate cried, 'We've had fun!'

'Yes,' Joss said.

Kate gripped the arms of her chair and leaned out of it towards Joss. 'Then why?'

Joss didn't like the look of Kate, or her tone of voice, but she had to go on. She'd known it wouldn't be easy, she'd expected Kate not to see, to be hurt, to take it personally. She said carefully, trying not to get excited, 'I just have to go back. It isn't you, it's nothing to do with you, but I can't live like this.' She paused, and then said emphatically, 'It isn't real.'

'Not real!'

'No.'

'Not real for a mother and daughter to live together and eat together and have jokes and go out together, not *real?*'

'That's real,' Joss said stoutly, 'but that's not the truth, is it? Living here isn't real and you're acting —'

'*Acting?*'

'You aren't living,' Joss said, amazed at herself. 'You're just getting through the days.'

There was a silence. Kate got up and pushed past Joss and went to the window. She looked out of it for a long time, it seemed to Joss, and then she came back to her chair, and sat down, and said in a very controlled voice, 'You've been talking to James. Haven't you?'

'No,' said Joss, 'nor Uncle Leonard.'

'Then why are you talking like this? You've never talked like this.'

'I am now,' Joss said. She took a breath. 'I made a chart. It had twenty-eight squares on it, for days. I coloured one in every day. I did the last one today and that made a month. I told myself I'd live here a month and I wouldn't even speak to James or Uncle Leonard, and I wouldn't go near

Jericho, and I haven't. But I'm going home now.'

Kate put her face in her hands. She whispered through them, 'Why?'

'Because it's more like a family there.'

'With James?'

Joss couldn't immediately reply. She said, 'It's my room and stuff,' after a while, but she knew it was only part of the answer.

Kate said, 'I can't believe this.'

Joss looked straight at her. 'Why don't you come too?'

'Oh *no* —'

'Why not? James'd have you back —'

'I don't want to go back. I'm free now, can't you see? That's what all this is about. I thought you saw, I thought in the last month, while we've been so happy together and you've been so nice, I thought you understood —'

'No,' said Joss. 'I still think you're daft.'

Kate clenched her fists. This must not turn into a row.

'Would you stay with me, if I found somewhere else to live, somewhere you chose with me?'

Joss's heart sank; she hadn't bargained for this. She held on to the chairback. 'No,' she said.

'I see. So the only place where you will graciously consent to live with me is in Jericho where you know I am unhappy?'

'I'm unhappy here,' Joss said. 'Why can't I choose as much as you?'

'Because you're still a child,' Kate said, without either meaning to, or much conviction.

'Don't give me that,' Joss said with scorn.

'Is it Mark?'

Joss sighed. 'No.'

'You don't like him —'

'I think he's a creep, but that's not why. I *told* you why.'

Kate stood up. She looked fragile and wounded, and the sight of her made Joss feel terrible. 'You want to go because even though I'm your mother I can't make you feel that this is home.'

Joss was silent. She wanted to say something affectionate, but didn't know how without sounding apologetic, and that, some strong instinct told her, would be fatal. She looked down at the carpet, an old imitation Turkey-patterned carpet, and began to count the stiff flowers in its border.

'Oh Joss,' Kate said brokenly, 'Jossie —'

Nine, ten, Joss counted. She ached to say sorry. Eleven, twelve, thirteen, turn the corner . . .

'What has James got I haven't got?'

Anger spurted up in Joss, drowning all softness. She leapt from her chair, turning it over.

'He doesn't ask for things!' she yelled at Kate. 'He doesn't ask me, and he didn't ask you, either!'

Then she flung herself out of the room, and down the dark stairs to the hall, and the front door to the street. From behind the closed door to the conservatory, she could hear Mr Winthrop's passion for this week, Peggy Lee, who was singing, 'Where did they go, all the good times, all the flowers and the wine?' Joss opened the front door and let it slam behind her so deafeningly that Peggy

293

Lee stammered and Mr Winthrop came out of his lair and began to shout abuse at Kate, up the stairs.

Joss had forgotten Hugh. When she had paid off the taxi, and lugged all her bags and her duvet up the steps, and pressed the doorbell, she expected James to open the door. She was just going to say, 'I'm back,' and then wait. But it wasn't James who opened the door, it was Hugh, in a pale-blue shirt and white trousers. James, Joss thought contemptuously, wouldn't wear white trousers, not white, not at his age.

'Good Lord,' Hugh said.

'I've come back —'

'So I see. Does Kate know?'

'She gave me the money for the taxi.'

'Hell's teeth, she *sent* you back.'

'No, she didn't,' Joss cried, growing angry. 'She wanted me to stay, but I wanted to come back.'

Hugh stooped for the nearest bags. 'I suppose you'd better come in.'

'I *live* here,' Joss said furiously.

'Yes, but I thought you'd stopped —'

'Why are you still here?'

'Oh God,' Hugh said, 'I don't think I can stand this.'

Muffled by her duvet, Joss pushed past him into the hall. 'Where's James?'

'Out.'

'Where's Uncle Leonard?'

'In the garden, having tea. With Beatrice —'

Joss ran down the hall, dropping her duvet on the floor, and out through the kitchen into the garden. Uncle Leonard and Miss Bachelor sat under the willow tree at the corner of the little lawn. Uncle Leonard was wearing his panama hat with the black ribbon and the split brim.

'I'm back!' Joss shouted. 'I'm back!'

They both looked up.

'What a bloody awful surprise,' Leonard said. He put out shaking, speckled hands.

'Josephine!' Beatrice called. 'How stupendous.'

Joss ran across the grass and collapsed at their feet.

'Why's he still here?'

'Hugh? Can't think. Perfect nuisance —'

'Josephine, is this an orthodox visit, does your mother —'

'Where's James, when will James be back?'

'You look worse than ever. Miserable child. What d'you want to come back for? Had some peace without you —'

'James has gone to an exhibition of modern art with Mrs Acheson —'

'*Bluey* —'

'Extraordinary name.'

'Nice little bum, though, not like —'

'Leonard!'

'I really tried living there,' Joss said. 'I did, honest. It was nice with Mum but it wasn't —'

They waited.

'We were pretending,' Joss said.

Beatrice beamed at her. 'You have been tremendously missed.'

'Not by me.'

Joss looked at Leonard. 'I didn't miss you either.'

'What d'you come back for?'

'To get away from Mr Winthrop.'

'Who is Mr Winthrop?'

'Mum's landlord. He smells.' She grinned at
Leonard. 'Nearly as bad as you.'

'Bloody impertinence.'

'Why has James gone out with Bluey? She's married.'

Leonard and Beatrice exchanged glances.

'She has been very kind and she is extremely
accomplished domestically.'

'Yeah?' Joss said. She scrambled to her feet.
'Which room's he in? Not mine, I hope —'

'Hugh? No. Mrs Cheng has guarded yours like
a lion.'

'I'm going to look at it. At my room. Then I'll
phone Garth and Angie.' She went skipping off
across the grass.

They watched her. 'Dear child,' Beatrice said
in a voice not at all like her usual one.

'Give over,' Leonard said in disgust. He glanced
at Beatrice. 'If you get sentimental, you old fool,
I'll spit in your tea.'

Julia sat in the sitting-room, and reread Hugh's
letter, for the eighth or ninth time. It was hardly
a comforting letter. It was full of reproach, it

seemed to Julia, reproach thinly disguised as self-reproach. He was only writing, Hugh said, because she had begged him to, because she had said she needed something more tangible and permanent than these unsatisfactory telephone calls which left her so distressed.

'You would be much less distressed,' Hugh wrote, 'if you could just leave me alone for a little while. I can only behave badly, in your terms, at the moment, and it would cause much less pain if you didn't provoke me into any behaviour at all. Don't get me wrong — I'm not happy here, I'm just in a kind of limbo and that's all I can ask for, just now, all I can cope with.'

The whole letter was like this, elusive and circular. It came back in the end simply to a rejection, a rejection of her, Julia, and, by implication, all she stood for, the home she had made, the standards she had kept up. The only element excluded from this wholesale rejection was of course the twins, and Julia had begun to feel, with a faint stirring of spirit, that Hugh couldn't just indulge himself over the twins and not accept what went with them, i.e., her, and their life together. She didn't doubt for a moment that he genuinely adored and missed them, but the longer he was away, the vaguer, for him, grew the reality of the twins, and the stronger their appeal as little perfect, forbidden, angel children. They were, in fact, far from being angels just now; they were being simply frightful. They had decided to disobey even Sandy, and to revert to a kind of anarchic baby behaviour, refusing to talk properly and tearing books up and throwing food about. The sadder Julia became, the worse their behaviour grew. Julia's newest fear was that Sandy would give notice which, unsatisfactory though she was in many ways, would be just another upheaval in the twins' desperately disturbed lives.

Julia put the letter down. She took a gulp of wine from the glass she had brought into the sitting-room with her. When she had first read the letter, locked in the lavatory after breakfast, she had wept bitterly and felt all the old familiar anguish and despair. But now, after so many re-readings and a day at work, she felt distinctly less abject. She considered this. Why should she feel any different? Hugh, after all, had said nothing different in his letter, he'd simply reiterated his own helplessness, the helplessness she had found so touching and poignant, so heart-breaking to watch. But she didn't feel so touched tonight. She looked at the letter, but did not pick it up again. She found she didn't want to pick it up, that the sight of it made her feel rather cross.

She went out to the kitchen. Sandy hadn't cleared away the twins' supper properly and there were crumbs and stray peas and milk spills on the table. Julia walked past the mess, and opened the fridge to find the white wine and refill her glass. She considered boiling herself an egg, and decided she couldn't be bothered. She opened the fridge again, and found the end of a wedge of Brie and a tomato, and carried these, without

298

a plate, back into the sitting-room. On the way back to her chair, she trod on Hugh's letter, and this gave her a tiny flicker of triumph. I do believe, she said to herself, biting into the Brie, I do believe that he's now as sorry for himself as I was for him, even this morning. Why aren't I now, why don't I feel like I felt in the loo after breakfast? What is it, Julia thought, letting tomato juice and seeds run down her chin, what is it that suddenly makes worms turn?

She bent down and put the half-eaten cheese and tomato deliberately on Hugh's letter. Then she crossed to the window and looked out at her early-summer garden, blue-grey and blue-black in the fading light. She leaned forward until her forehead rested on the glass. That lunchtime, she had had a planning meeting with Rob Shiner, about the second series of *Night Life,* and to discuss a new idea Julia had had about following the lives of three Midlands children, from different backgrounds, for five years. After the meeting, Rob had said come and have a sandwich. They were always having sandwiches together, Rob and Julia, and she said yes, gratefully, because having a sandwich with somebody else would prevent her from rereading Hugh's letter. During the sandwich, Rob asked if she would have dinner with him.

'Dinner?'

'I think,' Rob said, 'that you need a bit of cheering up.'

Julia said, meaning it, 'How nice of you.'

Rob refilled her glass with mineral water. 'And selfish. I'd like to have dinner with you.' He looked at her. 'The way you've coped recently, the lack of whingeing, puts you, to my mind, into the wonderful category, and I like taking wonderful women out to dinner.'

Julia had hesitated. Her mind had been so filled with Hugh that it took some time for it to get into another gear and think about Rob. She looked at Rob. He seemed absolutely the same, amiable, slightly battered, middle-aged modish in his leather jacket and jeans. She said, 'I'm rather out of practice.'

'Don't be coy.'

'I'm not —'

'He left you,' Rob said. 'He won't say if or when he's coming back. Are you going to live like a nun until he deigns to decide?'

Julia drank her water.

'I'm divorced and unattached,' Rob said, 'you're separated. We're free agents. Your self-esteem could do with a little fuel.'

That was what did it, Julia decided now, leaning against the cool glass, that remark about her self-esteem. It had plummeted unquestionably in recent weeks, simply plunged into self-despair, just like the women at Mansfield House she had interviewed for *Night Life* who'd said (and she could hardly comprehend them then) that, in the end, after years of being beaten, you come to believe that it's all you're fit for. In her turn, she had come to believe that Hugh was in the right, and that she had, by her nature, by her very existence, done him an injury and was therefore to blame for his state of mind. But what had she really done? She peeled her forehead away from the window and frowned out into the garden. She had been sympathetic and supportive and had proved herself able enough to earn enough to keep them all. She had not reproached him, not once, not even when he got so disgustingly drunk at the supermarket in Coventry, and she had suddenly discovered, at lunchtime with Rob Shiner, that she wasn't at all averse to being given a pat on the back.

'If a man had done what I've done,' Julia said loudly to the empty sitting-room, 'if Hugh had done for me what I've done for him, he'd be a hero. Nobody's going to tell me I'm a heroine, so I'll take any crumbs of praise I can get, even from Rob Shiner.'

She bent down and picked up the letter by its two shorter edges, so that it made a hammock for the remainder of the cheese and tomato, and carried it out to the kitchen waste bin. Then she wrote a stern note for Sandy telling her to clear up the kitchen before she went to bed and left the note leaning very visibly against the milk jug. Tomorrow she would get the twins up herself, and there would be proper breakfast with no snatching and spilling and grizzling, and then she would drive to the studios, and tell Rob Shiner that she would be pleased, really pleased, to have dinner with him.

James lay propped up in bed reading Boswell's account of his Highland journey with Doctor Johnson. They had just had dinner at Inveraray Castle, where the Duchess had snubbed Boswell, and been enchanted with Doctor Johnson. If James didn't exactly feel enchanted, he felt a very great deal better than he had felt for months. He had had a very enjoyable afternoon, and had returned to find the house trembling with rock music and Joss frying sausages in the kitchen.

'Hi,' she said. She wouldn't look at him.

'Jossie!'

She said something he couldn't hear. He went over to the radio and pressed the 'Off' switch and silence fell on the room like a douche of cold water.

'Have you come back for supper?'

'I've come back.'

'To stay?'

'Yeah,' Joss said, turning the sausages unnecessarily.

'Have — did you quarrel with Kate?'

'I couldn't live there.'

James came round the table and put his arm across Joss's shoulders. She stiffened, then relaxed.

'I oughtn't to say I'm pleased, but I'm going to. I'm pleased you're back.'

'Me too,' Joss said, furiously turning.

'What's the deal, part-time here, part-time with Kate?'

'Nope,' Joss said. 'I'll see her like before, but

I live here.' She bent over the counter beside the cooker. 'I said she ought to come back too. But she wouldn't.'

There was a pause, then, 'No,' James said. Joss shot a look at him.

'What d'you mean?'

'I mean — maybe that's over —'

'Over?'

'I asked her to come back. When she came for you. She was very clear that she didn't want to, so I'm learning, trying to learn, to live without entertaining any hopes like that ever again.'

'Jesus,' Joss said.

The door to the garden still stood open. There was a stumbling clatter outside and Leonard stood, framed in the doorway.

'Ah! There you are. What d'you make of this, then? Bloody child.'

The bloody child now lay, to James's great contentment, in her room across the landing, rolled in her duvet. Her return could not, of course, be as simple as all that because there would have to be discussions with Kate, and arrangements, but the bottom line was that Joss's flattened toothbrush was back in the bathroom and that the nine o'clock news on television had been interrupted constantly by Joss and Leonard squabbling as of old about the volume. Hugh had been quite kind to Joss at supper, and had only grown huffy when James had refused to elaborate, in every detail, on his afternoon with Bluey Acheson.

It had been a very happy afternoon. At the

303

exhibition of modern art — her choice, not his — they had wandered through a cornfield twelve feet high made of burnished metal and hung with immense coloured-glass butterflies and flowers. Bluey had adored it; James had thought it was very silly.

'But silly is adorable sometimes.'

'Not when it masquerades as serious.'

'But this doesn't! It's a tease.'

'Then it's a very pretentious tease.'

'James!'

'I don't have to like it, you know, just because you do.'

'I don't need you to like it, I just don't want you to dismiss it.'

'Oh,' James said, taking her hand, 'I do like this kind of amiable bickering. I've missed it.'

Bluey didn't take her hand away, and tried, unsuccessfully, not to let James drop it a few minutes later. He didn't attempt to take it again, either, all the way back to Observatory Street, but just walked beside her holding his jacket over his shoulder, because of the sunshine, and talking to her and smiling and being, oh dammit, thought Bluey, just so dear and delicious.

She led him through her little house to her tiny garden, and sat him by a wall, in order to admire her clematis, and brought him iced lemon tea in a glass. She told him about her childhood in Chicago and about going to college and getting married because all her friends were getting married ('That sounds improbably old-fashioned,'

James said, and Bluey cried, 'But it's true! It's true for girls brought up like me! Feminism didn't really touch us') and then about coming to England and finding it all so foreign. She smiled at James.

'You seem really foreign. Even though we both speak English.'

He looked at her consideringly. 'You don't seem so foreign to me, just extremely fresh and new.'

'New enough to get away with a bit of impudence?'

'Try it.'

'Would you talk to me about Kate?'

'Ah,' James said. He put his tea glass down on the little white wooden table at his elbow. 'I think I wouldn't. I don't think it's impudence to ask at all, but I'm at the stage of convalescence where I don't much want to remember being ill.'

'I just can't help being curious.' She looked at James. 'Are you curious about Randy?'

He began to laugh. 'Oh dear,' he said, 'I'm afraid I'm not. Oh Bluey,' James said, 'you really are so sweet,' and then he leaned forward, and took her shoulders in both his hands and kissed her on the mouth.

Chapter Fifteen

Mr Winthrop lay in wait for Kate. He had turned Peggy Lee down to a whisper and the electric fan heater right off, and left the conservatory door ajar, so that he wouldn't miss the sound of her key in the lock.

Mr Winthrop had had a visitor that day. An extremely respectful, bespectacled, soberly dressed young Nigerian had knocked at the door, and asked if Mr Winthrop had rooms to let. Mr Winthrop said he might have, he couldn't say. The young Nigerian had opened his briefcase and showed Mr Winthrop all his papers; he was a postgraduate law student, whose course was to start the next academic year, but who had come to Oxford early, to work in the law libraries all summer. There was, Mr Winthrop noticed, a Bible in his briefcase, and he looked both clean and studious.

'D'you have friends?' Mr Winthrop demanded.

'Not yet,' the young Nigerian said, 'but I will make friends at the church.'

Mr Winthrop took him up to Kate's room, using the key he kept for occasions such as this.

'Fifty-five pounds a week, electricity and telephone extra,' Mr Winthrop said.

The young Nigerian looked at Kate's room, at her cushions and pictures and her breakfast coffee mug sitting on the table among papers and books and an empty milk bottle holding a single orange lily. He said, 'It's a good room. When is the present tenant going?'

'Any day,' Mr Winthrop said. 'She's given me a lot of trouble.' He looked up at the smooth black face behind the shining spectacles. 'I don't want any trouble. No women or children.'

The young man moved his dark clean hands in a deprecating gesture. 'I live a quiet life. You can always refer to my college.'

Mr Winthrop thought of the glimpsed Bible. 'No singing? No tambourines and praise de Lord nonsense?'

The Nigerian was quite unoffended. He smiled. 'Very quiet,' he said.

Mr Winthrop led him downstairs again.

'Come back on Thursday and I'll let you know for certain.'

'Deposit?' the young man said.

Mr Winthrop's eyes bulged. He made an immense effort at self-control. 'Thursday'll do,' he said.

He ushered the young man out into Swan Street.

'I wouldn't like,' the young man said gently, 'to inconvenience a lady.'

Mr Winthrop thought of Kate. He snorted. 'Don't you worry, he said. 'She's no lady.'

Now that Joss was back at Richmond Villa,

Angie and Emma came home with her after school a lot. Garth, for some reason, didn't. Privately, Joss thought it was because it embarrassed him to find Bluey there, cutting Uncle Leonard's hair or making chicken pie. Joss had some sympathy with Garth's feelings; she also had some plans for Bluey.

Whether Bluey was cooking or not, Joss retrieved her share of the shopping responsibilities, and usually took Angie and Emma with her, to help carry and so form an audience for her growing housewifely accomplishment. They shopped partly in supermarkets and partly in the covered market, where the atmosphere was jollier and produce didn't lie gasping under plastic. When they had finished, Joss treated them to a Coca-Cola or an ice-cream with money taken from the wooden barrel in the kitchen at Richmond Villa. The barrel had quite a lot of money in it these days, because of Hugh's contribution, and could easily, Joss considered, run to cans of Coke or Italian-style cornets.

On their way to receive their rewards one day, Angie said, 'Hey, look at that kid.'

They stopped and looked. Inside a hamburger bar a small boy was pressing his nose and tongue against the plate glass. As his mouth was partly full of whatever he was eating, the sight was repulsive. It was also, to Joss, oddly familiar. She craned forward.

'Hey,' she said, 'it's the twins.'

'What twins?'

'Hugh's twins.' She turned and thrust her carrier bags at the other two. 'Take these home. I gotta see the twins.'

'Bloody hell —' Angie said, in indignation.

'Go on,' Joss said, 'I won't be long. Don't be a pain.'

She darted away from them across the pavement and into a hamburger bar. Sandy sat at a window table, smoking and reading the paper. Beside her Edward drew in a pool of ketchup with a potato chip, and George drooled against the window. Their table was littered with used plates and paper cups and trails of salt and sugar.

'Hi, twins,' Joss said.

Edward turned round and squealed. George peeled himself off the window and flung himself at Joss in ecstasy.

'I'm Joss,' Joss said to Sandy. 'I know the twins.'

'Rather you than me,' Sandy said.

'Joss!' the twins shouted, 'Joss, Joss, hello, Joss, hello, hello!'

Fielding them, Joss slipped into the fixed seat opposite Sandy.

'Are you the nanny?'

'I'm Sandy,' Sandy said. 'D'you want a coffee?'

'I'd like a milk shake,' Joss said, 'banana.'

'Me too,' said the twins at once.

Sandy regarded them. 'Shut up,' she said. She heaved herself to her feet. 'Mrs H. can stand you a milk shake.'

Joss watched her lumber off to the counter.

'Want to know something?' she said to the twins.

They lolled against her, and waited. Their faces were filthy.

'You know where your dad is?'

They looked at once alert and apprehensive. 'Daddy? Our Daddy?'

'He's at my house,' Joss said. 'He's staying with me.'

Their faces filled with wonder. 'In your house?'

'Yeah. Just for a while.'

'In the house where you live? The house with steps on?'

'That house.'

They began to giggle, their eyes as bright as squirrels.

'Is he in your bed?'

'No fear. He's got his own bed.'

'Our daddy? The daddy of us?'

'Your very own daddy.'

Sandy came back with a tall glass of foaming creamy stuff, and three straws. She put the glass down and handed a straw to Joss and one to each of the twins. 'You don't mind them having a suck, do you?'

Edward knelt up on his seat in order to plunge his straw in deeply. Through sucking, he said, 'Daddy's in Joss's house.'

'I know,' Sandy said.

'Then why,' Joss said indignantly, 'didn't you say?'

'I didn't know who you were, did I? I didn't know to say —'

'Will he come back?' George said.

Joss took a deep draught of milk shake. It tasted just as she expected, deliciously, powerfully, synthetic. 'Yes. He'll come back.'

'You better watch it,' Sandy said warningly. 'Who are you to get them all excited?'

'Joss is a big girl,' Edward said.

'I'm fifteen.'

Sandy gave a mild snort. 'Fifteen!'

'Our daddy's called Hugh.'

'I know.'

'Can we see him?'

'Soon,' Joss said, suddenly guarded. They were only babies, poor twins, only babies. 'But I'll tell him I've seen you. I'll tell him we had a milk shake.'

George suddenly dropped his straw and began to scramble off his seat. He clutched Joss's sleeve. 'Coming with you.'

'Me too, Edward coming too,' Edward said desperately.

'God,' Sandy said, 'now look what you've done. Of course you can't go with Joss, you've got to come home to Mummy.'

Joss put her arms round the twins. They were crying now, huge round tears sliding down their smeary pink cheeks.

'I haven't finished,' Joss hissed at Sandy. 'I know what I'm doing. I just haven't finished, that's all!'

Mark Hathaway was marking an indifferent set

of essays on Sylvia Plath's poetry. Mark adored Sylvia Plath and prided himself on teaching her illuminatingly, so that when a class failed to respond to her, as this one clearly had, he was inclined to tell himself that he was wasted teaching second- and third-rate minds in a provincial tutorial college. He thought he would mark just over half the essays, and then reward himself with a glass of wine before he struggled on to the end. If he finished before ten-thirty, he would go round to Swan Street to see Kate.

Things with Kate were going much more satisfactorily since Joss had gone. Immediately after Joss's departure, Kate had been very thorny and inapproachable, but without Joss there to rival him Mark had been content to wait, with an air of sympathetic understanding, until Kate felt better. After five or six days, Kate had come round to West Street, and, without actually saying sorry (which Mark would have preferred) was very sweet and pliant and affectionate. The next night, he had waited for her after work, and gone home with her and they had met Mr Winthrop in the hall.

'Where are you going?' he'd said to Mark.

Mark opened his mouth to answer, but Kate was too quick for him. 'To my room, which, as I pay rent for it, is my *private* room.'

That had been a very successful night; one of the most successful they had ever had, and Kate had not even mentioned Joss. It had left Mark with the feeling that their relationship was entering a new phase, a phase in which Kate would be as interested in him, for the first time, as he had been in her, for a long time. This feeling made him very much less resentful that last week's magnificent teaching of Sylvia Plath's poetry had fallen on stony ground.

At the end of the ninth essay he wrote, 'I wonder if you have deliberately misunderstood the imagery?' It seemed to him an elegant rebuke. He put his red pen down, and ran his hands through his hair and tipped his chair back so that he could stretch luxuriously. Someone knocked at his door, a small knock, not familiar. Without moving, he shouted, 'Come!' and it was Kate.

Mark sprang up. 'Kate!'

She looked bothered. She said, 'I'm sorry just to come round like this.'

'Why be sorry?' he said. 'I'm thrilled.' He took her in his arms and kissed her and then he slid her cotton jacket off down her back and arms and led her to the sofa.

'I've been thrown out,' Kate said.

'What!'

'Old Winthrop's thrown me out. He said I had the morals of an alley cat and I made a noise and he could get much more money for the room.'

'Only the last is true —'

'He wants me out by Friday.' Kate bit her lip. 'It was a horrible interview.'

Mark took her hands. 'Poor Kate. Poor Katie. I'm so sorry.'

She looked at him. His eyes were shining.

'You don't *look* very sorry.'

'Well, no —'

She tried to pull her hands away but he held them, and he was laughing.

'What's so funny? Me being abused by a disgusting old man and having nowhere to live?'

'You have got somewhere to live.'

Kate's mind flew madly, instinctively, to Jericho. 'You can't mean —'

'I mean here.'

'Here!' Kate screeched. She pulled her hands away and whirled round on the sofa, as if looking at Mark's flat for the first time. 'But this is yours, I mean, you made this for you!'

'I expect I'd have made it for you if I'd known you then.'

'Oh Mark,' Kate said, turning huge eyes upon him. 'That's so kind, but —'

'But what?'

'Doesn't — doesn't it make us a bit permanent?'

'Sure does,' Mark said grinning. He leapt up. 'I'm going to find you a drink.'

'I don't need a drink —'

'Yes, you do. To celebrate with. Look, there's heaps of space. I'll buy another of those louvred cupboards for your clothes, and fit it in over there, and as you know I already own a nice double bed and at least two spoons and two mugs and two glasses.' He swooped over the back of the sofa and seized her. 'Katie,' he said, his face alight, 'Kate, come live with me and be my love *all the time.*'

Kate said faintly, 'What about independence?'

'There's no point to independence when you've found the right dependence. I love you, Kate, as if you didn't know.'

He sprang away again and came back with two glasses of pale wine. Kate took hers.

'Smile at me.'

She attempted to.

'Hopeless,' he said. 'Aren't you happy? Aren't you relieved?'

She took a swallow of wine. She thought: Kate, you're being ridiculous, what's the matter with you? It's a lovely flat, you've had fun together, you don't want to live on your own after Joss and you can always leave if it doesn't work. Besides, what else, you stupid, muddle-headed cow, do you intend to do? I hate it without Joss, she cried out silently, I hate it, I hate it, but what else am I to do? How do I keep her if I don't let her go, even if that sounds like advice from the problem page of the tackiest sort of women's magazine? I've got to live, I've got to have some warmth, some kind of contact, someone to matter to, however little or strangely. She took another gulp and looked up at Mark.

'You're lovely to offer,' she said, 'I'd love to. I'd love to come here. And I'll try terribly hard to be tidy.'

'It's Julia,' Julia said down the telephone. 'I wonder if I could possibly speak to Joss?'

James said, 'I'm so sorry but she's gone round

315

to see a friend —'

'The thing is, she saw the twins today, in Oxford. They weren't supposed to be in Oxford at all, as a matter of fact, but that's not really why I rang. I just wanted to know what she thought of them, if they'd said anything to her about anything. They're being awfully difficult just now, somewhat naturally, and I need all the help I can get to try and understand how to —'

'Julia,' James said gently, interrupting, 'I'll get her to ring you when she comes in, shall I? Later.'

Julia's voice changed. 'I'm afraid I won't be here later. Could I ring again tomorrow? The thing is, you see, that I'm going out to dinner.'

Hugh lay on his bed, smoking. The window was open to the street and, apart from the noise of an occasional passing car, there drifted in the sounds of summer-evening living, people talking and the snip of shears, and music and the hiss of a garden sprinkler. James had suggested to Hugh that they go out for a drink, but Hugh had, to his own surprise, not felt like doing that. He had felt, instead, a desire to be by himself, and to take stock of things.

He also felt, which disconcerted him profoundly, rather chastened. If he was honest, he had never much liked Joss Bain, who seemed to him an archetypal adolescent unredeemed by any promise of improvement. When she had reappeared in their clubbish male household at Richmond Villa he had felt at first both exasperated and intolerant about her presence, particularly as James and Leonard appeared, inexplicably, so pleased to see her. But as the days wore on, despite her disordered habits in the bathroom and her ghastly music and her careless lack of feminine grace, Hugh had to admit that there was a considerable personality underneath the oversized jackets and undersized trousers and, what was more, a personality that was — bizarre, this, no other word for it — rather *upright*.

He stubbed his cigarette out and told himself that he couldn't have another one just yet. When was yet? Ten minutes? Twenty? Shut up, Hugh said to himself, shut up. He put his hands behind his head to imprison them, and crossed his ankles.

'Grown-ups can do whatever stupid thing they like to each other,' Joss had said to him after supper, 'but they shouldn't do it to kids, not little helpless kids.'

She hadn't been at all afraid of him, not in the least. She had simply started on him, while they were washing up.

'They kept saying "Our Daddy? Our Daddy?" You should've heard them, they don't understand. How can they? You ought to put them first till they can look after themselves. It's OK for me' — slight swagger here, Hugh observed — 'I'm old enough to do what I want, but the twins are only little kids. And that nanny. She's OK but it's just a job for her, she doesn't really care what they're thinking. That saucepan isn't half clean, look —'

Hugh had attempted a defence. He had tried to swing the authority of his age and experience, and to point out how little Joss, inevitably, knew of the delicate, dangerous, damaging affairs of the human heart. He thought the discussion would be easier for him if Joss lost her temper. But all she did was ignore him.

'I'm not interested in you. Or Julia. That's your affair. All I care about is the twins. So'd you if you'd seen them.'

It was, Hugh told himself, the tunnel-vision zeal of the true campaigner; don't admit any secondary evidence, however relevant, in case it confuses the prime issue. Yet even thinking that wasn't much consolation, particularly as it was he, Hugh, who in the end lost his temper, flung the washing-up brush on the floor and shouted idiotically, 'So what do you suggest, you sanctimonious little prig?'

She said, 'You ought to go home,' and marched out of the kitchen.

James had come in then and attempted, in a maddening, Jamesish way, to say anodyne soothing things that both calmed Hugh and exonerated Joss from interference and rudeness. But even Hugh could see his heart wasn't in it, that, if hung upside-down out of a high window with the threat of being dropped if he didn't confess honestly, James would have admitted he thought Joss was right. He dawdled about the kitchen for a while, putting things away, or at least going through the motions, and then suggested a drink, but the suggestion was plainly made in the spirit of offering a child with a hurt knee a lollipop.

'No thanks,' Hugh said, and went up to his room.

It was still quite light because supper at Richmond Villa was always early. Hugh hated eating early and nobody could explain to him why they did eat early here. James had said perhaps it was a hangover from when Joss was small. Or perhaps it was better for Leonard's ancient digestion. He hadn't sounded as if it were at all important, but it was important to Hugh because it seemed to him deeply uncivilised not to treat eating, especially at night, as some kind of celebration. Julia always . . . Hugh unfolded his hands and reached for his cigarettes. If he thought about it, Richmond Villa wasn't really very civilised anyway, there was no coherence to life in it, no elegance, and even its chief attraction, James, wasn't really concentrating, especially now Joss was back and that pretty little American was in and out doing her domestic science diploma bit. Oh hell, Hugh thought, thinking suddenly of the twins and rolling up into a ball on his side in agony, oh hell, oh bloody, fucking *hell*.

The door opened softly.

'Are you all right?' James said.

'Of course not,' Hugh said. He reached out and crushed his cigarette stub into an ashtray.

James came into the room and stood looking down at him. He remembered doing the same thing once, over forty years ago, in Cambridge, and finding that there wasn't just the hump of Hugh in the bed, but the hump of a girl too, a girl wearing nothing except, James recalled with sudden vividness, a green ribbon round her neck.

'Julia just rang,' James said.

Hugh flipped over and half-sat up. 'Julia? Why didn't you call me?'

'She didn't want to speak to you.'

'Christ —'

'She wanted to speak to Joss. The twins told her they had seen Joss. She wanted Joss's reaction.'

Hugh began to scramble off the bed. 'I'll ring her back —'

'No,' James said, 'you can't.'

'Can't?'

'She's gone out to dinner.'

Hugh stood up. 'Gone out to dinner? Bloody *dinner*? Who with?'

'I don't know.'

'A man?'

'She didn't say.'

They looked at each other.

'Do you,' James said, 'want that drink after all?'

A customer had been rude to Kate. He wasn't drunk and he wasn't, Benjie said, a sadist, he was just someone who'd had a bloody awful day and was simply on the look-out for an innocent person to vent his fury on. Kate had listened to him, white-faced, and then had collected up the rejected dishes of food in silence and returned with them to the kitchen. Then she and Benjie listened while the customer turned on Christine and refused to pay for what he had ordered, and slammed out of the restaurant.

Christine came down the spiral staircase.

'What did you say to him?'

'Nothing.'

'He said you were offensive.'

'I said nothing at all!'

'He said you accused him of muddling his order and being in the wrong about what he had ordered.'

Kate cried, 'I never spoke to him after his order! I just stood and took it while he called me incompetent and stupid and not fit to hold down a job!'

Christine, who could never bear the smallest incident that might in any way threaten her business which represented, as she often said, her identity as much as her livelihood, said disagreeably, 'Well, perhaps he had a point.'

'Oy,' Benjie said, 'steady on. Cool it.'

'I brought him what he ordered!' Kate shouted. 'You can look at my order pad!'

Christine glanced upward. *'Please* do not shout.'

'Leave it,' Benjie said. He glanced at Kate. 'Why don't you? There's always some awkward buggers, aren't there? We're just lucky we don't get more.'

'Please mind your own business,' Christine said.

Benjie made a face at Kate, and ambled back

to his stoves. Christine stood aside and made a gesture towards the staircase. 'I believe you have work to do.'

'I don't have to do it,' Kate said angrily, 'for people who won't stand up for me when I'm blameless.'

'Too true,' Christine said. 'Hurry up.'

Kate climbed the staircase in a turmoil. The most luxurious thing of all, at that moment, would have been to have walked out, through the crowded tables, and into the street, and not come back. But even in the midst of the blaze of anger at Christine's injustice, Kate felt a small, cold core of misgiving. She was in the right, certainly, but oh — oh, she was still so vulnerable. She picked up her order pad, and moved to the window table where a young couple had just settled themselves, jacket and bag all over the floor just as Christine hated and not hung up on the hatstand.

'I wonder if you'd mind if I hung up your things for you?'

The young man looked up from the menu at her. He had sandy hair and small round spectacles and he looked at her as if she were not a person at all, but just a waitress.

'Suit yourself,' he said, and shrugged.

Later Benjie said he would walk Kate home.

'I'm OK, really, I'm fine now.'

'I'll come all the same,' Benjie said. He stopped on the pavement to light a cigarette. 'You don't want to pay any attention to her, you know. Susie never did.'

'I'm not as tough as Susie.'

Benjie took her arm. 'She always gets windy if she thinks she's lost a customer. She thinks it'll spread like wildfire round Oxford, that she runs a lousy restaurant. You don't want to bother, Katie. It's only a job.'

'But with Joss gone, it's a bit more than that —'

'You watch it,' Benjie said, steering her past a swerving clump of cyclists. 'You don't want to think like that. You get in people's power if you think like that. Me, I do a job to pay for my fun. No job, no fun. Simple as that.'

'I was having fun —'

'Sure you were!'

'I'm moving in with Mark,' Kate said.

'You never!'

'He's got a lovely flat, we get on really well —'

Benjie dropped her arm. 'You want to be careful, you want to be really sure.'

'What do you mean?'

'Well, you lived with James, didn't you, and it didn't work out and you really knew James, steady sort of bloke, but you've only known this Mark guy a few months. I think,' Benjie said, taking her hand this time, 'I think you gotta hang free for a bit. That's what I think.'

The room in Swan Street felt as if it knew she was leaving it, so it had withdrawn itself, ready for Mr Akwa. In any case, since Joss's departure it hadn't felt the same, it had felt full of disappointment rather than promise and optimism. The last few days, while Kate had imagined, with a nervous excitement, living with Mark Hathaway, she had felt a certain indifference to Swan Street, almost a callousness. This evening, the room simply felt fragile, as if it represented no security at all beyond the purely physical shelter to be found in any old hotel room.

Kate sat down and took her shoes off. After a while, she got up again and turned the light off, and sat there in the not-quite darkness of the light coming in from the street outside. Benjie was of course right. You had to see elements of your life — your job, your relationships, your home — quite straight, for what they really were, not for what you wished them to be. She was used to Pasta Please and she liked Benjie, and she had liked Christine, but that was all. She had adored Swan Street, but it had died on her. As for Mark — Kate closed her eyes. Was she trying to make Mark into something that he wasn't? A Joss-Mark, even a James-Mark? Was she, if she was scrupulously, beautifully, honest, going to live with Mark because he had decided she would and she was absolutely sick of making decisions?

That was what freedom came down to, in the end, wasn't it? Making decisions, one after the other, huge ones and trivial ones, day in, day out; what to eat and wear and do, who to love, where to go and where to live, whether to emigrate or to buy red shoelaces instead of brown. And if you gave up on deciding because you simply couldn't go on, for misery and fatigue, and you said to another person — as she was saying to Mark — OK, you take over, you decide for me now, then you were surrendering your self-control, a measure (how big a measure?) of your independence. That's what I'm doing, Kate thought, that's exactly what I'm doing. Because I've lost over Joss, I'm letting myself just give in. I don't have to live here or work there, in fact, I mustn't. If I start giving in, I won't stop because I'll think it's all a punishment for failing over Joss, that I'm not fit to have her, that I shouldn't have had her, that I should be grateful for anyone who'll have *me*. She opened her eyes. The room swam a little and then steadied itself into familiarity, armchair and table, upright chairs, lamp, cushions, chair print. She felt about for her shoes. It was after eleven; late, but not too late.

'What are you saying?' Mark said. He had showered just before Kate came in, and he was wearing a dark-blue cotton dressing gown, cut like a short kimono, and his hair was wet.

'I'm saying that I am very sorry to change my mind, and to disappoint you, but I've decided that I can't come and live here, after all.'

'Why?'

'Because it would be wrong and it would ruin our relationship.'

'Wrong?'

'Yes.'

He moved towards her. 'What sort of wrong?'

This was taking more courage than she had reckoned on. Kate said, 'Because I don't want to make that kind of commitment. I'm not ready for it, and perhaps I never will be. I think I agreed to come because I was reacting from having lost Joss. I ought to tell you the truth. It's only fair.'

'Fair?' he said.

'Stop it —'

'Stop what?'

'Asking these little questions like someone in an American police movie. I'm really sorry, Mark, but I'm also very sure. I shouldn't have agreed to come and I —'

'Shut up.'

'Mark, I'm trying to explain —'

He said, 'You aren't coming because you don't love me,' and then he hit her.

She felt the blow thud into the side of her face. She was perfectly astonished. She opened her eyes and mouth in protest, but he hit her again, on the other cheek, and then he seized her by the shoulders, and ran her backwards, stumbling, against the blank wall by the bed, and began to bash her head against it rhythmically, bang, bang, bang. Her eyes flew open and shut and her breath came in gasps, and she could see his face quite clearly but miles away, dark and set. Then all of a sudden, he wrenched her sideways and flung her across the bed, the bed where they had often made love, and walked slowly across

326

to the opposite wall and leant against it, his back to her, and simply waited in silence for her to gather herself up, and to go.

Chapter Sixteen

'Where is she?' Helen said. She stood in the kitchen at Mansfield House, still holding her car keys and her bag.

'We put her up in Pat's room. With Pat and the baby. It was all the space there was.'

'When did she come?' Helen said, slowly letting the bag and keys fall on to the table among the cereal packets and toys.

Midnight, they said, or a bit after. She'd woken them up, Linda and Ruth said, they'd heard her from their room above the front door and they'd thought it was Pat's boyfriend again who'd been a menace all week. Ruth had looked out of the window and seen a woman waving, a woman she didn't know, having only been at Mansfield House a month, but Linda knew her.

'It's Kate!' Linda said in amazement. 'It's Kate!' and flew downstairs to undo all the bolts and chains and let her in. They had taken her into the kitchen and made her tea, and Ruth had found some arnica ointment and had smeared it on Kate's face. She didn't say much, she just shook. All she said that made complete sense was that she had a headache, so, when Pat came down to make up the baby's feed, they said could Kate

328

doss down on the extra mattress in Pat's room.

' 'Course,' Pat said, yawning. She peered at Kate. 'I see I don't need to ask what happened to *you.*'

They had given her aspirin, and a hot water bottle because of the shaking, and had put her to bed on the floor of Pat's tiny room while Pat fed her baby and read one of the holiday brochures which were her passion. Then Pat had gone to sleep and Kate had lain awake listening to her breathing, and the baby snuffling, and stared out into nothing for hours and hours and hours. When she fell asleep at last, it was into that racked and unnatural slumber to which even the most pro-tracted wakefulness is preferable, haunted by men-ace, through which the wails of Pat's baby wanting its first feed of the new day came thin and an-guished, like the screams of a cat being tortured.

'Who's seen her today?' Helen said sharply. She sounded as if she was annoyed, as if someone in the room was to blame.

Pat was sorting out an immense plastic basket of communal washing. She didn't look up when she spoke. 'I left her asleep. I put Jason in Linda's room for the morning. She was dead to the world an hour ago.'

'I'll go up,' Helen said. 'I'll go up and see her. Someone make a mug of tea I can take up to her, would you?'

Kate lay on her less-damaged side with her eyes shut. Her head throbbed and banged and the skin

329

of her face felt raw and several sizes too small. Helen bent over her.

'Kate?'

Kate turned, very slowly, wincing.

'Ow.'

'Oh Katie,' Helen said, kneeling by her on the floor. 'Oh poor love. You poor love. What happened?'

Kate shut her eyes again. 'Mark,' she said.

'I've brought you some tea. Here, I'll help you sit up. Did he only get your face?'

'Only my face!'

Helen slid an arm under Kate. 'Remember Linda? Two cracked ribs and a broken wrist as well as a face like yours.'

It was terribly difficult to sit up. Kate's head felt as if it were a huge, wobbling, painful balloon only lightly attached to the rest of her.

'Was it sex?' Helen said. 'Was he one of them?'

Kate said, 'No. I changed my mind about living with him, moving in with him. That's all.'

'Living with him!'

'I got Joss back. But she wouldn't stay. So I thought I'd live with Mark.'

Helen groaned. She settled herself beside Kate and handed her the mug of tea. Kate took it and held it tightly, to stop her trembling from spilling it.

'Don't lecture me,' Kate said. She tried to look at Helen, but her neck was stiff and wouldn't turn, and the eye nearest to Helen was so swollen she couldn't see out of it properly. 'Remember telling me how lucky we were because we'd never been hit? Well, now it's only you that's still lucky.'

'We'll get you down to the surgery later. Get John Pringle to have a look at you.'

'It's only bruises.'

'Kate!'

Kate's voice rose. 'It isn't the bruises that hurt! At least, they do, of course, but they don't hurt like what's going on in my mind hurts!'

'You must stay here, of course.'

'I'm supposed to be at work —'

'You can't work like this, Kate.'

Kate remembered. 'I had a row with Christine last night —'

Helen stirred to a kneeling position. 'I'll sort out Christine. You leave Christine to me. D'you want someone to collect your stuff? I'm sure Linda would.'

'I don't know, I don't know what I want —'

'Would you like to come back to my flat?'

Kate tried to smile. 'No. No thanks. I'm better here with the others.'

Helen got clumsily to her feet. Even through her own distress, Kate felt that Helen's author- itativeness was not exactly in top gear this morn- ing.

'We'll organise your stuff, Kate. And I'll go round to Jericho and tell Joss.'

'Joss!' Kate almost screamed.

'Of course,' Helen said, 'of course she's got to know.'

Kate's face puckered like a child's. 'Oh my God,' Kate wept. 'Oh, what have I done now, what stupid bloody mess have I made now?'

Leonard had cut himself, shaving. He often did this now, so James had offered to shave him which had made Leonard furious. He had agreed, with torrents of foul language, to allow a nurse from the health centre to come in twice a week to bathe him, but the suggestion that he could no longer shave himself was an insult not to be borne. He was so angry and upset that James cursed himself for even having mentioned it.

'I'm sorry. Really I am. I should have kept my trap shut.'

'Bloody right you should! Bloody right! I may not be as steady on my pins as I once was, but I'm not a drooling imbecile!'

The result was that Leonard remembered James's tactlessness every morning when he started to shave, and his unsteady hands shook further with rage. His thin old skin tore like tissue paper, and by the time he had finished — a very irregular business anyway — the basin in his bedroom was spattered with blood, and his furious face was tufted with blobs of cotton wool.

'You look like snowman,' Mrs Cheng said. It wasn't a joke, because she never made any.

'Go to hell!'

'You want use electric razor —'

'When I want advice, you slit-eyed barbarian, I'll ask for it!'

Joss simply put a bottle of disinfectant by Leonard's basin.

'What the hell's that for? Am I supposed to drink it?'

'I don't care what you do with it,' Joss said, 'but if you don't put it on your face you'll go rotten like a bad tomato and stink.'

'Tomato,' Leonard muttered, dabbing disinfectant unevenly over his cheeks and chin. It stung and he flinched. 'Bloody cheek. Tomato!' He put the cotton wool down and surveyed his face. 'What a sight, what a miserable, mucky old sight. They ought to put you down,' he told himself 'that's what they ought to do. Kindest thing. That or send round one of old BB's friends with a plastic bag and a bottle of sodding happy pills.' He dressed slowly, stopping frequently for little rests. Mrs Cheng had tried to help him with his socks once, but he had lashed out at her with his long, yellow-white bony foot, and she hadn't tried again. He put on his old man's vest and pants, a wool shirt ('What d'you mean, summer? What's summer got to do with being frozen to the marrow?'), his capacious corduroy trousers, his yellow knitted waistcoat and a cardigan and finally, with much moaning and heavy breathing, thick green socks and heavy brogues.

He got up from the side of the bed with difficulty and looked at himself in the mirror. His bare throat troubled him. 'Look like an old turkey, a diseased old turkey.' He found a spotted cotton handkerchief and knotted it clumsily in the neck of his shirt. 'Knock 'em in the aisles, old boy,' he said to the mirror, and bared his teeth at himself in disgust.

He limped out on to the landing. From the kitchen came the clashes and bangs of Mrs Cheng's weekly attack on it. Otherwise the house was silent, James having gone up to London for the day (alone, Leonard wondered?), Hugh having disappeared on some mysterious errand and Joss being at school doing her French exam, poor little bleeder. They had left him a tongue sandwich for lunch and, at his request, one of those passable little trifles in a plastic pot. When he had eaten them, Beatrice was going to come round and play bezique with him. Nobody under seventy knew how to play bezique any more.

He went down the stairs very carefully and slowly, planting the rubber bung at the end of his stick on each step before he lowered himself on to it. He thought he might do a little watering, in the garden, of the pots of petunias that Beatrice had planted so that, when she watered them this afternoon, he could wait until she had finished and then say, 'I did those this morning, you blind old bat.' He reached the hall floor at last, and began to chuckle.

The doorbell rang. At once, the kitchen door flew open and Mrs Cheng sped out, drying her hands on the overall she always wore for working.

'I'll go,' Leonard said.

She hesitated. 'You mind your manners —'

The bell rang again. 'Impudence!' Leonard said and creaked towards it.

On the step outside stood a large handsome woman dressed, to Leonard's mind, like a member of the Anvil Chorus, all scarves and shawls and jewellery. She said, 'Are you Mr Mallow?'

'Yes,' he said, 'and I don't want it, whatever you're selling.'

She had a formidable air. She said, 'My name is Helen Ferguson. I'm a friend of Kate's. May I come in?'

'Why?' said Leonard.

'Because I've something to tell you about Kate that I'd prefer not to tell the whole street.'

Leonard felt an unwilling surge of admiration. He stood back to allow Helen in — all of her, he noticed with satisfaction, just the kind of amplitude he had always gone for, if only she hadn't been dressed apparently in bedclothes — and then led her into James's study. He pointed to a chair with his stick.

'Sit down.'

She sat, in a gust of some exotic scent Leonard couldn't identify, and looked at him composedly.

'Mr Mallow, I run Mansfield House, the refuge where Kate used to help out, if you remember.'

'And?' Leonard said.

Mrs Cheng made Leonard sit down at the kitchen table. He was mauve-white and his face was working.

'Hit her about the face,' Leonard muttered,

'banged her head on the wall! Kate!'

'I get you brandy,' Mrs Cheng said. She went to the cupboard where the drinks were kept. She felt none too steady herself and the sight of Leonard scared her. She took the brandy bottle over to the table and poured a thumping measure into a glass. Then she sat down and gazed at Leonard.

'No bone broken?'

'No,' he said, 'but what can she be feeling?'

He reached out and took one of Mrs Cheng's hands. 'I've got to tell James now. And Joss. Joss!'

'Miss Bachelor help you.'

'Yes,' he said, 'yes.' He took a gulp of brandy and then brushed his eyes with the back of his hand. 'It's a wicked world,' he whispered, 'it's a wicked, *wicked* world.'

Mrs Cheng covered his hand with her other one, and pressed it hard.

'You don' need to tell me,' she said.

Julia left it until nine o'clock before she telephoned Richmond Villa. With luck, by nine o'clock Hugh would be watching the television news and Joss would answer the telephone. Joss did. She answered it in a tiny, far-off voice which Julia assumed to be Joss's notion of sounding laid-back.

'Joss? It's Julia. I'm so pleased to catch you because I heard you'd seen the twins in Oxford and I just wanted to ask how you thought they were.'

336

There was a pause and then Joss said, 'Oh fine,' in a dull, empty voice.

'Really? Oh, I'd be so pleased to hear that because Sandy said they got terribly upset and cried all the way home.'

'Did they?'

'Yes. She said they had started to get upset while you were all together, but she wasn't very helpful about what you'd all been saying that might have upset them, so I wondered if you could tell me a bit more?'

'No,' Joss said. 'Sorry,' and burst into tears.

'Joss, what is it? What've I said, what's the matter?'

'It's Mum,' Joss said. Her voice shook. 'She's got beaten up. Mark hit her. I went to see her and she looks awful, *awful*, and she won't say much and James isn't back until later —'

'Oh Joss,' Julia said in horror. 'Oh poor you, poor Kate. Are you alone? Where is she?'

'She's at Mansfield House,' Joss said. 'She says she's OK. Hugh's here. Uncle Leonard's gone to bed, we had to get the doctor —'

'I'll come,' Julia said. 'Sandy's here and you shouldn't be alone.'

'I'm not alone, I'm OK —' She broke off. She was not OK. She felt desperate, guilty as well as shocked because she hadn't wanted to stay with Kate, even though Helen had suggested it, she'd wanted to get home, away from all those little kids and the women and the smoking and Kate's terrible, unrecognisable face and hopeless eyes. 'I'll

337

get Hugh,' Joss said frantically to Julia. 'He's right here, I'll get him —'

'Julia?' Hugh said, a few seconds later. He sounded quite normal, neither defensive nor melodramatic.

'Oh Hugh,' Julia cried, 'what's happened, what's going on?'

'Quite terrible. Kate has been beaten up by a lover and thrown out of her digs and is at that refuge she used to help at, the one you filmed. Joss is like a scalded cat, Leonard's had to be put to bed because his blood pressure went through the roof and he began to hyper-ventilate. Mrs Cheng is still furiously hoovering because she says she has to, to keep her mind off things, Miss Bachelor has finally gone home after three-quarters of a bottle of sherry and no one knows when James will be back. Julia,' Hugh said, 'I am not unsympathetic to any of this at bottom, but this particular evening isn't one I'm in a hurry to repeat.'

'Aha,' Julia said.

'What d'you mean, "aha"?'

'I mean, the biter bit,' Julia said. 'You expect the whole world to make your problems a priority but are thoroughly put out when anyone else tries to do the same.'

'Julia!'

'Well, it's true, isn't it?'

There was a pause. Hugh found himself exceedingly anxious both to keep the conversation going and to avoid a row. The crisp Julia at the

338

far end of the telephone line was disconcerting.

'I was wondering —'

'Yes?'

'If — if I could come and see you and the boys. On Saturday, perhaps?'

'Sorry,' Julia said, 'I'm editing all Saturday.'

'Sunday?'

'Sunday would be fine.'

'For lunch?'

'After lunch. About three.'

'Who's coming to lunch, then?'

'Nobody is. I just don't want to have to cook Sunday lunch when I've been working until late the day before.'

Hugh longed to ask if she had enjoyed going out to dinner, and even more, to know who she had been out to dinner with. He said instead, 'Julia, I've been doing a lot of thinking —'

'Not now,' Julia said briskly, 'now is poor Kate. And Joss. I offered to come over. Shall I?'

Hugh could not bear her not to come over for *him*. 'We're OK,' he said with difficulty, 'we'll manage. Nobody can do anything for Kate for a couple of days, and Joss'll be all right when James is back.'

'I'll ring James in the morning,' Julia said. 'Will you tell him? And I'll see you on Sunday.'

'Yes,' Hugh said. From nine miles away, Julia could visualise his face as he said it. She strove for a sensible tone in her own voice.

'Good-night, then. And love to everybody. And sympathy.'

339

She put the receiver down and went to sit at the kitchen table, her head buried in her arms. She tried to picture Kate, and the scene in which Kate had been beaten up; she felt she owed it to Kate to try and sympathise as vividly as she could with what had happened. Poor Kate, poor little defenceless, damaged Kate, whom she used to feel so wary of because of what seemed to Julia too many deliberate and purely fashionable un-orthodoxies in the way Kate lived. I know different now, Julia thought, I know so much I never knew before even if I hate how I've had to learn it. She had said this to Rob Shiner over dinner and he had replied that there was a William Blake quo-tation to that effect, a quotation about wisdom being bought in a desolate market where none came to buy, and Julia had thought that William Blake had got it precisely.

It had been a pleasant dinner with Rob Shiner, but no more than that. Away from his professional setting he seemed cosier and duller, as if he couldn't bring the adrenalin that fuelled his work-ing days to charge time off as well. He had taken her to a very glamorous restaurant and given her delicious things to eat and drink, and been kind and attentive and flattering and, in the end, boring. She didn't want to laugh once, all evening and when, inevitably, he tried to kiss her good-night with some fervour, she found she certainly didn't want to laugh; she wanted to groan. She had gone up to bed leaden with food and drink and gloom and had lain awake for a long time thinking about

William Blake, and that there were few things she could think of at that moment that were as desolate as plain old disappointment. Nobody, she thought, shoving her pillow about in the hope of making it into a soporific shape, nobody ever gives disappointment the credit of being a prime force behind wayward behaviour. But it is. Disappointment is what's the matter with most of us and Kate at the moment must be absolutely consumed by it.

She lifted her head out of her arms now and looked across the kitchen. On the cork board hanging behind the door she had pinned the boys' latest paintings from nursery school, all ships and aeroplanes and trucks. 'They won't paint people just now,' Frederica had said, her eyes swivelling significantly. 'You do understand, don't you? I'm not going to insist, not just yet. You do see?'

I see more than I did, Julia thought, and much more, I begin to think, than people like Frederica. I shall get the twins to do a painting for Hugh, for Sunday. They can do a painting of *me*.

She got up and went back to the telephone and dialled. The other end it rang and rang and rang before it was finally answered.

'Mansfield House,' a tired voice said.

'Is that Linda?'

'No,' the voice said, even more tiredly, 'it's Janice.'

'My name is Julia Hunter,' Julia said. 'I rang up to ask about Kate Bain.'

Janice sighed. 'Hang on. I'll see if I can find her.'

'No,' Julia said, 'don't do that. Just say Julia rang to send love. Just give her my love.'

James said he would stay with Joss until she was asleep. Her room had, by her choice, virtually no orthodox furniture in it beyond her bed and a chest of drawers, so he did his best to make himself comfortable on her bean bag. This wasn't easy. The contents of the bag seemed to him both intractable and elusive, either bunching themselves into rock-hard mounds or running away altogether leaving him sitting virtually on the hard floor. The annoyance of this struck him as a most apt metaphor for the tribulation of his feelings. At least, he thought, looking across at Joss's carefully still body in bed, he knew what he felt about her.

As for everything else, nothing, not even things that looked straightforward, had turned out to be other than complex and delicate. He had had a charming day — at least, nine tenths of it had been charming — going to the Tate Gallery with Bluey Acheson who actually *liked* painting of the last forty years and could explain why, and then having lunch at a restaurant she had read about and then going (his suggestion) to the Sir John Soane Museum where she had been enraptured by the classical dog kennel. That had all been as easy as pie, sunny, friendly, happy, with just the right amount of flirtatiousness to make the expedition pleasingly different from any that one might undertake with an aunt or a godfather or anyone, indeed, who was not charged with the possibility of emotional or sexual adventure. It was only in the train going home that James had looked up from the evening paper and had caught on Bluey's face an unmistakable look, a mute confession she wanted him to save her the trouble of having to make out loud. As the carriage was absolutely full, James had simply smiled at her and returned to his paper with mingled feelings of delight and despair. Hurray and damnation. Bluey had watched him and thought: He must, he must; everybody else around me is living their lives, so why shouldn't I live mine the way I'm meant to, the loving way?

At Oxford Station, she took his arm. He said they were going to find a taxi.

She didn't want the day to end. 'Can't we walk?'

No, he said, they couldn't. The taxi ride was a little tense, and at Observatory Street Bluey said in a small sad voice that she supposed he wouldn't stay for supper. He smiled at her. He kissed her cheek, standing there on the pavement in full view of all Observatory Street, and said he wouldn't tonight, but that didn't mean he wouldn't like to, very much, some other night. You coward, he told himself. 'I've enjoyed myself today,' he told Bluey, 'more than I have for ages and ages and ages.'

She had smiled gallantly then, and gone into the house, and James had set off for home only to be overtaken after fifty yards by Garth, racing after him and saying sir, sir, may I have a word with you, sir? Of course, James had said, but then Garth could get no further and James, seeing the trouble, spoke to him warmly of his father's academic distinction and then took him to an Indian restaurant on Walton Street for lamb korma and a discussion on the possible futures of the world, the planet and Garth Acheson.

He hadn't got in until after ten o'clock. Half an hour after he got in, he went out again, and drove to Mansfield House. He doubted that he had ever felt more physically or psychologically shocked by anything in his life as he was by — not so much the sight of Kate, as by the realisation of how she had come to look like that. He was only there for ten minutes, in the kitchen, sitting at the table with a mug of coffee. Kate sat opposite him. She had tried to smile. She had said she was very tired and very wound up all at once, and that the doctor had given her three sleeping pills for the next three nights because of this. Nothing was broken; she was just bruised.

James had been close to tears. He had felt full of fury, a really savage red rage at Mark Hathaway, and full, at the same time, of a longing to help and a sensation of helplessness.

He said gently, unsteadily, 'Will you come to Richmond Villa? So that we can look after you? To reassure Joss?'

Kate shook her head, and winced. 'Thank you. Thank you, James, but I won't do that. I'll stay here, I'm fine here.'

'Please,' he said.

'No,' Kate said. 'I'm all right, really. They know what to do here, with people like me. They know me.'

Lying twisted on Joss's bean bag, James felt again his urgency that Kate should come back to Richmond Villa. Of course she must! If he, James, hadn't let her go in the first place, hadn't indulged her in a restless moment, she would never have been exposed to this kind of arbitrary brutality. He must make up for that, he owed Kate recompense for that, of course he did. But — did he? Why did he feel guilty? Was he guilty? Had he looked at her across the kitchen table at Mansfield House and simply been unable to bear the spectacle, the bare evidence of her suffering? Did he feel love then — or pity? What was it that made him wish that Kate, rather than Hugh, was now sleeping in the other front bedroom, across the landing from poor old Leonard, wheezing from shock in his flannelette pyjamas? Did he really, truly, love Kate still, or was he now simply consumed with guilt and pity? Oh pity, thought James, oh terrible, sirenish pity. I mustn't insult Kate with pity.

He listened. Joss's elaborately quiet breathing had relaxed into natural little snorts and snores. With difficulty, James turned himself on to all fours, and then got slowly to his feet. He stood looking down at her, at her ruffled crest of hair, her poor multistudded right ear, her still-childish hand clutching the duvet. At least I know what I feel for you, James thought, I feel rather what I feel for Leonard, only stronger. I feel great love, dear Joss, and frequently an equally great exasperation.

At five in the morning Cat took advantage of Miss Bachelor's open window, and brought her a shrew. It was not quite dead, so he played with it a bit, for her benefit, on the rug by her bed, and woke her up.

Beatrice put on the light, and peered.

'Intolerable Cat!'

Cat looked offended. The shrew, now dead from fright or prudently faking it, lay on its side, snout and eyes closed. Beatrice got out of bed and went downstairs for a dustpan and brush. When she returned, Cat had vanished, leaving his trophy behind, in reproach. Beatrice swept it up, and dropped it out of her bedroom window, on to the concrete path below where, with any luck, Grace would fail to see it in the morning before she trod on it.

Beatrice had a headache. She knew pefectly well why she had a headache and was inclined to think she deserved every thud of it. She took the brush and dustpan downstairs again to the dismal cupboard where they lived with the carpet sweeper and the ironing board, and then went into the kitchen and made herself a pot of tea to take back to bed with her. The sky was light already, the Friday sky. The one thing to be said for Friday was the arrival of her copy of the *Times Literary Supplement*.

Back in her room, Cat waited. Where, he said accusingly, was his shrew?

'I have no patience with your games,' Beatrice said, putting the tea tray down and climbing back into bed. 'You mistake cruelty for sophistication, which reflects poorly on someone as intelligent as you are.'

Cat jumped on to the bed, after her, and trod about all over her knees, pushing his broad head hard against her hands.

'Stop it,' she said. 'Settle down.'

He inserted himself between the quilt and the top blanket, and rolled himself against her legs, purring sonorously, heavy and satisfied.

'You are a good companion,' Beatrice said, pouring tea, 'I will say that for you. You are independent and characterful and you have a sense of humour. It is time, Cat, that I reminded myself that once I was proud to think that I, too, could boast all three.'

The last six months had been the richest in Beatrice's life for many, many years and she had not only revelled in them, she had rejoiced to revel. She had started by being interested and ended by being enamoured, of a house, a way of life, a group of people, a man. She had fallen into a luxurious habit of seeking amusement and stimulation and food — for an infatuation, Beatrice told herself firmly — by simply going round to Richmond Villa. She had gone all the time in the last few months, trotting regularly round like the paper boy or the milkman, persuading herself that she was valuable and necessary. Well, last night had changed all that. Last night, hearing about poor Miss Bain and drinking, unquestionably, far too much sherry, had been like being slapped in the face when she was a child and getting a fit of the silly giggles. There had been an inevitability about the last six months, its inexorable series of events, happening one after another like dominoes falling over in sequence, which had begun on that wet January night when James had knocked her off her bicycle. Well, Beatrice said to herself, drinking tea and looking at the postcard reproduction which was pinned to the wall by her bedhead of Dante demonstrating the whole pattern of the universe to the city of Florence, with an open copy of *The Divine Comedy* in his hand, well, Beatrice, now you have to get back on your bicycle and pedal off again; and to some purpose.

Chapter Seventeen

On the third day after her arrival, Kate moved into a first-floor room at Mansfield House with Sonia and her children. Sonia was coffee-coloured and calm, as were her children, two small girls who scarcely spoke. Kate felt she was intruding.

'You come on in,' Sonia said slowly. She indicated to Kate a bed by the window. 'You like that one? This refuge, this is the best time of my life. I'm learning how to be close to women.'

Sonia had killed her husband. She told Kate so within an hour. 'You better know, then we needn't speak of it. I killed him in a violent situation but I should never have stayed till things were that bad.' She looked across at her daughters. It was impossible to tell what lay behind their huge brown glass eyes. 'All I want is to pass on to them the strength not to let themselves ever be controlled or destroyed by anyone.' She glanced at Kate. 'It's good he's not alive so I don't have to force myself not to go back to him no more.'

'But —'

'It's terrible, loving someone,' Sonia said. Her voice was almost too calm, trancelike. 'I won't love anyone again. Not ever again.'

Kate made up the bed by the window. Sonia's daughters watched her in silence.

'I clean, mornings,' Sonia said, 'at the girls' school. This room all yours then, to do your own thing.'

'Thank you.'

'When you used to come here, I was new here, I didn't know you, but I used to think I wanted to be like you. Nice home, nice man. But I don't think that no more. The only way to have a nice life is to stay free. That's the only way to self-respect.'

There was something very depressing about Sonia. Her voice was steady and low and it went on and on and on. Her children, when they did speak, spoke in whispers.

'I only tell you this,' Sonia said, over and over, 'so we don't speak of it no more. That's all. You can't appreciate anything without self-respect, not being a woman, not your children, not anything. How can you have self-respect with a man treating you like that? How can you stay away from a man if you love him? Love's a terrible thing. It's a drug. It makes you want to please a man. How can you please yourself if you're always trying to please a man? Where's self-respect if you don't please yourself? You never know anyone till you've told them you love them. I won't do that again. I won't tell anyone that I love them. If you love someone you think you can help them, cure them. It's wrong to think that. You can't make no difference. I won't think that again.'

Linda and Ruth had been to Swan Street and packed up Kate's possessions. They had met Mr Akwa who had said politely that he hoped he had not precipitated Kate's departure. Linda said she thought he was probably the only man who hadn't. Mr Akwa had bowed and looked puzzled. A few days later, Kate received a card from him, with a ten-pence piece Sellotaped to it, that he had found under the armchair.

There was too much stuff to fit into the rooms with Sonia and her children, so Linda and Ruth stowed the rest away in plastic bags, in the basement. Neither of them said, Just for now, or, For the time being, and Kate was grateful for that. It was impossible, just now, to think further forward than the next half-day, or at most the next night, with Sonia's voice beginning again, quietly and relentlessly in the dark.

'I only tell you this so we shan't have to speak of it again —'

Kate went down to Pasta Please. It was plain that Christine found it very difficult to look at her, even though her face was much improved. Benjie gave her a bottle of vodka.

'You want to get that down you,' he said to Kate, 'and then you want to do a bit of thinking.'

Christine said she would keep Kate's job open for three weeks. Susie, now pregnant and waiting for her software salesman to decide whether or not to leave his wife for her, had come back to fill in Kate's job, 'And if you decide on a change in three weeks,' Christine said, 'she can cover until I find someone else.' She was kind to Kate, but in a faintly exasperated way, as if she had known something like this would happen all along. 'I hope at least you've finished with Mark now.'

'Oh yes.'

Mark had sent flowers to Richmond Villa. Joss put them in the dustbin.

'And his note,' Joss said, 'I didn't even open it.'

'It wasn't yours to throw away,' Kate said.

Joss scowled. 'You can't want to hear from him!'

'I don't. At least, I never want any further doings with him. But I want an ending, an explanation. There might have been something in that note.'

Joss brought it the next day, creased and stained from the dustbin.

'I only ask you,' the note said, 'to remember that I loved you and still do. But I know there is no future.'

Kate crumpled it up. 'You were quite right,' she said. 'The dustbin was too good for it.'

Joss looked round the room. Sonia and her daughters' clothes hung on wire hangers from hooks all along the walls because she had kindly emptied the only cupboard for Kate. Kate had not wanted her to, had begged her not to. 'I like to,' she said. 'As I told you, I'm learning to live with women.'

'You can't stay here,' Joss said.

352

'Helen offered me her flat.'

'Helen! You can't live with Helen!'

'I know that.'

Joss watched her. She looked better, much better, and the bruises were fading.

'The trouble is,' Kate said, 'that Helen's very shaken. I don't want the others to think I'm her sort of pet, but she keeps coming to look at me as if she feels she's had a close shave herself.' She looked up at Joss. 'Don't get this episode out of proportion, Jossie. It wasn't actually very much and, if I'm honest, I could have seen it coming.'

But Joss didn't want to hear. She put some sweets for Sonia's children on their pillow, and kissed Kate hurriedly, and went down to the second-hand bicycle James had just bought her from an advertisement in the *Oxford Mail*, which she had left carefully padlocked to a lamp-post.

When the twins first saw Hugh they couldn't speak. They fell upon him, and wrestled with him, each twin to a leg, with pent-up, suffused faces, but they couldn't say anything. Hugh found he couldn't say anything much either. He staggered with his clamped human leg-irons to the lawn, and fell over on to the grass, so that he could reach down and tickle them, to make them let go.

'You were in Joss's house!' George shouted accusingly.

'I was,' Hugh said, 'I was indeed.'

He scooped George up, and then Edward and held them hard against him and Edward whis-

353

pered, 'Daddy, Daddy, Daddy, Daddy,' in a fierce monotone.

'Don't cry,' George commanded.

'I'm not —'

'You are!'

Edward inspected him. 'You are!'

'I'm so pleased to see you.'

'You don't cry when you're pleased,' Edward said scornfully.

'Sometimes you do if you are terrifically happy.'

'We cried at Joss,' George said. 'We wanted to come to her house.'

'Do you like Joss?'

They looked suddenly shy and nodded violently.

'So do I,' Hugh said, 'but with some apprehension. Don't you think it's time I had a kiss?'

Their faces were hot and damp and soft. They clung to his neck with limpet hands and kissed him and kissed him and Hugh resolved upon the instant to behave forthwith like an Italian father who always kissed and caressed his sons, and not like an English one who was afraid to.

Julia came out of the house carrying a tray with tea things on it. The twins hung on to Hugh and watched her.

'Go and help Mummy,' Hugh said.

'What help?' Edward said in his new contemptuous voice.

'Help her take things off the tray to put on the table, and find a cushion for her chair.'

'Don't have to —'

'Don't want to —'

They looked at him warily.

'There's been a lot of this,' Julia said.

'If you don't help Mummy I shall take you up to your room like babies and put you to bed.'

They crawled sulkily away from him towards Julia and stood up on one leg each and began to bang mugs about. George dropped a plate of biscuits.

'Pick those up.'

Very slowly, he trod on them.

'Right,' said Hugh. He stooped over George and lifted him under one arm. 'Bed. Bed is the only place for rude babies.'

George began to roar. Edward followed him. Julia said, anxiously, 'Perhaps they should stay where they can see you —'

'They can see me out of their bedroom window.'

He marched off across the lawn carrying George and dragging Edward. Once out of sight of Julia, the twins stopped crying and began to snivel. Hugh led them upstairs and sat them on their beds.

'What a pity,' Hugh said gravely to them. His heart smote him. 'How sad.'

They looked away from him.

'I shall leave you here, and when you are good, in about ten minutes, I will wave to you from the garden and you can come down and say sorry to Mummy and we will start again.'

George put his thumb in. Edward began to twiddle a piece of hair above his ear.

'Ten minutes,' Hugh said and went back down to the garden.

'I've told them that I will signal to them when they can come down and say sorry. That gives me a chance to say sorry first.'

'Don't —' Julia said. She was wearing jeans and a soft pink shirt she had had since Hugh had first known her, and her spectacles.

'I desperately want to come back,' Hugh said.

She looked at him through her spectacles.

'Do you?'

'We suit each other,' Hugh said. 'I wouldn't suggest going on just for the twins, *even* for the twins, but we do so well together, don't we?'

She sat down on a garden chair a little distance from him, and lifted her hair in both hands and dropped it neatly and smoothly down her back.

'I am terribly ashamed,' Hugh said. 'I have to confess that I genuinely, thoroughly, felt as I did, when I left, but I don't feel that now. Not a shred of it. I should never have taken it out on you.'

'Your letter —'

'I hope you burned it.'

'I virtually did. Why did you write it if you didn't mean it?'

'I was in a habit of thinking, I suppose. I can't even remember now what that habit felt like. Julia, I love you. I really love you. Don't you want me to come back?'

There was a long pause and then she said, 'Of course I do.'

He held his breath. She said, 'I've been furious with you, you see. Furious and fed up. I will not be penalised for behaving well, punished for being kind. Do you understand?'

He looked down at the lawn. 'Yes.'

'I went out to dinner with Rob Shiner,' Julia went on. 'It was so dull. And I found I didn't have the heart for an adventure but' — she flashed a look at him — 'I don't want to be exploited for wishing to stay faithful either, or for being the chief wage-earner. I must emphasise this because it's important. I love you and I want to be your wife but I won't, do you hear me, I *won't* be punished again for being a good and loving wife. Right?'

Hugh was scarlet. 'No,' he said, so low that she could scarcely hear him.

'Can we come now?' the twins shouted from behind the safety bars of their bedroom window.

'Can they?'

'I love you,' Hugh said to Julia urgently. 'Can I get that through to you? Do you realise that I really, truly, love you?'

'Please,' the twins shouted. 'Please, please, please, we're good now, goody good, please, please, please —'

'Yes,' Julia said.

Hugh turned towards the house. 'You can come now!'

'Vivienne Penniman rang. So did those people from Rapswell. They're having a Country and Western evening —'

'Oh,' Hugh said, making a little dismissive gesture.

'And a friend of Rob's wants to talk to you about an idea he has for a series on taboos —'

The twins erupted out of the garden door, squealing like piglets.

'The first thing,' Hugh said, 'now I'm going to be at home more, is to get rid of that Sandy.' He was laughing. He ran forward to field the twins. 'The one with the fat hair!'

Kate lay on her bed in Sonia's room. Sonia had taken her children swimming, to the Marston Ferry pool, with a whole group of other mothers and children from Mansfield House. It was a hot afternoon and the air was full of hummings and buzzings and so still that the thin blue curtains at the window hardly stirred. Kate had started by gardening — the garden was rank with neglect — but the heat and a headache had driven her back inside. She had drunk two glasses of water, and then she had gone up to Sonia's room — nothing would make it other than Sonia's room — and had lain down on her bed and closed her eyes.

Julia had been to see her yesterday. It had been difficult to talk because there seemed to be nowhere to do it without clamorous toddlers or whirring washing machines or discussions about whether the police should be summoned to deal with Pat's boyfriend. Julia had looked tired but happy and had said that Hugh had come home.

'You said if I waited, he'd come,' Julia said. She held Kate's hands. 'You were right. But I had to get angry with him first.'

She had been lovely, Kate thought, gentle and lovely. She had asked, inevitably, what Kate would do next.

'I'd love to know, but I don't. You see, you've got a career and I've only ever had jobs. I'm not complaining but I'm not such a fool that I can't see the difference.'

Julia had offered to find her a job at the studios. Kate had hesitated. 'I can't be out of Oxford, you see. Because of Joss.'

'Oh Kate —'

'It's odd, isn't it? They all seem to gravitate to James; Joss, Miss Bachelor, Hugh, this American woman.'

'I don't know James very well —'

'I don't know Hugh.'

Julia laughed. 'He isn't very complicated —'

'Why did I leave the charmed circle, Julia? What was I doing?'

'Obeying instincts,' Julia said, 'like we all do. That's one of the things I've learned recently. I used to think that all you had to do in life was decide, and then your behaviour followed suit. But it's harder than that, isn't it?'

'Much harder,' Kate said.

When Julia left, she said, 'Don't forget about the job. Think about it.'

The trouble is, Kate thought, lying behind her closed eyelids, that I don't quite know where to start thinking. Everything seems asleep, even my instincts. All I know, the only petty, irrelevant little thing I know is that I can't stand Sonia much longer; I'm even beginning to feel a twinge of sympathy for her dead husband. I suppose that's a start, I suppose that at least shows I'm still alive.'

'Miss Bain?'

Kate's eyes flew open. In the doorway to Sonia's room stood an elderly woman in wire-rimmed spectacles and a brown-print summer dress. She carried a sad brown cardigan over one arm and was slightly out of breath.

'Miss Bachelor!' Kate cried, springing off the bed.

'I don't wish to disturb you. Please don't get up. I simply wished to reassure myself about you.' She moved the cardigan from her right arm to her left and held out her free hand. 'How do you do? We have never met.'

Kate looked round. 'There's nowhere for you to sit!'

'And what is the matter with a bed?'

'Do you mind?'

'Why should I mind?'

Kate's hands went to her face. 'I — I don't know what to do with you, I've been so — so —'

Beatrice sat on Sonia's bed. 'We should have met long ago. I wish you would lie down again. I'm sure you have a headache.'

'A bit —'

'Please,' Beatrice said, 'we must dispense with

getting to know each other. We must simply know.'

Kate subsided on to her bed again. She pushed herself back until she was leaning against the wall. Opposite her, Beatrice sat upright.

'Miss Bain —'

'Kate.'

'Thank you. Kate, my conscience is not at all clear. I feel in a way — and this is one reason for my coming — that your leaving Richmond Villa had something to do with me, and I am most anxious that your return is not impeded by my continued presence there. I shall not visit the house any longer.'

Kate gazed at her.

'Am I right?'

'Yes,' Kate said. She had a sudden longing to put down her burden, to return candour for candour. 'I was jealous of you. You were so clever and unusual. You caught James's imagination. But there was more to it than that.'

Beatrice's face betrayed nothing. 'Of course. You felt you had lost control.'

'How do you know? I did, but how could you possibly know that?'

'I am a human being too,' Beatrice said with a glimmer of a smile, even though I may scarcely look like one. I know the terror of feeling the power to choose is slipping away. So little of what we do is governed by free will, although we like to tell ourselves the very opposite. It makes us feel superior beings. The truth is that we are in large measure victims of our genes. Hence the struggle, the unending struggle.'

Kate moved forward on her bed until she was leaning towards Beatrice. 'I'm so stupid, so stupid not to have got to know you —'

'You can only decide what seems right at the time. Hindsight is a menace to self-respect.'

'You mustn't stop going to Richmond Villa,' Kate said suddenly. 'They love you there, you're so good for them. Joss loves you, even though you call her Josephine.'

'I have no taste for affected androgyny,' Beatrice said. 'She is a credit to you. You are an admirable mother.'

Kate ducked her head. 'I don't want her to be scared by what's happened.'

'Of course she must be scared. Scared enough to realise that there are still men around who cannot accept that society has moved on in its attitude to a woman's place. But you need have no fear that Josephine will be damaged by what has happened to you. She is a very resilient person. She is also much attached to you. If it is possible not to take her electing to live at Richmond Villa too personally, I should try to do so. Sometimes it is impossible for two people endeavouring to be similar protagonists to live together.'

'Oh,' Kate said impulsively, 'you are such a comfort!'

Beatrice looked away. She put out a hand and brushed at the caterpillars of candlewick on Sonia's bedspread. 'And you need not worry about that charming and competent American person either.'

'Garth's mother?'

'Indeed.' Beatrice gave a little smile.

'Could you explain more?'

'No.'

'Oh,' Kate cried, 'you are tantalising!'

'I mean to be comforting.'

'How is Leonard?'

'Very shocked over you, but better now. What, I wonder, in his young life, persuaded him to masquerade as a monster when he is nothing of the sort? The English public school system? Would you,' Beatrice said, 'would you come and see me?'

'In your room? With all the Marys —'

'All the Marys?'

'Joss said your room was full of Jesuses and Marys.'

'Ah,' Beatrice said. She stood up. 'Just one more thing.' She looked down at Kate. 'You are a person in your own right, you know. You don't necessarily — not necessarily at all — need a man to complete the equation, any more than I consider myself to be only half a human because I am childless.' She held a hand out to Kate. 'Please don't see me out, I can quite well find my own way. Come and visit me soon. And take heart.'

Kate stood up and took her hand. It was thin and dry, the palm like smoothed out, once crumpled tissue paper.

'Suppose,' Kate said, holding Beatrice's hand, 'suppose I find that I've — that I've broken something?'

'That, of course, if it's the case, can't be helped. But you will never know unless you take the trouble to ask.' Then Beatrice took her hand away and went out of Sonia's room, and Kate heard her going carefully down the stairs.

Garth Acheson had been only a little soothed after his Indian supper with James. There was no doubt that James was a great guy, but his greatness made things harder for Garth because he could quite see, and didn't want to, how James's greatness appealed to Garth's mother. Garth admired his father very much, but he would never have said that his father was approachable. He never had been; he just wasn't the kind of dad you could mess around with. Garth thought that you could probably mess around with James quite easily, and with that Hugh guy, who'd been living there, and they were both years older than Randy, so clearly the ability to fool around was not a matter of age, but of temperament.

Garth adored his mother. He had seen from the beginning that she hadn't liked Oxford much and he felt that Oxford was at fault for not appreciating her. Thus he was truly grateful to James for doing what Oxford had declined to do, but he now felt that James was doing too much of it, and he wasn't at all sure that he had made this plain to James, out of his own gaucheness and ineptitude.

That Bluey adored being appreciated by James was absolutely evident. Garth couldn't believe that his father hadn't noticed, but his father noticed things round the house, like Garth's running shoes lying in the hallway or a dripping faucet, rather than human things. Garth longed to say something to Bluey, but he was afraid to, not least because he didn't want her to stop looking like she was looking at the moment. The person to tackle, the only person to tackle, was Joss.

But Joss wasn't the easy prey she once had been. Garth couldn't believe what had happened to her in six months; it was wonderful, but it was a bit scary too, and sometimes he thought about the first time he'd noticed her, carrying Miss Bachelor's shopping, when she was just a scruffy kid. Quite a little kid. Now she was surrounded by friends at school, and seemed to take half of them home each day, including a thin, dark boy called Nat Temple who was hopeless at sport. Nat Temple didn't seem to be very far from Joss ever, these days. Twice, Garth had noticed, they were wearing identical sweatshirts. However, Nat Temple or no Nat Temple, Garth had to get Joss on her own, somehow, to discuss with her the problem of Bluey and James.

'I have been to see your mother,' Beatrice said.

Joss, having finished her exams, was lying on her back on the grass in a grey singlet and voluminous orange shorts and her ubiquitous boots, reading a magazine. She flipped the magazine down.

'Hey!'

'Don't use such meaningless exclamations,' Beatrice said. 'Does that indicate pleasure or mere surprise?'

'Pleasure,' Joss said, sitting up. 'She's great, isn't she?'

'Yes,' Beatrice said.

'What did you talk about?'

'You.'

'Me?'

'Yes. You. I said you were a credit to her. I told her I believed you to be resilient.'

'What?'

'Look it up,' Beatrice said. She had come to see Leonard, but he had been ordered to rest in the afternoon, and was not yet up. 'Do you,' Beatrice went on, 'feel responsible for your mother?'

Joss rubbed the hair on the back of her head upwards towards the crown. 'Sort of.'

'Having met her, I think she is one of the rare parents who would not wish you to.'

'She ought to be kept safe,' Joss said. 'She needs a bit of looking after.'

'By you?'

Joss began to unlace one boot, pulling out of the brass eyelets yards and yards of heavy black bootlace. After several minutes, the opening was wide enough to pull out a black-socked foot. Joss

366

took the sock off and looked at her green-white bare foot.

'Yuk.'

'Are you listening to me?'

'I'm thinking,' Joss said. 'The thing is, she wants her independence and I want mine.'

'There's such a thing as compromise.'

Joss began to inspect between her toes.

'Do not do that in front of me, Josephine!'

'Some things you can't compromise over,' Joss said, lying down again and waving her bare foot in the air. She then raised the booted one and held them there together, side by side, for comparison. 'You can't compromise about where you live.'

'Can't you?'

'Nope.'

'So what do you do?'

'One of you gives in to the other,' Joss said. She lowered her feet to the ground and lay there quite flat, with her ribs making faint ridges in her singlet.

'Josephine —'

'I don't want to talk about it any more,' Joss said. 'You can talk things into not happening.'

Leonard appeared in the open doorway from the kitchen. He waved his stick. Then he limped over to Joss and stood looking down at her.

'Idle trollop. What do you think you look like?'

'Trendy. Ace trendy.'

'Where's that spectral youth of yours?'

'Gone to have his ear pierced,' Joss said, 'the other one.'

Leonard lowered himself into the chair beside Beatrice's. 'Hugh's come back to finishing packing. Guess what he brought me. A bottle of brandy. A litre! A whole sodding litre!'

Joss rolled over. 'What've I got?'

'Greedy little bleeder. How should I know? He and James are planning a valedictory pint. Sentimental rubbish. Makes you sick, doesn't it?'

'No,' Beatrice said, 'it makes me content. I am not in the least ashamed to enjoy a happy ending.'

Joss began tearing up little clumps of grass, 'Me neither,' she said.

Garth finally cornered Joss by ambushing her on her way to school.

'Hi,' she said flatly, as if he did it every morning.

'I need to talk to you,' Garth said. 'I've been trying to get you alone for days, just to talk to you.'

Joss was chewing gum. She said, still chewing, 'Talk, then.'

Garth hesitated. They had about four minutes before they reached the bus stop and got inundated by Angie and Emma and Nat and Pete and Trudy and all that lot, which left him no time for a gentle run-up to his central point. He just had to lope along beside her and say it straight out.

'It's my mother. It's about my mother and James.'

'Yeah,' Joss said, 'I know.' She stepped sideways for a second and spat her gum accurately into the gutter.

'I'm worried, Joss. I'm real worried. I mean, my mother's married and —'

'You don't have to worry,' Joss said.

'I don't? But they go places together, I mean, they'll be seen, they'll do things —'

'Not for long,' Joss said. She turned and gave him a brief, happy smile. 'Not for long, they won't, because something's going to happen, something to stop it.'

Chapter Eighteen

Hugh and James sat at a small table on the pavement outside the King's Arms. As it was after the end of the university term, the pub had more tourists in it than students and, in consequence, a less energetic atmosphere. They were both drinking bitter, which they had now drunk together for over forty years.

Hugh had told James he'd been a lifeline and James had said that the feeling was mutual.

'I'm horrified at how close I got to thinking I could easily lose a wife and children —'

'In a manner of speaking,' James said, 'I've lost a wife. And I seem, in another manner, to have gained a daughter.'

'There's a self-sufficiency about you, James.'

'Is there?'

'It's what draws us all like magnets. We think you've got the secret, the elixir, so we think if we come and live right next to you we'll somehow learn how you do it.'

James took a swallow of beer. 'When Kate first left, I thought I'd die. I wanted to.'

'Why the hell didn't you say?'

'The only person there was any point saying it

to was Kate. Nobody else could have helped.'

'And now?'

James raised his head and looked past Hugh, towards the Sheldonian Theatre, against whose railings a group of French schoolchildren were trying to pile themselves into a pyramid, for a photograph.

'Things change,' James said. 'It's part of the healing process, I suppose. You wrench your feelings about to try and heal yourself, and then you alarm yourself by finding that, at least in part, you've succeeded.'

'You mean you can train yourself out of loving someone.'

'I mean,' James said, 'that the agony of loving more than you are loved can abate if the source of its nourishment is quite cut off. To persist deliberately in loving without return seems to me selfish and self-indulgent. If someone you love tells you, in so many words, that you injure them by insisting on going on loving them, isn't it purely loving, in the most generous sense, to try and curb yourself? And then, are you to blame if, to some degree at least, the curbing works?'

Hugh leaned forward. 'I want to be sure, for my own peace of mind, that you're OK. You look OK —'

'I am,' James said. 'Sometimes I think it's very odd that I should ever feel happy, and of course there are many times when I don't but fundamentally I —' he stopped. He glanced at Hugh. 'Perhaps my self-sufficiency is really just detachment, that male sort of detachment that makes women so wild.'

'Women!'

They smiled at each other. Then they pushed their chairs back, grating them on the pavement, and got up and picked up their jackets, and sauntered away together down the Broad, to where Hugh had parked his car.

A young woman at the next pavement table watched them. 'See those two?'

Her companion took off her dark glasses and peered. 'What about them?'

'I've been watching them and it was really weird, the way they were talking. Like two women. But you know, I don't think they were gay. Isn't it odd? I really don't think they were.'

Her companion put her glasses back. 'Too old, I shouldn't wonder,' she said.

When Kate went round to see Beatrice, she took a slim sheath of deep-blue iris, and a packet of shortbread. Beatrice put the iris into a brown-glazed jug, the kind Kate remembered her mother using for making custard.

'The last flowers I was given,' Beatrice said, 'were also blue. James gave them to me, three hyacinth, growing in a pot.'

'Yes,' Kate said, 'I remember.' She sat in one of Beatrice's unwelcoming chairs and Cat sat on the rug at her feet and surveyed her, and weighed up the chances of being rejected if he sprang on to her knee.

'All your Marys,' Kate said, looking round. Cat sprang. 'Ow,' Kate said.

'Throw him off,' Beatrice said. 'I am afraid he is overindulged.'

'I like him. He just surprised me.'

Beatrice was making tea with water from the electric kettle she had brought up from the kitchen for the purpose. 'He is a professional surpriser. He devotes much thought and energy to surprising my sister-in-law, but I fear,' Beatrice smiled into the teapot, 'that those surprises are deliberately malevolent.'

'Joss told me. Joss told me that you and your sister-in-law don't get on —'

'Ah,' said Beatrice, stirring the tea, 'ah, but what I am sure she didn't tell you was that we are sustained by our little feud. She has the power of a superior financial position and I have the power of a superior intellect combined with Cat. We are really very well matched.' She came and sat down opposite Kate. 'I am pleased to say that I can hardly see a bruise left on you.'

Kate touched her face. As if in sympathy, Cat put up a broad paw and touched it too.

'Oh, how sweet!'

'Not sweet, I'm afraid,' Beatrice said. 'His charm is always calculated.'

'I wanted to show you something,' Kate said. She stooped over Cat to her bag, which she had left on the floor by her feet, and took out of it a folded newspaper cutting. She held it out to Beatrice.

'St Edmund's is advertising for an under-matron. For the junior house. It's residential.'

Beatrice took the cutting and opened it out, and read it.

'I'd like to be with children,' Kate said, 'and I'd have the school holidays free. It's not at all well paid, but I've never had a well-paid job in my life, so that's no obstacle. And I'm the age they're looking for.' She hesitated. 'I wonder — I wondered if you would help me with a letter of application and — and if you would write a reference for me —'

Beatrice folded the cutting up again. She looked at Kate.

'Of course I would. I doubt you would need any help in applying but if you feel you do I should be only too happy. But Kate, I thought that you were proposing —'

Kate made a swift interrupting gesture with both hands. 'Yes, yes, but this is my insurance policy, this is —' she stopped. Then she said firmly, 'This job is what I shall do if I find I've burned my boats.'

'I see,' said Beatrice. She got up to pour the tea. 'I understand you perfectly.'

Bluey had at last got James to herself. Randy was in London at a two-day seminar, and Garth, who had made a new friend in the son of one of Randy's colleagues, was having his first-ever lesson in real tennis, on the court in Merton Street. Tuesdays were the nights that Leonard went out

to play bridge with Beatrice, and Bluey knew —
via Garth — that Joss had gone to Angie's house
to help paint her bedroom. They were going to
do it with something called colour-washing, Garth
said, which meant diluting the paint right down
and then slapping it on the walls in watery swathes
with huge great brushes. 'She won't make any
kind of job of it,' Garth said, but his tone of voice
wasn't critical, only wistful and a little sad.

Bluey had chilled some Californian chardonnay,
and made a bowl of guacamole, with corn chips
to dip into it. She had put a pink cloth on the
table in the garden, and the straw-coloured wine
and pale-green guacamole looked very pretty on
this, with white china, and wineglasses, and three
Iceberg roses, from the climber against the house,
in a little Victorian vase Bluey had found on an
antique stall at the Wednesday open market.

'You can't refuse just to come and have a drink
with me,' Bluey said to James.

'I don't want to refuse,' James said.

She had tried not to build on this, not to take
his live words apart, unpicking them over and
over, and then stitching them together, again and
again, to see if they couldn't be made to come
out larger, more significant. If he said he didn't
want to refuse to come, then surely that meant
he wanted to come very much, which surely, in
its turn, meant that he wanted to be alone with
her, which surely . . . Or perhaps he just meant,
I don't want to disappoint you as clearly this means
a lot to you. Did that then mean that coming

wouldn't mean as much to him as he knew it would to her? Honestly, Bluey told herself, honestly, you're enough to drive yourself insane.

When James arrived, he kissed her on her mouth, but lightly. He had not brought anything, and although there was absolutely no reason why he should have done, Bluey felt a small disappointment. Even a spray of honeysuckle from his garden: *particularly* a spray of honeysuckle from his garden . . . He admired her garden.

'I've learned a lot from Beatrice. It's almost incongruous that she should have such an eye for plants, but she does. I even begin to think I could get quite interested. A very suitable interest, no doubt, for an old man.'

'You're not old,' Bluey said.

'Well, I'm a lot older than you, and a lot older than I was, and the process continues.'

He made approving noises about the wine and the guacamole and asked the name of the roses in the vase. He told Bluey about Hugh and Julia, and how Hugh had brought the twins round to Richmond Villa to show them where he had slept, and how excited they had been, and awed, not by being where their father had slept, but where Joss did. Joss had let them bounce on her bed and had given them glasses of Coca-Cola with scoops of ice-cream floating in it, which had made them quite drunk.

He told her about Leonard insisting that Mrs Cheng should have a pay-rise, and Mrs Cheng trying to show her gratitude by turning out

Leonard's drawers and cupboards and being bawled out for it, and about Joss's new campaign that they should have a dog. He told her about a new pupil he had, who was seriously intelligent and a joy to teach, and about a newspaper piece he had been asked to consider writing, about whether society should be encouraged to turn back to loving its neighbours, rather than worriedly, impotently, loving the remote and endangered rain forests of the Amazon, or the faraway threatened dolphins of the Yangtse River. He went on for so long that, in the end, Bluey could bear it no longer and cried out, 'James! I want to talk to you!'

He looked at her. 'Dear Bluey,' he said, 'I know. I want to talk to you. That's why I've come.'

'I love you,' Bluey said. 'It's no good, James. I just love you.'

He leaned forward and took her wrists in his warm grasp. 'I know you do.'

'And you don't love me back.'

'Not in the way you want. I'm not in love with you, and I don't want to be in love, Bluey, harsh as that may sound.'

'With me?'

'With anyone.'

She thought: I don't feel any pain. What's happening, why don't I hurt? She said, 'Is it because of Kate? Is it too soon?'

He was still looking at her steadily. 'Certainly, Kate was not very long ago. But I think, to tell

377

you the truth, I'm rather tired. There's a supposed condition of being heartsick. I think I just may be heart-tired. I've loved being with you, I love your company, you cheer and charm me but I cannot seem to put myself into a higher emotional gear than that.'

'And you don't want to?'

'No,' he said, 'I don't want to.'

She waited for him to say that soon, she wouldn't want him to either, but he didn't. He slid his hands down her wrists until he was holding her hands, which he squeezed before he laid them down together in her lap.

'Have I made a fool of myself?' she said.

'Not in the least.'

'Did you come tonight to stop me starting?'

He smiled at her. 'I came tonight to stop you building castles in the air, which you had peopled with deeply ordinary old chaps whom you had dressed up in shining armour.'

'Oh James,' Bluey said.

'I'm going now. You have made me very happy and done me a power of good and —' he paused, then he said, 'and I think I've said quite enough.'

When he had gone, Bluey went back out into the garden with a tray, and put the glasses and bowls and the wine bottle on it, and carried it back to the kitchen. She put everything away — guacamole and wine in the fridge, corn chips in an airtight box, glasses in the dishwasher — and then she sat down at the little breakfast bar, because the pain had suddenly, finally, come, and wept and wept into her folded arms.

Sandy the nanny was quite equable about being dismissed. She had seen her dismissal coming, for a long time, slowly over the weeks while Hugh was away, and at a terrific speed since he'd returned, and so it was no surprise. She'd imagined that Julia would tell her, in the kitchen, giving a Juliaish list of reasons why she had not proved satisfactory, a list on which Edward's shrunken Fair Isle jersey would no doubt prominently figure, and she had rehearsed her lazy and impertinent expression for wearing during this scene.

However, it was not Julia who spoke to her, but Hugh. He didn't corner her in the kitchen, either, he summoned her to his study where he said in a perfectly friendly, smiling, rather alarming way that he was quite sure she would be happier in a less isolated job, with more people of her own age about, and that he and Julia were releasing her at the end of the month in order that she might be free to find such a position.

She smiled back at Hugh. It was a smile that hid a degree of confusion that slightly disconcerted her. It was OK, she said to Hugh, lounging elaborately against his desk, she'd go at once, on Friday. A girl at the pub had offered to let her share her flat in Cowley, and she was after another job in any case. Hugh, who didn't believe a word of it, said he was so pleased to hear that,

379

and wrote her a cheque for a month's wages.

Sandy went upstairs and looked at her bedroom. She had never liked it; it wasn't the right kind of room for anyone her size. She'd miss the twins a bit, she had to admit it, but Mr Hunter was right; it was lonely working with kids. She hadn't liked the look on his face when she said she'd got another job; at least the part about the flat in Cowley was true, or trueish.

She sat down on her bed and looked at the cheque. She looked at Hugh's signature; he'd got nice writing. He was a funny bloke, all that trying to stay young and the wisecracks and then going all to pieces when he lost his job. Sandy wasn't ever going to take a job that seriously, not she. She'd make enough to get by, to have a few drinks with, have a good time, anyway for the moment. Maybe in the end she'd go back to Suffolk, but not yet. There were things to do first, things like going down to the pub tonight to see Steph about this offer in Cowley, and doing a bit of ringing round, about jobs. Steph might be able to help about that, too. She'd said, a couple of nights ago, that that Italian place, Pasta Please, was advertising for a waitress. Steph said it was a nice restaurant. Sandy thought she'd heard that too, though she couldn't think where. She got up and looked at herself in the mirror. A prospective employer couldn't object to you any more on grounds of sex or race or colour or religion, but could he, Sandy wondered, object to you on grounds of weight?

Garth Acheson thought real tennis was a bizarre game, but he loved it. He loved all those dozens of tennis balls and that weird, historic-looking old racquet and using terms like 'Chase the last gallery!' He played as often as his friend Matthew could get the court, and then he went home with Matthew afterwards and they watched television together and teased Matthew's sisters and made themselves extraordinary meals out of whatever food happened to be around. Matthew's parents were not conventional in any way. Matthew's father had a passion for early music, and made the instruments for it, as a hobby; and Matthew's mother had clearly never arranged a flower or sewn a button on in her life.

When Garth got home after several hours in Matthew's house, Observatory Street seemed to him unnaturally orderly and clean by contrast. Matthew's mother was probably not much older than Bluey, but her appearance was clearly of no consequence to her and she was simply letting it fend for itself. Garth had once opened the bathroom cabinet in Matthew's house looking for some Alka-Seltzer after a remarkably unsuccessful culinary experiment he and Matthew had made with onions and bananas and curry sauce, and found that the only shampoo there was labelled 'For Dogs. Anti-Flea'. Bluey washed her hair every three days, and all their clothes the minute they took them off.

It was therefore something of a shock to come

back to Observatory Street one early evening and find that his bed hadn't been made, that the breakfast dishes were still on the kitchen bar, and that Bluey was sitting on the sofa watching television, with her shoes off.

'Ma?' Garth said.

'Hello, darling.'

'You sick?'

'No,' Bluey said. She held out a hand to him. She looked a little pale, and she hadn't tied her hair back as usual, but otherwise she looked quite normal.

Garth came and sat down beside her. He reached to pick up the remote-control to the television and switched it off.

'I spent most of the day with Daddy,' Bluey said, 'and then I got back here and I just couldn't face the chores so I said to hell with them, I'll watch television.'

Garth froze. What had she spent the day with Randy for? She never spent time with Randy. Had she gone to tell him that she didn't love him any more, that she loved James?

'Why did you have to go see Daddy?'

'He called me. He called me right after breakfast,' Bluey said sadly. 'That old college doesn't want Daddy for a second year. The exchange programme has just run out of money. Their guy's coming back from the States and we have to go home.'

'Oh my God,' Garth said.

'He's so upset,' Bluey said. 'He thinks if they'd

really wanted to keep him the second year, they'd have found the money somehow. He's really cut up. He just went in this morning as usual and they just told him. Just like that. He said he went straight to find a phone to call me.'

Garth hung his head and stared at the carpet between his feet. He couldn't visualise his father humiliated, he couldn't imagine Randy being checked like this. Randy had always been a man who just went on and on and if there were obstacles, those obstacles knew sure as hell they had to get out of his way.

'Poor Daddy.'

'I know,' Bluey said, 'I took him walking. I don't really know where we went, but I just took him and he just came. We had lunch someplace off Holywell Street, I don't remember the name. He kept saying, "I have you, Bluey, don't I, I have you?" He's never said anything like that to me in twenty years. I made him go back to the laboratory in the end. I said, "You've just got to go back in there and show them you're still smiling." He didn't want to go. I had to kind of take him there. It was so sad, Garth, so sad. I felt just awful for him.'

'Do you think it was really the money?'

'I don't know. I don't know it helps to know. I think all we can do is say bye-bye to Oxford and go home. I wanted to make a nice dinner for Daddy but for once in my life I couldn't face it. We'll go out and pick up something to eat. Later, when Daddy comes back.' She looked up at the clock. 'He said he'd be back, latest, by seven.'

Garth said, turning to her, 'I never thought this was what you'd say to me.'

'No,' Bluey said, 'I know.'

'I thought it would be James.'

Bluey slipped her feet back into her shoes. 'I wanted it to be James, Garth. But he doesn't love me. Maybe he was right to tell me so. Maybe Daddy and me —'

Garth took her hand. She clutched his.

'It's time we went home,' he said.

She looked at him. She nodded. He gave her a little grin, and moved sideways so she could put her arms around him.

'Fact is,' Garth said, 'fact is, Ma, Joss doesn't love me, either.'

Kate set out for a walk across Port Meadow. This was an exercise in nerve-steadying. She walked for a long time, and, because it was the lunch hour and a niceish day, there were lots of people to look at who were walking too, or lying on the grass trying to sunbathe with their office clothes pulled up and down and apart in a way, Kate thought, that contributed nothing to the sum of human dignity. There were also people with dogs. Kate stopped at one point to watch a man talking to his dog, which was whirling round and round like a gimlet, with its head in a hole.

'Whassat then, whassat?' the man was saying. 'You gotta mouse there, then? Or a mole? Or a beetle? Whatchew got then?'

The dog took no notice of the man and the man took no notice of Kate. After a while, she left them both, and retraced her steps out of the Meadow, and turned south, walking down the long brick streets to Jericho, past terraces the colour of ochre and beef tea with Gothic detailing and heavy stone architraves, and tiny gardens full of starved shrubs, and bicycles.

It was in her mind to go into Mr Patel's shop and buy something, not so much for the sake of buying something as to see Mr Patel and speak to him and watch his polite dark face light up at the sight of her. But in the end, she couldn't do it, and walked past his shop, and on down Walton Street, past the pillars of the Clarendon Press to the corner she had always liked where the old painted grocery slogans had been left on the walls. 'Try Lumley's 2/6d Tea' they said, and, 'The Finest Turkey Coffee 1/4 lb Canisters'. She'd always visualised the canisters, little rectangular tins with pictures of sultans on them, and fountains, and the veiled ladies of the Ottoman court in gold and red.

She walked the last two hundred yards very slowly. By the time she reached Richmond Villa, the sun had gone in and a still, high, grey sky held the early afternoon very quiet. She went boldly up the steps and pressed the bell.

'Kate,' James said, opening the door. He didn't seem surprised. 'How nice.' He stood aside to let her come in and then he bent and kissed her cheek. 'I thought you'd come,' he said. 'It's been

385

on my conscience that we haven't talked about Joss in an official manner.' He bent again to look at her face. 'I'm so glad. I see you're much better.'

She followed him. The kitchen looked exactly as usual. On the table lay a broken jug and a tube of glue, and the newspaper.

'I'm trying to mend that,' James said. 'I didn't think I awfully like it, but when it got broken I found I did. Joss's friend Trudy broke it, silly child, trying to demonstrate how easy it is to walk with a pot on your head.'

'Where's Leonard?'

'Resting,' James said. 'He always rests after lunch now, unless there's a Test Match. He'll be so pleased to see you. Would you like some coffee?'

'I'll make some —'

'Will you? How nice. Are you really better?'

'Yes,' Kate said, filling the kettle and plugging it in. She came back to the table and watched James trying to fit the pieces of jug together. 'Look. That bit goes there. James —'

'Of course, how dense I am. Yes?'

'I've been to see Beatrice. I had tea with her. She came to see me at Mansfield House.'

His face lit up. 'My dear Kate! How terrific. I'm so pleased.'

'I feel I ought to say sorry, somehow —'

'I'd much rather you didn't.'

Kate moved away. It was not easy, standing near him, not easy not to touch him and she couldn't touch him before she . . .

'What do you think of her?'

'I think what you think,' Kate said. 'I think she is a real original. And very brave.'

James bent over his jug. 'She is an example of true courage, don't you think? Bearing the steady wearing-down effect of daily life without complaining. She might get angry, but she doesn't whine.'

'Do you think I whine?'

Unaccountably, and to her consternation, James looked embarrassed. 'No,' he said, 'no. I don't think you whine.'

'James —'

She halted. He went on juggling pieces of china about in an absorbed way that was not at all encouraging. For a moment, a split-second, her heart failed her utterly, but it was over as soon as it had come. There was nothing for it but to go on. She must do what she had resolved to do, what she had come for, whatever the cost to herself. She would never forgive herself if she hadn't at least tried, and nor could she go on with any kind of unanswered question cluttering up the way ahead. Because there always was a way ahead, even if it wasn't the way you had imagined. I won't look back, Kate thought, I won't succumb to 'if onlys' . . .

'James,' she said again, more firmly. She left the kettle and the mugs and the waiting spoonfuls of coffee, and came back to the table, and sat down opposite him. Then she took a deep and steadying breath and let it go.

'I've come to ask,' Kate said, 'if you will marry me.' Her question fell into silence like a stone down an empty well. It was only a tiny silence, but so complete that it told her all she needed to know.

She leaned forward. 'James,' she said, 'James.'

He looked up at her. She tried a smile. She said, 'I've left it too late. Haven't I?' and then she waited for his confirming nod.

The employees of G.K. HALL hope you have enjoyed this Large Print book. All our Large Print titles are designed for easy reading, and all our books are made to last. Other G.K. Hall Large Print books are available at your library, through selected bookstores, or directly from us. For more information about current and up-coming titles, please call or mail your name and address to:

G.K. HALL
PO Box 159
Thorndike, Maine 04986
800/223-6121
207/948-2962